unimagined research! plus vast
imagination —

See pg 241   pg 284

one family's writing over 1,100 yrs,
Religious emotionalism

7/13   Joan Burke
18 33th aves
780.58204

Remarkable Silence

An Archaeological Thriller

By Karen Wills

eBook ISBN:9781484149294

Published by Gyrfalcon Publishing, Inc.

First Edition: April, 2013

This book is dedicated to all
victims of religious intolerance.

Table of Contents

Prologue

52 AD

The aged woman set the scroll near the center of the scarred table. Unsteadily placing her quill in its worn holder, she sighed. She had indeed grown old. Wearily brushing a strand of white hair from her drooping eyelids, she conceded she lacked strength to struggle with another word, much less sentence. Perhaps the God of the Hebrews would grant her another day. Her smile at such an idle thought wrenched to a grimace. Like many educated Jews she didn't worship the tribal deity who robbed and terrorized unlettered peasants. She'd lived too long to believe in a god who brought little comfort and no justice to infinite forgotten sufferers. She doubted one who allowed the Roman oppressor and the bloodsucking priestly class to exist.

As a skeptic, she scorned the religion of her fellow Jews, its allurements both strength and weakness. Some used old Hebrew beliefs as a future dream to numb the present's cruel reality. The priests used the stern Hebrew God to justify authority, income, and power. In turn, Rome squeezed the last coins from its Jewish subjects.

She stared into limitless depths of the night sky. How many Jewish mothers had lost sons and daughters in this 'Holy Land'? How many Jewish loved ones had been fed to the flames of doomed revolts and religious conflicts? She'd seen hundreds of vibrant young men reduced to rotting meat on Roman crosses, hundreds of young women added to long slave lines.

She scanned the study walls with faded eyes beholding clay tablets that recorded the generations of her ancestors. Here was their story, Israel's true history. Was it foolish to carry on this family tradition? She couldn't alter past or present and would soon join her dead ancestors. Under the Roman sword every day was merely another day of grief. Tears wended down her gaunt face. Nothing would bring back her three beloved sons: brilliant James murdered many years ago by the priests in Jerusalem, more recently brave Nathan slaughtered by the Romans in a nameless rural revolt. But before the others, the first lost had been the dreamer who lived in an imaginary world where angels dwelt and God spoke. She called her writings after that beloved first born son.

She named them the Jesus Tablets.

Chapter One

For if the truth of God hath more abounded through my lie unto his glory; why yet am I also judged as a sinner?
Romans 3:7(KJV)

Men become civilized, not in proportion to their willingness to believe, but in proportion to their readiness to doubt.
H.L. Mencken

August, 1995 A.D.

The lanky figure of Henry Cross stood on the highest point of the dig, big hands browned so dark he could be native. He raised his head with the eagerness of one often scanning horizons. The sun levitated red blanching to white every morning here at Sepphoris, Israel, searing the anthill activity of a normal workday.

Native foremen oversaw laborers speaking several languages. Sun-bronzed graduate students recorded every centimeter of earth removed and noted every item the soil had concealed for centuries. With no certainty of key discoveries, usually the only guarantee remained relentless heat and powder-fine dust invading each plane and crease of sweating bodies.

Dr. Cross of Harvard University's Archaeology Department had been assigned directorship of the Sepphoris excavation nearly fourteen months earlier, an ego-boosting windfall. At only thirty-three, decades younger than the other site supervisors, he led well, listening attentively and making fair decisions, apt characteristics since the dig exceeded two hundred fifty employees. Now, tension led to a scowl. His gray eyes lowered and he walked toward the laborers hard at the task he'd assigned them. It would be another long, but revelation-filled day.

***

Everything had changed two weeks ago, Henry had been standing some distance from grid number 73 when he heard its crew foreman exclaim. Henry barely made out the word "Allah". Then the foreman barked orders over the excited babbling of his crew. A native worker clambered out of the hole they'd dug and ran toward Henry while shouting in Arabic, "We have found something, Director! We have found something big, very big!"

Henry followed, almost running over the rough ground in spite of his usual self-protective skepticism of any discovery having career-building value. When he arrived at the spot, however, the crew continued digging frantically while keeping up happy conversation. A truly good discovery would mean a big reward. The broad-faced crew foreman grinned, pointing at the excavation. "Dr. Cross, whatever this is, I've never seen such a thing before, and I have, as you know, much experience on these digs."

Henry squinted against the sun's glare and squatted at the edge of the hole. The men had unearthed an asymmetrical stone, the lid to a square vault. In spite of himself, he shivered in the heat. Voice shaking in anticipation he ordered, "Lift the lid."

The men used crowbars to pry the lid off, sliding it away on the level ground by their shoulders. Inside the uncovered vault, obviously constructed for long term storage, lay stacks of clay tablets. The lid design prevented ground water entry, and the bottom corners of the vault had drainage holes for any water leakage. The protected tablets rested on stone spacers.

Henry jumped into the excavation and measured the whole amazing thing, breathing hard. The vault measured four feet deep by eight feet long and five feet wide, carved from solid rock, a major commitment of time and capital. Someone involved, someone of ancient times, not only had money, but cherished whatever the tablets contained. "Congratulations, gentlemen," he said, voice cracking with the thrill of it. "You've just earned a month's wages in one day."

It took three days to count, measure, and remove the five hundred and forty-eight Tablets from the vault. Henry ordered them taken to his and Alice's home, to be carried directly to the study. Intensely excited, all skepticism gone, he knew he'd found something potentially significant. Alice, a foremost expert on ancient languages, would help him determine just how significant.

***

Now night had dropped onto the dig. Henry, striding home toward tawny, his long-limbed wife Alice, shivered in the cool air, breathing loud in the still darkness. The recent discovery had shaken him, bringing back old, hard memories.

It all went back to religion. Raised by fundamentalists in Western Nebraska, Henry understood them in a way most of his colleagues never would. He recalled the emotional appeals to God's "unchangeable Word" and the constant need to "be right" with God. An image struck him, one of many since the tablets' discovery: a man's big-knuckled fist pounding a scuffed pulpit while his rumbling voice ordered those seated below to be "saved by the blood of Jesus" before it was "eternally too late." Just remembering, Henry relived through a clutch in his belly his wide-eyed child's fear of eternity in a scorching hell. As a bookish teenager, he'd pulled away, hungering for objective science and real, tangible evidence.

Now he studied the stars, wondering what might happen when this new discovery became public knowledge. Except for the Dead Sea Scrolls, nothing of such magnitude had been found in Israel. The biblical conquest of Canaan already disproved, recent digs revealed only Palestinian settlements between the thirteenth to eleventh centuries B.C.E., autonomous agrarian villages bonded by kinship. Nothing suggested settlers from Egypt or the Sinai. Yet empires were based on the biblical God-endorsed Exodus. Jews, Christians, and Muslims laid sole claim to the truth.

Religious foundations were about to crack where Henry stood. He shivered and thought how cold the night had become. Would his and Alice's lives be in danger? His hurried footsteps crunched on the baked earth. He forced himself to stop again and breathe, sweating under the canopy of eternal, unshakable stars. He didn't want Alice to see him so apprehensive, weakly fearful. Looking up, he pondered the endless cosmos: black holes, white dwarfs and pulsars, change and transformation. Perhaps only astronomers should be preachers.

***

By the time the next morning's sun hung its fire over the Galilean hills, Henry and the Sepphoris labor force had been working for an hour. As she rested her tan arms on the window sill, the first sweat beaded on Alice's strong Nordic features. She once again marveled at the organization needed to unearth what the ancient mound concealed. Workers gridded off the area in layered sections, each systematically uncovered under the watchful supervision of a grid foreman, depth and location of all finds recorded, each artifact labeled and placed in a secured vault.

West and southwest, the physical and intellectual battleground of Israel caught glimmers of the deep blue Mediterranean twenty miles away. In spite of ongoing tension, the setting held beauty along with its spiritual history. So many had, and still would, die for it. Alice lifted her hair from her neck running a familiar question through her mind. *Who were the Israelites and whence had they come?*

Alice's Midwestern professorial father served as a Methodist deacon. Her mother said grace on Sundays, but the family maintained an academic reticence about faith. Alice didn't understand how anyone could make religion her sole reason for living. In her upbringing, while belief in something was assumed, whether acquaintances were Catholic, Jewish, or Protestant mattered less than achievement and intelligence. Here in Israel religion meant infinitely more.

Her Sunday school and confirmation classes taught of vast palaces for King David and King Solomon. She took that as, well, gospel. Yet, pursuing paleography, the study of ancient languages, she learned that no evidence showed David or Solomon ever lived. Compared to Egypt, Babylon, and Ur, Palestinian archaeological finds had been modest. When

Egyptian civilization existed for at least two thousand years, the raw, scattered, twelfth century Palestinian settlements were still constructed of mud and stone. Though compiled at a time and place where Jesus should have been well known, the Dead Sea Scrolls disappointed Christians as not a word mentioned him. Where was proof of his existence?

Always changing, ancient languages gave clues as to when written work was created just as Shakespearean era writing is distinguishable from our modern era. If written after a recorded event, a biblical work couldn't be prophecy. However, the Bible often claimed to be prophetic. Such spiritual vertigo unnerved her. Who, steadied by biblical assurances since childhood, could peer into such a dark chasm without plummeting?

Christians placed spiritual hope in Jesus' resurrection. Muslims based so much of their beliefs on Moses, not to mention the Judaic tenets. What if this new discovery proved the Bible false? Henry, raised in a much more religiously straitened circumstance than she, seemed calm. Alice, child of liberals, unaccountably felt threatened.

Alice splayed her fingers on the window sill, fighting agitation. She labored at a disadvantage here. Typically, linguists perused materials delivered to climate controlled rooms equipped with the latest technology. Now she struggled in primitive, dust pervaded conditions. Still, from the first day she'd loved the suspense whenever a worker turned over a single trowel in the timeless Holy Land. At first she hungered to read the mysterious tablets. Now part of her wished the relentless Galilean wind had ground them to dust. The making of a career was one thing. This was so much bigger and more dangerous.

Workers had taken painstaking care in transporting the Tablets to the Cross home's study. As on-site linguist, Alice's job was to transcribe their contents, recording their basic genre. She had her first close look at the Tablets on the fourth morning after their discovery. She remembered the way the Tablets were stacked in the vault, the impression of almost reverent care and symmetry, each centered precisely on the one beneath, every stack straight, square, and parallel.

She'd sensed these would not be the vainglorious boasting of an ancient despot, so common in ancient Middle East writings, no ravings of some old king inventing a history to match his ego, no exaggerated longevities, no elaborate genealogies, no claim of divinely endorsed dynasties, no boasting of harems, or counting of enemies' body parts. She didn't know why she knew but did. These Tablets would not be the droppings of roosters strutting and crowing on dung piles. These were serious.

Long tables were brought in to allow the Tablets to lie side by side in the order they'd been stacked in the vault. Were they in chronological order? Studying the lowest layers on her first day with the project, Alice saw Hebrew influence; writing Hebrew on clay must have been laborious. Someone wanted the longevity baked clay provided. She started at the table containing higher layers covered in Greek lettering.

One with an unusual border drew her eye, the impressions clear. The use of Greek in Palestine commonly associated with Alexander the Great, whose conquests introduced his language to Palestine, Egypt, and the entire Middle East around 325 B.C.E., would have occurred long after Egyptian. Hebrew and Greek were fluid languages, each capable of expressing detailed thought and complex narrative.

A word could mean different things depending on its era as well as context. She proceeded cautiously even when the words first seemed understandable. There were significant dialectical differences among Macedonians, Thessalonians, and Athenians. Greek on clay tablets was unusual, although often prominent on papyrus and occasionally leather. This tablet showed every characteristic of being Koine, common street level Greek, also the language of the New Testament. The New Testament showed diversity, some books in very good Greek, others of lower quality.

Some tablets displayed the same outline. A single word or short sentence appeared in the upper left hand corner, in the second line another short sentence. The body started on the third line, like modern correspondence. These sentences might furnish or reflect a name or source, the first word here a Greek form of the common name, Mary. The next phrase read 'of the tribe of.'

Alice paused; the last word was an Egyptian proper name, Mosis, commonly associated with a god's name. Egyptians often shortened such names. Then she had it. "Mary of the tribe of Moses."

As she translated the reference to both a Mary and a Moses, she caught her breath. With her heart racing, curiosity trumped caution. Her eyes darted almost against her will to the next words: "The mother of Jesus, known as the Christ." Alice froze, then pushed herself to stand, weak-kneed. She reread the words. No mistake. Whoever wrote this introduced herself as the mother of Jesus, the mother of the man millions call Jesus Christ.

Alice moved toward the open window, crossing her arms to still their trembling. She drank in air. Was this possible? She could not be first to read such a discovery. She looked out onto the hill of Sepphoris, feeling no joy, only fear, and she had never known real fear. A feeling of dread settled, as the room's heavy, dark furniture floated around her. She called out the window in a strained, high voice, sending for Henry. She waited, head on her arms on the sill.

Dust blew across the ancient landscape in slender fingers and whirling eddies as if to clear the land of these puny intruders so foolish as to seek Sepphoris' secrets.

***

When Henry arrived, Alice walked into his arms, shaking her head.

"What is it, sweetheart?" he asked.

Alice pointed at the Tablets. Haltingly, she explained her morning's work and findings. Henry moved to the table, pulling her with him. His background in ancient Middle East languages didn't match hers. Nevertheless, he had no trouble coming to the same conclusion.

He removed his hat, nervously rubbed his cheek, then sank down in an old wooden chair, suddenly exhausted. "I think I've been coming to this all my life. My God, what have we found?" He straightened abruptly, the professor taking over, and spoke again in his characteristic steady voice. "We have to be suspicious. It might be a hoax. But, deep down I have a hunch they're the real deal." Henry picked up a pen, rolling it slowly with his fingertips. "I want us to translate them ourselves. At this point, we still control what happens."

Alice tried to use an equally deliberate tone, but her voice quavered. She rested a hand on his shoulder. "It might not be that easy. There might be linguistic problems I can't solve. Language experts work in teams for a reason. I have to admit, too, I'm petrified."

He held out his hand. She grasped it. Finally, he spoke in that quiet voice that never failed to give her confidence. "We're scholars. These tablets are either meaningless or a stunning revelation. In either case we have to see it through. We're here for a reason. Maybe it's fate. If we release the news too soon we might never know what's in them."

Alice squeezed his hand, and then smiled. All that purity. She'd married him for it. She bent to kiss him and went back to work. That was the beginning of the translations of what later became known as The Jesus Tablets. Alice would translate. Henry would keep the site running smoothly.

The end would not be so orderly.

Chapter Two

Alice's initial hunch was right; each writer followed a form, beginning with the writer's name and titles. The tone seemed calm, objective, as if by an older, educated man who felt no need to impress or flatter, only to distill a lifetime's observations and experience.

The first identifying line read, "Eli, third son of Shem." The second, "The thirty-sixth season after the escape." Then the body began. Alice originally fretted that this could be pseudepigraphia, writing falsely attributed to another, normally Jewish writings attributed to an Old Testament figure claiming divine inspiration. However, this made no such bold assertions. Eli was a biblical name, but nothing implied this writer was a biblical character. Alice recorded that in her notes and concentrated on reading, allowing herself to flow into the story.

***

"My name is Eli. I write of my friend, Moses, a man to remember. We saw and did much. These writings record the history of Moses and the larger community of which we became part. I am Egyptian by birth. It grieves me that my body will be laid to rest far from my homeland. It is the will of God that my end will come in these lonely highlands of Palestine. Who am I to argue?

"I was born in the 42nd season of the reign of Ramses II in the city of Thebes. My family was of some importance, although not wealthy. Our wealth lay in service to the Pharaoh, my father serving with distinction as an officer in the Pharaoh's army. My family included scribes, lawyers, priests, and others of worth. My mother bore my father three sons and two daughters. I was the last son, my sisters younger than I. Thirty-six seasons have passed since I have seen them. If it is God's will, I shall see them in the afterlife. I miss them.

"I can never forget my childhood teacher. Alto, a crippled elder, had been a scribe to both the Pharaoh and the priesthood. He had traveled with the Pharaoh's staff on military and civil trips. He committed himself to my education, stressing language, religion and politics.

"Alto instructed that government serves the elite by convincing peasants it exists for them. He insisted that two forces above all controlled the many for the benefit of the few. The first of these was raw physical power, the second, even more powerful, superstition and religious fear of the unknown. How useful to convince the uneducated classes that life after death would be paradise in order to take their minds off the drudgery of their lives.

"Alto insisted what can be seen, read, and heard is not necessarily the truth, for all those can be manipulated, adding that governments reveal truth by accident. Governments tell and do what perpetuates power. Propaganda is just another name for history. Without Alto's wisdom, my life would have been less fruitful, and my followers could not have survived. I bow my head in thanks to God and Alto. Pharaoh Merneptah, took the throne after sixty-seven years of the reign of Ramses II. At this time, my troubles began.

A man is determined by the women of his life. My first encounter with a woman was nearly my last. I had been a junior officer on the planning staff of the Pharaoh's army for two years. We studied the various routes used by the main army to maintain Egypt's holdings. Our enemies were Libyan tribes north and west of the delta, and the rising power of Assyria in the northeast. Too, there was a new invasion in Southern Palestine by a strange group we named the 'Sea People,' raiders who struck along the Mediterranean coast. Troubling to us, they increasingly held Egyptian territory and formed occasional alliances with our Libyan enemies. I accompanied our forces on missions to hold our lands in Palestine as well as to the Northern Delta area to evict raiders growing stronger with time.

My secondary duty was to serve as master of languages, I seldom saw combat. Fluent in most of the regional languages, I could speak and write Akkadian, Hebrew, Aramaic and

Phoenician. I questioned prisoners and translated all manner of foreign documents, studied maps and planned strategic operations. I learned of the geography and inhabitants of those areas. I associated with supply officers and grew knowledgeable in the needs of armies on extended operations. Our forces were strained on many fronts. Increasingly, victory occurred only by superior planning. I gained promotions, my future secure. How quickly fortunes change. My turning point: the beautiful Leleah.

"Leleah, enviably, was cousin to the High Priest of Egypt. I, on leave in Thebes, first saw her at a religious festival. Our Egyptian week lasted ten days and on the tenth day most enjoyed a day of leisure, feasting and observing religious rituals. My eyes wandered across the crowd and fell on her. Fifteen, tall, strong as a cypress, she turned her wide-set amber eyes to me, their effect like a blow.

"Beginning then, I only existed to learn of her. A member of the highest social class, she was betrothed to one of the five leading Egyptian generals; therefore, untouchable. Alas, youth in love is never practical. I used one of her slaves to communicate with her. Leleah met me in secret places.

"I flattered myself into believing her love equaled mine. Of course, our affair could not remain hidden. Her outraged father informed my commander our trysts must cease, or I would meet the direst end. My furious superior assured me the general would not spare one who intruded on his property rights. My wise commander assigned me to two months of operations against the Libyans in the Northern Delta. I craved Leleah constantly. Our hours of passion grew in my memory. "I deserted. In Thebes, I sent Leleah word to meet at our trysting place. We lay together. At that moment of greatest joy: disaster.

"Rough hands seized me. A military unit had found us. Without hesitation, Leleah ran to the commander, thanking him tearfully for rescuing her from this madman who abducted and raped her. Mute with shock, I was unable to speak in my own defense. They took me away. Confined with base criminals, beaten daily, I remained unable to make a word come out of my mouth to answer my interrogators.

"My hands shook so I could not write. Leleah testified she hardly knew me and had discouraged my advances. She had seen me privately only to communicate her engagement and wish not to see me again. Stripped of all rank and privileges, I stood condemned to slavery. Forbidden to know my whereabouts and threatened with death if they ever tried to find me, my heartbroken family departed, never to see me again.

"Guards took me to the city of Ramses, the Northeast Delta, to the brick making gangs, where I became one of a crew of forty. We labored to meet a daily quota of two thousand bricks. Our taskmasters were under dehumanizing pressure to reach quotas. They used the lash freely since the daily quota was beyond most. They killed anyone unable to make predawn muster. The strongest only lasted about eight years.

"Life meant horror. Criminals served their lives in tormenting heat and humidity as a warning to the general slave population. One day melted into another. What brought me out of my mute journey to the grave was Moses, a giant I slept beside in our slave shed. Moses became the best friend I ever knew."

***

When Henry came in Alice sprang up and pointed to the Tablets. "Moses," she crowed, "Moses is mentioned here by a writer who knew him. It's proof, isn't it? Primary evidence! He was real! The foundation of Jewish, Christian, and Muslim faiths and we have the first hard evidence."Henry sat at the table and read. Alice stood behind him, fingering the shaggy hair at his neck. Her thoughts turned from Moses to the tale of Eli and Leleah. She slipped her hand into her husband's shirt. He grinned. Her sense of dread had given way to the thrill of their unprecedented discovery.

Later, lying together, they chuckled. Henry had put her off until he'd read all of her translated Eli section. Then he whirled her around the study and into the bedroom where their excitement carried them through the lovemaking.

"Did you ever love me the way Eli loved Leleah?" she teased him.

"Yes. Youth in the throes of passion is probably always the same. We were lucky. I remember exploring you as though I'd discovered a new continent. My new world of Alice."

She curled against him. "Eli sounds real. Speech can be lost to post traumatic stress."

"Of course. Even better, his knowledge of the military problems in that ancient time support his being one of the educated service classes. But you do realize Moses wasn't found by a princess in the bulrushes?"

He felt her tighten in his arms. Then she sighed, "Oh, hell."

Chapter Three

Moses," Eli's narrative continued, "enslaved at birth, did not know his parents. A giant, he nearly killed his former owner when the foolish master attempted to whip him. Moses resisted the authorities so violently a dozen men had to struggle to subdue him. When a slave, I watched him snap sun-hardened bricks like twigs in his hands. He seemed older than I, but knew not his birth date.

"I owe my life to Moses who helped me rejoin the world. After six months I could speak, telling him of my fall because of a woman. I also described distant lands and customs. The idea of freedom caused his face to shine. Moses was a brilliant man in spite of his lack of formal education.

"I slaved for one year before planning my escape. Life under these conditions mattered not. I would end mine if escape failed. Labor at the brick works made me strong, but strength subjected to grueling labor and a poor diet would soon fade to mewling weakness. I risked all and invited Moses to join me. To my relief he enveloped me in his huge arms, committing his life to our attempt. It took nearly another year of preparation before we cast our lives into God's hands; although, Moses had no belief in any god.

"We stored a portion of our daily grain rations under our pallets of rags until we hoarded food for thirty days. Gaining sufficient water supplies proved a greater challenge. We lived eighty miles from Lake Timsah and one hundred miles from the north side of Bitter Lake. Our route should take us to the wilderness of Shur northeast of them. Once there we could decide where to go. Moses had never been out of Egypt, so would depend on me. There were Egyptian soldiers trained to seek runaway slaves. The escape must occur at night when obscure darkness and cooler temperature favored runaways.

"I showed Moses how the stars would lead him out of Egypt if I were killed, sketching maps in the bricks as we worked side by side, then brushing each away with a stroke of my hand over the muddy surface. Moses' great potential for learning emerged.

"We leapt at our opportunity when it finally arrived. News races through a slave community, and the latest rumors sounded bad for Egypt. The Libyans had broken through the Western Delta defenses. Nearly all the troops in the Eastern Delta moved west at a fast march to stem the Libyan tide. Even our taskmasters worried. The talk hinted that all slaves might be transferred south until Egyptian forces gained strength. Moses' sad face crinkled into smiles when I told him that night we would escape. Our last day at the brick works was the longest I knew. My life could end within hours if God did not grant us success. Luck would prove as vital as planning once the operation began.

"When darkness rendered work impossible, we slaves returned to our lice-infested quarters. Moses and I retrieved our food supplies and waited for sounds of sleep overtaking exhausted men. I stealthily took my bundle outside, pretending I had to relieve myself. Moses followed. The taskmasters often gathered in the evening to complain and tell jokes over cheap wine. Slaves could be left unguarded, the desert its own deterrent. We crouched beside the occupied shed, waiting until they drank themselves into silliness. We distinguished six taskmasters by the timbres of their rough voices.

"Finally, one announced that it was time to find his bed. When he was about twenty paces from the door, I grabbed him from behind, covering his mouth with my hand while Moses snapped his neck. We lowered him to the ground, taking any weapons and coins before laying his corpse in a depression near the hut. Within an hour, four more taskmasters ended their lives by Moses' huge hands. Finally, only one remained. I pounded on the shed door, and in my best military voice commanded in the name of the Pharaoh that it be opened immediately. The door swung wide, and Moses gripped the last neck. Those sounds of snapping vertebrae echo in my memory.

"Our water problems were solved since the skins were already filled for the next day. We each took five gallons plus our supplies wrapped in bedding rags and struck out to the northeast, armed with sword and dagger. At dawn, troops would track us.

"I used every trick learned from military experience. When we crossed delta stream water we left a trail going toward the sea, then waded upstream for several hundred meters before half running northeast. We walked on the hardest surfaces, keeping to rocky ledges. I rejoiced when the wind swirled up, erasing the trail we left in sandy spots as the sky lightened in the east. I located a place to hide during the heat of the day. We spread our rags, camouflaging them with sand. When the sun reached its zenith, six mounted soldiers rode from the direction of our flight, stopping often, searching for tracks and passing parallel to us only two stone throws away.

"We watched them move on to the northeast and remained motionless until dark, then crept out, hoisted our supplies to our shoulders, and continued. Noting increasing signs of habitation, we arrived near the Egyptian community of Succoth, a fortress town located on a main trade route to the Syria-Canaan region, the most dangerous leg of our escape. The Mediterranean Sea lapped sixty miles to our west; the Gulf of Suez about eighty miles east, leaving a heavily patrolled corridor, the Egyptian army's first line of defense against invasion from the north. Forces also constantly looked for runaway slaves. Troops would be on highest alert for enemy attacking from Syria.

"I decided on the land bridge between Bitter Lake and the Gulf of Suez, a mining area known for desolation and primitive native raiders. There were three small military outposts: Migdol, Zephon, and Suez itself. We had to slip through this southern route. Before dawn we hid near Lake Timsah in a heavily patrolled area.

"Throughout that day we alternated watching. About midmorning, Moses woke me with a touch. A combat patrol traversed four hundred meters off, drifting in our direction. The nearer human eyes approached our camouflaged hide, the easier to spot us. When they reached two hundred meters, we slipped our swords from their scabbards, resolved to die fighting. I heard the grousing so common to low ranking soldiers on unpleasant duty. However, at a word from their commander the complaining ceased. As the patrol neared, I placed my hand on Moses' arm, afraid he would roar into combat before we had the slightest chance.

"I could see their faces. Fate decreed their officer called a halt with the soldiers no more than fifteen meters away. I smelled horses' sweat and feared the beasts would somehow betray our position. The soldiers dismounted to stretch their legs and tighten the cinches on their riding pads. Time dragged exquisitely. The officer mounted, scanning the area in a 360 degree concentration on distant vistas. He ordered his men to mount, and they drifted east.

"The balance of the day passed as on wings. Sleep came easily to two so worn. During my watch I observed foot soldiers marching toward the Delta at a forced pace to reach the Libyan offense. At dusk we struck out south by southeast in the foothills. For the next three days we saw no troops until our final, unguarded jump-off position near Bitter Lake's southern tip.

"We each had less than one gallon of water left. This night we had to cross heavily occupied ground. Seven miles to the lake, then ten of lowlands to the foothills of Shem, all heavily guarded and fortified. As the sun lowered we clasped hands, swearing to escape or die together.

"When dusk settled we left our hide. Stars poised above as we arrived at Bitter Lake. We heard sounds of men giving orders and constant background murmur as they drifted in and out of buildings. When Sirius joined the other stars, I touched Moses' shoulder: time to move. I depended on military habit to place the guard lines at predictable locations.

"Lower ranking soldiers served on guard duty. I gambled our lives on their sort lacking the experience and dedication of high ranking officers. We crawled past several guard lines with two left to cross before we reached the north side of Bitter Lake. Finally in front of the main guard line, but still behind the undiscovered final listening posts, I could not shake foreboding. On hands and knees we inched forward, every movement thought and rethought before a limb moved. Finally, I saw the listening post. These men were not talking. We inched on our bellies. About ten meters in front of the guard pits, I let myself feel the first wave of hope, a grave mistake.

"Something exploded in my face with loud clacking. Movement and noise surrounded us. Some things flew while others ran in random directions. From both guard posts came, 'Halt!' I nearly stood and bolted, but thanks to Moses I did not. Still in the frozen prone position, he gripped my leg. To my astonishment he started to make the most melodious trilling sounds, rising and falling in unusual cadence, having the effect of being somehow present yet fading at the same time.

"One guard said, 'It's those accursed quail again. Listen to their racket.'

"The guard from the other listening post asked, 'Should we investigate?'

"The response was a bored, 'Nah, listen to the quail still on the ground. If it was anything important, the damned things wouldn't still be there.'

"Moses had mimicked an entire flock of sleepy but nervous quail! He pushed me forward. As we progressed, Moses made that melodious sound fainter and fading. Finally we dared rise to our hands and knees and scuttle another two hundred meters. At last we rose to our feet and embraced, overjoyed, breathing free air.

"Still ten miles from the foothills of the Shur wilderness, we dared not luxuriate in success. We risked exposure on the flatlands fronting the guarded Egyptian border. With only two more hours of darkness we strode north as fast as possible without overheating. Thirst threatened. We had less than one gallon of water between us even though we had been frugal. The flat ground eased walking, but as the stars disappeared daylight could ruin us.

"Should we press on and chance being spotted on the flats, or seek concealment for the daylight hours? Dawn's advance decided us. We needed a hide. We searched for any reasonable depression, but...nothing. The sky lightened so fearsomely. We chose a roll in the surface of the flats twelve inches lower than surrounding ground. We tried to dig down but mounting light stopped us. We spread our cloaks, then crawled under them, praying to remain undetected. The sun burst over the skyline while the foothills and promise of real concealment lay yet two miles distant.

"We appeared as ragged skeletons, filthy with chalky sand and alkali dust, burned reddish black, our lips blistered and cracked. Our skin shriveled and stuck to itself. We had only allowed ourselves miserly sips of water. Tortured by thirst, we might not survive the day on these sun-baked flats.

"We struggled to even whisper. Words sounded beautiful, so starved were we to share our emotions. I told Moses it was my honor to be his friend. I did not know whether we would survive, but I loved him. If we survived, our escape would be legendary. Moses touched my cheek with his huge hand, grateful to be free.

"I made out pieces of the crude road running north along the Red Sea then on to the small

oases of Marah, Elim, and El-Tur. Egyptians used the last to serve the mines with their high slave numbers. Egyptian caravans would be large for protection from desert raiders. I, too, would soon take the path of the sword.

"I looked across the remaining flats toward the Shur Wilderness foothills. Even if we made it there it would not necessarily get us water. Then I caught the movement of two horsemen traveling at a steady walk in single file toward us. The second looked backwards on occasion, dragging something along the ground. As they moved closer I thought it must be a bush or branch. I could not discern his purpose. The lead rider only studied the ground ahead.

"Then I knew. They searched for human tracks across the road in either direction from the Egyptian border. This would tell the Egyptian commander if his lines had been watched by enemy scouts or whether anyone had crossed from the Egyptian side to the wilderness. Any tracks would be followed up by mounted troops intent on capturing enemy scouts or escaped slaves. Had we crossed that road in darkness, we would not have spotted the faint brushed surface and these man hunters would have alerted the main forces quickly; two half-dead escapees could not have evaded capture. Burning rays turned these dry flatlands into an oven.

"I felt dizzy, nauseated, dying of thirst. We took swallows of our priceless water. We would hold it in our mouths and roll it over our swollen tongues before allowing it down our throats. Fear clamped my heart. Our enemy, that blazing torch in the sky, cast fire into our very bones. We decided to swallow water only when dizziness became so severe as to threaten consciousness. I began to understand the old myths that spoke of a burning hell where sufferers dwelt forever. Surely no god could be so cruel. Despairing, I recalled images of the blue Nile. What cool water my mother gave me from the family fountain.

"No air moved. Even breathing became painful and laborious. Mute, we lay side by side gripping each others' hands. We had agreed that a slight squeeze would inform the other that life was still present. If the other did not respond, he must be awakened and forced to take a sip of our dwindling water.

"Death crept closer with every degree the sun rose toward its apogee. The slightest squeeze of a hand measured life. Surely, no lovers ever transmitted hope and anxious expectation more than we by that almost indiscernible contact. All breath held until one knew the other still breathed. We felt our lives sinking into the sand in the drops of sweat traversing our dusty bodies, finally slipping to the earth.

"The big hand lay still. I rolled to my side to grasp Moses' head. Groaning, I poured drops from my bag in his mouth. No movement. I rubbed his forehead. With more urgency I massaged his throat and poured more until some trickled down. This time an eyelid fluttered, so I shook out the drops. Finally his lips moved. I wanted to shout with relief when his eyes opened. At last his eyes opened again and I forced him to drink more even though he shook his head. I poured at least two pints of water into him and waited, dreading the onset of convulsions.

"No hopeful father ever waited for a son from his wife in labor as I waited for water to restore Moses. Water, the mother of life. Water, the God of Creation. I could soon hear his sounds if I put my ear to his lips. In a short while I heard him clearly ask, 'Why?'

"I clutched Moses with a grip weak as that of a nursing baby and whispered, 'In five more hours the sun will set. Be strong, Moses. Stay alive. I have a plan.'

"The next five hours were a horror. Twice I revived with Moses trickling water down my throat. Our touches sustained us. I dreamed I drifted through a large house. When I looked out the window I saw how beautiful the stars were. I awoke to find myself under a roof of rags, and cold. I shook Moses' hand vigorously. Night had arrived, and we lived.

"We drank the last of our water. Staying away from the brushed path we paralleled the road to the terrain I sought.

"We approached a narrow spot where solid rock covered the road, leaving no tracks. A broken boulder sat on the north side, drifted sand at the corners. We would try to buy our lives with money, having taken what the guards carried when we killed them, a modest sum of silver. Daily scouts would be on the lookout for anything dropped by other troops or infrequent travelers. What would attract attention more than a cheap moneybag? I spilled the glinting coins.

"Moses would crouch behind the rock, while I watched from a small rise. When I saw approaching scouts, I would cover him with his cloak and sand. The guard would focus on the trail until he spied the coins. That's when both riders would race to them. Moses readied to charge the lead rider the moment his right leg started to slip down from his horse. The second man would not have time to draw his sword.

"As the stars vanished I climbed the hillock. The sun ascended with that abruptness that only occurs in the desert. Finally, riders glimmered in the distance. I made out three. I raced down to warn Moses of the additional man. I covered him, then ran to my depression, drew my sword, and covered myself with my cloak.

"They approached until the lead rider pulled up and wiped his brow. The second rode up abreast of him. Forward they came, pace after pace. Was it possible these fools would not even notice the coins? I had nothing to fear because in that instant the riders saw them. Each tried to beat his friend in dismounting. We charged.

"My sword struck my rider between his neck and shoulder. He crumpled as Moses cleaved the other two. I grabbed the last two horses' reins. Moses captured the leading mount, plunging with terror. We removed the water bags. After Moses drank, I took a large drought. So sweet. So welcome. We buried the bodies to hide them from buzzards.

"The scouts carried bows and quivers along with cloaks that they wrapped themselves in during cold desert nights. They also yielded four gallons of water each. Placing our lives in the hands of the gods, we headed north into the uncharted country of the Sinai Wilderness. The farthest mountain in sight looked at least twenty miles away. Foothills merged into a maze of canyons and cross drainages. At last we could rest in the shade, sheltered by steep canyons, pursuit no longer possible.

"The diamond-shaped Shur wilderness formed part of the Sinai Peninsula. Its southern apex the junction of Gulfs of Suez and Aqaba, its northern apex reached the Dead Sea, the distance north to south about two hundred miles, about one hundred twenty miles at its widest. Egypt had little interest in this desolate wilderness, its mountain peaks rising around three thousand meters. Scorching in summer, arid, full of scattered scrub brush and sparse bunch grass, vast stretches of ground like hairless skin. Violent flash floods during infrequent rains compacted thin, impenetrable soils so what water there vanished in massive runoffs. Raiders often struck merchants using the land bridge between the Dead Sea and the top of the Gulf of Aqaba. Egypt's interest lay in copper and turquoise mines in the Southern Sinai between Elim and El-Tur.

"The Red Sea's glimmering beauty impressed us. Water might be located along a main trail. The natives might not notice two northbound travelers. Shade in the lee of the hill made this paradise compared to the flats. A gentle breeze murmured that this wilderness held the answer to our future.

"We traveled in the cool night air. Soon our faint trail joined a larger one. We made out foot prints signaling recent use. Before dawn we hunted for a concealed spot in which to lie up, our goal to find water. Life did exist in these arid mountains. Occasionally we glimpsed a type of hare, and goat like creatures on rocky reaches. Later I learned that regional natives called them Ibex.

"We slept for the bulk of the day in a sheltered spot. In late afternoon we awoke, waited for moonrise, and proceeded, stopping after a long time on the edge of a huge basin several miles long, really a rock funnel. Skirting the edge of the drainage, we descended. It narrowed, extending finally under a massive rock ledge, a monolithic slab. Cool air rose, not from shade alone. This ledge formed a roof about twelve feet above ground, the mouth of a cave into the next mountain.

"Our eyes adjusted to the dimness, permitting exploration deeper into this cool cavern. After about sixty paces our most desperate need was met: a pool of clear water at least sixty feet wide, in places the bottom observable but in others too deep to fathom. Runoff of this huge basin coupled with the rock ledge sheltering the water from rapid evaporation made this possible. We joyfully agreed. We had found a home for now.

"The water was fresh and cold, but we camped at a spot of concealment away from it where we could keep the water hole under observation. Such a treasure could not be unknown. Although the thought of local savages worried us, Moses and I began a several week period that we both looked back upon fondly for the rest of our lives. We hunted and explored around our camping site. During midday we rested in the shade and in the evenings returned to our main camp. Rest healed us after our harrowing escape from Egypt. Hunting yielded enough to live on. Moses and I grew stronger than we had ever been.

"Our evening conversations ranged broadly. Moses displayed a subtle mind, showing a strong interest in theology in spite of his atheism. He extracted nearly everything I had learned from my old teacher, Alto. The concept of a King of Gods fascinated him. Just as with the Egyptian Pharaoh, there must be a most powerful God. The only real God. I shared Alto's cynicism that religion was merely a tool to control the masses. Moses agreed.

"However, Moses noted there were many different gods. Some Egyptians described a kind, beloved god, and some Assyrians described a stern god most feared. Many solved this problem by worshipping numerous gods, some good and some bad, just like people. I explained the old idea of conflict between two gods: one good and one evil. Bad acts were caused by the influence of the bad power. Moses rejected that, announcing that the King of Gods would have created everything. God would have to be responsible for the existence of the evil power as well as for any acts he allowed the evil power to do. How could a good God permit evil to happen?

"We spent long evenings wrestling with this. Moses reasoned that perhaps God was not all powerful. I suggested that bad things happened because people had done bad things. Moses responded he had done nothing to deserve being a slave. 'Did I ask to be born a slave rather than a king? Does any human ask to be born, determine his homeland, or even determine his own reasoning powers? Are these things not solely in the hands of God?'

"I countered with the concept that the wrong might have been done by one's parents or forefathers. Moses responded, 'What system of true justice would blame an innocent man for another's crime?' Moses declared it impossible to worship an unjust god.

"Moses held nothing sacred, and would explore any subject. He did not hesitate to attack the problem of causality, pointing out that in Egypt he made bricks; therefore, he was the creator of that brick. If a normal human saw that brick lying on a road he would agree someone had made it. Moses' problem: who made Moses himself? To say that a God or gods made Moses only took the question back one more step. For the ultimate question was: Who made God? When I objected, insisting we had to stop somewhere, Moses merely replied: 'Why?' I had to admit I did not know. Moses asked, 'Is man justified in placing the title of God upon whatever we do not know?' We agreed these discussions raised more questions than they answered.

"Moses turned to the ideas of truth vs. utility. He reasoned an idea could be useful and yet not true. For example, the idea of God might be politically useful, yet God did not exist. A false idea could be useful. I agreed. It puzzled him that a lie could sometimes serve a higher good. Moses asked who decides what is right in a situation. I responded that the person in the situation made the decision. Moses answered with the disturbing question,

'If that is true then why do we need God?' I confessed I did not know.

"Days passed. We discussed how to rejoin civilization. Each wanted a better life: a wife, children, and possessions. Being recaptured and forced into slavery haunted our nightmares. Most avoided such a fate by being part of an extended family, clan, and tribe. Those units bound members to come to each other's aid because of honor and blood. Without that, Moses and I were vulnerable to any who outnumbered us. The challenge: to retain our freedom yet gain some group's protection, to be more than just assets to be taken.

"One afternoon Moses pointed. A small troop about three quarters of a mile away headed toward the water hole from the northeast. We first feared Egyptian troops, but soon saw they moved with the random ease of wild animals, paying no attention to any leader. As they drew closer I counted seven. Each carried a dagger, sword, and bow, their clothing as ragged as ours. Some of their clothes appeared Egyptian; however, most were of homespun. Members took random turns being in the lead like a pack of jackals. They went to the pool to drink, reappeared, conversed a little, and seemingly intended to camp overnight. They obviously felt safe. As the sun sank, they posted no guards. We picked out bits of sentences bracketed by long silences. We could understand them, but the dialect had a slightly different rhythm than we had heard before.

"What was our course of action to be? There seemed no point in attacking. Ideally, they would welcome us warmly and take us to a larger group, to be treated as free men, a hope not probable enough to risk our lives upon. When Moses turned to me, a gleam in his eyes, announcing he had an idea, I listened. It was mad, but I had nothing better.

Chapter Four

"His plan did work and this is how the rest of our lives' unfolded. We waited until dark before descending from our sanctuary. I crept within forty meters of the sleeping forms. Each of the seven slumbered. Satisfied, I returned to Moses. His plan, incredible in its boldness and simplicity, might work.

"From the edge of a massive rock sixty feet above the sleeping forms, one could look directly down on them. Intrigued, I forgot about our danger if the drama Moses staged failed. My first exposure to Moses' genius for conquering the primitive mind began as we waited until moonrise when the elements seemed to grow restless. The moon rose only half full, and wind through boulders whispered and moaned in alternating rhythms. During brief periods of calm, silence arrived, so sudden the men awakened briefly to glance about with trepidation. More than one rechecked his weapons.

"As the moon ascended, Moses grasped his ten foot long walking staff. He spread out the cloak he had taken from one of the dead soldiers to frame his gigantic head and body. His red hair and beard, like the flowing mane of a wild stallion, accentuated his huge shoulders and chest. Moses nodded for me to begin. We embraced before I went to my spot.

"I circled the camp to where I could see the sleeping men as well as the huge rock where Moses crept. Several sleeping people tossed as in disturbing dreams. The eerie night stiffened the hairs on my neck. A wind shifted from the west toward Moses. Even the elements acquiesced to him for what could be our last rash act. Like a polished performer, Moses stood tall upon the edge of the sixty foot stone, crying in a sonorous voice, 'Who are these that dare violate the peace of the Almighty God of Heaven?' This had an immediate effect on the sleeping men who rolled from under their cloaks, reached for weapons, and turned to see the figure on the rock. Moses, perfectly silhouetted by the risen moon, his cloak fully extended in the wailing desert wind, looked terrifying. All but one dropped his weapons. The moonlight reflecting off the rocks expanded his figure. Majestic, slow, he pointed his staff at the man who still held his weapon. In a voice laced with haughty laughter Moses bellowed, 'You, a worm of the dirt, would dare to raise a weapon against the prophet of the Almighty God?' Not waiting for an answer, he extended his arms to the heavens. In a supernaturally powerful voice he prayed, 'Will the Almighty God show mercy to this man, or shall I point your staff of power and erase this evil?' As if on cue, the wind died. I almost forgot my part.

"From my deepest being I cried, 'Moses, Moses, my faithful son! Listen to my instructions! Withhold your hand, for these will be my chosen people! Great things shall they do if they obey my commands. You, my faithful son, will be their leader! Once again Moses pointed his staff at the weapon holder and in a firm but kinder voice said, 'You have been spared, my brother. Lay down your weapon, for now you serve the Almighty God of the heavens.'

"His weapon clattered to the ground. Again Moses implored, 'Is it today you begin to reclaim the world from sinful men?'

"I answered in my deepest voice, 'Today, a great tribe will form and in time a great nation. They must follow my commands. If they follow not my voice, I will destroy them.' Thankfully the canyons made my voice sound as if it came from dozens of directions at once. The terrified men knelt, foreheads on the rocks. They struck their chests, imploring to be spared.

"The wind returned with a howl and Moses ordered the prostrate men, 'Arise!' Fearfully, they obeyed. Moses' hair and beard flowed in the wind; the edges of his cloak rose creating the image of a huge bird of prey poised to strike. The picture of power, he ordered, 'Remove your sandals, for the ground you stand upon is holy. The one true God has decided to spare your lives.'

"The men quickly shed their footwear.

"Moses continued, 'Soon I will return. Prepare a fire for my servant. Now I must pray to make you ready.'

"All heads nodded.

"Moses added, 'Blessed will be your children's children because of what God has given you tonight.' Because of the angle of the cliff Moses had only to take one step back to disappear. I rejoined him, babbling that his performance had been magnificent. Moses gave me the rest of his plan, and I could only shake my head at its audacity. My friend poised on the edge of greatness and history.

"Now Moses had to conform the seven to his will, perfect calm and poise his only weapons. As we approached the camp, Moses, a moving wraith, wrapped his body and covered his head with the cloak, face hidden. He paused on the flickering line between blazing campfire and receding darkness, asking, 'Are you willing to become servants of the one God?' Again, they fell to their knees and none spoke. Accepting silence as obeisance, he approached each and asked his name. After the man answered, Moses gently told him to rise, now chosen by God. The seven glowed with conversion.

"Moses next explained that every male of God's army must have the sign of his willingness to bleed and sacrifice for the Lord, that the only true God required blood and pain before He could give peace and security to those who accepted his protection. Moses then solemnly performed the rite of circumcision upon each of those simple men. The blood, pain, and surrender of the act of circumcision formed a bond to God and Moses that I failed to understand. Moses the genius did. I thanked Egypt for performing the same act on Moses and me for hygienic reasons when we were infants. When the last man had had this bloody rite performed upon him, Moses gathered the foreskins. He held them aloft in his huge blood-stained hand and spoke in his tremendous voice. 'Accept these faithful men who have entered into your service.' He cast the foreskins into the fire, the bleeding men so mesmerized by the ritual and surrounding drama they gave no indication of pain. They would have walked off a cliff at Moses' command. Aware of the ancient Egyptian art of hypnotism, I had never seen such a convincing performance. I was still unaware of the power of the symbols of blood, flesh, and fire. Only Moses intuited that with them he could lead these feral men into a new nation.

"Moses directed me in private to convey his instructions to his new disciples to lead us to their home camp. His enthralled followers assured me they could travel in spite of the recent circumcisions. Moses enhanced his aura of mystery and otherworldliness by keeping his face cloaked, allowing only one person before him on the trail. He communicated with his men only by gentle touches. He halted the group four times through the night and upon his knees intoned lofty, solemnly delivered prayers. We traveled most of that night, the guide leading us east toward the highest peaks.

"We made camp at dawn. Before eating, Moses broke silence with a prayer of thanks, petitioning his God for our safety. This pleased and reassured the seven. Moses then retreated to a visible spot out of earshot, sitting without sound or movement. With appropriate humility, I brought him his meal. The real test would be when these men rejoined their home group. Larger numbers of uninfluenced people might make it more difficult to continue this spell.

"Two more nights of travel passed. Moses amazed me with his ability to immerse himself into the role of a divine prophet. What were these wiry savages? The tallest stood no higher than my shoulder. None weighed over one hundred ten pounds of bone and sinew. A unique mixture of wildness and innocence characterized them. I had to learn about them if the gods were to grant us long lives.

"After the third night the men wanted to press on to their main camp. Now in a large mountain basin, we had been descending for some time. At first I glimpsed a head around a rock, then the flicker of a shoulder. Surrounded, I struggled for composure while Moses, a stately figure of mystery, strode toward his destiny. Finally I viewed outlines of a crude campsite, about a dozen ragged tents made from some type of hair. Our guide halted and whistled a hawk's cry. People swarmed from behind each boulder and tent. My hand moved to my sword.

"Moses, massive, hooded, surveyed the group. Then his arms rose, hands reaching for something unseen. It seemed everyone would expire for lack of breath. At first, I heard only a verbal cadence. Slowly and steadily the chanting sound rose. Moses repeated words over and over with ever greater volume and intensity. 'Are these your chosen people? Are these your chosen people?' Until at last with a sudden shout that echoed across the mountains Moses cried, 'Yes! Yes! I hear your voice! These are the ones! Praise to the one great God! Blessed be these eyes of your servant who has beheld the salvation of your world! Bless these unworthy hands as I look upon your chosen tools! Yes, Lord! I will obey your command! I will teach them and they shall be great! Gold and silver shall be given to them!' Moses lowered his hands and spread his arms as if for an embrace. In a powerful yet tremulous voice he said, 'Great will be the fruit of their loins! Empires will fall in their hands like ripe fruit!'

"Mouths agape, we fixed our widened eyes upon this prophetic giant. Immediately, the hooded form turned as if toward a hidden voice, and then roared, 'Yes! Yes! I will warn them of the evil one. The one who opposes the Almighty God of Heaven! I will tell them that blessings will flow like a mountain spring if they obey your commands! But if they do not!' At that moment he seemed to swell, his expanding cloak barely able to contain his shuddering body. 'God forbid! God forbid!'

"Moses wheeled slowly toward the petrified crowd and wrathfully raised his staff, the tip leveled at them. In tones of blackest doom and horror he said, 'If you resist the one God, then God will destroy your tribe. God will destroy your sons and daughters! God will cover their flesh with maggots' and sores! Your wives will wither like grass in the desert sun! Your enemies will rape your daughters before your eyes! Your eyes will be gouged out and you will be led to slavery! Beware my children, for the power of God is great and He will not spare the unfaithful ones! He will send them to a place of darkness where they will live forever.'

"As if to emphasize the fate of any intractable children, Moses strode over to a boulder at least three feet in diameter, seized, and began to move it. Before my unbelieving eyes, dirt cracked from the edges. Inch by inch it rose. Like a colossus Moses held it overhead. He raised his eyes to heaven and said, 'All praise to the Lord! This is how you will destroy your enemies!' He cast his massive boulder down where it shattered. Instantly the forceful Moses transformed back to the mystery prophet. He raised his head as if to better hear the hidden voice and humbly said, 'All praise to the Lord. I will pray for your servants.' He turned to me and said evenly, 'Come, Faithful One, let us pray for these children of God.' Moses addressed the crowd. 'Peace to you, my children. My peace I give to you. We will begin the work of the Lord upon our return.' This newly minted prophet strode away with me in his wake. I thought, *'If this is our beginning, what will be the end?'*

"We stopped a short distance from the barbarians. Moses knelt, his back to the campsite, telling me to kneel facing him. This would allow us to see in a full circle and confer while appearing to meditate. I told him I had never seen such a feat of strength. We compared observations about the size of the encampment and the number of fighting age men, agreeing there were around thirty men and forty women, the number of children harder to determine.

"Although unconvinced these men were controllable or trainable, I did agree that we had gone too far to stop. We repeated our oath that we would live or die together. When we returned to camp I followed six paces behind my 'master'.

"As Moses stepped before the assembly I sensed tension, so stationed myself to his left side, the weakest to defend. Moses felt it, also. He gripped his staff in his right hand. It would take a priceless second to replace with a sword. My heart sank. He did not realize the danger. Instead, with great dignity, Moses intoned, 'The mighty God of all Gods. The King of all kings. The Lord who will show mercy upon those who serve him and wrath upon those who resist him. The Lord is the great Yahweh. Yahweh, the Lord of hosts. Your children's children will shout this name upon the walls of conquered cities. They will rest beside still pools of water. They will eat fruit without labor. For you are the chosen ones. You are the blessed of the Lord!'

"Then Moses paused as if he had suddenly heard a voice beyond mortal men. With a deep sad voice Moses asked, 'Is it true, Lord? Even here among your chosen ones? The evil one is among us?' Moses scanned each face for any spark of resistance or glare of hatred. I felt the sticky calm that precedes a storm.

"A man stepped forward and half turned toward his companions. Older than the rest, he bore scars on his right hand, his sword hand. He spoke with hardened scorn, 'Who is this God? I see him not! I have led you many years. I, Akad, son of Char. Whom will you follow?'

"The crowd wavered. Three men moved to Akad's side while the rest looked down at their feet, shifting restlessly. My hand gripped my sword hilt. Moses moved with deliberation toward the resisters. I shadowed him. He spoke in a voice resonant with danger, 'Yes, whom will you follow? Will you listen to the voice of the evil one or will you obey the one and only God! I warn each of you as I now warn Akad. Within one minute only the faithful followers of God will live and God will kill without mercy any who resist! With the mercy of the almighty God I give Akad the first choice. What shall it be, life or death?'

"Akad's hand neared his sword. He would have at least a full second before Moses could draw his weapon. I could not reach Akad in time. To my horror, Moses pivoted a half turn to lean on his staff. Sword out, I strove to reach Akad even though I would be too late. I saw in the corner of my vision Moses uncoil like a viper. Akad's sword had almost cleared its scabbard when Moses' staff smashed the other's head like a pomegranate. As that staff continued its arc the three others toppled like straw. All but Moses had failed to reckon with the deadly reach of his ten foot staff. I killed two of the three as they struggled to regain their feet. Moses grabbed the third by his throat before the resister could recover his weapon. With his left hand on the man's throat he raised the thrashing man by his neck and faced the crowd, his dagger in his right hand. He said, 'Thus die the enemies of the almighty God!' as he plunged his dagger into the victim's heart.

"Moses ordered the bodies removed, then the men to gather before him. His command was simple: any man who wished to serve the Lord was to accept circumcision immediately. To refuse was to die. When flames licked through gathered wood, Moses ordered all to kneel while he held the bloody pieces of flesh skyward toward Yahweh. 'I commit these souls to your service. I shall obey you.' At that moment, Moses cast the foreskins into the flames, and the smell of burning flesh seared into our memories.

"Then Moses showed the leadership I would witness over years. He raised his hands to heaven and said, 'Accept these offerings of circumcision as a pleasing odor to Almighty God.' He then placed his hand on the head of each kneeling person and asked his name. As each answered, Moses quietly asked if he were willing to commit his life to Yahweh. Each affirmed, and upon that affirmation Moses asked the person to rise and become a member of the army of Yahweh. Many rose with tears of happiness. When Moses had accepted each to the cause of Yahweh he ordered feasting prepared for the evening hours. All not involved in preparation were encouraged to rest for the festivities.

"When the red sun melted below the horizon, the savages emerged from their tents and awnings. The women brought our food of bland goat stew and bread so Moses could ask Yahweh's blessing. He stood saying, 'My kind and gracious God, we gather together this evening to share in the bounty that you have provided. Help us be worthy of the gifts that you have given to us.' After that the people ate. Moses and I sat close together. We noted separation of the sexes. The men, sinewy and trim, kept their black hair cut at mid-neck length and the hair out of their eyes by cutting it across their foreheads. The women allowed their hair to grow to mid-back. Both genders wore tunics reaching from neck to mid-thigh, cinched at the waist with a cord. Their copper complexions clear, the attractive women lacked grooming. Many wore silver bracelets and necklaces. The men wore sandals, but the women walked barefoot. The thirty-one men were confident, the twenty-nine women modest. The fourteen children ran wild, with matted hair and festering sores.

"As people finished eating, Moses stood and inquired, 'Did Akad have any women and children?' A handsome women stood, eyes on the ground, a girl child clinging to her leg. Moses then asked if Akad had any brothers yet living. One of the original seven stood. Moses brought the woman and the brother close together before the people and placed a massive hand on each of their heads. With a strong voice he declared, 'May the wife of the dead man be joined to the dead man's living brother. This is the law of Yahweh the almighty God. Now and forever.' Turning to the widow, Moses said, 'Behold your husband. Share his tent and serve him well.' All present accepted this.

"The recent widow was now smiling and being congratulated by her friends and family. Fortunately the other three dead had not married. My admiration for Moses, who realized a woman had no place in society without a man to protect her and her offspring, continued to grow.

"Moses instructed that a small tent be set up for him on a rise three stone throws from the camp. That night we spoke. He would have to establish firm rules and ritual behavior to consolidate his leadership. However, we agreed that change should come slowly. After all, God must not appear to change his mind often. I would befriend the people to learn their habits and customs. Moses, would project a daunting, but approachable demeanor. Alto's lessons in political leadership might save our lives.

Chapter Five

"Sunrise sprang into light with no incidents. Moses assigned one younger man to help me inspect the camp. Water arrived from a combination of runoff and an artesian well, the volume and pressure low. My companion said it had gone dry in the past when evil water spirits seized the spring. The food situation encouraged me, at least seventy-five bushels of wheat stored in a cave, enough coupled with the sparse returns of hunting to sustain us for six to eight weeks. My companion explained that several extended families formed our group. Ours was one of many spread throughout the wilderness, all forming a loosely connected tribe, with intermarriage common. Blood and group loyalty formed their value systems.

"In the evening men returned from hunts and women assembled with them. Moses again prayed to Yahweh before we ate our poor food. Afterward, Moses, taking a new direction, told the assembly about God's promises to his chosen people. He appeared to go into a trance in which he received directives from God. He told the people how God had promised to make them into a great nation, and that all the nations on earth would be blessed because of the people here this evening. Yahweh would, in time, give them a promised land, paradise beyond description, 'a land flowing with milk and honey.' The soil would be rich beyond compare and covered with fruit trees; indeed, fruit could be picked from any limb. Every person sat entranced by the image Moses spun. Moses described grapes so large that a single bunch would require two men to suspend it from a pole to carry it home. I watched many lips move at his irresistible description of the sweet taste of the grapes.

"There would be meat every day and quail would fly into camp so no one need bother hunting. Waterfalls, running brooks, sparkling lakes, and gentle rains would abound. Every motion of Moses' hands and every impassioned word instilled the grassy vistas in the people's minds. When he addressed the women who labored so hard in this wilderness, he told them that baking bread every day would be unnecessary. God would make a daily supply, called manna, grow within reach on bushes.

"Moses strode back and forth across his rocky stage. When he laughed in ecstasy because of what God promised, the 'chosen people' smiled and laughed with him. Dreams became their reality, and hopes truth. Moses, master story teller, placed this image nearly in their grasp, but suddenly wept as in greatest sorrow. To my amazement, others started to weep even before Moses explained his problem.

"To have all these things, the people must obey Yahweh without question and never thwart his prophet. Moses pleaded with this Almighty God. He swore that he would help the people and guide them onto the correct path so they might claim this paradise. Soon he was chanting, 'We will not fail, we will not fail,' and the people joined him. He began clapping with his broad hands in time with the words. Within seconds everyone chanted and clapped in unison. Moses' charisma carried us. If only Alto could see Moses. The old cynic would have smiled approval at this charlatan. What if all civilization began in fraud like this? Was fraud the forerunner of law?

"In the evening tribal members gathered for stories told and retold so many times their origins had been lost to memory. Moses rose and stated he, too, had a story. Brilliantly, he created the story of how God worked in history to prepare his chosen people.

"He told the eager listeners that God had called one of his forefathers, Abraham, to begin the chain of events that ended here. Abraham was born in Mesopotamia, vaguely known by these savages as a country far to the northeast. God took Abraham on a roundabout trek to a land called Canaan, several hundred miles north of us. Some of the men nodded wisely. They knew about this land of Canaan.

"Moses' God made a deal with Abraham. If Abraham would obey God's commandments, God would give Canaan to his descendants. The first sign of obedience was the mark of circumcision on every male of God's chosen people. Each male had to be circumcised at once. This satisfied our male audience who had met this first requirement. Everything demanded obedience to God, but more particularly deference to God's messenger -- Moses. Obedience equaled the bedrock of civil control. How Alto would have been fascinated at this living example of government being born. Alto would have been sardonic about these primitives' never wondering why God would want a piece of skin off a man's penis as security on a holy contract.

"Moses closed with an example of God's rage when disobeyed. Moses invented two cities, Sodom and Gomorrah, their denizens so evil as disobey God, a sin...the worst offense.

"Sin was an important concept. First Moses made homosexuality a horrible sin. The practical reason: the need to breed warriors. Carnal knowledge without family commitments discouraged work, duty, and responsibility, destroying the family unit and leaving children without parental discipline. Without these, civilization cannot be maintained. Sodom and Gomorrah reveled in disobedience and homosexuality. God warned the inhabitants, saved the obedient ones, then destroyed the cities by fire from the sky, wiping out the sin with the sinners. His listeners shifted, terrified of the wrath of their God, yet somewhat proud of his power. In my heart, I asked how anyone could imagine a God so heartless. With this lesson driven home, everyone retired for the evening.

"The next day my guide grew more loquacious. The savages existed by raiding the main road leading to the Egyptian mines, the same upon which Moses and I killed the scouts. Basically, the attackers scattered loaded supply animals into the wilderness, where they tracked and killed the beasts. Bread being the staple for slaves working the mines, the usual cargo was wheat. This captured wheat coupled with the fresh meat from butchering the pack animals formed our main food supply.

"I encouraged him to explain how they fought. Apparently each fought separately with low losses. The rule of the club determined the raiders' leadership, thus the quick acceptance of Moses. I pondered whether this selection made it impossible to advance toward civilization. The most intelligent might not be strongest. This tribe's behavior had been unchanged for hundreds of years. Individuals only owned weapons, jewelry, and clothing.

The group shared everything else. However, destitute people had the right to take necessities from any member owning an excess. The man possessing two swords had to give one to a man who had lost his. In fact, the giver gained status by his deed.

"My young guide continued reticent on sexual and religious matters. I offered a silver charm in token of our friendship and respect. After he accepted it for his mother, he explained the status of women as being chattel of the male head of their family who was to feed, shelter, and protect his dependents. Women and children were property, a wife valued for practical reasons. First, she lay with him. Second, if she produced sons that brought status to the father as more sons meant more warriors. Sons also provided for their parents in their old age.

"Daughters were marketable. If a man desired a woman he must bargain with her father and pay a bride price. The greater the beauty the higher the price. However, fatalities of war left a surplus of women. Polygamy placed unattached women under the care and responsibility of a man. To afford more than one wife enhanced status. Single men lay with certain unattached women who depended on the group for food and shelter. Adultery, on the other hand, was taboo, the adulteress always killed by stoning. If a single man violated another man's daughter, he invited bloodshed. The tribe valued and honored virginity. Also, it was shameful for a man to sell his wife. Moses would have to find a balance between property rights and carnal desire.

"In the evenings Moses constructed a compelling history. The principle rules of conduct in his stories built a scaffold for government in the wilderness. One story of blind obedience concerned this fictitious Abraham. Abraham had a son, Isaac. Wanting to test Abraham's loyalty, God told him to take his only son to the top of a mountain and sacrifice him. At the last moment, God saved Isaac just as Abraham raised his arm to plunge a knife into his son's bared chest. Moses made Abraham out to be a hero. The people seated at Moses' feet nodded in approval of such faithfulness. Plainly, religious fanaticism condoned murder and madness.

"Another evening Moses related an unlikely tale of his childhood and early life in Egypt. He had been the child of slave parents, chosen while still in his mother's womb to be a prophet of Almighty God. Moses described a cruel Egyptian pharaoh (leaving this pharaoh unnamed since he never existed) concerned about an excess of male slaves. This pharaoh decided all male babies born of slaves should be drowned. Upon his birth, Moses' mother concealed him for three months, then furtively placed him in a basket hidden in the Nile's reeds. While bathing in the river, the pharaoh's daughter discovered him. In this fable, the daughter had a kind heart and raised Moses, giving him all the privileges of being her son. Moses, however, was picked by this selective God to defend and deliver the downtrodden. Upon seeing a slave being beaten by his owner, Moses killed the owner and fled the country. I, his faithful servant, accompanied him.

"Of course, that plot is a well known legend of an orphan found by a princess, then raised in noble surroundings. The child grows into a hero who defends the weak even at the cost of his own position, versions found in folklore of many civilizations. The concept of a slave owner killing his own slaves is as unlikely as a livestock breeder killing his calves. This slave owner would have sold surplus slaves and kept the money. Nevertheless, it convinced these barbarians Moses had been selected by God for a special task. Find the chosen people and lead them into the promised land of Canaan.

"At that moment a young boy blurted, 'Father Moses, how did you get away from the Pharaoh? What happened next?' His frantic mother tried to silence him, frightened of what Moses would do at this interruption.

"Stately Moses accepted this childish outburst. 'What did I do? No, my child, it is what Almighty God did. My servant and I, fleeing across the desert, reached the shore of the Red Sea when I saw the chariots of the Pharaoh's army behind us. I prayed, 'Almighty God, if it be your will, deliver me from the Pharaoh's army so I might find your chosen people.' Suddenly an angel stood between us and the army which consisted of numbers of chariots with archers milling in confusion as a pillar of clouds came between them and me.' Moses raised his hands skyward and laughed in jubilation at what his Almighty God did next. 'God told me to point my staff to the opposite shore. Praise the

Lord! Praise the Lord! The sea split open and a dry road opened for us to cross!' Moses paused to allow the image to sink into his enthralled listeners. 'Then we crossed speedily until reaching the far bank out of the bed of the Red Sea. The army of the Pharaoh saw the dry road with the water piled up on each side and rushed to cross.' Tears trickled down Moses' beard. His voice cracked. 'I was so afraid. But a voice from heaven called to me, saying, 'Fear not, Moses my faithful prophet. I, Yahweh, will protect you. Tell my chosen people how I preserved your life.'

"Then Yahweh said, 'Stretch out your staff toward the Pharaoh's army.' Moses dropped his voice to an awed pitch. 'I stretched out my staff and in a moment the sea swept over the pharaoh's army, destroying them all!' His audience gasped at this awesome sign of God's power. Moses paced on the rock stage, trying several times to stop and speak, but acting as if words failed to convey his emotion. Finally he paused and said, 'That is how Yahweh spared me to lead you into the Promised Land.' Moses silently walked to his quarters, an absolute master of constructive deception.

***

"To these desert dwellers all objects and living things contained spirits, a few good, others evil, the cause of everything. Even the many neutral could be offended by careless behavior. Dead people's spirits carried danger. The sun, moon, lightning, and storms had potent spirits. Evil spirits held sway during darkness. Food or gifts: an arrow or spear might appease a spirit.

'What,' I asked, 'was the most effective offering?' My guide turned evasive. Why so sensitive? He finally responded that blood pleased best. 'The evil spirits feed on blood, so I offer them other living things so they won't feed on me.'

"Chilled, I asked, 'Is more blood better?'

"Yes, sacrifice of more is best.

"Is sacrifice of a goat more valuable than of a dove?'

"Yes."

"Would human sacrifice appease more than animal sacrifice?"

"My companion focused on the distance. 'Spirits smile at human sacrifices.'

"My stomach churned, but I thanked him for the gift of his knowledge. I ended our talk for that day, needing to be alone with my sudden revulsion.

***

Moses gathered the men. Yahweh's chosen people must now prepare for war. Conquest of the Promised Land would take sacrifice. Yahweh would send a message when we showed readiness

Moses told the men at the evening assembly amid much prayer and praise to the one Almighty God that the time had come for a raid. On the third evening, we departed as the sun sank.

"It took two nights traveling south to reach the place for our base camp. From it we could spot supply movement. At least three thousand slaves worked the mines, consuming tons of grain each day. Supply caravans must travel here often.

"On the fourth evening a caravan camped ten miles east with approximately one hundred loaded donkeys. Two officers with four soldiers guarding them rode ahead of the donkey column with twelve sword and spear laden foot soldiers along its two mile length. Six rode at the dust clouded rear, protective cloths across their faces.

"That evening Moses gathered the men and assured them that God had given the enemy into their hands. God would fight with us. Any fallen hero would go to paradise and be legendary.

"Near dawn I divided us into two groups of twelve, our main weapon the bow and arrow. No man was to use his sword unless necessary. We would attack the men rather than flush the donkeys. If successful, we would have time to control the spoils. I placed the first group where the lead six mounted Egyptians would be out of sight of the rear. I placed six archers on each side of the road, covering each with a skiff of sand. Twelve men prepared to attack the rear element.

"Finally the enemy appeared, donkeys shuffling, sniffing, and plodding. The hoof of the officer's horse stepped next to a red stone assigned as our signal. Twelve fighters rose from the sand, each hitting his target. When the stricken hit the ground our men leapt on them, daggers flashing. The rear Egyptians also stepped into their mortality.

"Swiftly, one warrior stationed himself on each end of the pack string. Moses and I supervised the removal of weaponry and valuables from the dead. The lead donkey was captured and the pack string, led by one of our men, began threading its way deep into the recesses of the Sinai Wilderness, that maze of rocky fingers and canyons. Moses directed the grain stashed in separate locations. We released the donkeys to avoid carrion attracting birds of prey visible to the Egyptians. The biggest raid they had ever suffered would not be taken lightly by the Bitter Lake commander.

"None in our camp could recall a greater capture of enemy spoils accomplished without loss of native blood. This was accepted as a sign of Moses' authority. To obey Moses was to obey Yahweh.

"Moses ordered a celebration with feasting, music, drums, flutes, rattles, and dancing. He sent runners to outlying groups of our extended tribe, extolling our success and offering to share our spoils, as well as an invitation for any warrior to join us. The joining warrior would receive a full set of arms if he consented to the laws of Yahweh. Moses also made an offer to any group leader to join us as a lieutenant if he so submitted. From twenty-two fighters we increased to sixty-two. All accepted the religious rituals Moses demanded, including circumcision.

Chapter Six

"Over the next months we struck relentlessly. Even added Egyptian manpower did not prevail against us. Moses began mapping the Sinai to broaden his knowledge of our wilderness. He also assigned men to dig cisterns in drainage spots for increased water storage. Gradually he transformed a barren deathtrap into a fortress with hundreds of concealed cisterns.

"Sometimes I wondered at Moses' daring in nightly stories. This almighty God created the world in six days and rested on the seventh. Moses' God even created light before the sun! Why a god would even want a world puzzled me. And why would an all-powerful God need to rest? Moses told me that if anyone asked a truly serious question, he deferred to the mystery of God, and the questioner usually accepted that.

"One evening, Moses told his flood story. The idea that God would destroy all earthly people because of their evil seemed to be God's fault just as much as the people's. Didn't he create them, and if all knowing must have seen they would do evil? Moses' Yahweh created a flawed being he later had to destroy. Then that short-sighted God blamed those who never asked to be born for the entire fiasco! Moses merely laughed, saying religious beliefs are immune to logic. People only need to believe themselves Yahweh's chosen.

"The next night Moses related how humans descended from one man and one woman. All their children and their children's children were then held eternally responsible for a violation made by the female. Moses crowned this story by making a talking snake the culprit of the lady's transgression! I criticized Moses afterward. He wagered me that even more advanced people would believe it. I protested that no intelligent person would believe a snake could talk and no judge would hold a descendant responsible for the act of a forefather. I argued God had to be responsible because He made the human, the snake, and the temptation. What responsible father would allow his children access to something fatally dangerous? Moses laughed off my arguments, saying I still did not know how the worshipful could embrace almost any idea that shored up their wants and beliefs.

"I continued to learn from my young guide. As we strolled above the camp, he told me these people had a death centered religion. As I had learned from old Alto, agricultural communities tended toward easy going fertility gods, sexual and love based. My present community was a warrior one which lived by violence. Its gods were temperamental, fickle, and violent, the world hostile and fearsome.

"They dwelt amidst evil. Ignorance contributed to a fare of perpetual doubts and fear of the unknown. Since people saw images of dead friends, family, and comrades in their dreams, the dead must live on in the spirit world. Speech in a dream was a message from the spirits, absolutely true, a recurring dream ominous. Moses used dreams. A leader could claim a political change necessary because he received a message from his deity in a dream or vision.

"Because the tribe prospered under Moses' leadership, no gods required human sacrifice. Cults in many countries did have mad ceremonies that partook of sacred blood and flesh. Even Egypt carried memories of this morbid practice of human sacrifice from before the dawn of its civilization. Any guilt about Moses manipulating these people toward a higher civilization disappeared when I considered such depravities. I committed to any deception if it ended human sacrifice.

"Our community now numbered two hundred twenty-five. Moses mapped and converted the Sinai into a nearly impenetrable stronghold, raiding trade caravans from Arabia going to the Mediterranean Sea. We guaranteed immunity to a few fortunate traders for accurate news of other nations. Moses molded a society focused upon his leadership. Slowly our people made traditions of myths that forged their identity. Now we had to create civil law concealed within religious dogma. The natives' awe of all-powerful Yahweh would yield civil government. Laws accepted and reinforced by habit would give us an identity to resist integration into other cultures.

"The deep silence of the desert contributed to solemnity one evening. As always Moses had a small fire built ahead of and slightly below him that cast his shadow in a maze of wild patterns on the cliff behind. Adults and children cringed when he raised his arms to make a point.

"Moses declared the world locked in mortal combat; on one side the Almighty God, on the other an evil god. The forces of the first consisted of angels in the spiritual realm and his obedient followers on earth. The forces of the evil god consisted of vile spirits called demons and those on earth who disobeyed Yahweh. You were on the good side only if you obeyed Almighty God. Disobedience was sin. Moses the Prophet declared that to be good, you unquestioningly obeyed your prophets.

"An obedient life earned eternity in paradise. A disobedient life earned eternal misery in a dismal underworld. Yahweh judged each individual by deed. Listeners trembled at being under Yahweh's eye. Any setback came from failure to obey God. God received praise when things went right, but the individual or group got the blame when things went bad. The political leader could not lose. This cosmic combat myth was a masterpiece.

"Moses and I resolved to sculpt a legal base sound enough to command other cultures' respect, yet short enough for our illiterate people to memorize. One day, seated away from the others, we put ten laws in order of importance. The first dealt with the existence of many gods, too complicated and confusing. Moses needed absolute authority. We composed a simple statement. 'You shall have no other gods before me.' Reverence for only one God would instill identity enough for our group to resist assimilation into other cultures with many gods. What a sweeping religious idea!

"My military exploits convinced me that to destroy a conquered nation's temples and statuary devastated it, causing loss of faith. Our One Almighty God stood above idolatry. We could travel more efficiently without idols. Therefore, the second law: 'You shall not make or worship idols.'

"Still on the theme of protecting our God's image, some mocked or ridiculed gods. Therefore, we devised the law, 'You shall not profane your God.'

"We needed a reminder of the benefits of obedience. Moses reflected that Egypt had all kinds of gods who never helped him. I said when I was a slave I would have worshipped any god who let me rest in the shade during the heat of the day. Moses smiled and stated our fourth commandment, 'On the seventh day each rests on God's command.'

"While I came from a loving and orderly home, Moses had no family. We viewed parents as responsible for their children who in turn owed them obedience. We agreed 'Honor your father and mother' was more than adequate.

"The matter of carnal behavior came next. We decided that sex between a man and an unmarried woman was a violation of the property rights of her father. Thus bride's price and custom would safely handle the offense as long as violence was not done. Adultery was not simple as it led to endangerment of family, thus society. After much debate, we merely stated, 'Adultery is forbidden.'

"Obviously, no society could allow its citizens to murder each other so our sixth law was simple. 'You shall not murder.'

"Since theft endangered property we made the simple law of, 'You shall not steal.' Here, of course, we meant within the group. Raids would continue.

"Moses brought up the question, how will leaders learn the facts so justice can be done? The curse of the legal system is falsehood. Moses agreed that that seemed to address the heart of the matter so we wrote down, 'You shall not give false testimony.'

"For our final law we desired a general principle addressing the root of much of man's evil toward man. Coveting something of another's without the integrity to acquire it within society's rules was destructive. We settled on, 'You shall not covet your neighbor's possessions.'

"Thus we derived ten short laws to help our society mature toward civilization. Drawn into concern for our people's future welfare, we two began abandoning self-interest.

"Moses disappeared on increasingly long hikes, leaving before dawn not to return until story telling. He sought a setting for our Ten Commandments. Finally Moses took me to a singular peak.

Leading around the mountainside, he at last asked, 'Can you hear it?' I listened but detected nothing. He said, 'Wait. You will hear.' It started so low one strained to pick up the source, then slowly increased from a whispering moan to a keening cry, only to fade with haunting laughter.

"I could only ask, 'By the gods, Moses, what is its source?' He motioned me to follow. We rounded a corner and stood on a huge crater's edge, cliffs forming sides riddled with caves, cracks, and concavities. Wind blowing through caves and tunnels coming out the other side of the mountain gave birth to the sound. The mountain was a giant wind instrument. I imagined the effects on a night with a partial moon. The sound disappeared for brief intervals leaving the impression our mountain lived and breathed.

"Moses led the way across the basin toward the cliffs. Shining spots of melted volcanic sandstone patterned the rocks. We entered the cave. Sunlight poured through a gap in its roof. Moses stood in the center of the light-flooded spot and instructed me to walk out into the basin and view his image. The cave mouth framed his giant figure. The light became an intense beam magnifying his size. Further, the sand spots patterned the shallow cave with sparkling images. When Moses spoke, the walls amplified his voice. He had discovered the dais to deliver our Ten Commandments.

"Days passed. Finally Moses instructed the people to gather one day's supply of food and water. When the camp awoke at dawn, Moses had gone ahead. The rest of us started at noon, our marching warriors surrounding the women and children. We traveled no faster than the slowest, including women with babies and toddlers.

"As we approached the highest peak, neighbor glanced at neighbor in unspoken fear. We neared the mountain as the horizon gulped down the blood red sun. The wind freshened. We heard moaning from the mountain. The lead warriors halted, and it took all my persuasion to convince them to follow me forward. As long as they did, the rest of the column continued, perhaps afraid to be left behind. Twisted formations on the cliffs became grotesque silhouettes, but the people descended with me into the basin. The wind gusted with monstrous force as the mountain, screaming in fury, seemed outraged that these puny humans dared its depths.

"By this time the women wailed. Cringing warriors drew swords. I ordered all to be seated. People cried that Moses was dead. I assured them he was safe and would appear on the dais. Under my breath I damned his absence, fearing the terrified people would stampede.

"At that moment a partial moon sailed over the cliffs. I stood before the trembling people and said, 'Almighty God will strike down any who move.' My hair tingled. Sparks and threads of twisting light sprang across the crowd. Lightning lit the sky, thunder rumbling. In the silence afterward, I heard Moses. 'Do not be afraid, Chosen People. The one Almighty God commands you to listen!'

"Another flash of sheet lightening streaked the sky, and Moses the giant mounted a huge stone. Lightning-lit cliffs sparkled. The mountain moaned. Moses appeared and disappeared with each flash; the cavern came to life as if lit with a thousand spots of flame. Lightning branched again, revealing Moses, staff and arms outstretched to the heavens. During a pause in the lightning, Moses spoke from the dark, 'Yahweh commands 'You shall have no other gods except me!' Thunder followed on cue. Moses awaited another moment of sheet lightening and asked in a rumbling voice whether the chosen people understood. With terrified cries the assembled answered that they did.

"With perfect timing Moses coordinated lightening, thunder, darkness, and silence to awesome effect while reciting the Ten Commandments. One by one the people answered in tearful cries that they understood. When he finished, the world hung suspended. Flickering lightening illuminated Moses with lifted arms and staff. Finally he spoke, 'I give my chosen people the sign of my heavenly anointing. Feel my gift of life-giving water that will bind you and your children's children as my chosen people forever.'

"The people froze in fearful expectation. Then I heard a soft sound... a spat of rain and then another and another. Everyone lifted arms in the air praising this miracle and sign of divine affirmation. Moses exhorted, 'Each of you grasp the hand or cloak of the person ahead of you and God will lead you down this mountain.' And that is how it happened. I led, and all the people held to each other in the dark as if blind. We groped our way off the Mountain of God.

"Upon returning to our main camp, the people burned or destroyed all idols and religious objects. Moses instructed each adult to memorize the Ten Commandments.

"Moses gave more minor commands; for example, the concept of clean and unclean. The people lacked basic cleanliness. Moses explained that God was perfectly clean and nothing unclean could have his approval. Therefore, the idea evolved that being clean was the same as being holy. We taught hygiene, grooming, and healing. As a result, the community began to suffer fewer infections. The women used combs to help each other untangle their tresses. Our followers advanced along the trail to civilization.

"Moses gave me the title of High Priest. I performed weddings, burials, and other functions related to our spiritual needs. Moses held the title Prophet. I transferred cases of complex issues to him as our leader. Being a priest is easy. People felt better just by talking to one willing to listen. When young lovers confided in me, I worked to arrange their marriages. If the father insisted on too large a gap between what the suitor could pay and paternal demands, I often made up the difference from the God's treasury. The idea of a God's treasury came from the design that twenty percent of all spoils taken in raids belonged to God, the other eighty percent shared equally among the attacking warriors. In that way, money and goods for God's work remained available.

"Time passed. In two years we altered our raiding. We had concentrated on supply trains taking food stuffs to the Egyptian mines. Now we expanded our operations to the north. The Egyptians began moving many slaves with the food shipments. When our troops attacked, we threw spears to the slaves calling them to fight for their freedom. They promptly attacked their masters, doubling our force.

"Moses ordered that no slaves be killed unless they resisted us. All were given the option of going their own way with weapons and supplies or serving Yahweh. Over the years those who chose to stay proved to be some of our bravest soldiers. By these means and many others we grew. Moses also began ordering raids on northern pack strings hauling metals and precious stones, mostly turquoise and copper, to military posts. This shift occurred because he established markets with illicit traders in the Northern Sinai who brought us iron. New iron hammers and chisels allowed easier cistern construction. In addition, Moses shared plunder with independent Sinai tribes, slowly absorbing them into our emergent group.

"The world to which I once belonged changed. Invading Libyan tribes had not been crushed in the Egyptian Delta. The Libyans formed a dangerous alliance with the Sea Peoples, fierce warriors from northeast shores of the Mediterranean. No one knew why they began to settle and raid the entire Levant coasts of the Eastern and Southeastern shores of the Mediterranean. Rumor had it that they left their homelands after some natural disaster. Others suggested an even larger horde of peoples from the northlands displaced them.

"Pharaoh Merneptah put down revolts in three major city-states, Ashkelon, Gezer, and Yenoam in Canaan. The peaceful reign of Pharaoh Ramses II ended. Hittites north of Canaan remained strong. Their empire counterbalanced Egypt's efforts at expansion. I worried about my father and friends in the Egyptian military.

"Growing numbers of families fled the coastal areas of Canaan into the Dead Sea hills. Egyptian taxes were reducing peasant farmers to starvation. Canaan naturally divided into dozens of small kingdoms where each potentate lived in grandeur. The peasants were crushed between Egypt and the little kings who, losing laborers formed a pact forbidding peasant emigration. Many peasants took the outlaw trail to the Canaanite highlands and joined other escapees. All that occupied our thoughts.

Chapter Seven

"Canaan formed a rectangle about ninety miles wide by one hundred fifty miles long. If one divided it into three even strips running south to north, the western strip would be fertile and blessed with both land and sea trade. The middle would be marginal farming land with little trade. The eastern strip would be arid, poor farming, and low population. Galilee's area was the true breadbasket. This community became our destiny.

"Moses desired a young woman named Mirian while I chose to wed Sarah, sister of Shim. We married our wives on the same night. That evening the moon sailed with special beauty and clarity. Moses and I hoped our married lives would be as full and clear. The marriage vows were simple, the celebrating as modest as our social station permitted. What strange twists and turns my life had taken to bring me to this night of love.

"Life flew by after our marriage. Dark-haired Sarah grew ever more beautiful and serene, bearing me two sons and two daughters. Moses and his wife had three robust sons, youthful reflections of their proud father. My first, Abraham, was a tall, thoughtful youth who inherited Sarah's common sense and tranquility. Abraham and Joshua, Moses' oldest son, were inseparable. I often smiled when Sarah pointed out how similar the boys' friendship was to the love Moses and I shared.

"Moses and I spent many hours discussing their training and education. I insisted our children be literate. Moses eagerly agreed as his life had been limited by his inability to read and write. Naturally, our sons had to become proficient in military arts to gain respect in this martial tribe. Moses charged me to direct their education. Much of our materials were letters and journals of Egyptian soldiers killed during our raids. Thankfully our contacts with traders also enabled me to obtain more literature from the cultures around us. This broadened the children's horizons, preparing them for the day our tribe would join the larger world.

"I insisted my daughters also be literate. Moses understood illiteracy was another form of slavery, that tyrants encouraged ignorance. It pleased me to observe our children learning well, strong in reading, writing, and mathematics. Abraham was particularly studious, capable of penetrating thought and subtle analysis. I was sometimes taken aback at the ability of my young son to ask mature and challenging questions. Abraham could dig out the weakness of any argument or situation.

"Like all other men of our tribe, now one thousand strong, our sons began military training at age twelve. Joshua threw himself into the martial arts with the abandon of those born to the sword, while Abraham approached military training with the methodical attitude he brought to studies. Our eldest sons turned fourteen, becoming men with military duties. We turned them over to seasoned commanders instructed to place them in direct combat with no repercussions if any of our sons fell in battle. No favoritism would be shown them, promotions dependant only on merit.

"Our sons grew taller and harder, each scarred by minor wounds in raids. Joshua, who loved combat, quickly earned promotions. Abraham did as well. Commanders noted how he accomplished his objectives by careful planning, losing few men.

"How swiftly one ages. Twelve more years passed. Streaks of white appeared in Moses' great mane. Like an ancient stone, he sharpened in face and frame. To me, my grave wife grew ever more beautiful; I never tired of her. Our youngest sons died in combat. Moses and Mirian had also lost their two youngest. I, thankful that women did not go into combat, was blessed with one grandchild.

"Moses and I had joined a people more animal than human and formed the bud of a civilization. Our tribe achieved an identity and history. We held a common religion and language. At times we wondered at our success in forming an ethical system of government based on mythical Yahweh. Without reservation, this tribe believed they were His chosen people, and soon Yahweh would take them to a promised land. This bound them together to face troubles with the confidence in his control.

I wondered how many civilizations had been held together by a belief in a god just as mythical as our Yahweh.

"Our surviving sons had done well, Joshua one of our four military generals. In that office he showed great leadership and judgment. His seasoning was partly thanks to Abraham, now our leading military planner. As is common among men who fought side by side in battle, Joshua and Abraham had saved each other's lives. Such experiences bond men closer than blood.

"Using the forces of combat, marriage, and religion, we merged various splinter groups of raiders into one body. Through the telling and re-telling of Moses' stories the people had accepted without question the truth of this past. In time, fewer remained who could boast they were there when Moses spoke directly to their God.

"A number of the men regarded as learned specialized in memorizing and telling tribal history. These storytellers competed to determine who could best move the audience. From the original tale of God parting the Red Sea so Moses and I could escape, the story grew to Moses leading hundreds of the original tribe from slavery. The story of the Ten Commandments grew until mountains shook and the heavens split from divine power. Moses was no longer an escaped prophet from Egypt. Indeed Moses was so important he spoke to the Pharaoh himself and demanded his Chosen People be released. Many times older people stood to testify as to how Yahweh acted in their lives. Driven by emotion and longing, they believed in the described request. Chance or coincidence no longer existed; Yahweh caused and controlled everything.

Storytellers evolved a whole Yahweh theology. Arguments increased about what Yahweh would or would not do.

"My religious duties burgeoned beyond my ability to meet them, so I appointed priests from the ranks of storytellers even though I feared their developing into a powerful idle class. We decided priests could not own property or be paid. All priests would have the civil and military responsibilities of others. If the priestly class were ever permitted to benefit materially or financially, we feared merciless exploitation of their followers.

"Another problem: What would happen to justice if leaders actually believed themselves instruments of God? Zealotry might crush civil authority. Moses in choosing those who handled governing, pondered such danger. Officers like Joshua and Abraham organized our military. It seemed, no longer young, we had just escaped Egypt, and now our time was nearly over. We sat on a rock overlooking the main encampment, marveling at the progress of our people.

"Still, support of our warriors and families depended on Egyptian mines. Winds of change swept from the North. Traders told us trading ventures were suspended, no longer profitable or safe. Since Egypt lost control of her foreign subjects, the kinglets of Palestine pressed their peasants ruthlessly. More and more refugees fled to the Canaan highlands. The Sea Peoples gained power, and wrestled land from the Hittite Empire, now in decline. Moses, having lost none of his shrewdness, sent agents in various guises to the Mediterranean coast and Egypt. They scrutinized the Canaan cities of Gaza, Joppa, and Tyre, coastal cities international in outlook where our contacts among the old traders would serve us well.

"From Memphis and Thebes we gained the most fruitful insight as to Egyptian strengths and intentions. Egypt tantalized me. How tempting to seek my family! I longed to return to the land of my youth. Nevertheless, I did not. Why would I want to know if any of my friends or family had been killed in our raids?

"Our agents to Canaan described a dismal picture of power and prosperity in decline, lives of leisure rather than of commercial risk. Those with money often hoard it in times of political instability. Men of ability are reluctant to enter governmental service when they observe its corruption and dishonor. This, of course, guarantees that the government will be increasingly corrupt and inefficient.

"Our agents from Egypt also told us it still struggled, incapable of defeating the Libyans, the Sea Peoples, and the Hittite Empire. Although yet proud, Egypt was conceding territory as she tried to shorten her defensive lines, her military in decline, Libya and the Sea Peoples threatening her very heartland. Egypt had decided to close the Sinai mines in the near future. I will never forget Moses striding among the men reassuring them and thanking them for their service, adding the present situation was both a challenge and an opportunity. He posed the ultimate question: 'Since Yahweh is with us, who can be against us?' Nods of affirmation followed.

"Our tribe would leave the Sinai in three months for the Canaan highlands, the only area still uncontrolled by a major power. It would be simple for Moses as a prophet to receive a dream or a vision instructing the people the time had come for Yahweh to fulfill His promise to take them to the Promised Land. Religious beliefs have social use. The Yahweh myth would motivate this tribe to depart our wilderness for a wider, more habitable world.

"Moses and I felt light-hearted. After all, we were old men, what hurt could the world inflict? Most of life lay behind us, a liberating state. The tribe had civil and military leaders to carry on. Our religious and historical myths would give unity and identity for the transition from raiding culture to peaceful agricultural society. We regretted violence we had inflicted, but how could we have avoided it if we wished to survive? We had created a government to control violence in a just manner. Violence should diminish as we progressed from predators to farmers. My remaining ambition became to eat bread raised on our own farms. Moses only yearned to cast his eyes upon lands green with vegetation and place his hand in a stream of rushing water.

"As in old times, we spent hours discussing religion. To our mutual surprise we had both reached the sense of a divine source in spite of the fakery of our Yahweh legend. After all, life did encompass such mysteries. A Creator seemed more plausible than a fickle God. On the other hand, both Moses and I had experienced intimations of divine approval or disapproval of our actions. Conscience and the inherent sense that we each would face a divine judgment could not be denied. We both confessed to having felt a spiritual presence or nearness, then laughed as we wondered what a real God would think of two old men pondering questions with no provable answers.

"Certain rights and wrongs seemingly had universal application: murder for one. It followed there might be universal moral laws as well as universal physical laws. If we believed in a judgment then God must exist in some sense. The drive to solve the mysteries of life made inventing God possible. However, undeniably life existed whether we sought to answer its questions with invented gods or not. In short, God might very well exist no matter how we used or misused the concept.

"Of course, many viewed their god or gods in other ways. Different cultures had different religions and only chance decided in which culture any human was born. Since the individual had no choice as to natal circumstances, it seemed unlikely he could be penalized for worshipping in the faith of his culture.

"Moses felt people should live lawful lives honoring a god even if doubting its reality. Religion gives hope, but can also enslave. Our infliction of mental and spiritual conformity upon this tribe disturbed us, but like many leaders, we aspired for the ends to justify the means. In any event, our past was unalterable. We hoped any existing God would forgive us. I, Eli, still retain that hope today.

"Moses chose six men, including Abraham, commanded by Joshua to scout the Canaan Highlands. We intensified raids on the Egyptian supply road. I told our priests the time approached when Yahweh would lead us to the Promised Land. Youths who had heard the theme of a Promised Land since birth had grown skeptical of such an idea. Privately, I rejoiced at their analysis, but actual movement toward the Promised Land would erase doubts. All were wakening to the importance of approaching events.

"Moses sent messages to valued trader contacts to gather sufficient pack animals and equipment to transport the necessities of two thousand five hundred people, these traders to gather at a point in the northern Sinai for final instructions. I marveled at his prescience. Over the years we had traded turquoise and copper to these same illicit traders for supplies. Nevertheless, he made certain a substantial percentage was converted into silver and gold. Our illicit traders made commissions from our mutual dark dealings with which they could retire in choice surroundings.

"A month passed. Our sons came home flushed with their first exposure to the outside world. Compared to the Sinai wastelands, the land of Canaan seemed paradise, rich with vegetation and water. Trees greened the land. Its inhabitants, all escaped farmers, depended for protection on remote terrain. Nearly everyone spoke dialects of one language. The beauty of the native women with their greater height and lush size intrigued our young soldiers. I wondered whether sexual attraction existed so a real God could prevent people from becoming too separate. Subtle indeed might be the means of such a God.

"The Canaanites would welcome our military help in defending against enslaving governments from which they had escaped. They would share their abundant land and agricultural knowledge. The Canaanites, possessing freedom of property and religion, prohibited slavery. Moses would have to tone down our teachings so our tribe could live in peace with people of other creeds.

"Our leadership agreed a move must be made, leaving only decisions about our route. After four weeks of raiding supply trains, our troops disengaged and returned to prepare for travel. Moses sent runners to inform our illicit traders that we required the pack animals in six weeks near El-Thamad. Joshua and Abraham plotted our route from there. My son Abraham proposed we carry only seven days' supply of food, consigning most of the donkeys to water duty. Although the risks were high, we had no choice. We placed our lives in God's hands.

"During the evening sessions, Moses informed the people the time was at hand to travel into the Promised Land. He retraced the well-believed tribal history of Yahweh's chosen. Yahweh in his wisdom had allowed enough time for us to gain in strength and numbers. Elders nodded when Moses recounted earlier times when the tribe had been little more than scattered elements of near-starving raiders. But, Yahweh had formed a nation so strong even Egypt could not defend against our warriors and was closing her mines. The time to enter the Promised Land had arrived. Moses again called it a land flowing with milk and honey. He explained the challenges and dangers ahead. Lives would be lost, but those lost journeying to the Promised Land would be honored for generations. Enemies of Yahweh, strange people, would try to hinder our keeping the land, but Yahweh tested and rewarded those who stood behind their leaders. We must remember Yahweh had chosen us. Once again Moses successfully used our mythical Yahweh to reinforce political necessity.

"For our arduous travel across arid lands, we would be fortunate to move seven miles per day. Our daily water requirement neared thirty-two thousand pounds for the people alone. At least three hundred twenty pack animals carrying one hundred pound loads would be required per day. Likewise the daily grain allotments would be at least two thousand five hundred pounds, four hundred pack animals needed to supply even one day's requirement of food.

"The donkeys would need at least three gallons of water each per day as well as grain. In all this totaled five thousand five hundred gallons of water per day and two tons of grain. That meant we needed at least one pack animal apiece for a two month journey. The distance to the Northern Highlands of Canaan would be two hundred miles as the raven flies. Unfortunately, humans must walk on earth. By the time the tribe followed up and down slopes and around natural land obstacles the actual distance would be closer to two hundred fifty miles.

"The old, sick, and women with children would suffer. The dust stirred up by the tread of thousands of feet and hooves would hang like a suffocating fog. The sun would beat relentlessly. Night travel would not occur because the tribe could not defend itself in the dark.

"Since the largest threat remained Egyptian forces along the Mediterranean, we chose the safer eastern drainage of the Dead Sea. We had to pass through a land of the Edomites who thinly occupied the area north of the Sinai Peninsula. Depending on the rains, they alternated nomadic to settled lives. We hoped to barter for permission to cross their lands. Nomads view land much as sailors view sea. It really belongs to no one.

"The second major people would be the Moabites who mainly lived on a plateau fifteen by sixty miles east of the Dead Sea. We would not pass through their most populated sites. We anticipated their grant of passage with no fighting. North of Moab were the

Ammonites who had inhabited their area for hundreds of years. We would cross the Jordan River at the southern edge of Ammonite influence. We hoped to avoid fighting.

***

"The tribe began its move north from the Sinai toward the land of Canaan, our exodus like a chain of migrating ants strung out for two miles. Every person from oldest to youngest carried clothes and food. Men of fighting age shielded the marchers led by Joshua and the other military leaders. The enthusiastic walkers started at an unsustainable pace. Many secretly carried personal effects they had been ordered to leave. Soon, heat and the terrain tamped down excitement. Heavy burdens littered the trail behind us. The column strung further out despite soldiers' urgings to stragglers. We were still well within our Sinai stronghold and could afford more straggling than would be tolerated later. At first people visited, but as the day wore on talking declined as the weary concentrated on putting one foot before the other. Our first death occurred by early afternoon. An old woman dropped between one step and the next. Within days, news of a death in the column would cause no surprise or wonder.

"The maze of thin trails through the Sinai became more defined as we continued toward El-Thamad, nothing but a small spring fed by a sub-terrain seep; still, enough to make it an important crossroads. Our destination after El-Thamad would be Ezion-geber, a little used, remote port, located at the Northern tip of the Gulf of Aqaba. Ancient Ezion-geber had resources to support fewer than a hundred inhabitants, the toughest outcasts of the human race. Murder was a minor offense. We would follow north one hundred miles through desert country, ornamented with the bones of those who died of thirst during storms or mishaps.

"For twenty-two days we struggled. Serpentine trails wound over and around countless obstacles. The dying, bereft of reserves, would sink to the ground wordlessly as if not wishing to disturb others. I dreaded each steep mountain, wondering how many beloved lives that particular tower of rock would claim. Each day the encampment roused from the hollows that had served as shelter. Each night stupefied people huddled for warmth. As days passed, only muted words of encouragement could be heard.

"I watched many parched husbands pretend to drink from dwindling water bags, then urge wives and children to drink deeply. Mothers did the same so children could gulp the life-giving liquid. Often one or both parents perished. Many times I turned away so none saw my grief. Perhaps part of the hope for a kind God is based on the feeling that such sacrifices deserve a reward in a next life.

"On the twenty-third day the storm hit. Early that morning, instead of rising with halts and starts, the wind blew stronger and stronger, so fierce by midmorning we struggled to walk against it. As we fought to cross a finger of the mountain, we saw a boiling gray curtain on the horizon, an approaching wall of swirling sand. Moses sent a runner to warn everyone to take shelter. Donkeys brayed. We hunkered in the lee of a boulder cluster before this monster smote us with heat and utter darkness. The sand and dust pelted our robes, stripping away any exposed skin, the dust so fine our eyes burned.

"We breathed air heated in a great furnace, crushing all sense of time and place. It filled my heart with dread that the tribe had scattered, each member locked in a solitary prison of sand with only the ruthless wind. Moses and I shared a water skin. I drifted as in a trance, returning to that deadly day we spent upon flats outside Bitter Lake. How ironic that Moses and I would die of thirst so many years later. Hundreds of us must be without water. Hour upon endless hour passed. Our water was gone but the storm raged in its relentless assault. Dying with Moses, I felt a strange content. How easy to drift to death.

"Then silence. I swept our robes aside and beheld a world of windless skies! I shook Moses back to consciousness. He struggled to his feet, a rousing colossus. My joy at being alive plummeted when I saw his blood-covered chest, a trickle seeping from his mouth. Moses insisted we attend to survivors. He would explain the blood later. He wiped his face and strode off to rescue the living.

"A few had risen and strove to regain their bearings. Some helped others. Many could not stand. Little water remained. Our only hope lay with men in transit who could now catch up and replenish our supply. To our joy, some soon did.

"After the two day storm, scenes of elation for the living and mourning for those lost took place. The men went from rock to rock trying to rouse people drifted over with sand. Some revived with water. The blinding nature of the storm produced sad ironies. Children were found dead only feet from surviving mothers because neither could hear the other. Short distances committed one to death and another to life. Sarah and Mirian survived.

"Moses was everywhere, giving orders to those capable of action, a tower of compassion for those who mourned. Up and down the column he strode, giving kind words and embraces to the despairing. Hard decisions had to be made as to who was too near death to receive our limited water. None had strength to bury the dead. Joshua ordered us to start again. A battered people limped and finally halted one mile away from the tragedy. Famished, the column prepared food. El Thamad, with water and shelter, lay eight miles away, miles that separated the quick from the dead. Was religion a reaction against the mystery of meaningless life and the irony of certain death? Yet our people so desperately needed hope. Does not a leader do his best to give his people hope?

"Moses blamed our devastation on evil forces that would do anything to block God's chosen. He alluded to the mystery of Yahweh. Our dear ones rested in a place of happiness beyond understanding. Occasionally Moses claimed the deceased went to heaven before their natural time because God sought company or needed services. I did not question Moses' ways. He understood our peoples' needs in a way I, amazed at how his platitudes helped the tribe endure, did not.

"Finally Moses and I sat, secluded on an outcropping, gazing on the tribe below. Moses said for over a year a painful growth had been forming in his chest, and he had been bleeding occasionally from his mouth. Mirian knew. He still intended to see our people to the Promised Land. I desperately urged he might recover with proper food and rest. Moses placed his hand on my trembling arm and shook his massive head, saying he needed my help to finish his earthly task. I wept as he held me. How impossible to live in a world without Moses! It should have been me comforting my beloved friend. I had no right to indulge myself when he asked for my help. I said I would do anything to help him however he wished. We sat as so many times, and watched the sun sink. I vowed to myself to preserve his memory. I prayed to a God I never believed in. I asked that Moses never be forgotten. We descended the mountain, our greatest challenges before us.

***

"It took two days to journey the eight miles to El-Thamad, sheltered in a large ravine. Because of its location below the surface of the surrounding terrain El-Thamad had both shade and protection from the elements. More importantly, El-Thamad had the spring. Its denizens traded in water and contraband. Shelter could be bought by any fugitive. Talented criminals found employers.

"Our traders arrived with eighteen hundred donkeys before we descended from the Sinai Mountains. A local delegation approached the head of our column to ask our intentions. Moses assured the locals we would pay for all water and be gone in one day. We came in peace. He treated these outcasts well. After we left, El-Thamad would return to its lonely, dusty isolation.

"We rested for a day, these asses all that could be obtained. Joshua placed guards around the people as they rested and slept in the shade. I approached a local leader to find someone with medical skill, saying the person would be paid well, but must be skillful and discreet. My host studied me, then gave a time and meeting place. When Moses and I reached it the local bade us follow him. We halted before a rock crack that extended into a cliff. A tall gaunt figure, face deeply pockmarked, stood before us. After studying Moses with sad eyes, he nodded, asking us to enter. Our escort departed.

"The crevice opened into a room flooded by sunlight from a breach in the rock ceiling. Vessels of powders and liquids filled rock shelves. Surgical tools lay neatly on a separate cloth-covered shelf. A collection of scrolls heaped on another. The healer asked Moses to lie on a rock table for an examination. Moses asked the scarred man how he knew he was ill. The skeletal man merely smiled and explained he had been a court physician in the past. I thrilled to be in the presence of a man of education and culture after so many years among the unlettered. This sallow specter questioned Moses while running his hands over the great old frame. Occasionally the pockmarked man found a scar or even a tiny build-up on a bone and correctly stated when the injury occurred and its precise nature. The stranger asked Moses how long he had been a slave. When the surprised Moses did not answer the physician apologized, saying the bones showed hard physical labor in childhood, seldom seen in free men, adding that everyone in this place had secrets. He frowned as he explored Moses' lower chest.

"The physician told Moses to sit and explained that Moses was afflicted with a lung tumor. There was no known cure since it would spread to other organs. Patients usually died during operations or of infection afterwards. Moses would die in two to three months with or without surgery.

"I grasped my head in agony and wept. Moses placed his hand heavily upon my shoulder, a silent reminder of my duty and promises. The doctor proffered drinks in little cups. As we swallowed the slightly bitter draughts, I felt soothed. Moses declared his pain vanquished.

"The doctor walked to a recess in the wall, and returned with two vessels, one large, the second small. He explained we had drunk opium from the Black Sea region, produced from the pods of an unusual plant. Moses should drink from the larger vessel only when discomfort became unbearable. The amount necessary to relieve pain would increase with the disease. The amount given us should allow travel until the end. When the blood flowed steadily or in large amounts every few minutes, death was imminent. On the final day, even opium would not give respite from pain. At that point the physician held up the smaller vessel and said drinking this would quickly end all torment. Moses reached for and held it in his giant hand, asking what liquid could transport a human through the gates of death so easily. The doctor answered it was a mixture of wine and hemlock from the North Mediterranean shores. Moses laughed, with his ever youthful voice, remarking how few had the luxury of dying with the taste of fine wine on their lips. The doctor smiled, resting a hand on Moses' shoulder. 'Spoken bravely and truthfully. I am glad to help such a man.' He said opium sometimes produced visions and users claimed access to divine understanding. The important thing was that it killed pain and he had never known patients to report unpleasant visions. The physician addressed me, saying only a true friend would stay with Moses through all to come.

"That evening I sought company from the cold stars. How many before me had gazed into the remote heavens and wondered if life had meaning? Had all this mysterious matter and life always existed? It is so human to believe a force created it. But when our hopeful hearts reached for that idea we also had to recognize it seemed impossible God did not have a beginning. Was it simply human nature to stop at the idea of God because it offered such soothing hope? Do only the thoughtful few say, 'Yes, the idea of a kind God is good, but what existed before God? Do we confuse hope with reality?'

"As I reclined on a boulder, yet warm from the sun, I thought how trivial all these beliefs seemed as I gazed into the limitless firmament. If there was a God, He must be far, far larger than my selfish, piddling imagination. Would Moses be remembered? Would a God welcome him to that home Moses had described? Could one gain God's favor? How was a man expected to find such a mysterious God? As I rose from the rock to return to our encampment, I had no answers. God, if he existed, kept remarkably silent.

"We crossed the desert toward Ezion-gebert. From there, the tribe would turn north through the inferno of the Wadi Arabah. The rough trail, on higher ground which formed part of a land swell blocking the northern advance of the Red Sea, wearied us. Once we reached Ezion-geber and turned north we would enter the Negeb Desert, a mix of ravines, wadis, and broken ground, desert, and badlands flanking the Dead Sea. Rain, when it did occur, caused deadly flash floods. Over eons, a large depression formed, the Dead Sea Rift, the Sea of Galilee and the Dead Sea parts of it. I had heard of Dead Sea waters so salty a man could not drown in them, only float.

"When we reached Ezion-geber, similar to El-Thamad, Moses assured the locals of our peaceful intent. We picked up the trail north immediately, not straining their meager resources by camping. They had never seen such a host cross this remote spot. Living in the open desert without means to clean ourselves reduced us to sun-burned leather draped in stained rags.

"These native denizens, outcasts and criminals, calculated their chances of a successful raid. With narrow eyes they noted our weapons, bright and visible. However, they doubted this many people could survive the trip across the Negeb. More than one killer glanced at our weary column, then at the broiling sun, wondering whether its fiery talons would do his killing for him. If we weakened or made a mistake these jackals would tear us to pieces.

"They disrobed our women with their hungry eyes. Only our armed men prevented the rape and slavery of our wives and daughters. No longer protected by the Sinai wilderness, we risked exposure to a merciless world fraught with heartless men and desert.

"The Negeb is a poor place to find water, the only constant source the Jordan River two hundred miles away. Our food requirements from where they were until we would reach the Jordan were over half a ton of grain a day not counting feed for our animals. Every pound of grain and water had to be carried from storage in the Sinai. Each step north was that much further away from food stores and cisterns.

"At first, the terrain continued high because we had to cross the great land uplift that blocked the eastern branch of the Red Sea. However by the end of the second day we started to descend into lowlands of the southern Dead Sea Rift, the soil so powdery the slightest disturbance, much less the feet of two thousand people, caused it to boil up and hang in the air. We inhaled it, coughing without respite. Dust settled on our tormented bodies, increasing thirst. By the end of the third day we endured nineteen more fatalities, by the sixth forty-two.

"Moses bled often, the heat and pervasive dust inflaming his lungs. By mid-afternoon he sipped opium at least every hour. How painful yet awe inspiring to see the gaunt giant continue striding across this desert with growing intensity, his entire being focused on seeing this tribe to water and safety. After we camped, Moses barely slept. Often I dozed at his side only to awaken to see him gazing into the night sky. I begged him to rest because we depended on our bodies' ability to endure. Moses smiled agreement, and at times he pretended to sleep for my sake. Too soon the blazing sun would shatter the night sky. Another day on the desert.

"We were far into the punishing Negeb. However, the Jordan River was less than one hundred miles away. That haven of water obsessed me. Some water haulers went north to the Jordan to fill their empty vessels. The first convoy back brightened our column with hope as they described their first sight of an actual river. Raised in the Sinai, they had seen only slight rain and runoff.

"We soon entered country claimed by the Moabites, a powerful culture. Thankfully, our scouts reported little activity. But Moses weakened. We could conceal his distress no longer. He confided in Joshua, stressing that the tribe not be told. Moses marching day after day in this valley of death appeared inhuman. He often sipped the medicine, reset his jaw, and kept going forward. The flesh melted from his giant frame, yet his hair remained a wild mane of white, gray, and sand. With matted hair hanging between his bony shoulders he resembled an old desert lion, a starving beast of prey. Sinews stood out on his arms like burned black ropes. I most remember his eyes, glowing with intensity. Many times I believed they saw images I could not. No pain seared enough to stop him, as if he wrestled Death itself in order to die in one certain place and time.

"In the evenings we huddled together, speaking of our youth, reliving the savage scenes of our survival. Moses pondered whether he was just preceding me into an afterlife. He promised if such a thing were true he would prepare a place for me. He speculated that death might be just a shallow river, beyond its dark waters fair shores, green with grass and shaded with apricot and pear trees. I said I was unworthy to be his friend. He replied if not for me he would have died a slave. Dying as a free man was worth any hardship. I gripped his hand, committed to see him to his final goal. Again and again I swore my private vow to get Moses to the Promised Land, and see that the world did not forget.

"It took nine agonizing days to reach the Dead Sea. The column paused often as people raised exhausted eyes to gaze upon its water. Even water not potable was a sight of joy to us survivors of the Negeb. Along the shore, minerals left from evaporated water formed shapes and figures, salt fantasies of every conceivable shape.

"Moses coughed and bled heavily, increasing sips of painkiller. He seldom spoke, although much of the time he leaned on me, his great arm around my shoulder. Joshua tried to assign men to help me with Moses, but I refused them. As long as I could go forward I would see Moses reach the Jordan. What a sight we must have presented, two old men clinging to each other, stumbling northward, the ravaged giant leaning on my thin frame, both filthy, our rags barely covering us. Our peeling skin blistered with running sores. Our lips swelled and cracked. We gasped for breath. Somehow, faltering, we continued.

"At times Moses could rally and walk unsupported. How much was sheer will and how much was his pain killer I know not. I wanted to thank the healer. It seemed unfair that worthy people like Moses not receive a just reward. Then I would remember the words of my old mentor, Alto, when he explained how easily we confuse our hopes with reality. How difficult to see the hands of a kind God under our present conditions and with our present losses.

Chapter Eight

"When it seemed life could not torture us with any more, a scout reported that a Moabite party wished to speak to our leaders. Moses straightened and ordered that Joshua be called. It did not seem possible this drooping tribe of nearly two thousand might have to battle men as well as the elements. Moses ordered a runner to tell the Moabites we would permit a party of twelve to approach our column. Moses smiled, laying his hand on my arm. I readied my sword. Moses had the same glint in his eyes as when we killed the Egyptian scouts on the supply road so long ago. Here he stood as an old lion with matted mane and scarred, diseased body, but still a dangerous foe. I drew strength from that as the Moabites arrived.

"The Moabites appeared slightly better fed than the desert variety of human dregs. Their short, burly leader's calloused hands showed no sword scars, only calluses of a full-time farmer and part-time raider. Joshua arrived with several tested men and addressed the Moabite who stated that this land was theirs and none were permitted on it without permission. Joshua responded that we harbored no hostile intent and planned to leave their lands at the Jordan River. The Moabite leader seemed uncertain as he glanced over our column and the warriors who flanked it, calculating our strength behind his small, stony eyes. The Moabite asked Joshua of his position if the Moabites denied passage. Joshua replied that we would fight. The Moabite then gave an ugly laugh and said, 'With what will you fight? Starved scarecrows like him?' He pointed at Moses. Joshua's sword was halfway out of his scabbard when Moses raised his hand halting him.

"Speaking calmly Moses said, 'Let us reason together. Is it not too hot to do battle today? My son Joshua still has youthful passions.' Staring directly into the Moabite's eyes he said evenly, 'First impressions are often wrong and sometimes dangerous.

"The Moabite seemed to waver.

"Moses continued in a conversational tone, 'We have over a thousand warriors. The Egyptians could not kill us. The desert could not kill us. If you try to kill us, the cost will be high. You are a farmer are you not?' Without waiting for an answer he continued, 'I myself wished for a life of honest toil and the peace of the evening fields. Sadly, my hands have shed blood too many times.'

"The leader's eyes dropped to Moses' huge scar-crazed hands. 'Of course, I am old now and ill. I would like to see the Jordan River before I go the way of all flesh.' Moses continued without apparent offense, 'I apologize for my appearance. Our trek across the desert was difficult.' Shifting slightly, Moses said to the Moabite leader, 'Do you have a son here? I would like to feel the grip of a Moabite man in the flower of youth.'

"Before the leader could answer a stocky young man stepped forward and sneered, 'Here I am, old one. Shake the hand of a real man. I bed three women a night!' Once again I thought nothing would prevent Joshua from killing them all after this affront.

"Moses chuckled and replied, 'Perhaps Moabite women are not lusty. One of ours can easily satisfy any man.' Moses slowly extended his hand. In fury the young man stepped forward and gripped it. This Moabite concentrated on placing all his strength through his right arm, the sleeve stretched tight. Sweat appeared like warts on his forehead. How could Moses endure? Moses replied to him as to an infant, 'Surely such a man as you has a better grip? I had more strength as a youth. But perhaps I am too old to remember.' With that statement, the intensity in his eyes burned to white molten metal. The air filled with energy. A force seemed to rise from the earth and I watched Moses expand. Under his cloak cords of sinew rolled and gathered across his huge chest. It seemed his right arm swelled into stone, and all eyes moved toward his hand. No one breathed. His fingers tightened. Blood drained from the Moabite's hand, then his face. I heard his bones crack and the scream torn from his throat. The horrified young man fell to his knees as the hand of Moses continued to contract. The Moabite leader remained silent. I wondered why the father didn't spring to his son's defense.

"Finally, Joshua leapt forward and said, 'Father, release him!'

"For several moments it seemed Moses did not hear. Then, without releasing his grip, Moses turned toward the Moabite leader and said, 'Will we have peaceful access across your lands at a fair price? I am old. Will you allow a dying man to see the Jordan River?'

"The Moabite leader answered, 'Release my foolish son. The braggart has met his reward. You and I can reason together!'

"Moses slowly returned to his former status as a sensible old man. The injured youth was led off. The Moabite leader turned reasonable indeed. As farmers, the Moabites could use many donkeys. Moses generously promised their amazed leader that once we crossed the Jordan our tribe would send back two hundred. Moses gave six donkeys loaded with valuable trade goods to him at once. The two parted the best of friends and all of us again appreciated the genius that belonged to Moses alone. Finally, I knew Moses and I would live to see the Jordan.

***

"The column resumed its march beside the Dead Sea. Hour after hour Moses and I struggled north, his left arm around my shoulder, my right around his waist. The sun's heat seemed to redouble as if it wished to halt our movement toward the Jordan. Onward we shuffled through dust that entangled our feet and blinded our stinging eyes. Moses and I would stop when we heard Joshua telling us we were at the camp site. His voice reached me as a thin sound whispered from afar. We would sink down against the nearest rock, leaning on one another.

"We found bread in our hands and would try to get some down our throats. The people feared for us and did everything to help. They delegated small teams of volunteers to precede us, even picking up stones we might stumble over in our weakness. I had no way of knowing that the seeds of legends were being born in the tribe as they watched us refuse to die.

"We endured nine days before reaching the Jordan. The sun was live flames searing all exposed skin. Objects formed and reformed in swirling patterns to dust-infected eyes. Wind tore at our cloaks and blew sand in all directions at once. My biggest memories are of littlest things. The taste of dust as one fell to the ground, the gritty feel of Moses' staff as I used it to pull myself erect. The flavor of sand mixed with blood from my split lips; the feel of Moses' ribs as he grew so thin. Victory was claimed if we could take the next step through the dust.

"Most of all, I remember Joshua saying, 'Only one day more. Can either of you understand me? Father, we are nearly to the river!' His voice annoyed me. Why disturb a slumbering old man? Then a rough hand jostled my shoulder. With great effort I opened my eyes to see Moses gazing at me with his weary smile.

"At last I understood! We had arrived almost to the river! I noticed the setting sun. We were in camp. Joshua was here. Abraham was here. Although he could barely turn toward me, Moses smiled. Incredibly, I laughed. Impossibly, Moses' eyes started to dance. Exuberantly, he chortled with me. What a scene it must have been for Joshua and Abraham! Their two old fathers trying to laugh, breathe, and cough all at once.

"There seemed nothing left of Moses but blood, bones, and flaking skin. Only his eyes revealed the Moses I knew. Then the sight of the fresh blood on his face and neck punched me to reality. He wiped it away. 'Eli, my old friend, every man must die and my time is almost here. If there is a peaceful place after death, I will prepare a room for you and will be waiting.'

"I leaned against his chest for his embrace. My cheek rested against the blood-encrusted roughness of his clothes. I wondered at his comment about preparing a room for me. What a strange idea after so many years in the desert! I placed the thought aside as I forbade my eyes to weep. The weak beating of his heart pulsed within my ear.

"On that last morning, Moses swallowed opium before he could rise. Joshua and Abraham met us as we started on the trail and said we should reach the river that afternoon. This gave me fresh strength and hope. I enticed Moses to drink more pain killer, and helped him with his drinking bag. Today was his final trial. The drug gave him succor.

"After days of silent marching, Moses desired to tell me his dream of meeting with God. In fact, Moses said, he did not think it was a dream at all. I responded with practical questions as to what God looked like and what they talked about. Moses tried to chuckle at my simple questions, but mostly just coughed and bled. He was able to say that God laughed a lot and had explained many things. He was nothing like vain mortals imagine. God said he did not have a man like body or any human weakness. Moses confessed he had been ashamed that he himself had used such ideas to control and lead. God seemed to understand and merely laughed saying humans always made up things He was supposed to have done or said. Even exhausted, I thought the idea of a laughing God was new. Of all the powers and strengths our God might have, I had never pictured Him with a sense of humor.

"I remembered what the healer said about visions being common among those taking this drug and wrestled with the idea of playing along as one might with an intoxicated friend. However, Moses had not been this lucid in days. I knew that dying people often rallied before surrendering to death, and I decided to be honest. I suggested his conversation with God might have resulted from the drug. Moses agreed that was possible, but it appeared as real as our conversation. I asked what made him think it was not merely an illusion. It took Moses time to gather strength to reply, but he finally said, 'Because He gave me answers.'

"I mentioned to Moses that we must be within three miles of the Jordan. As we struggled down the trail, Moses finally got out that God loved all life equally with no favoritism.

"No favoritism! Could this be why pain and death seemed so random? After all, I thought, what is favoritism anyway if not selective treatment? Wasn't it just human hope and vanity that we expected God to intervene whenever chance impinged on our lives? What is life except births and deaths? To a God of all life would it make sense that one be more valuable than another? Did it make sense that God would have a favorite life form much less a favorite people? Could it be that God seemed so distant because He refused to value one life over another? If God created all life, should it be such a surprise that He loved equally? In a single blow Moses swept away all myths that God loved one people and hated another. All political advantages and individual vanities were destroyed if God loved all life equally. There was no God of the Egyptians to pit against the God of the Hittites. There was only a God for everyone and everything with no favoritism.

"Finally I asked Moses why he thought God spoke to him. After all why would God choose to do so? Moses did not know. That broke down my reserve, and I asked Moses if there is life after death. Moses said the answer to that was yes, but he did not know exactly what it was like. It seemed clear that death was not the end, and he felt God implied death was a change toward a completely different realm. Moses did say there was a type of judgment but that the result would be corrective change rather than the human fantasies of physical punishments and burning hells. We fell silent, struggling to keep up with the others. Finally Moses said there was nothing more he remembered except a general sense of God's humor and acceptance. Thus ended our strange discussion. Moses spoke of it no more.

"We turned west to a land greener than I had known in decades. As we descended the river drainage, the air cooled. We gazed across a shallow, verdant valley. A sparkling band of flashing blue traversed this paradise: the Jordan River. Awestruck, we savored the beauty. This was a Promised Land.

"Wild oak, cypress, and poplar trees, tall grass, and low blooming plants lined both sides of the Jordan. Scattered spots of anemones, tulips, black irises, and oleander lit up the grass blanket with bright yellows, reds, and blues. Vibrant butterflies dipped over the colors as we drew near our people ahead. They cheered, shouting our names. I don't know how Moses found the strength, but he hoisted his staff and continually waved to them. Then they strew grass and flowers upon the trail. Thus after so many years in the desert, so much hardship, Moses and I felt soft plants beneath our feet as we approached the river.

"The Jordan sang with delicate melody, gliding over rocks and slipping through overhanging foliage. The water near the bank almost reached our knees; such a wonderful cool feeling as it swept around our legs. I supported Moses as he bent to drink deep. I then helped him, restored and radiant, stand erect.

"The throng hushed. Plovers sang and other birds chirped above us. Leaves and grass rustled in the breeze. Moses removed his arm from my shoulder. He clasped my hand. With effort, he lifted it high. Hands above our heads, we turned to our tribesmen. How the hills rang as nearly two thousand survivors cheered our deliverance. Everyone converged on the river to wash battered bodies and celebrate. No amount of life or sorrow to follow would ever lessen the joy of that glorious day.

"Moses weakened quickly. All his fortitude had focused on seeing his people to the Promised Land. He bade us farewell, drank the fatal liquid given to him in Ezion-geber, and passed through death's portal. At his request, we buried him without ceremony in an unmarked grave beside the Jordan. The life of Moses that I have faithfully recorded is true and accurate. I, Eli, was there, and I mourn him to this day."

Chapter Nine

Alone in the study, Alice wept over Eli's last entry. Part of her wanted to wail. Only the presence of the Arab cook in the kitchen stopped her. Her tears darkened the Tablet, and she smeared them away. Exhausted and nursing a headache after weeks of translating, she cried for the pathos of Moses' death at the Jordan, so near in some ways to what she'd learned in Sunday school. Still, it didn't match the Godly Moses. A stinging loss, but then again she'd grown fond of these two benevolent connivers.

Besides, the biblical God, worse than Moses' lifesaving hoax, was a mass murderer: women, children, even babies slaughtered in the Old Testament because their religion was "evil". As a child, she'd accepted such iconic cruelty, simply filing it away as part of her Judeo-Christian identity. What would she think now if a political leader killed every first-born of a nation just to show he could? Wouldn't she recoil, horrified? Yet, according to her Sunday school teacher, Mrs. Graben, that's what God did to the Egyptians. Now, the Tablets blatantly proved that angry God did not exist. Then why did she feel unsettled? Why the panic attacks she'd been having almost from the start of this labor? Was she afraid of God? People? Was she afraid of people or for people? If only the real God could be found! If the Tablets had such an effect on her, a sophisticated scholar, what would their effect be on those who, with contented faces shining in spiritual well being, attended church each Sunday?

She put all the work in order. As she did, she pictured the boy Eli and his crippled teacher sitting outside under palms for class. Eli's cynicism comes to some educated people. Is cynicism really the state of being educated? If so, she should have been more probing. Did she feel cynical now? Not really, and that mystified her, too.

Yes, she should have probed more, but she had plenty of company. Millions held the Bible was written by honest, informed, devout historians. However, these Tablets exposed them as schemers just like any modern politician! How obvious now that every book of the Bible stemmed from mere mortals' agenda. It benefited King David to be approved as "a man chosen by God". What an endorsement. How easily ancient leaders created whatever image they wanted. According to these Tablets anyway. She kept circling back to the same question: How would the world react to these Tablets? Humanity required spiritual hope, comforting security.

Alice's face tinted as the sun, gone from blazing white through her window to cherry-red, flattened over the western horizon. She had to get out of the study with its dark furniture and walls like yellowed ivory. She scribbled a note to Henry, directing him to the kitchen for his chicken kabob supper, saying she needed a long evening walk in the Sepphoris hills. She should stay, but they seemed to be moving in parallel lines these days, seldom touching, only communicating about the Tablets.

As she trudged toward the hills she sighed, massaging her knotted neck. Youth in the throes of passion such as Eli with Laleah create such catastrophes. She remembered her early days with Henry, how joyously they claimed each other's bodies. She had hoped for a child, but that hope failed. Perhaps they were destined for something else. These incredible Tablets.

Archaeology was Henry's child. Henry was now in his true element, having long ago accepted his state as a borderline Christian by virtue of admiration for Christ as a great teacher. But he couldn't accept all things biblical. Pulling her heavy sweater close, Alice failed to think about her brief absence from the study earlier in the day to attend to a minor crisis in the kitchen.

***

Henry sat in the study that night after a lonely meal of over spiced kabobs, also moved by Eli's final words. The longer he read, the more he felt almost electrically charged. If this were true, Moses gained control over a primitive tribe by chicanery and force. The Exodus story was proven a fable, fabulous to use the same root. Except. All the communities existed at the time. Could the Tablets solve the old debate about the actual path of the so-called Exodus? Scholars had long noted the vagueness of

Exodus route. Three routes had been debated: the Sunday School version of the crossing at the Gulf of Suez; Exodus: 14, which put up to three million people near Migdon; or the story starting at Numbers:33 which is silent about the Egyptian army's defeat and merely states, "They passed through the sea into the desert."

The selection of Moses by God, the idea of a chosen people, and a land promised by God were fables. Henry, never altogether unchained from his fundamentalist background, felt a meteor of freedom soar through his psyche, or was it vindication? For the first time he was at emotional as well as intellectual liberty. Still, what would be the effects on others? Alice's growing upheaval over the Tablets took him aback. How deeply our early teachings take root.

His mind reverted loosely to scholarship. The impossibility of a populous Sinai Peninsula goaded endless study of the Biblical account. Three million people plus their flocks couldn't have lived there for forty years with no forage. Climatologists agree the desolate environment has existed for millennia. Also, unable to remember how long since he'd asked himself such questions, he admired Moses and Eli's theological and philosophical discussions. Alice's personal note at that point said, "Damn it. It soothed me for years to latch onto cultural answers to religious questions."

He'd had time to ponder Alice's initial report and sent Sam Stein, his department chair, a coded fax. Secrecy meant everything until the material could be stamped with unimpeachable validity. At that point the Tablets together with all the transcripts and site reports could be turned over to Chairman Stein and Harvard, what happened next the realm of others.

Henry rubbed his eyes to force sleep away, stretching against the back of his chair. Would it be that easy? What if the authorities decided to suppress the information? Could he, a dedicated archaeologist, remain silent? What was his duty to these documents' writers? They'd labored, perhaps even suffered, to create and preserve this wealth of information. Could he, or anyone, rightly suppress it? Wasn't commitment to truth greater than potential upheaval? At the end of his soul search he swore fealty to the god of integrity.

He had just so committed himself, when the door opened and Alice, dark circles under her eyes, walked in. "I can see that it's going to be world shaking," she said, standing in front of the desk in the study, glaring at Henry seated behind it. "But the words here shake me, too. Words have such power." To Henry's astonishment, his sophisticated, intellectual wife burst into tears.

He rose and put his arms around her, rubbing the top of her tawny head with his chin. "It's a vindication of my rebellion back home," he said.

"I wasn't raised for this," she whispered. "I didn't think I believed so much anymore, but it was always my fallback position, my insurance, what I could go back to."

"To save your soul?" He smiled gently.

"To define my identity in the world."

"Markers of sorts. Basically saying, 'Do not cross this line of behavior...of belief."

"More like buoys at sea, Henry. The books of the Bible told me, 'Don't go too far on the open sea, little boat. Don't lose sight of us."

"Now we sail on the sea of uncertainty. But this has been given to us, Alice. We'll have to navigate by new signs."

"I'll navigate by the stars for awhile. When I go for my nightly hikes, I'll lift up mine eyes to the hills and all that. It helped tonight. My emotions keep darting back and forth over this."

"Well, studying the firmament was good enough for the likes of Galileo," Henry said.

"Sure, and look what happened to him." Alice forced a smile, blew him a kiss from the doorway, and went to their bedroom.

Henry almost joined her, but Eli's words pulled him back to his desk. Sepphoris slumbered like a giant with a free conscience. Henry poured water, drank, and returned to the Tablets.

Chapter Ten

"This reminds me of the Dead Sea Scrolls," Henry said to Alice, seated at the kitchen's trestle table over strong coffee and oranges next morning. In 1947, an Arab boy herding goats on the west side of the Dead Sea idly cast a stone into the mouth of a shallow cave, surprised to hear pottery breaking. Eventually eleven caves with ancient manuscripts were found in the Khirbet Qumran area.

"We've certainly heard enough of the rumors," Alice said. Claims of suppression and even some destruction. There'd been debate as to ownership and how the larger academic community could gain access to the scrolls. Many expressed dismay and finally suspicion at the snail's pace of the process. One deep belief held that certain manuscripts contained damaging evidence against Judaism and Christianity. Since the Essenes who hid the scrolls were critics of their time's religious establishment, this was not implausible.

Then strange things happened. Academic dissenters were quietly dissuaded to drop the issue of Dead Sea suppression. Vocal professors gained promotions or retired early. One did not talk about the glacial pace of the Dead Sea Scroll translations if one wanted a long career in ancient Near East studies. That era's active participants died off. Spouses of prominent critics of the Dead Sea scenario were rumored to have received large offers for diaries, records, or manuscripts the deceased might have written concerning the Scrolls, none ever published.

***

In spite of her efforts to be light through the days and nights of translating, Alice developed a haunted look. Gray circles shadowed her eyes as she unveiled the ancient words. She remembered how Jesus allegedly said, "The truth will set you free." Ironically true, but believers would be "free" in a spiritual vacuum. This Jesus story was far from the idyllic Good Shepherd who comforted millions. She grew distracted, translating the Tablets each day, arranging her output, taking her long, solitary, nocturnal meanderings. "Like an owl," she muttered.

Her interest in languages came from a love of words and how people used them. A turn of phrase could delight her. Now, in spite of the importance, she took no joy in the work.

As she walked the ancient hills, stopping to study the panoply of stars each night when she'd finished work, she wondered at her past naiveté. Leaders always wrest control over power and image. The current presidential scandals in America should have been her wake up call. If a leading politician would lie to the American citizenry about a sexual dalliance, what would an ancient despot like King David get away with? King Solomon was just a ruthless dictator who even used his own people as slaves. Given the blatant greed of television evangelists, was it so surprising that ancient priests manipulated their audiences?

When she considered the brutality with which Muslims suppressed other religious groups in Third World countries, or thought of the Spanish Inquisition, should she be surprised that ancient priests would also denounce other religions as "enemies of the true God?"

***

Henry believed he had everything under control. His strategy of not discussing the Tablets seemed to be working as curious students' questions declined. Alice was doing a tremendous job. So far Henry found no major issue of translation to differ over. She'd calculated from references to Ramses II that Eli penned his history in 1274 to 1212 BCE, and Henry agreed.

Despite his accounts' rogue implications, Eli's descriptions of these primitive folk rang true. Mixing religious simplicity with a magical world of spirits remained common in primitive cultures to this day. Explorers noted it not unusual for primitives to see them as gods or divine messengers. Although Eli's writing predated the Bible, Henry saw links to it: the duty of a man to marry his brother's widow, reference to The Promised Land, huge clusters of grapes, the quail legend, the phrase "milk and honey," Moses told dramatic tales that later appeared in the Bible to give a primitive tribe a sense of history. Henry shook his head, remembering the dark clouds that history spread across his own childhood.

One night he felt the old familiar need for Alice, who left the house each evening without inviting him. He urgently wanted to lie beside her, to tell her in words and with his body how much her translations meant to him, and how he wanted to comfort her. One of her personal notes while translating had said, "Where is my biblical Moses? This destroys the foundation." When she returned, he closed the study and stepped into the cool dimness of their room. She turned toward him and held out her hand, pulling him to the bed. For that night, their work and all its repercussions could wait.

Of course, the Tablets inevitably remained the focal point of Alice and Henry's world. They discussed them, elation alternating with fear, although Henry tended to the former and Alice to the latter, and each even thought of them when they made love. Henry resented the daily duties of supervising the dig. Only evenings were his for fiercely joyful study.

Stein began to assert pressure. After only three weeks of reading Alice's translations, Henry received a fax from his chair demanding news. Clearly Henry's department head needed information soon. Henry would have to fax him again soon with a progress report.

***

One morning, Alice rose before Henry. When he stepped into the kitchen, she hoisted her cup in greeting. Strong morning coffee was the best here in the Middle East. "Did you dream?" she asked.

"I'm too tired to dream these days."

"Moses had them going with his nighttime visions, didn't he?" she asked.

Henry poured coffee for himself and sat down. Alice seemed easier now with the truth bomb they'd uncovered. "In the Bible," he said, "dreams start with Abraham: he received the idea of the

Promised Land that way along with the idea of a chosen people. Jacob dreamed the ladder to heaven, Joseph dreamed, David dreamed, Solomon dreamed, Ezekiel and Daniel dreamed. In Matthew Jesus was conceived by the Holy Ghost in a dream. The New Testament book of Revelation was John's dream."

"I dreamed about human sacrifice last night. It was that creepy section with Eli talking to the guide. Of course, I know children were sacrificed to the god Molech. The Old Testament scorned horror shows like that."

"Even so, all blood-based religions are rooted in human sacrifice."

Alice winced. "Sure, throw communion at me."

"'Eating flesh and drinking blood' is just as modern as last Sunday's services for Christians."

She frowned. "What about those Ten Commandments?"

"Born to give primitive people their first laws. It's funny. All this was just storytelling for political control, and I can't understand why I'm offended. After all, why should ancient leaders be any more honest than our modern ones?"

"I know. But it's a way to make sense of it all, isn't it?" Alice ruffled his hair. "I'm starting to feel comfortable with the truth. It's so grown up."

He stood, and they walked outside, blinking in the harsh light. "What we've found will add tremendous new detail to the whole Moses story. Just the cisterns explaining how they had water. There wasn't enough water in the whole Sinai to keep such a horde alive for a day. Eli is right on the money about distances, place names. Their searching questions are more credible than the Old Testament's fantastic stories."

"There's nothing else like it in Middle East literature."

"Truer words were never spoken. Except perhaps by Eli."

***

That night, after a dinner of lamb stew and pita bread, they picked up the morning's conversation over rich red wine.

"I used to think about the Spanish Inquisition," she said. "If the Catholic Church hadn't had such power it couldn't have happened."

"Don't forget the Middle Ages. The Catholic Church literally owned one third of Western Europe."

"What a pair of nerds we are. Does anybody but an archaeologist talk like this over a romantic dinner?"

"No. You're just lucky."

"I'm wistful. Even if the truth is best, I feel nostalgic for the old certainty."

"I'm not nostalgic at all. I grew up smothered in all that certainty. I only want to be sure of the truth."

She sipped the wine and smiled. "Everybody wants that. Maybe some just want to take shortcuts."

"Enough, my lady nerd. I'm sure of you."

She laughed.

He became serious. "For now, we're the only two living souls who could have this conversation. The great, true story of Moses."

"I didn't expect the nobility," she ventured. "People should know. What will happen to these Tablets?"

"Ah, the big question. This is a treasure beyond price to scholarship...to the truth. On the other hand, these Tablets strike down foundations of Judaism and Christianity...to some extent even Islam."

"After reading Eli's story, I feel a responsibility to him, Henry. They wouldn't suppress this, would they? Aren't we, all of us, dedicated to the pursuit of truth?"

"Bearers of awkward truths have always paid a high price. How brave are you? How brave am I?" Henry rose, rubbing his eyes and walked to the window. "Sunset already."

"I know it sounds strange coming from me, but I have no real regrets and neither should you," Alice said, putting an arm around his waist. "Tonight, we should feel blessed. We've been given this enormous gift. Stein will be here soon. Yes, we'll lose some control, but we'll be able to share the responsibility, too."

Alone in the study, Henry returned to his desk and waggled a pen back and forth, feeling the strain of the last weeks. The

Tablets weighed down his body, his conscience, and his soul. Surprisingly, he felt the need of prayer. Head bowed and hands folded he prayed to a God of the Universe. Master and maker of endless galaxies. Creator and sustainer of all life. Intelligence beyond comprehension. Source of hope beyond all fear and trial. He prayed for courage and wisdom. He prayed for help. He prayed not as a child, but an enlightened man seeking strength to do his duty.

In that obscure room in Sepphoris, Henry sensed that God was truth and encouraged seekers of truth. To find the absolute truth was to plumb God's depths. Henry felt assured that a seeker of truth was the most faithful and loyal disciple God created. The author of all truth could only be God the Almighty. To hide the truth would be to hide the face of God. A searching mind was an unearned gift. Not to use it to ferret out truth within the maze of shadowy falsity was to deny the ultimate giver of that gift. Refreshed, Henry now knew his path. He had work to do.

What Henry didn't realize...the Tablets had a life of their own; forces gathered around them. Had he foreseen the future he wouldn't have felt so complacent. Quickly making notes, he saw Alice striding back to the house from her stroll in the hills, a lovely, animated silhouette in the milky moonlight.

Chapter Eleven

What harm would it do, if a man told a good strong lie for the sake of the good and for the Christian church? `[...] a lie out of necessity, a useful lie, a helpful lie, such lies would not be against God, he would accept them.
Martin Luther

We should always be disposed to believe that which appears to us to be white is really black, if the hierarchy of the church so decides.
St. Ignatius Loyola

During the weeks of Alice's Eli translating, the relentless sun presided over Sepphoris' student laborers. The work day started with native workers and college students filtering to their assigned sectors. Among the latter strolled one Andre, a skinny, boyish twenty-six-year-old. A Harvard grad student in Mideast anthropology, he'd obtained a dual major in ancient languages and psychology at the Catholic University of America in Washington, D.C. with a full scholarship from the Baltimore Diocese. Devout Catholic parents nurtured his fascination with religion and the ancient Mideast.

Andre's main talent in life turned out to be a gift for discerning lies. That led him to psychology. His college professors conducted tests to validate his talent. Andre could, they determined, identify a liar with ninety-two percent accuracy. The psychology department urged him to stay in D.C. under a grant for further tests, but Andre, feeling a call to the priesthood, declined. The Christian story with its ability to comfort the afflicted and reform behavior fascinated him. He knew the tale of Jesus, poor unlettered country boy confronting powerful secular authorities then dying as a moral hero of the poor was a well known plot in many cultures. Andre recognized its folktale characteristics, but it appealed to his tender nature nevertheless.

His Uncle Charles, a priest of the Jesuit order in Baltimore, often visited Andre's parents. Uncle Charles's mysterious aura made him an object of awe. As Andre grew older Uncle Charles handed reading lists to him which he consumed. By age fourteen, Andre had honed his gift for lie detection. Father Charles never seemed to lie so achieved almost godlike status to his nephew.

Andre now believed only the Church with its mythology and dogma could prevent civilization's collapse. After all, Sepphoris was dust, but the strong Church remained. Professor Cross, always even-handed in his study of ancient cultures and artifacts, became a role model. Time and again Cross would emphasize the close link between religion and civilization, stressing how impossible it has always been to find a developed culture lacking spiritual beliefs. Another factor in Professor Cross' favor: he never lied.

In Israel, Andre took up with Michael, a sunburned, withdrawn grad student from the Deep South. Michael's father, powerful in upper reaches of the Southern Baptist Convention, ministered to a thriving Atlanta congregation. Michael's parents groomed him from early childhood for the same calling.

After work Andre and Michael hiked the nearby hills, debating eternal questions under the star-rich Galilean sky. Friendship deepened, slipping into intimacy. They often sealed their evening meanderings with joyous sensuality. Michael's parents faced a disappointing future. Their boy would never be a Baptist minister.

In addition to the work at the dig, Michael and Andre, along with others, enjoyed evening discussions with Professor Cross who could weave religion and archaeology into a stunningly rich, complex tapestry, expounding on past controversies as new evidence emerged from the Mideast to conflict with mainstream beliefs. Cross held the sessions twice weekly in his study. These informal evenings ended abruptly with the discovery of the Tablets in Sector 73. Cross announced that his work load had increased too much to give the extra time. Asked if this were because of the Tablets, he answered with a brusque, "No, they may be a disappointment," and changed the subject. Andre went rigid at the lie. Even Henry feared he'd been unconvincing.

Andre puzzled next day as he sifted the dry soil in his section. The Tablets must be the critical issue. After all, Dr. Cross had been honest all these months, even on sensitive topics of politics and religion. There must be something astounding in the Tablets to make him tell a

whopper. If their contents were unimportant, Dr. Cross wouldn't care. Then there was Dr. Alice Cross. Evening after evening she wandered the site alone. Formerly, she and Dr. Cross had walked hand in hand. He'd liked seeing them laugh at private jokes. Whatever had been discovered in the Tablets altered the couples' life.

Andre committed himself to stalking evidence. In seemingly idle conversations, he learned who was at Sector 73 for the discovery. Michael became a willing co-investigator. Working separately, they gathered information, cloaking questions as casual discussion, raising no suspicions. Abi, the sector leader who'd helped Dr. Cross prepare the Tablets for transfer, provided the most helpful recall. An illiterate Arab in his thirties, Abi obviously had keen powers of observation. For centuries his ancestors lived or died based on vigilance and solid memories of surroundings. A respectful Andre took mental notes as the Arab described the Tablets' script. Andre concluded it must be Hebrew. Astonished that Abi could recall shapes in such detail. Abi explained how he studied the top Tablets while he waited for Dr. Cross. This mysterious find was of great interest to Abi, who'd run his calloused finger over the marks. With that same finger Abi duplicated them in the dust outside the laborers' barracks. Andre's heart leaped when he recognized Hebrew. Occasionally Andre would add a mark that would be a logical Hebrew correction, and Abi's head bobbed eagerly.

Abi remembered that the markings on the last looked different. His crooked finger drew some of those marks, and Andre realized they were Greek. Odd. He'd never heard of a Greek find written on clay tablets. Drawing the marks in the dust, Abi insisted one series appeared many times. To Andre's astonishment the word Moses appeared in Greek. Abi solemnly told Andre he'd felt the hand of Allah every time he traced his fingers over those marks in the clay.

Out of the dust of Sepphoris the figure of Moses arose and confronted contemporary humanity. In the desert heat, Andre shuddered in a sudden icy draft.

Chapter Twelve

Next morning Andre mulled over the information he and Michael had gathered. Everything boomeranged back to the Tablets: the secrecy, the lie, the change in Alice Cross's behavior, and the long hours of study by Henry Cross. Andre had to see the Tablets for himself. The hours when they lay unread came after Henry Cross ended his studies late at night and before morning when Mrs. Cross went on duty...at least three hours. Andre, who'd never done an illegal thing, now contemplated breaking and entering. The mystery of it...just so intriguing. The memory of Abi's finger tracing the word Moses in the sand triggered a gnawing hunger in Andre.

The Cross home was unguarded since armed troops ringed the camp's periphery. Andre remembered the study key rested in a glass stuffed with pencils and paper clips on the desk. Otherwise, it went into a Cross pocket. Andre needed that key. Stealing it was possible, but that would just warrant the lock's replacement and tighter security. How could he make a copy without the key itself?

His thoughts turned to Georgey, a white haired, sunken-cheeked Arab who worked in his section, rumored to have lost everything in the Yom Kipper War when Israel annexed coastal properties owned by generations of his family. He'd worked for the English as a young man and knew, though seldom used, their language. He now did light work, sifting dirt through a sieve to check for pottery shards or small artifacts. His hard eyes had seen hard times. Thin, unsmiling, Georgey was a tough old man.

Andre chose to be direct. Taking Georgey a bucket of soil to sift, he placed a twenty dollar bill on top. Andre murmured that he wanted to talk after work near the laborers' barracks. Georgey nodded slightly.

Early that evening, they sat leaning against a building, watching the still radiant sun sink in the lavender sky. Others scattered into small groups. Nothing would be suspected about Andre being there. In low tones he said he needed to copy a key, but didn't have the key itself. Georgey waited long to respond. Finally, he asked in perfect Queen's English whether Andre could get an imprint of it. Andre grinned. It might happen. Georgey traced his old finger through the dust. "In Israel, among the Jews, such a thing is very dangerous. It would cost five hundred American dollars."

Andre sifted dust through his fingers. "If you get a key, and the key works, I'll pay your five hundred."

Georgey squinted against the evening glare. "I will need $200.00 cash and a picture of you. Then I will begin."

"Why do you need a picture?"

For the first time Georgey looked directly at Andre. "The picture goes to some friends of mine. If you are a member of the Israeli Secret Service, they will know who to kill." Then and there Andre glimpsed the deadly world living under the thin veneer of civilization. Next afternoon he made the transfer to Georgey. The Sepphoris wind came up sharply as the money and photo changed hands.

***

The Tablets' mystery drew Andre toward a world more dangerous than he knew. Since all work ceases in Israel for Shabbat, most Arab laborers go that day to visit loved ones. Georgey joined numerous travelers who left the camp Friday at sunset. Even the Israeli Mossad, good as it is, is not all-powerful. Georgey wasn't among the thousands in modern day Israel who have dossiers. An old laborer didn't warrant use of limited manpower.

Georgey didn't consider himself a terrorist, only a victim of aggression and land theft. An Arab received little justice in Jewish courts, and Georgey was far too prudent to plant bombs, leaving that to younger, more passionate men and women. Instead, he joined thousands of Palestinians who contributed information to Harakat-al-Muqaama al-Islamiya, commonly known as HAMAS, the new Palestinian alternative to the PLO. Many Palestinians felt PLO leader Arafat betrayed the cause by signing a peace pact with Jewish Prime Minister Rabin in May of

1994. Rabin was later killed by a right-wing Jew, and Hamas was busy trying to kill Arafat for his half of their perceived betrayal. Hamas killed nearly a thousand Israelis in ten years. Georgey turned to his Hamas resources to copy the key.

Even had Mossad been aware of Georgey's sympathies, it would've been difficult to trace his actions thanks to separation of Arab and Jew into districts as well as entire towns. This, coupled with the Arab tribal, clan, and kinship mentality, made penetration of these barriers elusive. When Arabs disappear into their ethnic warrens, they evade surveillance. Orders are then passed verbally with many layers between the person who orders the act and the person who places the bomb.

Georgey couldn't just walk into a lock shop asking for services. Such places were watched by Israeli security, but his younger brother knew someone who knew someone, simply how illegal and dangerous things are done. However, there are rules. It was one thing to seek questionable services, but certain death to ask how the service was provided. No fool, Georgey gave Andre's photo to his brother for safekeeping and life insurance. He also placed the request for materials with the matching dollars. Next morning he received a small block of a plastic-wrapped malleable clay-like stuff with instructions. Once removed from the plastic wrapper, the substance would dry rock hard in thirty minutes, plenty of time to take side and edge impressions of the key.

***

By noon of the first working day after Shabbat, Andre held the block in his hands. Now for the imprint. Michael was equally caught up in the cloak and dagger of unapproved key copies and mystery tablets. The young plotters agreed the impression must be taken during the day while Alice Cross worked in the study. A feasible plan had to provide at least a couple of minutes' access to the master key without alerting her. It helped that the room was a study with shelves of academic reference books. Cross allowed access to them by students looking up information for thesis or dissertations. Andre and Michael decided both would go to the study on midday break asking to check a point needing clarification. With two of them and only one Alice Cross, some diversion might arise for making an impression of the key.

Professional agents would have been appalled at their simplicity, but luck smiles on fools. During the afternoon heat at the site, a thirty minute break was called, allowing everyone the chance to sit and enjoy a cool soft drink. Workers used restrooms, read, or visited.

Andre and Michael casually walked into the study and asked Alice if they could look at the *Anchor Bible Dictionaries* to settle an argument. She, surprisingly harried, recognized and greeted the pair, merely waving them to the bookshelves behind her. Andre took a volume down, and as he pretended to scan, spied the key in its glass on the old desk. There seemed no opportunity. He signaled they should leave. As they started out, Alice was jolted out of her studies by a crash and a cry issued from the kitchen.

She disappeared down the hall. In seconds Andre had the master key, pressing it into the unwrapped clay. In thirty seconds the task was accomplished and shortly Alice returned, shaking her head in exasperation at the interruption. Her concentration seemed so intense; they doubted she'd remember they'd been there at all. In half an hour the block turned stone hard, and the clay bearing the key impression rested in Georgey's grubby pocket. Mossad could only wish its operations were so easy.

Later Georgey spoke to his contact and waited while his message wended the Byzantine underground of Palestinian résistance. Next morning he faced a serious young man, and answered his probing with extreme care. The soft voiced questioner wanted to know about the purpose of the key request. Georgey described Andre and Michael in detail, saying he didn't know what the key was for, but it didn't seem likely the two were petty thieves. The young man seemed intrigued. A devout Muslim, he detested theft. However, unrelated minor details could be vital.

The interview ended. The questioner thanked Georgey for his assistance and told him the key would be made. Finally alone,

Georgey had the sensation he'd held his breath for the entire interrogation. Such a polite, dangerous young man.

***

Late that night a man with a heavy beard below bleary eyes focused on his agents' field reports. Here was an odd thing, two American students conniving to obtain a key for something at Sepphoris, a minor request, but puzzling. Sometimes minute things led to essential knowledge. The reader, Ramadan Shakaki a sub-commander of the Izz ad-Din al Qassam Brigade, the military arm of Hamas, passed this on to his superior.

***

Impatient, Andre spied on the study light each night, touching the key Georgey provided, now in his pocket. He would have an answer soon. The night he finally made it in, the study lights went out at 2:08 a.m. An hour later, Andre stood tensely in the darkened hallway. In stocking feet he tiptoed to the study door. His left hand felt for the lock while his right pushed in the key. He doubted it would work, but the door swung open.

Andre slipped in, closing it soundlessly behind him. Alone in the silent darkness, he made his way to the desk. With a tiny penlight he examined the items on it. On the right side was a file folder labeled "Dr. Henry Cross," a pencil slipped into a folder pocket. On the left was a much thicker file that said, "Dr. Alice Cross," with "Private" underlined. Andre memorized Henry Cross's folder placement to return it in exactly the original position. After this precaution, he opened the folder and began reading. Less than ten pages long, it contained only notes and comments. As sentence after sentence unrolled, Andre recoiled. Clearly, this was a commentary, its subject Moses and a primitive tribe. Notes indicated these Tablets would blast organized religion. Andre read the complete folder and replaced it. It was now near 3:30 a.m.; his skin crawled as if he'd spent an hour in a lion's den.

Several hundred pages filled the Alice Cross binders. Andre had only thirty more minutes at most. Here the mystery began to unfold. She did thorough work beginning with a general outline. Authors ranged from the biblical Moses to and through Jesus known as the Christ: narrative with history, comprehensive Hebrew and Koine Greek. Internal linguistics flawless. Alice Cross noted historicity as high. Andre couldn't have been more astounded if he held a nuclear bomb in his hands. *Father in Heaven! What could this mean for the Holy Mother Church?* Time was his enemy. He had only a few minutes left to begin the translation narrative. With pounding heart and unbelieving eyes Andre made a brief start before he had to quit. Replacing the folder, he slipped through the study door, locked it, and crept outside. Only death could prevent his return.

***

Michael was astonished at Andre's news. How would this affect his father who preached the gospel all his life, not to mention the hundreds of ministers who shared his beloved Southern Baptist Convention? What would a different Moses, but most important Jesus, mean to his family, himself, and the rest? Even though Andre had only read the Moses portion, he was aware these translations reported to and through the life of Jesus. Rumor had it that Dr. Stein would arrive soon. That explained Henry Cross's late hours. Andre needed a wiser head. He would write to Father Charles. Michael also worried, unconvinced that Andre should write anyone about the Tablets in case the information became too widely known. He had no way of knowing a common Israeli situation would complicate the scenario even further.

Georgey, unaware of Andre's late night entries into the Cross home, still observed Andre and Michael up to something. He did know the two seriously discussed whether to write to someone in the States, puzzling because what private letter would be worth arguing about? Finally, Georgey overheard Andre say he would post a letter tomorrow.

That afternoon two Palestinian suicide bombers gave their lives to Allah resulting in fifteen fatalities in Jerusalem, among them six American tourists. The Israeli government prohibited all Americans from public travel until investigation by the Secret Service. Dozens of Palestinians were rounded up and grilled, facing long periods in jail or curtailment from travel, the dreaded closure that meant hunger, health care problems, and lost incomes.

The closure only stopped Andre's posting from the nearest mailbox. However, the Israelis allowed Sepphoris Palestinian laborers limited travel. Georgey agreed to mail the letter from Tel Aviv because Mossad read all American mail sent from Sepphoris. Any letter mailed from a larger urban area wouldn't be opened. Andre tipped Georgey heavily.

A copy rested in the hands of the Supreme Commander of Hamas by midnight.

***

No one noticed the scrofulous beggar picking through trash cans in southern Gaza City. Few ventured into this area called the Quarter of the Lost, a bombed-out slum harboring victims of life and war no one wished to know or claim. Broken men came to live out their last few months before their remains rotted in skeletal ruins. No one cared to count the murders here.

The beggar wore the ensemble of demented homeless: a ripped and filthy woman's scarf; a torn suit jacket; Egyptian military trousers that stank of urine. The old beggar hobbled along stopping to hack, spit, and catch his feeble breath, his cane a broken crutch. He carried a large woman's purse with a broken strap. No one could have felt anything but pity watching this lost soul wander through shattered buildings barely held up by a few rusty bars of reinforcing steel.

The rancid beggar disappeared into the broken bowels of an old factory with a maze of rooms and hallways. Outer doorways faced streets and alleys continuing for hundreds of meters. It would take months for a cartographer to plot the routes, but the stooped beggar knew this area. Sheik Ahmad Yassin, brilliant and dangerous, the Supreme Commander of Hamas knew its every inch.

Born in Jordan to a prominent family, he attended private schools in Great Britain doing so well his family sent him on to the United States to Columbia University. The handsome young Arab flourished, traveling America widely, his onyx eyes widening at the wealth and freedom capitalism produced, but noting extreme poverty, too. However, he was young, rich, and the others' plight skimmed under his preoccupations. At UCLA Yassin tied his studies together and earned two PhD's, one in business management and another in psychology. California was a cornucopia for the egotistical, sensual young Arab. Yassin joined in the sexual freedom of California in the 70s and early 80s. Carefree California girls contrasted so with his country's reserved women. American women, so delicious, so available. Almost as compelling as the UCLA library.

The Jewish problem in Palestine reverberated at times like a slight headache. He rejected invitations from Mideast student organizations to join protests against Zionist aggression. Throwing rocks at Israeli tanks seemed a foolish way to die. Leave him to study in the UCLA library by day and enjoy the delectable pleasures offered during soft California evenings. No one seeing Yassin then could've guessed he would become the Israeli Secret Services' most lethal adversary.

The Prophet Mohammad's words formed the web and fiber of his culture, but he disdained much of the Koran as primitive. September 17th, 1986, whipped him around one hundred eighty degrees.

He was ill, feverish, and had been home for days, unkempt and bored. Unusual for him, he felt the loneliness common to expatriates. His brother had been urging him to come home and make the pilgrimage to Mecca. Almost idly, Yassin began reading his grandfather's Koran again. He closed his eyes and drifted, slipping into an overheated sleep, when the vision struck.

***

He stood on a vast ridge in Jordan looking west over the Dead Sea. Voices shrieked and sobbed. Although they begged for help, he couldn't find them.

Frantically Yassin tried to run to those imploring him, but couldn't reach them from his high ridge. Finally Yassin cried, "Allah, help me!" He was lifted to a mountaintop near the Mediterranean. Wind swirled so terribly he feared it would cast him from where he stood. The world hushed. Yassin confronted scenes: police beating children, women, and old men; soldiers kicking helpless people who fell in fear and exhaustion; shooting men trying to defend their wives and children; women screaming as clothes were torn from their bodies; bulldozers crushing homes; boys shot defending their homes with hand thrown stones. Homes looted, ancient cemeteries desecrated as tanks rolled over family markers. Endless barbed wire fences grew higher and higher. Countless Arabs mingled tears with blood as they clawed at the barbs.

Yassin dropped to his knees. He cried for means to help these defenseless ones. Then a majestic voice boomed. "Yassin, have you seen enough? Have you heard my people in Palestine? Will you save the children? Will you cast out the infidel who plunders my people?"

"Who are you?" Yassin whimpered.

"I am Allah, God of your forefathers. I sent the Prophet Mohammad to them. Out of the desert I called my people. Out of the desert I called my warriors of justice. The Arabs and the Arabs alone are my chosen. I forged my people to carry my holy sword. I brought water to the burning sands. I am Allah, and there is no other God beside me."

Yassin pressed his throbbing forehead to the earth. "What would you have me do, Lord? I am unworthy."

Then came the tender tone. "You are my chosen warrior. The fight will be long and arduous. Nonbelievers must be vanquished and cast out of my sacred land. Pray. I will lead you."

Yassin rose. He extended his arms toward the sufferers shouting, "I am coming!"

***

Dizzy now and chilled, he opened grainy eyes with a start to find himself still on the bed. He wept. It was too real. Not a dream. He clutched his grandfather's worn Koran in both hands, pressing Allah's word against his forehead. From that day on, the playboy scholar, now chosen warrior, served Allah.

Chapter Thirteen

Among friends Yassin still played the cheerful hedonist. Privately, he pored over the Koran, a supplicant for guidance. He scrutinized even minutia of the history, politics, geography, and current conflict in the Middle East. Israel's strengths and weaknesses were crucial. The United States financed it with approximately two billion dollars annually. Secret CIA funds allowed channeling of two billion more in military hardware. Israel advanced beyond Arab governments in technology. On the other hand, America needed Arab oil like a suckling child needs milk. Plus, the Vietnam conflict eroded public support for war. The more extended a bleeding war in Palestine, the less likely America would continue backing it.

His furtive reading in the library showed him how Mossad squelched Palestinian uprisings. Arab leaders' led from the front which made them easy targets. Analysis convinced him of Arab forces' inability to conquer Israel or these Western infidels by conventional methods. A day would come when Arab nations had both the money and will to buy essential hardware, but only unconventional warfare would end United States' support of Israel. Vietnam proved a dedicated guerrilla army could defeat a powerful, conventional one. However, Mossad's fine and deadly net pressed guerrilla operations hard.

Only superior organization could counter the Jewish Secret Service or the American CIA. Yassin had found his true gift and destiny. He researched the complex world of intelligence and espionage, studying histories of both the CIA and the FBI, British efforts with the OSS, the French underground, and the Russian KGB. He studied the American Mafia and the Italian Red Army. Yassin researched German methods of World War II, especially the deadly Gestapo. Next on this comprehensive list were underground groups like the right wing Minutemen, the racist Black Panthers, and the Irish Republican Army. He included Marxists, nationalists, idealists, and even serial killers. Yassin hungered to know what made each group tick, how they organized, and what really worked. How did they escape detection, and what brought their downfall? He read espionage novels. Indeed, creative writers gave him some of his best ideas. From a mountain of data Yassin distilled a few pounds of organizational gold. Five years later, he returned to Palestine. Allah willing, his would be a terrorist menace honed to perfection.

The playboy matured. Now Yassin impressed his father with his desire to establish an export business in Gaza City. His father's funding and his own American contacts helped establish a promising business. Mossad, with a dossier on every Arab who studied in America, watched him. Several who approached him with invitations for political activity had actually been Mossad members. Their reports logged his disinterest. Since he spoke three foreign languages fluently and was related to prominent figures in the Jordanian government, he did warrant a close look. Mossad's periodic checks found Yassin rather vocal about the need for Palestinian tolerance, often suggesting to friends that time would solve everyone's problems, a dangerous view since Hamas and the Hezbollah occasionally killed Arabs not sympathetic enough to the cause. Yassin neither married nor paid for prostitutes, strange for a man who'd been renowned as a heartless playboy.

Mossad's Yassin file slammed shut after a fire bomb annihilated him and his Mercedes. Twenty-three bombs exploded that day and fourteen people lost their lives as radical Palestinian groups signaled their fury by fire and blood. An Israeli radio station received an anonymous call from a Palestinian taking credit for killing Yassin as a collaborator with Jews. Mourning relatives buried his body, burned beyond recognition, in Jordan. Eight months later, his estate closed, Mossad placed his dossier in the Inactive Deceased file.

Mossad didn't find out about Yassin's unusual life after death. With the modest name of Pebbles, he rose to Supreme Commander of Hamas. The Koran teaches that Allah honors a humble man. With his genius for wreaking death, destruction, and sorrow on all infidels beginning with Israel, but ultimately meant to include the arrogant United States, he struggled against pride. What he didn't acknowledge even to himself was that successful strikes led him to ecstatic heights he'd achieved before only with the release of sex.

By the time Pebbles had masterminded assassinations of seventy-nine Mossad agents, he struggled for humility motivated not just by the Koran, but practicality. Pride led to high visibility, and visibility meant death. Pebbles had Allah and his mission. He talked to no one, and used no telephone, fax, computer, or radio. Yehiya Ayash, the commander Pebbles replaced, had been known as The Engineer. Mossad traced a phone call and killed him. Pebbles eschewed modern technology. His weapon was his mind.

It took him years to reach this position. A person code-named Pebbles had asked for a few agents and an assignment. The Hamas leadership suspiciously sought a meeting. His answer: "No meetings." Would Pebbles talk on a phone or radio? Again, "No." Pebbles wanted agents and an assignment. The Hamas leadership scoured the area for him. After months, agents assigned this task admitted failure after days spent watching never-nibbled bait. Yet the Hamas leadership still received Pebbles' chiding messages. When would they stop wasting time and send him agents and an assignment so he could fight the Israelis?

Hamas finally assigned five expendable agents and a risky task. Included in the five was at least one suspected informer. Within three weeks, to the astonishment of Hamas leadership the mission succeeded and two of the five agents sprawled dead on the street with the word Mossad carved on their foreheads. Still skeptical, Hamas filtered more agents to this strange leader. Under Pebbles' invisible guidance, inept agents grew skilled and good agents better. More success. Hamas began to catch up with Mossad.

Mossad leadership raged against its growing losses. Suspecting an impenetrable cell growing within Hamas, Mossad threw resources into solving this mystery. Even when Hamas agents were captured, their minds wrung out by torture and drugs, they revealed nothing because they knew nothing. Pressure increased as Israeli political leaders met death through assassinations so varied it seemed unlikely to be the work of one mind. But, behind all Mossad's losses stood the ruthless Pebbles.

Deep within concrete ruins, he masterminded triumphs. Money came easily to this Mideast cauldron. America and the Jewish private sector gave Israel hundreds of millions annually. However, oil rich Arab nations gave millions to Palestinian resistance fighters. Iran alone provided an annual one hundred million.

Pebbles formed connections with Hezbollah (the Party of God) based in the Bekaa Valley in eastern Lebanon. Here many of Hamas' best operatives received training, weaponry, and explosives. Pebbles established a training camp near Khartoum in Sudan, Africa. Military experts from the Eastern Bloc as well as hardened veterans from the wars in Afghanistan, Iran, and Iraq poured expertise into the Hamas cause. Money isn't enough to win wars. Blood wins wars. Kill until the enemy's will is broken. Pebbles became the ever thirstier Lord of Blood.

Nothing less than obliteration of Israel and the decadent West could quench his parched needs. Israel came first, of course, but his thoughts drifted often to America, probing the vulnerability of vulgar New York where commerce ruled over spirituality.

Pebbles reviewed Andre and Michael's letters. Allah has guided a watchful amateur and here was the truth. *Truth comes from the desert, for out of desert regions came the Prophet and the blessed Koran.* Muslims long believed Moses and Jesus were two in a long series of prophets pointing the way to the true God, Allah. Satan and the Zionists had created stories with a mantle of righteousness. The Tablets would cause upheaval even among Muslims, but now Allah allowed his truth to rise from the soil of Sepphoris. There would be more harm to the infidels. Pebbles began to plan.

***

Those surveying the spawn of defeat need look no further than the twenty-three year old Arab woman, Amal, a Hamas member for four years. With delicate features and shimmering black hair, she should have held the world in her slender hands.

Unfortunately, she lived in the hopelessness of Ya'bad, a refugee town. Her ancestors, falsely said to have abandoned their land, were relocated at gunpoint. Jewish settlers filled the vacuum.

Only one of fourteen thousand Arabs in the concrete ghetto of Ya'bad, Amal learned to read and write Arabic from camp volunteers. Her great-grandfather built the camp under the unsympathetic eyes of his Jewish captors in 1948. The original tents gradually evolved into concrete slums. In 1976, Amal's mother gave birth to her on an army blanket spread on a cement floor.

Many of their men died during the Jewish-Arab wars, Amal's grandfather and father among them. Two of Amal's five brothers now languished in Israeli prisons. Two of the remaining three, not heard from in two years, had joined Hezbollah fighting against the Israeli Army in Southern Lebanon. Her youngest brother could not speak or hear.

Amal, code-named The Fawn, trained in Jordan with her brother. Their mother, dedicated to Hamas, urged them to fight. In Jordan Amal's trainers had doubts as to her suitability, but in time noted how her lovely hands never faltered, even when assembling bombs. As days passed, while Amal mastered the trade of death her beauty stirred problems. All men wanted her. Her disinterest held them at bay.

However, one moonless night Amal awoke to the tip of a knife at her throat, a rough hand smothering her. A voice growled, "Not one sound." Amal nodded, holding still while he rammed her nightshirt buttons into her chest, undoing them. The voice grew throatier, his hand kneading her bared breast. The knife barely moved.

Finally she purred, "Surely you have a better place for your other hand than on a knife." The sweating rapist, breathing coarsely, laid the knife by her head while his free hand caressed her thighs. Amal's shirt was well above her waist when she whispered, "I am ready. Hurry and take me!" Wresting off his clothes, he missed the flash of her hand as she drove the knife to its hilt below his Adams apple. Her cold eyes bored into his, which dulled with his rasping last breath.

At her Sharia trial Amal didn't plead for mercy. When the judges asked if she had anything further to say she said she had explained the truth and was ready to face Allah. Found innocent, she returned to her unit never to be molested again. The men warily avoided her.

In explosives, small arms, and field craft, Amal equaled the best. She had an affinity for precision shooting, asking sharp questions about methods of sight correction and long-range ballistics. She advanced to sniper training, learning to shoot with a scope-mounted precision rifle on stationary and moving targets from four hundred to eight hundred meters. She mastered the bullets' flight, effects of gravity, and wind. The first shot had to kill, no time for a second. The mind, body, and rifle must be as one. She gained control over even her heart's beating to make precision aiming possible. The kill was all, escape secondary. Palestinian fighters killed and died on demand.

Once concealed, Amal never moved. Even in unbearable heat with ants invading her clothes, she merged with the earth. The camp commander began the train of messages that eventually reached Pebbles who selected the next stage of Amal's training in Amman, Jordan.

Amal began her most challenging course of study which required giving up her innocence not to a man, but Palestine and Allah. From a sardonic Russian former model with icy blue eyes over rock hard ledges of cheek bones, she learned the arts of allurement, flirtation, lovemaking and personal analysis. Amal learned to be reserved, coy, or openly aggressive, attracting the right person in the right way. Insecure and timid men could often be won by a gradual friendship. The direct approach lured others. She studied textbook psychological profiles, the goal never only sexual contact, but potentially vital friendship and intimacy. Influential older men often yearned for friendship as much as, if not more than, passion.

Both her cool Russian instructor and male partners critiqued trainees which grew less excruciating for Amal over time. Depending on the subject's personality, Amal learned to enhance the experience with verbal and tactile stimulation. Older men might not climax, but must be soothed when that occurred.

Powerful men's wives might not be knowledgeable or willing lovers. She completed the course with high marks. All training completed, she clandestinely rejoined her mother at Ya'Bad until assigned a mission, her life committed to Allah and Palestinian liberation.

Three years later, Amal was informed that an interview for the position of servant for an Israeli general had been arranged for her by a charming Hamas agent, mistress of an Israeli staff officer. Many Israeli officers used Arab women for cheap domestic labor as well as mistresses. At Amal's interview General Kessler asked about her background. She admitted her father and grandfather met death in the wars, and she didn't know the whereabouts of her brothers, most likely also dead. When asked her views on the Arab/Jew conflict, Amal, eyes downcast, said it was tragic. She yearned for peace.

The general, a burly man with white hair, military bearing, and sad eyes, said that he, too, desired peace. He asked if she would truly enjoy being a domestic in his home and cultivator in his flower gardens. He wanted no sullen faces among his lilies. Amal answered she would happily work there because she valued the dignity of honest labor. The general's villa sat four miles from Ya'bad, but Amal assured him she would take pleasure in the exercise. The general promised to arrange the necessary documents, and excused her. General Kessler commanded the large Northeast District of Israel. All went according to Allah's plan.

Each day Amal, code named The Fawn, walked four dusty miles to and from the general's small plantation. The Israeli Army had evicted its Palestinian businessman owner in 1948. The general received the property following his service to Israel in the Arab war of 1967. Amal helped a Jewish cook with the meals, cleaned the house, and maintained the general's fragrant lily garden in late afternoons and early evenings.

The general closed each day sitting amid his lilies, breathing the deliriously perfumed evening air. Amal watered and maintained the garden in shorts and a tunic blouse. Soon the general blended an appreciation for her beauty with that for his lilies. Occasionally he invited her to join him under his shade trees to discuss landscaping and the profusion of botanical choices. He looked forward to these evening discussions with this diffident, dark-eyed girl.

Amal listened raptly to stories of his war days of the 1960s and 70s. He surprised her by sometimes expressing regret for the brutalities of war. Amal sympathized with her troubled general, assuring him she knew little about those difficult times, but hoped someday Arabs and Jews could live together again in peace. Amal showed interest in Israeli history without posing confrontational questions. This lovely girl brought light into her employer's life, and he equated her with the open female beauty of his soothing flowers.

The proud general had given up the pleasures of bedding women, but the keen yearning returned as he watched the graceful Amal. Amal subtly showed a long tanned leg or wore tunics missing a button or two while she bent to pick an errant weed, never hurrying. Secular, he hadn't experienced reverence like this since his boyhood on a kibbutz. Miraculously, she even listened to him.

The general's wife, always at the top of her own list, left for days at a time. She couldn't remember when her bull-like husband last initiated intimacy. Usually a few minutes of passive endurance with her eyes tightly shut relieved him. Thankfully, he hadn't asked often and over time stopped entirely. Wiser Amal saw that General Kessler was too sensitive and proud to endure his wife's condescension. It gratified him that a striking young woman with eyes the color of golden brown dates showed an interest in his life and hobbies, unlike his flyaway wife. On the few occasions he'd touched her hand Amal didn't pull away. In fact, she often gave a gentle squeeze in return. Amal waited. Allah would reveal the day and hour.

***

On an evening of an apricot setting sun and cooling breezes the general rested in his grotto, all tasks accomplished. Life had taken on vibrancy. His roast chicken had been exceptionally good and he enjoyed being served by light-footed Amal, her eyes downcast. His wife had fluttered away that morning for three days in Tel Aviv. After an hour or so reading a new history book in his study, he clapped it shut and strolled out to his garden. He looked forward to an evening listening to the warblers as night descended. As usual at this hour Amal watered and tended the white and rose-tinted lilies. Her body glowed like a ripe fruit. Listening to her nearly whispered songs of Old Palestine brought rare serenity.

He lingered in the deepening twilight, and called Amal over to the bower later than usual. She sat beside him on the padded bench. A glaze of sweat enhanced her olive skin with its glint of copper, redolent of blooming lilies and fertile earth. In recent days they'd frequently spoken in muted voices of the lilies' intoxicating scent. Amal's hand rested lightly on his as early stars emerged. Darkness cloaked the white haired man and the dark haired girl, rendering the bower more intimate. A partial moon glided above, casting its patina over the shade trees and garden. The white lilies glowed, virginal points swooning in dimness. The night gradually peeled away the general's years and worries.

He felt heat in his groin. Amal's hand hovered, then brushed that stirring. Without the slightest urgency or demand, but with the lightest of kisses she touched his cheek, then his neck with petal-like lips. Her fingers lingered closer and longer as his erection pushed upward. Amal slipped to the ground, loosened his clothes, and began lightly kissing and touching his inner thighs. The general gasped, nearly drowning in a sea of rising sensations. When Amal touched his erection with her lips she paused like a child to ask him if it would be all right. The General touched her loosened hair like a benediction. With the gentlest of hard-learned techniques, she gave the amazed old soldier the finest, longest, most delicate lovemaking of his life. Then she thoughtfully covered him and rested her head on his shoulder. With no claims on the general and with the invaluable talent of the desperate for locking such experience in a private room, she allowed him to drive her back to camp, hers from that night on.

***

Half a world away, Sam Stein, once known as 'Stocky' Stein to his bar mitzvah class, but now an internationally respected scholar, brooded over Henry's lack of response. Six weeks had passed with no news. The other expensive Israeli sites had come up dry. Uncharacteristically impatient, Stein nursed a paranoid sense of exclusion, and faxed a message geared to focus his wayward subordinate's attention.

Later that morning, Henry read that if he did not send timely reports, Stein would arrive to kick his bony rear all the way to the Mediterranean. Henry smiled, but knew he would have to give his boss something to chew on. He faxed a quickly composed reply to Harvard.

Stein's longtime secretary, Betty, read it first. Dr. Stein had been a bear lately, obviously displeased with Dr. Cross. Buzzing him with news of the fax, she was relieved to hear Stein's "at last" sigh.

Stein's chair creaked as he straightened. Cross had something. *My God, what could it be?* He all but salivated. To do real archaeology again would be worth facing the ire of the university comptroller! A key discovery! He could feel it. Grinning, Stein told a surprised Betty to book him a flight to Tel Aviv and fax Henry Cross his thanks and arrival time.

As Stein went whistling back to his office, Betty shook her head. *Dr. Stein is losing it!*

Chapter Fourteen

If the gods do evil then they are not gods.
Euripides

There is but one evil, ignorance.
Socrates

Later that morning, in his stark office, Big Matt Homes, Head of the Mideast section of the Central Intelligence Agency, studied a message. After fourteen years in Jerusalem, Homes empathized with all parties in tortured Palestine. Partly due to his sensitive heart, also to his fluency in Hebrew and Arabic, he was particularly adept at judging the reception given political decisions. Homes internalized as few could how deeply the United States was into the Middle East situation. The Jewish agony during World War II gave them credibility and claim to a land of their own. To say America was pro-Israel was an understatement. Nevertheless the United States, like Europe, increasingly perceived the Palestinians' undeniable grievances. Yet, Israel had reason for anxiety. Surrounding Arab nations would be elated to see her destruction. How to obtain peace in the Mideast: the excruciating question for numerous U.S. Presidents.

The basic dilemma was how to remain in good graces with the Arab world which owned the oil that industrialized America depended on, yet support Israel which shared Judeo-Christian culture. America needed normal trade relations with Arab nations. However, the volatility of the Mideast meant the United States needed a reliable military outpost (Israel) necessary for projecting strength if vitally needed oil supplies were blocked. Still the United States found it hard to support Israel, a police state of routine detentions, denial of free movement and due process to Palestinians.

The unstable Mideast threatened earth's survival. The Israeli Dimona site in the Negeb Desert manufactured over one hundred nuclear bombs by 1986. Wealthy Arab nations wanted nuclear weapons and the Soviet Union's break up made access to them possible. Terrorism might soon go nuclear. All this made the message intriguing. A CIA agent stationed at Sepphoris had sent a nano-second radio transmission to a receiver at America's Embassy in Tel Aviv. "Religious development of potential import. Will continue to investigate." The only other indicator was a rating of 4. Information at the CIA rated from 1 to 5 in order of importance. A classified cipher identified the agent. The CIA often fielded agents at digs. Anything to do with religion was volatile in Israel where America wanted no surprises.

***

On an early evening in Boston, Father Charles settled in his office to read the day's mail, pleased to see an envelope from his nephew Andre in Israel. *Youth always feels they can move the world.* He slit the envelope with an ivory letter opener, a gift when he completed his first tier of Jesuit studies. He drew out the thin paper and read under the soft light of his green shaded lamp. After the first sentences, he realized this was no social letter. Andre recounted everything he'd done and feared from his readings.

Even worse, Andre wrote that according to Dr. Alice Cross's outline it appeared Mother Mary felt her son, Jesus, suffered from mental illness. Andre feared for his soul as well as the welfare of the Roman Catholic Church. Harvard's Dr. Samuel Stein was rumored to arrive in Israel within two weeks. Apparently in response to this impending visit, Dr. Henry Cross was putting in such long hours that Andre had been unable to sneak into the study to read more. The last paragraph was a plea for guidance.

Father Charles refolded the letter, then knelt in prayer. His Catholic Church already faced serious troubles. The Church had coped poorly with scientific knowledge. Democracy and individualism eroded compliance with marching orders from a sexless old man wearing funny clothes in the Vatican. The American Catholic Church openly existed as a bastion of resistance to Rome. Issues such as birth control, women's equality, child abusing priests, strictures against priests marrying, divorce, and remarriage stirred dissent.

Father Charles rose to pace and think, a habit from his student days. Education and freedom were tearing down the prison walls of Catholicism. The Church had always functioned as a source of explanation for those yearning for answers for the mystery of disease, vagaries of weather, randomness of war, and horror of famine. The Church declared that most harm came when a subject broke a law. The peasant could understand this since punishment came when one defied a king or a chieftain. Of course, the Church found myths useful because the uneducated were used to hearing campfire stories told since prehistory. Myths of massive floods sent by a punishing God to kill all mankind; myths that all animals from all the earth survived the flood in a giant floating box; myths of talking snakes leading temptresses to disobey an unlikely god who walked in a garden; myths of divine acts such as parting the sea or causing the sun to stand still in the sky. The shepherd boy David slaying the warrior Goliath. Mary singing praises after divine impregnation. Touching stories, but stories nonetheless. The Church claimed these actually happened.

The Church found herself defending positions that science and logic gradually destroyed for thinkers. Plank by plank science dismantled the mythical ark as geography discovered continents with species that couldn't have swum to the ark. Archaeology discovered ancient records predating the Bible which bore remarkable similarities to biblical accounts. Astronomy revealed earth was not the center of the universe, and the sun could never have held still. Indeed, some of the Church's greatest minds argued the world was flat. St. Augustine's reasoning was that people on the bottom of a sphere could not see the returning Jesus. Scholars discovered signs of literary and political revision, destroying the Church position that Moses wrote the first five books of the Bible.

Censorship, the infamous "Index" which listed books Catholics were not permitted to read, was the Church's answer. That many forbidden books were the greatest works of science and literature couldn't be concealed forever. The "Index" was not disposed of until 1965, long after the world had rejected this insult. But these Tablets were something new.

Father Charles returned to his desk, running his hand through his white hair. He rubbed his temples. His faith was secure. His awe seeing the priest celebrate the Eucharist had never left him even when it was he now honored to perform this sacred rite. Belief in prayer and the presence of a forgiving God unfailingly sustained him.

At first, to be a Jesuit was synonymous with absolute dedication to the Roman Catholic Church and the will of her Popes, to be one of "the Pope's men." Eventually, Jesuits mastered and contributed to mathematics, hydraulic power, atomic theory, paleography, and even oceanography. In recent times most modern Jesuits were ashamed of historical parts some had played: centuries when thousands of medieval Jews were slaughtered, the senseless bloodshed of the Crusades, murder, genocide, papal corruption, and the Inquisition. Sophisticated Jesuits couldn't ignore the long, sorry list of corruption, immorality, and papal hunger for power and, worst of all, the church's silence during the Holocaust and Gulags.

The revolution of Vatican II in 1965, opening volley of a long war, was largely thanks to the subtle Jesuits. The underground maneuvering by Church factions was impressive in sheer callousness and cynicism. Father Charles had been directly involved with strategies to undermine papal power. Unfortunately, this struggle might become a battle to the death. No organization had more experience in Machiavellian maneuvers than the Jesuits. Over the last century they'd trained their ranks to prepare for this battle. Of course, the Jesuits didn't underestimate Rome either. Father Charles's conscience was clear. The Church must change to survive.

Behind this change were the Jesuits and clandestine forces within them. The deepest Jesuit cells wanted to wash the papacy away. Only then could dedicated men and women of God thrive, serving their communities free from the chains of Rome, helping the helpless, not having to abstain from sexual joy in order to serve God free of papal judgments impinging on cultures the Pope neither inhabited nor understood. Although the current Pope might love to disband the Jesuits, politically that would shatter Church unity. The Pope wouldn't like to be remembered as the one who made the Church's final fatal mistake.

Father Charles winced as he restudied Andre's letter. His dream had been to reform the Catholic Church, not destroy it. The weakened Church might collapse under the weight of this new evidence. He felt no threat to his own faith in the unknowable relationship between Jesus and God. However, most might be incapable of such faith. He wrote a reply.

"Your sins are forgiven. Mother Church needs you. I will contact you very soon."

It was also time to fax his Father General Jesuit in Vatican City. Father Charles wrote that the power of darkness was present. Would the Father General please pray for Father Charles? The code meant "Serious danger ahead. Please contact."

Chapter Fifteen

Men create the gods after their own images.
Aristotle

All religions are equally sublime to the ignorant, useful to the politician, and ridiculous to the philosopher.
Lucretius

Religion is regarded by the common people as true, by the wise false, and by the rulers as useful.
Seneca the Younger

Morning started early for Pope Jerome. Habitually he rose at 5:00 a.m. to begin a schedule that ran over sixteen hours. He ruminated as he braced himself for the day ahead. These nine hundred million Catholics were incredibly stubborn and thick headed, each culture demanding change and special treatment. Did these countries not see that Mother Church had to be the same for all? It seemed as if every common Catholic had become a politician, a theologian, or even an armed revolutionary! Every bishop rebelled against his cardinal, and every cardinal wanted to become pope. Even ordinary Catholic women clamored for the collar of priestly duty. He smirked. How sorry they'd be if they had to deal with what a pope had to. If only they would just be good Catholic mothers the world would be better off. Had not Mary been willing to serve at the foot of the Cross?

At least when he was Archbishop in Poland, priests and nuns obeyed him. The Vatican government could be as treacherous as the communists. Many a day Jerome felt God had made a rare mistake in seating him on this rickety throne of the Blessed Peter. He longed to see Jesus within the gates of heaven. Jerome felt a touch of peace that every day was one day closer to his Lord. If only everyone could grasp how the length of human life is so miniscule compared to life eternal with Jesus! Were poverty, misery, and suffering not the fate of Jesus Himself? How could a faithful Catholic truly be a child of the Mother Church if he did not obey his priests, bishops, and his Pope in Rome? Without obedience and a supreme authority, Catholicism could not survive.

The United States was a giant thorn. Feminists, homosexual priests, child abuse, all damaged the Church. Lay peoples' material wealth blinded them to their spiritual needs. With everything so relative, how impossible to convince them that eternal unbreakable laws flowed from the Pope, the Vicar of Christ Himself. Of course, sex obsessed Americans. Every Catholic girl of fifteen felt it her divine right to be on the pill. American women voiced their rights so aggressively some priests asked for transfer to more obedient areas.

Europe was nearly atheist, its materialism only exceeded by the United States. Although the Poles were 95% Catholic, nearly 70% opposed the ban on abortion. The same percentage felt the Church had too much power. Even Irish Catholics turned against the Pope in 1991 when they revoked the constitutional ban on divorce. Russia was lost, Africa a surprising bright spot. Unfortunately, Africa had always been a dark hole of misery and suffering. Of course, the Church didn't like to talk about profit, but it takes money to run an international concern. The Church sank millions into the Polish Solidarity movement and that had to come from somewhere. What a bitter pill that much of it had to come from the American Catholics. The United States challenged the Pope's authority at every turn, but capitalism produced a profit.

The Middle East, that death zone where so-called religious worshiped and killed each other in grim determination. The situation in Israel wouldn't be resolved in his lifetime or probably anyone else's. The rough and ready tribal faith of the Muslims seemed custom-made for extended warfare. The Catholic Church had poor success in the Muslim countries. Every child in the tragic, eastern Fertile Crescent seemed to be born with a rifle in one hand and a Koran in the other. Jerome had to remind himself that God in his wisdom would eventually provide a way for the Church to enter those suffering countries.

Asia looked much better, the Philippines actually rather good. Of course, places like China and North Korea would remain isolated concentration camps until God freed them from the crudest form of communism. A Pope must be a realist.

With resolve for a new day Jerome rang for his secretary. He frowned at the two inch deep stack of papers the smiling young priest carried, foretelling a difficult day. Jerome riffled through them, stopping at the Vatican intelligence report. Reading a troubling line, the Pope asked his hovering secretary what this particular section meant. With a quick glance the blond priest identified an intercepted fax from Father Charles O'Malley to the General Secretary of the Jesuits. Jerome was more than familiar with Father O'Malley, a flaming fag from Boston, a member of the Jesuit faction intent on overthrowing Papal power. Pope Jerome looked forward to the day when Satan would fry Father O'Malley's rear end. Unfortunately, Old Father Charles was a slick fox, never caught in a compromising situation.

"What do our moles think it means?" the Pope asked.

The young priest smiled brightly and said, "Our men in the cryptograph department think this is a warning of something bad on the Jesuits' horizon."

Well, thought the Pope. That improves the morning! Bad for the Jesuits meant good for him. With a sigh, Jerome told his smiling aide, in all probability himself a spy for some Vatican faction, to keep an eye on the Jesuits and let him know if anything more developed.

***

At the Sepphoris dig Alice, tense and rushed, translated. The actual translations were almost complete, lacking only the meticulous scholarship that establishes shades of meanings and possible hints of other evidence. These could be done over a period of leisurely months. The very last tablet was so unusual that Henry had asked her to place it with her personal possessions, with no reference to it in her translations. They could peruse it in greater depth later. Everything had to be ready for Dr. Stein. Alice worried about Henry, so strained and pressured. Hopefully he could catch up on sleep before his department chair's visit.

***

That evening Andre realized Dr. Cross wasn't in his study. Both Andre and Michael vibrated with curiosity. Andre had told Michael everything Alice's outline said as well as the gist of the Moses account. However, neither of them had read the rest. In particular, the Jesus account was ripe with mystery, and they could barely wait for the details. It was slightly after 2:00 a.m. when Andre slipped into the study. In stocking feet he silently moved to the study desk. He located Alice's manuscript translations by penlight and picked up where he'd ended at the Moses account. Every page devastated him as he read the real story of Israel, the intertestamental years and the story of Jesus. Jesus' mother wrote that story, but it included a brief writing by Jesus himself, complete and credible.

This discovered history portrayed Jesus as many things, but definitely not Savior, Lord, and God incarnate. It reduced the adored and venerated Mary to the pathetic mother of a pathetic son. There was no reasonable way of destroying the Tablets. There were piles of them, hard as rocks. Henry Cross would be on him in a matter of seconds. Even if they were broken, modern archaeology could reassemble the shards. Nor did Andre relish the idea of spending the rest of his life in an Israeli prison with a bunch of Arab terrorists. Uncle Charles would know what to do. Andre would just have to be patient until further instructions.

An amazed Michael heard Andre's account as they lay on a hilltop only a couple of miles from Nazareth. Andre remembered large sections of the translation verbatim. Michael groaned. *My father's entire life of ministering to his beloved Southern Baptists will be rendered meaningless. The whole thing is just too amazing. Jesus almost certainly walked across this hill and others nearby. Perhaps he gazed into the sky from this very spot. What must this sad mother have felt to find her son speechless, eyes glazed and arms extended toward the heavens? Perhaps she tenderly held him, begging him to come home to supper. Did she*

*patiently listen to his stories of paradise and his conversations
with God as she led him by the hand?*

***

Sam Stein felt buoyant as he drove his rental from Haifa east
to Nazareth, amazed at the improvements made in this troubled
country since he'd been here eight years before. The investment
in money and labor must be titanic. However, tension shimmered
with Israeli military omnipresent. You never knew when to
expect annoying checkpoints. You could round a bend and there
were the ubiquitous soldiers carefully examining cars and ID's.

Soldiers treated him well when they saw he was an American
citizen, but such treatment wasn't universal. Even from the
highway segregation showed: road construction clearly divided
between Israeli supervisors and Palestinian laborers. Stein, an old
Civil Rights worker, remembered driving through the American
South during the early sixties sensing that same current of restless
hatred. A secular Jew, he believed no society can long survive
with ethnic hostility. This was not a country at peace.

Stein cruised the 30 miles from Haifa, eager to uncover this
mystery. Turning off the paved highway onto the graveled
service road, he saw Sepphoris. It did indeed look like a bird
perched on the side of a small mountain. Workers appeared small
on the imposing hill. Even in the sun's glare, a brooding grayness
hung over the scene. An ancient menace clung to Sepphoris.

Pulling up to the Supervisor's residence, he'd hardly worked
his paunch out of the car when lovely Alice emerged from the
low house. She embraced him, saying she would send a worker
for Henry. She invited him into the small living room. Something
awry bothered Stein. Alice wasn't the same light-hearted woman
he liked so well, although pleasant, and saying the right things.
There was brittleness about her, a new nervousness. Dr. Alice
Cross was scared, trying to mask her fear behind a facade of
normalcy. Something flitted through Stein, too. For the briefest of
moments he, himself, felt an irrational flicker of fear.

Thankfully, Henry walked in. Stein quickly stood to shake his
colleague's hand while he also did his mental sizing up. Henry

had lost weight and appeared drawn. Darkness around his eyes spoke of tension and short nights. Since Henry had always been a slender man the loss of fifteen or so pounds made him cadaverous. Henry showed no fear, but seemed worried, uptight. Whatever had been discovered at Sepphoris put pressure and lots of it on the Cross couple. Stein decided to be patient, letting Alice and Henry pace the conversation.

After the obligatory exchange of pleasantries, Henry clapped his hands on his knees and stood. "Let me show you what we've got here."

"It's why I came."

Henry led the way into the study with its floor to ceiling library, long desk, and a worn couch buried in cushions along the pale study wall. Folders, binders, and documents covered the desktop. Next to the couch sat a large rectangular block four feet wide, four feet tall, and six feet long covered with a black plastic sheet. This had to be the object of his trip. Stein noticed Alice standing back as if not wanting to be too close. Henry removed the tarp and said, "This is the discovered library of Sepphoris."

Stein blinked. Tablet after perfect clay tablet sat stacked as neatly as gold at Fort Knox. Indeed, Stein felt like he was looking at the lost gold of El Dorado. He ran his fingers over the lettering on the tablets as he listened to the rest of Henry's words. "A complete history of ancient Israel from the days of Moses to and through the life of Jesus."

The first words out of Stein's mouth sounded stupid, but were all he could think of. "Lock the door." Henry walked over and turned the tumbler as Stein pulled out the desk chair. Stein asked, "Would both of you sit down? On the couch? Now, start at the beginning, and don't leave out any details."

Henry did most of the talking, explaining the circumstances of the discovery and everything that he and Alice had done since. He detailed how they'd split the work with him cross-checking Alice's work. Alice spoke of how she'd translated the entire collection, her work now in binders on the desk. Henry added that he'd reviewed the Moses section, but the cross referencing took time, and he'd only been able to scan the intertestamental and Jesus material.

"Alice, you're our linguist. What are your impressions of all this?"

"What I translated was unambiguous, authentic, and different from any known biblical account." She got up, smoothed her cargo shorts, walked to the desk, hesitated for only a moment, and then placed her outline in his hands.

Not a word was spoken for fifteen minutes. Every now and then his eyes widened or an eyebrow rose. At last he laid the outline on the floor and hunched toward them like a child sharing a secret, but hands clasped like a man in prayer. "If I got this straight, these Tablets contain facts, figures, and dates that rewrite everything biblical about Moses and Jesus? Furthermore, these Tablets contain sections apparently written by Mary and one by Jesus himself? In addition, am I to understand that in these is convincing evidence that Jesus was mentally ill and, in fact, never resurrected?"

For a second everything paused. Finally Henry nodded. "Those are the stone cold facts as we see them."

Stein said, "Alice, I've known you for years. I know you're a brilliant linguist. You're in the top ten living Ancient Mideast language scholars. I still have to ask. How certain are you that you're right?"

She answered in a choked voice. "I'm as sure as anything in life that these translations are accurate. I'm so sure I'm scared. And I can't say exactly of whom."

Turning to Henry, Stein asked almost fiercely, "What about you? I've known you since you were a farm boy come to college with straw in your hair. I watched you grow from brilliant student to a world class scholar. Are these Tablets authentic?"

"Yes. Not one sign of forgery. Every item checks out and many fill gaps in our information. Every piece of evidence, linguistic or historic, is consistent with authenticity. Everything is here for your inspection. I'm completely certain."

"Well," Stein said. "We know what this means. If authentic, this discovery will reform global thinking. Does anyone else know about this?" To his great relief Stein both shook their heads in the negative. "Okay, I have two days to read the transcript and spot check the Tablets. Alice, can you be available to answer questions as needed? Henry, you run the site as normal. When necessary, I'll call a conference and we'll hash out details and questions. In two days we'll decide what's next. Alice, let me set up at the study desk. When I wear out, I'll rest on the couch."

That's how the next step began, three rational people trying to do the right thing. Courageous and hopeful, they faced a future more dangerous than they could predict. The Tablets of Sepphoris appeared to be only clay. In reality, they held enough energy to destroy the world's faith.

For the first time in a long while Stein lived and breathed as pure scholar. Harvard Archaeology Department's reputation rested with this work. Nor did he take his responsibility to the faithful lightly. He had final responsibility for the Tablets. For her part Alice happily allowed Stein to lead. She respected his integrity. If it had to do with honest Mideast scholarship, Stein's rise from solitary voice of protest against Christian bias to founder of scientific archaeology was legendary.

As Alice watched Stein work she thought how much is owed these rare truth seekers. How many times they cleared the path of the debris of superstition and the entanglements of falsehoods by refusing to be bound by culture or custom. How many times had the quest for the truth placed them defiantly in front of kings and popes? How many of them had languished in prisons or been burned at stakes because they would not bend their knee to human error? History recorded stories of those who faced the power of the Church and State with nothing but confident integrity. They stood staunch before councils, parliaments, and inquisitions and stated simply, "This is the truth. I can do or say no more." Yet she knew that the war between reason and superstition would never end. A new Dark Ages could return.

Stein arranged his work, note pad on the right, Alice's outlines dead center, and the translation binders on his left. He read the translations, spot checking often against the relevant tablet. Stein was a speed reader, in this case crucial. He needed silence. Alice even removed her sandals and worked in stocking feet. The silence unsettled her. She preferred working with classical music turned low. Nevertheless, she read on the couch, available to answer questions.

Starting with the first of the Eli and Moses binders, Stein read steadily, pleased at the absence of errors. On a few small points there might be a slight debate on the shading of a word or phrase but nothing to challenge Alice's translation. Checking the tablet against the translation was the slowest part, so he requested only the most debatable or critical sections.

Chapter Sixteen

Pastor Robert Steward pulled out of the parking lot of Gold Ridge Southern Baptist Church, his silver Cadillac steadily picking up speed. He loved the sensuous power the luxury car gave him. Total silence combined with almost magical acceleration. Turning onto the Atlanta beltway he watched the indicator slide to 85 mph. He'd be home in twenty minutes, after the enjoyable commute from his busy church office to his home in Briar Estates.

Wealthy Baptists of the Old South comprised his congregation. The men projected confident power, the women that graciously relaxed self-assurance only old money can buy. Not for them to complain about social conditions or racial tensions. The old families lived as they had for generations with well understood yet tactfully unspoken codes: personal, social, and racial.

Like his father and his grandfather, he preached the gospel of Jesus. His family traced ancestors from the earliest plantation days, his father a prominent pastor who preached the stern, masculine fundamentalism absorbed by southern families for over two hundred years. When young Robert reached the ninth grade he enrolled in the Robert E. Lee Military Academy in Richmond. At the University of Virginia, he made his best career choice, successfully wooing Barbara Taft, only daughter of the Honorable Senator Andrew Taft from Kentucky. The Taft fortune was large and diversified. Over generations, Tafts made money by means legal and illegal, first making a fortune running slaves. During the Civil War they ran the northern blockade, selling rifles at high profits to the Confederacy. After the war, they bought land cheap from impoverished southerners and entered the reformed southern government. Power and profit sail the same boat.

The Taft line ended with Barbara. Therefore, Senator Andrew Taft and his diminutive wife had to make hard decisions. Although cool to the match at first, they observed Barbara smitten with this young Robert Steward, a fact the good Senator pondered. Investigation revealed the Steward family as prudent with money, responsible, and delightfully prolific. For decades, every Steward produced at least four sons. The Tafts hungered for grandchildren, not only for heartfelt reasons, but as heirs for an accumulated fortune that far exceeded Barbara's needs, all factors that rendered young Robert Steward more interesting.

They warmed to him, so polite and considerate. He carried himself with southern military bearing. Although the Senator realized that the ministry didn't promise a great financial future, their daughter wouldn't be socially embarrassed. When Robert graduated from Southern Baptist Seminary with his Masters of Divinity, he proposed. Barbara accepted on condition her parents give their blessing. After proper protocol, they did. As a wedding gift Senator Taft gave the young couple a Cadillac and joint bank account of three million dollars.

Robert realized the wealthy have spiritual needs as do the poor. He chose to serve the former while reaching out to help the latter. When the search committee of Gold Ridge Southern Baptist in Atlanta, Georgia, sought to replace their retiring pastor, he interviewed for the post. The long arm of Senator Taft reached beyond his native state. Robert was hired after a trial year and settled down to serving the Lord. To the Taft's great delight Barbara gave birth to a vigorous son in the second year of marriage. The optimistic Senator bought the new parents a twenty-seven room mansion with a domestic staff of six, a prophetic purchase. The next decade welcomed five more children, four chaotic boys ending with Michael, and one enchanting daughter. The domestic staff expanded. Mrs. Steward definitely needed the help because her offspring were well beyond the delicate Barbara's coping skills. The elder Taft transferred several million annually to his modest, grateful, and prudent son-in-law and daughter.

The young pastor strongly preached God's love and willingness to forgive. Pastor Steward suggested that wealth comprised both a gift and recognition of ability. He encouraged his flock to consider what each could do for those in need. On the other hand, Robert condemned those misguided souls who advocated unearned welfare, arguing that such schemes were communistic. Any such plan would merely remove money from the responsible and give it to the careless.

Basically, Pastor Steward preached that responsible people like his congregation were approved by both man and God. All faithful desperately want God to forgive their faults and welcome them into heaven. His grateful listeners gave Pastor Steward praise, support, and a great deal of money.

Pastor Steward had two outreaches, first to the affluent in the Atlanta area. He didn't seek to maximize his congregation. He sought only members of like class and means. So much alike, everyone got along. This allowed him the financial backing and Church support to reach Atlanta's poor. He specialized in helping the working poor. State and City services made referrals to him when they saw a disadvantaged intelligent candidate. If the Pastor spotted potential, the Church of Gold Ridge provided funds and housing for attendance at vocational, trade schools, or college. The Pastor would assist the newly qualified worker in finding suitable employment. Well-fixed Church members got the satisfaction of making a difference without having to associate with people who made them uncomfortable. Furthermore, the Pastor insisted that all charitable funds be dispensed and monitored by a separate accountant. When the Church realized that the Pastor donated every dime of his $150,000 annual salary, they were astonished. Southern Baptists are unaccustomed to saints.

Senator Taft lived to see four of his grandsons become successful businessmen with Michael only twelve when the old patriarch passed away. In the old man's will, he took care to see that all his grandchildren were amply endowed with cash and securities, still bequeathing forty million to Barbara and Robert, by now nationally recognized as a brilliant churchman, guest of several United States Presidents. Michael, the youngest, turned out to be the family anomaly, quiet and thoughtful, even placid as a baby.

Although the Pastor tried to play with Michael, he could never penetrate the boy's reserve. Nevertheless, the Pastor often read his son's writing when his wife showed it to him. The boy had keen sensitivity as if he saw what the rest of the world was too coarse or busy to perceive. The father noted how Michael often prayed alone for long periods. He began to hope this last son might have the Steward calling.

At twelve Michael began to read history, philosophy, and theology. Delighted, Robert withheld no expense to feed such curiosity. Michael had access to computers and book suppliers. By age fifteen, he'd accumulated a library of over five hundred volumes, all of which he read. He began to talk to his father about spiritual matters. The pastor continued his dream that Michael might follow in the ministry.

When Michael reached puberty, there were none of the usual bouts of puppy love or romantic pining endured by hormone driven peers. Like all healthy young people he had a curiosity about sex. However, pictures in *Playboy* and *Penthouse* magazines bored him. Michael didn't talk to his father, instead shelved the subject as irrelevant. A loner through high school and college, on the few occasions he did reach out to others, his intensity startled them.

The ministry attracted Michael with his compassion for suffering and empathy for loneliness. Questions of God and the daily mysteries of life fascinated him. However, the gospel of Jesus as presented by the Baptist Church seemed too harsh with sinners burning forever in hell. When Michael had an opportunity to do missionary work in Latin America after graduation, he took it. That reinforced his concerns. How could Christian countries have such hunger and exploitation? He saw starving children eating from the trash can behind the local Catholic rectory. That couldn't be compatible with the teachings of Jesus! When the chance to go to Israel on an archaeology dig came up, he accepted it to forestall the day of career decisions.

A father seldom knows his own son. It would have helped him understand the letter post marked, as Andre's had been to his Uncle Charles, Tel Aviv. Robert Steward still had high hopes for Michael even though the young man seemed in no hurry to attend seminary. However, the father had the wisdom to be patient, taking solace from a strong feeling that his son would be important in the cause of Jesus.

This was no ordinary letter, nothing about the weather or the commonplace questions about health and home. Instead it tersely told about an archaeological find, explaining its nature, the contents, and how the Tablets were being kept secret. Michael implored his father to use his influence to get them to America until decisions could be made as to their public release. The letter ended with a plea that something be done. Secrecy about the Tablets could not be maintained for another month.

The sunny afternoon seemed to turn dark. Pastor Steward prayed for guidance, for his son, for the church, and for the world. He checked his appointment calendar. Miraculously he had the rest of the afternoon unscheduled.

***

Stein woke, surprised at how deeply he'd slept, although tired enough to have slept hours longer. He gratefully took the cup of hot black coffee Alice offered. A few sips and he was ready. He spread the translations before him. He'd always struggled with biblical scholars' basic dilemma, the absence of physical secular evidence of any of the Old Testament characters, not a hint of Abraham, Joshua, Moses, Jacob or any of the rest of the cast, not even any trace of the terrible Egyptian losses at the parting of the Red Sea. Not a clue of massive Egyptian plagues, loss of an entire generation of first born, or the extermination of the Egyptian Army. Such harrowing events could not be lost to history. No evidence is no evidence.

Stein remembered Genesis 46 where Jacob is told by God to go to Egypt, and how in verse 26 it states the number of the entire group to be sixty-six. However, in a scant four generations the number of fleeing male Jews of fighting age as noted in Exodus 12:37 is six hundred thousand not counting women and children! Exodus could not have happened for a day much less forty years in the rocky desert of the Sinai. The Tablets detailed the horrors only two thousand five hundred people endured to reach Canaan. The numbers just didn't add up.

Chapter Seventeen

Stein continued reading. Abraham took up the history after his father, Eli, died. After Moses' death, the tribe mourned by the Jordan for seven days. They then met with Canaanite leaders, assuring them of their peaceful intentions.

***

According to Abraham,

"The hill people told how they raised barley, wheat, figs, and olives. In the fall the petty lowland kings often hunted the hill people more for sport than gain. This harassing hindered their harvest, making it hard to survive winters. With only clubs and slings for weapons, they planted in many small clearings, hoping some would remain unnoticed by their enemies.

"We saw we could benefit each other, they numbering the same as our surviving tribe. Their crops would ripen within a month, so this was the time of danger. Joshua suggested our men could rebuff the lowland kings, leaving the hill people to concentrate on bringing in the harvest.

"Joshua added that we would spread our hundreds of donkeys equally among all. Would the hill people consider joining our group to form one community? After much private deliberation, they agreed. We united. The main leader of the hill people promised allegiance with Joshua while each grasped the other's testicles, the ritual of taking testimony.

"Joshua planned to surprise the kings who had such easy hunting in years past. I inspected the crops which would be ample for all if safely harvested. True to the highlanders' words, as the grain turned golden our scouts reported the approach of three hundred armed soldiers and peasantry.

"Like children, the enemy wandered into our ambush. When Joshua made the high piercing whistle of a desert hawk, we fell on this column and slaughtered them without suffering a single casualty. When we returned with our plunder, many hill people fell at our feet and praised us for their deliverance. Joshua told them to rise because our victory was due only to our god, Yahweh.

"The petty lowland kings sent a second small army which we dispatched as well. Our people helped with the harvest. Near its end, five hundred foot soldiers and twelve mounted men, the sons and noblemen of the kings appeared. We let them come close. Then Joshua made the sound of the desert hawk, and we fell on them like ravening wolves.

"We beheaded the noblemen, tying their bloody heads to their horses' saddles. Joshua ordered the bridles removed and the horses turned home with a grisly message to their lowland lords. Our spoils were great, the grain harvested, and the harvest festival would begin with the next full moon.

"Joshua and I hoped the event would unite our two groups solidly. These Canaanites, more intelligent, taller, and heavier than our desert tribe, lacked the inbred tension of the desert dweller. They willingly shared from sheer goodness.

"Canaanite women voiced their opinions fearlessly to their husbands, unacceptable in the Sinai tribe. Daughters had more choice in a future husband than our desert maidens. Single Canaanite women flirted, not done among our tribe. Canaanites believed in a joyful life of easy laughter, whereas our desert fighters focused on the grim likelihood of early death. Still, our dark desert women's graceful silence and perfect manners charmed Canaanite men. Our women bore that aristocratic grace and restraint suggestive of sensuous lovemaking. The hot blood of the youth of both tribes would hasten tribal solidarity.

"Canaanite festival preparations were elaborate. Men hunted stags, hanging them to cool. Women and children gathered racks of firewood. As the first of two festival days neared, the Canaanites dug deep stone-lined pits. They buried prepared stags on layers of stones over beds of live coals to roast for two days. They baked gold-crusted breads and prepared grains, gathered nuts, olives, and grapes from the forested hills. Finally, the night arrived when the festival would begin as the floating orb of the full moon rose. Family tents occupied hundreds of quiet nooks near the central grounds, affording privacy for parents and children.

"As the sun slid down, the crowd hushed. Reverent families spread blankets and robes on the ground while watching for the moon's ascendance. This special hour reminded couples and families of the timeless beauty of everyday things: the special sacredness of the earth, the sun, and the moon, the joy of love, family, and companionship. I held my wife with even greater tenderness than usual.

"The fierce Yahweh, an invention of Moses, seemed unworthy of the gentle gratitude felt on this darkening hillside. How silly, I thought, that we pretend to be a chosen people when here it is so clear that love happens everywhere. Undoubtedly, harsh demands of survival encouraged people to yearn for special advantage.

"I wondered what calls us to worship. Tonight, at this moment, we all worshiped life. What did we feel and hope to extend if not life? Was it not life we yearned for after death? When we lost a loved one was it not the loss of life we mourned? When a babe was born was it not life we celebrated? When we feared death was it not the loss of our life we dreaded?

"A faint white glow brightened the night. Hundreds shifted to see the moon break earth's plane. Finally, the huge rim rose like a shimmering pearl. It seemed seconds until it hung, a white globe in the evening sky, bathing us all in moonlight. Lovers gazed in rapture. The chant arose, 'Praise is to the moon, the sun, and the bounty of our mother earth. Praise is to the Creator of all these things. Amen.'

"We lit bonfires. In minutes the cooks unburied the stags and the golden meat suspended from limbs for everyone to take cuts. Men carried goatskins of wine from shaded places, now hung so all could fill their cups. The Canaanite farmers explained how grape vines were the first crop cultivated in the highlands. Strangers and friends mingled. Gradually people settled in large circles surrounding dancing areas. Stringed instruments of unexpected complexity and drums of deep resonance appeared. Their sounds created such melody that couples rushed to the open space to dance. Only women danced in our tribe. Past midnight the dancing slowed, becoming sensual. As elders retired, the youth danced on.

"Canaanite men never sold their wives, but showed their affection with none of the desert master/slave relationship. Canaanite wives worked in all facets of farming. The warrior's wife lay with him and bore his children. To the desert warrior one female equaled any other.

"I fretted that our Sinai women would appear less capable than their Canaanite counterparts. In addition, our young women drank little wine which puzzled the hill people. However, when the dancing slowed, becoming more seductive, our maidens perked up. This was something they knew. Sinai women with no assets beyond desirability had performed erotic dances for centuries. My wife shook her head as if to indicate these Canaanite women were pretty, but clumsy. Images of her dancing reminded me of that truth.

"When I glanced at my father Eli, seated with my mother, I saw him smile. When the last Canaanite girl finished, he stood up in the firelight, telling the assembly our women also knew dances of love, and asked if the group would like to see one. This invitation amazed because our women were so reserved there had been whispers they must not enjoy lovemaking. Eli clapped his hands and called, 'Melee!'

"Melee, Eli's fifteen year old granddaughter, doe-eyed, ripe, and a delight to any man's eyes, sprang to her feet and ran to the center of the dancing area. One of our musicians lifted his flute. At the first notes Melee slipped her outer cloak off as gracefully as a flower opening at dawn. In a moment she transformed into a desert shaman. With graceful movements Melee entrapped every man as she rode the notes of that haunting flute like smoke on an evening breeze, every snake-like muscle controlled. With extended arms she could send a muscle rippling from one wrist to the other like a wave upon the sea. Her eyes turned colors in the firelight as she twisted into the music.

"Melee became a supple nymph of passion, her upper torso perfectly still as her hips undulated with the rhythm of love. About her throat lay a double set of linked coins, girdling her waist delicate silver bells. A triple set of slender silver rings wound around her ankles. With these, Melee radiated a perfect harmony of sultry invitation.

"As if in response to a hidden voice, the flute quickened as her hips moved faster and faster. The silver bells on her waist jingled more urgently with each second. Melee closed her eyes in desperate ecstasy. Glowing with sweat, she placed her hands on her furious hips as if to restrain their frenzy. Just as the tension grew unbearable, Melee stopped. With a very deep tender sigh and joyous smile, she gazed into the harvest moon as if into the eyes of a lover, a perfect statue of desire frozen in moonlight. The crowd was equally frozen. With perfect timing Eli broke the silence with a quick clap and Melee swooped up her cloak and disappeared within the circle of our other maidens. Finally the stunned crowd began to applaud. There would be no more doubt about our desert women's desirability.

"Camp roused well after midmorning, everyone sated with food, drink, lovemaking, and sleep. An ancient wisdom dwelt in this celebration. Meaningful life was inseparable from love. Being joyous led to good memories, and good memories repeated blossomed into beloved social traditions. It seemed healthier for a society to celebrate life than ponder the unknown of death. The rational Canaanites had advanced beyond us with our fearful preoccupation with Yahweh's demands.

"Next day elders of both tribes met in counsel. Joshua represented us. Methods of decision making varied. The Canaanites would only reach a decision after long discussion among their leaders. They had to reach consensus. The desert tribe left final decisions to Joshua alone because of his military leadership.

"These completely different theories of government and ways of thinking profoundly affected efforts to merge and form a common religion. Later, I saw religion's venomous power to divide. Finally, we agreed to part our Sinai tribe into twelve groups among the Canaanite population, the Canaanites to help the Sinai newcomers construct dwellings before the rainy season, Joshua to settle in the central area among the majority of Canaanite leaders.

"The Canaanites would teach the Sinai tribe the art of farming. In return, Sinai warriors would share military skills with their new Canaanite neighbors. I worked closely with Canaanite priests to understand and merge our religious outlooks. It was further agreed that the freshly merged tribe should have a new name to identify our new beginning. The selected name was 'Israelites' after a small, but valorous tribe that fought the mighty, Egyptian army two or three centuries before. The Israelites were destroyed, but their heroic deeds passed into folklore. Thus the name was reborn. We also used the name Hebrews because the word Habiru meant fugitives and we were fugitives from the desert mountains.

"Younger single members of both tribes intermarried quickly, the urge for love, sex, and family overriding all differences. However, adjustment proved hard for older desert warriors. They had lived by raiding and then resting, not doing manual labor. However, to become a farmer a person had to labor all the time. Clearing land with rude tools is backbreaking toil and a man's greater strength is essential. Desert women attended to every domestic need. Now both husband and wife faced a life of laborious planting and harvesting on a dawn to dusk basis. This did not come easily to desert men, their status based on courage and combat skills.

"It was amazing to see what else affected us. For example, in the Sinai the skies were bright, the weather scorching. Here in the Israeli highlands cold, maleficent clouds often cast across the winter sky, abrading our morale. Canaanite natives rebuked any who complained about excess rain because rain was vital for the crops. To complain against rain was to complain about the basis for human survival. Canaanite farmers feared complaining against winter weather might anger the gods. An angry god might cause drought and thus famine.

"Canaanites tended to be patient, used to the cyclical passage of time, content to wait months for wheat to grow from a seed to the whole grain. They made decisions at leisure. In contrast, warriors tend to be men of violent action, making decisions rapidly, making things happen immediately. Force is habit to a warrior, yet the farmer knows one cannot force a stalk to grow.

"Warriors often missed the pure intensity of combat and the brotherhood that occurs only when men fight shoulder to shoulder. To the warrior the plodding day to day labor of the Canaanite farmer reduced a man to the level of an ass. Desert men resented the gradual independence of their wives as they acquired the habits of Canaanite women. Nevertheless, I hoped two or three generations of intermarriage and common culture would meld the differences. Unfortunately, I underestimated the power of religion. The imaginary Yahweh returned to thwart our blending two cultures.

"Yahweh worship was a command religion, the Ten Commandments intended to outline our contract. God gave commands, the believer expected to obey, a formula passed on to the priests. Sadly, what began as a civilizing platform turned oppressive. The more a leader needed group compliance, the more drastic the punishment the strident leader claimed Yahweh would inflict on the disobedient.

"The Canaanites viewed their gods differently. God was simply life. Rather than obeying divine legislation, the Canaanite sought to cooperate with God in life's recurring cycle. The Canaanites did not think of themselves as unique, singled out by a demanding Creator, but as an equal part of a web of all living creation. The mystery of birth formed their center of existence. The recurring of spring, new shoots of wheat, prosperity of harvest, and the miracle of human birth inspired awe. Joyful sexuality and fecundity shaped their religion. The Canaanite system implied only vague hopes of an afterlife.

"This idea of cooperating with God led Canaanite men to cooperation in self-government. Power rose from the whole to selected leaders. In the Yahweh system, power went from the divinely appointed leader down to obedient followers. One man rule was exactly the slavery the Canaanites had fled the lowlands to escape.

"As men of the earth, Canaanites farmers also believed in what they could see and touch. Since farmers stay in one place, they worship local gods. Invisible gods have little appeal to tenders of visible grain and visible grapes. Warriors cannot carry large visible symbols of gods so the god of the warrior had to be invisible. Object worship offended desert people who focused only on an invisible divinity. Yahweh extremists scorned Canaanite 'idols' even though Canaanites maintained the object only represented the mystery of the god behind it.

"While Canaanites were not adverse to the concept of one main god, they could not accept his not having lesser gods to serve him. After all, who ever heard of a kingdom without underlings? But since these, too, lived forever in a divine world did they not also have to be gods? Furthermore, as a fertile, lusty people, the Canaanites were unimpressed by Yahweh's lack of a consort. What kind of a man or god would deprive himself of lovemaking? Canaanites viewed sex as a joy, a god-given gift. Sexless men and gods met with gravest skepticism, even repulsion.

"In the main, the problem lay with the desert people's Yahweh position. Extremists felt they were the only true chosen people, that only they were obeying the true god. Canaanites were disgusted with the Yahweh extremists who condemned venerable gods the Canaanites had worshiped for untold centuries. Yahweh extremist scorn of healthy farming community festivals dismayed the Canaanites. Worldlier, they viewed the exclusivity of Hebrew extremists, who would not allow their children to marry Canaanites, as foolish and insulting. Thus demonic religious hatred threatened our new Israeli community.

"To explain human existence, the Canaanites had developed a system of divine creators. Their supreme god was El, father of other gods and first cause of everything. El had a consort, Athirat. Their divine coupling produced lesser gods who produced others. El remained aloof from mundane matters. The god most important to the Canaanite farmer was Baal, son of Dagon. Canaanite priests viewed Baal as the grandson of lofty El. What captivated the Canaanite farmers is that Baal was the god of rain. Since seasonal water is essential to a farmer, they worshiped Baal as primary god. Baal also had a consort called several names the most common being Anat, Astarte, or Ashtoreth.

"The farmer understood the seasons, and that the rain 'died' at a certain time so crops could ripen. That same dead rain god came back to life in the spring to bring life-supporting moisture.

Belief in resurrection of various types was common among all known nations. Some desperately needed to believe that every word of these stories was literally true, while others were content to live with myth. Canaanite priests gave simple answers for complex mysteries.

"Of course, these farmers were uneducated, but practical. They wanted to worship in a manner acceptable to God with least effort. The farming community had a centralized location, nearly always on a hill with stone symbols for male or wooden symbols for female deities representing key gods. Usually Baal was a large upright stone, tall and slender, this virility symbol common throughout the known world. Nearly all nations had such symbols revered as fitting representations of joy and the promise of life. In many countries craftsmen made phallic figures of extreme realism, but such talents were beyond the time and means of Canaanite farmers. They deemed a raw stone mounted erect suitable for the masculine god Baal. The people went to the gods to pray for good fortune.

"The form of Ashtorath, often a small statue kept in a home, displayed multiple breasts representing abundant fertility. A female deity satisfied Canaanite women for their needs, particularly to bear children. Ashtorath frequently stood also on a hilltop or within a beautiful wooded glen where a tree was chosen to represent the beauty of long, fertile life. An Ashtorath symbol often sat on the same hilltop as the Baal figure. The Ashtorath monument would be a tall slender pole carved with figures to represent female tastes and adorned with fresh flowers. This combined the symbol of the erect phallus with female delicacy and beauty. The erect male organ was referred to as the 'staff of life', the female sexual organs as the 'gates of life.' Lovers tryst on these sacred hilltops and shaded glens. Barren wives might induce their husbands to couple at these sites, hoping the gods would grant pregnancy.

"Yahweh extremists eschewed understanding the Canaanite religion. Ironically, the intent of all was the same: to honor and acknowledge their creator. Both tended to worship their god less than petitioning for favors. Unfortunately, the wish to exclude other religions grew and sickened the community body.

"If all-important rains did not nurture our highlands, then one religious viewpoint would blame the other. Extreme Hebrew factions caused most division, mired in their belief that Canaanites worshipped idols and false gods. During good years, the extreme Hebrews kept a sullen silence, but in bad years they shouted Yahweh was punishing Canaanite false worship.

"After the first harvest I went with my father Eli to Moses' grave beside the Jordan, deeply moved as he broke a loaf of bread and spread the crumbs on the grave. We withdrew and watched birds gracefully land on the grave and eat them. Moses would appreciate this. Once again, my father impressed upon me the greatness of Moses and how history must preserve his name.

"I promised Eli to save his memoirs and add to them when I reached advanced age. As he lay dying, my father wished us well, whispering he hoped to see Moses. Whether he received his wish I do not know. I do know that with his last breath he smiled with radiance and uttered, 'Moses' as if in greeting. My mother felt it fitting he be buried next to Moses. I planted a young birch between their graves. Over the years I visited them. That sapling grew and flourished into a strong, sheltering tree.

"To set a good example, Joshua and I both took second wives, Canaanite women. I now have nine sons, the youngest seventeen, the oldest thirty, and four daughters. Like our fathers, we educated our children, both daughters and sons, at home. Most difficult was to decide which of them should know the truth about the desert Yahweh religion as our fathers had chosen us.

"In the end Joshua agreed to judge my children and I his for the necessary intellect. Joshua selected only my youngest son, Ishmael, and my oldest daughter, Jebel. From Joshua's fourteen I selected two sons and one daughter. Joshua agreed the memoirs of Eli be maintained with continuing history by my family line. Eli's memoirs were converted to the finest clay, fired by a Canaanite peasant, formerly a slave in a pottery establishment. We hoped that clay tablets could last for centuries. We stored them in secluded limestone caves behind tiny openings hidden by stones. My two chosen truth bearers became custodians of the Tablets.

"When we revealed the truth about the Yahweh religion, our gifted children told us they had long thought the true God could not be such a savage tyrant as Yahweh. It was silly to believe the true God would have any chosen people. Had not God created everyone?

"I, Abraham, am an old man. I have written in the hopes that the memories of Moses and Eli be preserved. If there is a true God it is in his hands whether these writings last. At the end of life how little we actually leave behind: children, memories, and little more. I cannot stop the endless wheel of eternity and accept the judgment of God. I would be pleased if someday another would read my account and lift a cup of wine to my memory. You are alive, and I am dead. Perhaps someday we will meet. Farewell from Abraham."

***

If old Abraham could only know what effect his, and his descendants' writings are about to have! It was Stein's duty to see these Tablets safely to the United States. The big question was how. He looked up at Alice reading on the couch and asked, "Could you by chance bring me a glass of wine?"

"Certainly." She padded off, still in stocking feet, and returned with a fruity local carafe. Guessing where he'd left off, Alice raised a glass with Stein in a silent toast to Abraham, son of Eli.

Chapter Eighteen

Amal settled into being General Kessler's mistress. Much had changed. She now lived in the domestic quarters of the general's home. Amal never questioned, never made demands, nor made any advances. When the general talked, she listened. When the general initiated lovemaking, she complied. Slowly but with steady steps, the general fell deeper in love with this tender peasant woman. Amal put the general's needs paramount, asking nothing, but scrupulously accepting whatever he wished to give, and he gave her much.

Becoming a live-in domestic enabled Amal to escape the refugee camp and provide money for her mother. The general signed documents that allowed Amal considerable personal freedom. Two days a week she walked nearby hills to pick from the profusion of wild flowers. Amal would be stopped by Israeli patrols, but her papers clearly established that she belonged to General Kessler.

Walking the countryside gave Amal knowledge of her operational area, within easy hiking range of three military bases linked by highways rich with military traffic. Amal located ambush sites that could afford a sniper good chances for success and escape. Still, the time might come when her life would have to be exchanged for an enemy's who must be eliminated. Amal prayed to Allah to accept her soul when she completed her earthly mission.

In the meantime, Pebbles had altered lifestyles of the Israeli elite. Politicians now frequently attended heavily guarded funerals of powerful friends, relations, and fellow government leaders. Personal acquaintances were incinerated in their luxury cars by fire bombs. Friends were killed by poison or cut in two by assault rifles on public sidewalks in front of their office buildings. Friends' bodies rested in closed caskets because their heads had been shattered by a sniper bullet. Behind it all were the actions of one unknown. Pebbles believed with Allah's help he would destroy all infidels, but first must come Palestinian freedom.

Early one evening the copy of Michael's letter to his father arrived on Pebble's desk. The Arab leader's eyes gleamed, black stones lit by fire. The Sepphoris site swelled in importance. If he could possess the Tablets, he could prove the Zionists had no God given claim to Palestine. It would be possible to prove their mendacity about Palestine's history. However, the Tablets were in a camp surrounded by two hundred Israeli guards, and it would take a truck to transport them. Stealing only the translations would be worthless because Zionists would simply claim they were fraudulent and no Tablets existed. The Jews must still be unaware of the Tablets' content. However, too many people already did know. Mossad would have the news soon.

Michael's father had potential to move fastest because he acted independently, thus posing the biggest threat. Who would the famed American clergyman contact? Killing the messenger would buy time. With a few marks on a slip of paper Pebbles set in motion his murderous plan.

***

At that exact moment, half way around the world another spy master reviewed his options. Chief Matt Homes, CIA, pondered what to do after perusing the reports of field agents in the Middle East. His Sepphoris site agent had sent a second message. From a rating of 4 on a scale of 5 the agent coded this information as a nearly unprecedented 4.5. The missile confrontation between Kennedy and Khrushchev over Cuba had only rated a 4.8. The agent's message declared making contact imperative and not to entrust a standard coded transmission. The agent suggested contact through option D.

To identify option D required the agent's assignment file. Homes directed his secretary to hand carry it from the operations room where every CIA operative was tracked twenty-four hours per day. Information arrived here to be analyzed and directed to the proper departments.

Homes read the file. As per his standard procedure it didn't contain the agent's name or photo, only verified this agent's first assignment in Israel. Still, nothing suggested a tendency to exaggerate. Scanning down the communication list Homes found option D. He grinned as he noted the method of message delivery: imaginative and unconventional. Section Chief Homes authorized his field agent to use it, then ordered the Sepphoris file hand carried to Chief Executive (and Senator) Albright this very morning. Within an hour a burst transmission was sent from the American embassy in Tel Aviv. This signal in turn lit one of two tiny bulbs, one red the other green, on a miniature radio transmitter somewhere in Sepphoris. In this case the green bulb shone. The agent who turned it off would use option D to communicate.

*　*　*

As a political appointee Senator Albright had imagined this job would be exciting as well as prestigious. Reality meant endless hours and soul crushing decisions only he could make. As a Senator he'd specialized in avoiding direct questions, a master at giving impressive answers that said nothing. Here hard decisions had to be made daily. Quiet men in gray suits often stood before his desk and could only be answered in a "yes" or "no." He was cast as judge, jury, and executioner by proxy. Plus he lost all privacy. Everyone in power was watched by someone and others watched the watchers. The survival of nations couldn't be risked on human frailty, reality on a planet peering into the nuclear abyss.

His boss, President Straihorn, scared the CIA chief; those oval office dalliances chilled him. Secret cameras and microphones in the White House exceeded those at Nashville's Grand Old Opry. The Supreme Commander also reveled in military power, his penchant for bombings well documented. The President also ordered killings of political enemies, crossing deep lines of loyalty in intelligence communities. It's one thing to use the power of office to kill enemies of your country, quite another for personal ends. All in all, the CIA chief counted the days until this basket case of a President's final term ended. Nevertheless, Straihorn had been elected legitimate United States President with the CIA bound to serve his leadership.

All these factors troubled the CIA chief as he read the Sepphoris report. Nothing could be done until the agent got the information out of that guarded camp. How often the most powerful could only wait. He lit a match and watched the report burn in his special furnace, ruminating that perhaps in his next life he would return as a professional golfer.

***

The popular President Straihorn's facets included one lurking behind the warm smile and charisma: a first rate Machiavellian mind. Decisive and efficient, manipulative and ruthless, he weighed his actions for desired results, success his only measure of morality. Winning is right, losing the ultimate sin. Presidential rules seldom adhered to simple codes of right and wrong.

Another feature of President Straihorn's personality sparked concern among intelligence agencies. The mental professionals' nearly unanimous consensus was that he suffered from advanced megalomania, an extreme desire for power and an uncontrollable urge to use it. Megalomania fed by narcissism can have negative sexual ramifications including exhibitionism.

In the nuclear age every President is scrutinized by a committee of psychiatrists selected from private practice and academics whose reports are reviewed monthly by the FBI and the CIA. Should either of these agencies determine the situation warrants closer review, they request more frequent reports. Both agencies were requesting weekly reports on President Straihorn.

Psychiatrists concluded that either the President didn't care about social conventions or couldn't control his sexual impulses. His acquaintances dying under questionable circumstances, many at convenient times for the President, disturbed agencies more. Nearly all had damaging information about his business, sexual, and financial affairs. Concerns peaked in 1993 and early 1994. The sexual scandal involving a White House aide raised compelling questions about his sanity, such indiscretions in the

Oval Office and subsequent lies to the American public were disquieting. He apparently liked being watched during carnal acts.

***

As much as the secret services knew about President Straihorn, they didn't know his thoughts as he sat in his oval office at 2:30 a.m. that spring morning in 1995. He often came alone to the oval office very late, sitting at his desk in the dark. He'd enjoyed darkness since earliest childhood. His best ideas came to him in dim rooms, the darker the better. As a teenager he hid in a lightless closet dreaming the life he would have when he finally left home. He also entertained sexual fantasies in those comforting confines, imagining locking himself in there with a submissive woman. Occasionally he'd thought about placing a woman in a locked closet to which he alone had a key. In his college years he played out that fantasy, thrilled by the sense of control over the frightened coed. He released her only after they had sex; the time spent planning that adventure well worth it.

Even as a child, the President believed in long term plans. He also loved secrets, the sensual thrill of clandestine strategies. Long ago he'd given up seeking to understand the reasons for his pleasures. He only knew he enjoyed feelings of supremacy when no one knew his plans. He especially liked to hint at secrets and watch others try to penetrate his guile. He had sex in this office frequently. The sense of risk was hotly erotic.

Awareness that daytime cameras transmitted every detail heightened arousal. Taking exquisite risks raised him to exquisite pleasures. He particularly enjoyed daytime sex with the door to the Oval Office ajar. The elements of public risk, observation from unknown eyes, and complete control over his sexual partner all added up to life at its finest.

Few suspected the infamous sexual scandal had been planned by the President himself. From the start he pushed the political reality envelope to its outer limits, without doubt his most thrilling plan. Even the boy in the dark closet could never imagine such an adventure. To dangle over the political abyss with one hand, yet pull out of such an impossible spot proved the ultimate thrill. He'd known from the start the romantic little aide could never keep their affair a secret. He jilted her with perfect timing, and her broken heart responded exactly as calculated. To expose his sex life to the nation and survive politically gratified more than anything he'd ever done. He'd even portrayed Congress as a bunch of sour prudes.

***

After work, students and laborers at Sepphoris went to the showers to wash off the grime from
the long sweaty day. They ate evening meals in the large onsite kitchen. After dining, both students and workers filtered away, many to enter into card games that transcend language and culture. Some played board games, chess being most popular. Literary students reclined on their bunks to read. Still others -- in time honored manner -- wrote letters home. More than a few played outdoor sports. The camp administration provided courts and fields for volleyball, softball, and basketball. The camp also had archery targets and horseshoe pits. Students and workers checked out balls, mitts, boards, and other equipment.

Of course, romances sprang up naturally. These couples would normally seek out secluded areas as twilight faded. Students who left camp in the evenings (excluding Palestinians not allowed that freedom) found privacy in nearby undulating hills and folds. Usually by 1:00 or 2:00 a.m. even those with the most passionate needs retired. Between 3:00 and 5:00 a.m. the camp slumbered, surrounded by two hundred soldiers. The American CIA agent faked sleep in barracks C., still amazed he'd stumbled on such critical information. The CIA in Langley, Virginia, gave this 4 plus warning credibility. The field agent's ingenuity surprised and impressed his handlers. He might be young, but made of the right stuff.

***

At 3:27 a.m. he slipped from his bunk with his towel and shaving kit and casually walked to the men's room. Entering a stall, he latched the door and removed a device from his kit similar to a small tape cassette. Indeed, to the untrained eye it would be difficult to imagine it different from any tape player anywhere, magnetic reels visible through a plastic window, normal press buttons in normal places. Pressing the buttons actually did nothing. It seemed broken. But pressing buttons in a predetermined order would show an alphabet printed as part of the plastic tape lid.

It was then possible to compose a brief message stored in a miniscule memory bank. Another button transformed it into a mathematical cryptic of random complexity transferred to a tiny section of magnetic tape no more than one-eighth inch in length. The tape itself would decompose in under twelve hours unless treated with an unusual, specific chemical. Sitting on the commode, towel draped over his head, the agent sheltered the device on his lap, writing with no possibility of his message being caught on concealed cameras.

Once the message was encrypted, the memory devices were erased. When the complete button was compressed, the cassette expelled a sliver of tape and cut it off. The agent withdrew a tiny hollow plastic sphere from the machine's back, divided it, and placed the tape in one half of the sphere, sealing the unit by compressing both halves together. Also from the back of the small machine he removed a metallic ball less than three-sixteenths of an inch in diameter, a miniature radio transmitter with a one hundred meter range. Satisfied, he tucked his encrypting unit back in his kit, flushed the toilet, and returned to his bunk by 3:49 a.m.

He listened for unusual sounds. Cupping the two small objects in his right hand he glanced at his watch, 4:16 a.m. He slipped out of his bunk and walked soundlessly to the side door, left open in the hot season making it easy to step outside into the barracks' deep shadow. The moon had set and luckily clouds shrouded the sky. He proceeded to the recreation room where balls, bats, and other equipment were stacked.

From under a bench he withdrew one long aluminum arrow. Removing the previously loosened target head he inserted a small piece of tissue paper with a message sphere and the miniature transmitter behind it. Using a tiny bottle of five minute epoxy, he re-glued the target head in the shaft. After the glue set, he picked up a camp archery bow he'd previously placed against the wall.

Working quickly, the agent removed six rubber bands stashed in a knot hole in the bench, each neatly cut in two. He tied them up and down the bow's string to reduce the twang of bow string to a whisper. Glancing at the sky, he nocked the arrow on the bow string; a cloud approached a bright star in line with his aiming sector. When the cloud's edge covered the star the agent brought the bow to full draw. With a final plea of, "Fly True," he released the secret of Sepphoris, and eluded espionage technology. The arrow silently sliced through the air in a high arc over Israeli soldiers' watchful eyes.

Perhaps it was only just that the truth of Moses through Jesus be delivered by an ancient means that would have been familiar to both. Impaling the ground three hundred meters away, that arrow struck a modern world unprepared for the Jesus Tablets.

***

Israel encourages and protects tourism. Every day hordes of international visitors fan out over the country after boarding vans and buses to experience the land where religious heroes trod. Armed with cameras and electronic toys, tourists stand in line to photograph scenes including Jesus' alleged tomb or the site of the mythical Sodom and Gomorra. Money from fools spends just as well as that from sages. Israeli locals are free to invent stories about every hill and pile of rocks. Indeed a religious historian would be amazed at the feats of walking the modest Jesus had accomplished during his short life. He must have had the foresight to visit many villages not

founded until centuries after his death. Locals are used to flamboyant tourists traipsing over rough ground in the elusive hope of a religious experience or at least a decent snapshot.

Because of all this, no soldier gave it a thought when a tourist van pulled off the Sepphoris road at dawn. Several tourists grappled with their tripods and began to photograph the pearly sunrise. Nor was it unusual when they began to walk the flank of the hill where each paused frequently to take photos. Few things are a more common sight in Israel than tourists fumbling through camera bags in search of yet another lens or roll of film. However, this time each camera was also a radio receiver panning for the signal from an aluminum arrow.

Finally, the heaviest tourist detected a faint green light in his viewfinder. Wiping his sweaty brow, he wandered in that general bearing another fifty meters before lifting his camera. The green light brightened. Walking left twenty meters, he took another reading, mimicking a fat man taking a breather. Six more paces and the green light grew brilliant in the viewfinder with no new bearing. He was within ten feet of the arrow. Setting his camera case down, he stooped to tie his shoelaces. Finally, he spotted a straight line under a shrub. A childhood spent hunting white tail bucks in Minnesota taught him few things in the natural world are perfectly straight.

In seconds the agent unscrewed the target head, removed the message capsule and transmitter, and placed both in a 35 mm film container. He shoved the arrow under the sandy soil. Slowly the heavy man clambered to his feet, slinging his camera bag over his shoulder. He drifted back toward the van pausing for a few last photos. At the van, he pushed a button on the dash that activated a strong radio transmitter. As the other searchers raised their viewfinders a bright red dot signaled the arrow had been found. Sepphoris' message moved closer to United States soil.

Chapter Nineteen

In two hours they arrived at the Tel Aviv Hilton. Just as the elevator door was sliding shut a white-haired woman stopped it, stating she was going up to 327A. It would have taken a trained eye to detect the slightest movement between the elderly lady and the fat man. He and his companions exited on the second floor to prepare for their flights back to America, never assigned to Israel again.

The elderly woman went on to the third floor. At Room 327, she unlocked her door and entered. There was no room 327A. She removed the microfilm sliver, placing a drop of clear substance on it. After thirty seconds the liquid dried to a hard clear coating on the tiny message from Sepphoris. Meticulously the woman worked the treated film into a ping pong ball sized threaded hollow lead sphere. Lead would prevent x-ray detection at airport security. She gift wrapped the sphere in a small rectangular box.

Even a highly trained eye could hardly realize any connection between the white-haired elevator rider and the glamorous woman in polar ray sunglasses who exited it carrying a single bag. She stopped in the gift shop to purchase a Yemenite filigree bracelet of silver and garnets, asking the clerk to gift wrap it before she strolled out onto the sun-drenched streets.

She flagged a cab to the American Embassy on Hayarkon Street. For the first time in her CIA career she had orders to kill anyone trying to stop her. Whatever she was carrying, her country must want it badly to risk killing in broad daylight in a friendly country. The CZ 75 9mm pistol in a pouch lining of her tote never felt heavier.

Light-headed with relief, she briskly passed alert Marine guards stationed at the Embassy doors, and asked the receptionist to inform Ambassador Morgenstern her niece had arrived.

Within moments her distinguished aunt, silver hair pulled into a tight chignon, greeted her. They walked together into the Ambassador's French décor office. When the door closed solidly behind them the Ambassador smiled. "Alexi, did you find a nice present for your mother?"

"I love Israeli jewelry," Alexi answered placing the package on the Ambassador's desk.

"Bad news, sweetheart. Your mom checked into MedStar Georgetown University Hospital this morning. Her jaw ached and she had flu symptoms. Those can be signs of a heart attack, so they want to be sure she's OK. No results yet, but come back to DC with me tomorrow. You can give her your present in person."

The Israeli Mossad probably listened to every word. Only two rooms in the building were certain to be free of electronic bugging: one the radio room, the other the conference room used by CIA handlers and the Ambassador for top-secret discussions. Electromagnetic machines bombarded them, scrambling all radio waves and electronic devices except those encoded by American operators. Even digital wrist watches couldn't operate in that environment, the radiation so intense it led to suspicion of links between this method and high cancer rates among Embassy personal. In addition, the code was generated by a random computer program maintained from CIA headquarters in Langley that changed the cryptic key several times each hour. Agent Alexi was, in fact, Ambassador Morgenstern's niece, and her mother was ill. Neither the Ambassador nor Alexi knew the illness had been induced by a clandestine change in her mother's blood pressure medication. Mossad's check of hospital records would indeed show her as a patient. Thus, the secret of Sepphoris left Israel at 4:04 a.m. in the diplomatic pouch handcuffed to the Ambassador's wrist. In eleven hours the microfilm so laboriously secreted out of Sepphoris arrived at Langley. Like a building hurricane, forces surrounding the Jesus Tablets gained speed, drawn closer and closer together.

***

Simultaneously, one of the world's most powerful men, Piet-Hans Tobenhien, the Father General of the Society of Jesus, known by Catholic insiders as the Black Pope, was a passenger aboard a Boeing 747 approaching Heathrow International

Airport. The Black Pope earned his name first because the Pope wore white vestments, the head of the Jesuits wearing the more humble black garb. Over centuries, Jesuit society heads also used ruthless methods to gain and hold power. The Jesuit Father General of his time foiled more than one pope.

A tall, powerful, stern-faced Dutchman with a heavy white beard and no nonsense manner, Father Tobenhien was also a scholar of international renown, the long time Rector of the Pontifical Oriental Institute in Rome. His specialty was Near Eastern Catholic rites. Hard and cunning, reticent outside the classroom, when he did speak, everyone including Pope Jerome listened. As Father General of the Jesuits, Tobenhien led twenty-six thousand priests in positions of power throughout the Catholic Empire.

He and the Polish Pope Jerome were mortal enemies. Father Tobenhien emerged from a tiny country noted for producing independent thinkers and stubborn personalities. The stereotypical Dutchman made up his mind slowly and then held his position to his dying breath. Class distinctions are despised by the libertarian Dutch. The Pope emerged from a society where class distinctions emerged from centuries of economic oppression, where Catholic hierarchy cooperated hand in glove with politicians.

When Father Tobenhien spoke of injustice he intended to do everything to correct it here and now. He didn't talk of betterment in the sweet bye and bye. Quite the contrary, Father Tobenhien intended to use church power and pulpit to attack forces and classes profiting from poverty. This rejection of the Pope in order to serve a greater God was the bloody battleground where Jesuits clashed with Polish Jerome. To the majority of Jesuits, absolute obedience is given to God and duty to his often helpless believers. To the Old Catholic Church absolute obedience was owed the Pope, ultimate duty is to obey him in all things.

Having lived for years in war-torn Beirut, Father General Tobenhien had enough of religious dictators leading followers into murderous acts against other believers. Each dictator claimed to speak for God. Whenever a man claims so, death and persecution follow. Only the voice of reasonable consensus could control religious passions in the nuclear age. One man authority of the vast Catholic Church had outlived its primitive past. Infallibility seemed archaic as the medieval rack or papal dungeons.

His afternoon discussion with Father Charles in Boston raised unexpected issues. If a discovery in Sepphoris denying the divinity of Christ proved true, ramifications would render the Catholic Church a palace with a paper foundation. If Jesus had no validity, neither did the apostles. Father Tobenhien looked out his airplane window and trembled. Thousands of priests would be without employment or training for secular jobs. Masses of believers would be adrift in disillusion, their Bible just another mythology.

Many times the Church took firm stands defending sacred claims. However, with the Renaissance, the Church lost each battle against truth, logic, and science. Beliefs in witches and demons faded as medicine learned facts about physical illnesses, mental illness, and mass delusions. Papal sacredness diminished with the mindless waste of life in the Crusades. The Church's defense of the flat earth doctrine caused such embarrassment the Galileo affair would never be forgotten. Imprisonment and persecution of early and later scientists clarified the Church's lack of insight to truth. Science disclosed a universe vaster and much older than that described in the Bible while the Church defended the earth being the center of the universe, even claimed the sun held still in the sky while Joshua slaughtered his enemies.

The split that left a Western and Eastern branch of the Church showed its leaders to be fallible mortals. History didn't overlook nor forget the Church's silence as millions of Jews died during World War II. Nor did it forget the Church's part in assisting Nazi war criminals escape justice. The church never excommunicated the Catholic Hitler.

The Church never revealed a balance sheet of its immense holdings. How could the Vatican justify the billions squirreled away in bank accounts worldwide, given in sacrifice by deluded believers? Yet bad as all this was, these Jesus Tablets could be worse. In spite of past blunders the Church could always claim to be the representative of Christ on earth and the ultimate spiritual guide to heaven. Too, the Catholic Church would not die alone. After centuries of killing each other in God's name, Protestant and Catholic would plummet together.

He surprised himself by acknowledging that his beliefs wouldn't be much affected. To him Jesus had always been an ideal to aspire to, a perfect man who showed how to live and relate to a corrupt world, who represented relief for the poor and suffering, a dream figure who fought for the oppressed by standing up to the rich and the powerful. A man dying for his ideals and religion had timeless romantic appeal. A man who would die for a stranger filled nearly every man and woman with awe and hope. The final link in the chain was for God Himself to die for His Father's children. Love at that level can only exist in the imagination, but is so enticing, the theme so noble and lofty it inspired and elevated the faithful. The story of Jesus gave humanity a precious myth. As Father Tobenhien pondered all this, he watched claw-shaped clouds below. The Church could never admit that it, too, only had hopes, dreams, and faith.

Father Tobenhien calculated how many knew about the Jesus Tablets. Andre and Michael knew; one or both may have told others. Henry Cross and his wife also, and probably Dr. Stein their Harvard department head. Stein was on site, and would communicate with others after returning to the United States. The Israeli Mossad would have acted by now if they knew. Anything reducing the Jewish claim to Palestine would endanger them. Probably no major player knew of the Tablets because no visible effort had been made to protect or transport them. Nevertheless, this secret couldn't be kept.

The heart of the problem was the tangible Tablets. Destroyed, their contents could be debated into eternity, but the Church would be safe. However, obliteration of hundreds of hardened clay slabs called for expertise and supplies. Arranging the death of the Cross couple and Stein was feasible, but would focus attention on the Tablets. Of course, the entire camp knew they'd been discovered even though lulled into thinking them unimportant.

The Tablets must be destroyed. Father Tobenhien considered reasoning with Stein to buy time until he could demolish them. Would money smooth the path? No. The well-paid scholar earned an international reputation for integrity. His career testified to his willingness to speak truth regardless of results. Such men had always been enemies of established religion. Although Father Tobenhien had never met Henry Cross, he'd read his writings. Cross was also of strong character.

Unfortunately, the United States government couldn't be counted on to be an ally. It had been surprisingly cool to the Catholic Church for decades and resented Vatican interference in world affairs. Most American Catholics chose not to mix religion and politics. The rejection of the birth control pill had ended the Church's influence with most Catholic American women.

President Straihorn posed a mystery. His sexual peccadilloes belied serious religious beliefs. At times he showed signs of despising all religious leaders. His meeting with Pope Jerome had been icy, the asexual Pope and the philandering President having little in common. Whoever could not be controlled by the Church could not be trusted. Pope Jerome himself must be Tobenhien's strongest ally. Even if hating each other, both sought Catholicism's survival.

How could they find the right person in the right place to destroy the Tablets? Since they were in Israel, he might work something out with that government. After all, Israel had a definite stake in the status quo claiming Palestine was based on a covenant made between God and the Jews.

If any of the Arab nations gained possession of the Tablets, the propaganda value would be beyond any price. International opinion might swing over to the oppressed Palestinians while the Jews would lose western nations' funding. Of course, if Moses were revealed as a charlatan, his God discredited, this might raise questions about Allah's validity which would slow Arabs down. One couldn't be sure.

Unfortunately, the Catholic Church and the Jews hated each other with deep, ancient passion. Since the Jews believed themselves the chosen people, they resented Catholicism's claim to be the only correct path to God. Nor had the Jews forgotten centuries of slaughter and persecution inflicted by the Roman Catholic Church. It would be difficult to close ranks.

Father Tobenhien prayed with all his Jesuit force of will and depth of piety. He prayed that God would not overlook the millennia the Church had sheltered the poor and the helpless. He prayed that God would forgive his weakness and that of the Church he served. He asked for an answer so simple seekers could find their way home to their Creator. He asked with the confidence of faith as he knocked on the door of his God.

After several minutes of this, the good Father smiled. God had answered. He knew the next step. The jet banked, beginning its descent to Heathrow Airport. After a brief layover in London, Father Tobenhien would proceed to Rome, once again to play its part on the world stage.

Chapter Twenty

I do further promise and declare, that I will, when opportunity presents, make and wage relentless war, secretly or openly, against all heretics, Protestants and Liberals, as I am directed to do and to extirpate and exterminate them from the face of the whole earth, and that I will spare neither sex, age nor condition and that I will hang, waste, boil, flay, strangle and bury alive these infamous heretics; rip open the stomachs and wombs of their women and crush their infants' heads against the wall, in order to annihilate forever their execrable race.
Pope Paul lll, 1576

We hold upon this earth the place of God Almighty
Pope Leo XIII Encyclical Letter of June 20, 1894

Stein had no idea how far the secret of the Jesus Tablets had reached. He only knew he was reading the most remarkable documents he'd ever seen. Stein shoved his glasses to his receding hairline. Reading beyond Abraham in the Tablets, he thrilled. King Saul would be revealed as nothing more than the first power-hungry dictator to rise from a peasant society, King David a politician who used religion to write history flattering to his reign, King Solomon a tyrant who enslaved large numbers of his own people to build his grandiose government buildings and expand his empire. The Temple business in Jerusalem would be revealed as a profit- making scheme foisted on a superstitious population to line the pockets of the religious and political elite.

Turning the pages, he perused the account of Abraham's son, Ishmael, who wrote of the Canaanites increasing numbers and land expansion, of peaceful intermarriage, but also of fundamentalists who became Yahweh extremists intolerant of the fertility god Baal worship and that of his consort Ashtarte. He also wrote of tension caused by fear of invasion by the

Philistines, whose iron weaponry beat the crude copper of the less advanced Israelis.

***

Ishmael, a priest, wrote, "Many feel the Philistine threat is a punishment for worshipping the gods improperly. This plays into the hands of the Yahweh extremists. Others feel only a strong central government can organize a common defense. I secretly fear that the religious and political extremists will merge and dominate. Such a pact would be difficult for the common people to resist. I fear this much more than I fear the Philistines.

"Our heritage has been passed down by storytelling, the figures of Moses and my grandfather, Eli, growing over time. Moses as leader of the desert raiders is especially romantic to farmers with their unexciting lives. Stories of the escape from Egypt and years in the Sinai have varied with each storyteller, but each has exceeded the last by larger and more vivid details. The history of Moses is far from the real world where he dwelt. Moses is now described as a person who spoke face to face with God. It seems pleasant to believe one's heroes walked with the gods."

Stein raised his head and worked his stiff shoulders around to front, then back. He'd hardly moved while reading. This ancient Ishmael had done more for modern understanding than he could have dreamed. This brief description of an ancient society undergoing severe growing pains was a treasure. The rough equality of desert raiders metamorphosed into a class and status conscious society. Here was a first hand description of a culture veiled by time, not authored by official religious or political leaders with something to prove or cover up. Ishmael, a person not of a vested class, had no agenda.

How Stein looked forward to telling Esther and their grown children about it. Perhaps it really was a mystery of God that these ancient tablets had been found. Was humanity now capable of facing a serious historical account that so contradicted popular religious stories?

***

Turning the page he began the next account written by Ishmael's son David who wrote of the loss of the Yahweh followers' treasured Ark of the Covenant at the battle with Philistines at Ebenezer. David wrote, "This drove the Yahweh radicals to a more frenzied rage. They claimed all Israelite setbacks were caused by the peoples' refusal to worship Yahweh, the only True God, overlooking the Philistines better weaponry and training. The Yahweh minority promised their ruthless Yahweh would save the people if they elected a king. Naturally, the zealots had someone under their control to offer, a strongman called Saul. To protect ourselves from outside domination we gradually became dominated by our own government. Centralization of power did allow us to halt the advance of the Philistines and better our military. However, taxes bloated and military drafts lengthened. Over time the ruling classes were far more concerned with their privileges than the welfare of their countrymen.

"Yahweh priests gained power as we humble ones fell from favor. The deadly pact my father Ishmael feared between a political class and a religious class came to pass. Now political leaders saw the strength of written propaganda and flattering stories were written on official scrolls.

"It was easy to convince illiterates that anything written is true. Thus began the myth that religious writings were literally the Word of God. Wealth trails power like a dog, and King Saul gained riches beyond measure. Three parties held power in Israel through an uneasy balance of interests: large landowners, the king and his circle, and the religious elite. This triad was still a minority. Most continued to worship their ancient gods of the earth, practicing the old rites of fertility. They feared Saul and the Yahweh priests."

The writer went on to describe Saul's growing paranoia, some justified, over attempts to seize his throne. Here the Tablets related the story of David's coming into Saul's favor while plotting with the Yahweh priests. Through propaganda they would exalt his exploits.

"Finally King Saul sought to destroy David, but wily David stayed one step ahead. The common people were told by whispering tongues how David was being unjustly persecuted by mad King Saul. Yahweh priests preached that God withdrew his favor from Saul, and chose David as His anointed one who would save us from domination and oppressive taxes. Even when David betrayed Saul, Yahweh priests justified treason. When King Saul finally died in battle fighting the Philistines, David seized power."

David introduced a dark violence-filled chapter. The Yahweh priests strictly punished those who transgressed against Yahweh's many laws. "Clay gods and goddesses were smashed, their shards buried in unknown places. Religious tolerance was treason to Yahweh fanatics. Love, romance, and sexual pleasures were considered evil since they were often enjoyed on the hilltops that once housed Canaanite sacred shrines. Yahweh priests deprived us of all joy, replacing happiness with the dour burden of endless laws and religious duties."

Government priests levied harsh taxes which drove farmers into foreclosure, making them nearly slave labor. "In time David allowed the Yahweh priests to transform part of Jerusalem into a centralized place of worship. Here peasants could be fleeced at leisure. Worshipping anywhere but Jerusalem was a serious crime.

"Through a military draft David enslaved many farmers. The King and the wealthy class took the spoils of war. When farmers drafted into David's army were killed, the government foreclosed on overburdened widows' property. Anyone who criticized the government went to the front to be killed. By such vile means, King David deprived his countrymen of their lands, women, and wealth. All this while, scribes spun stories praising David as kind, just, a favored son of God.

"Every vice and crime was shown in David's reign: adultery, rebellion, rape, fratricide, exploitation of citizens, and plundering wars of aggression. The merciless king declined into senility as his own family plotted to pull him down. Eventually, David yielded the throne to his bastard son Solomon, fruit of Bathsheba, a just revenge. King David had murdered Bathsheba's husband for the evil joy of despoiling his wife.

"Solomon secured his kingdom by killing any threat. As the years pass the Yahweh priests weave tales to justify murderous David and unscrupulous Solomon. Some simple people believe them, but most doubt. Perhaps the true God will one day free us from bondage."

Chapter Twenty-one

Stein laughed. "You know, Alice, this is the first primary source to actually describe King David."

She looked up from her reading and grimaced. "Such a portrait of evil. Nothing like the beautiful young hero of my Sunday School days."

"Nor in my Bar Mitzvah classes. This won't go down well with teachers of either of our faiths."

"No wonder the Bible goes on and on about their feats and virtues. All that business of Solomon being the wisest man on earth.

"Like the Hitler/Stalin propaganda...just earlier."

Alice sighed. "It hurts to see it writ so plain. I was happier before all this, Sam."

He chuckled. "Ah, yes. We all have that flower bedecked image of the Garden of Eden. We want to think moral giants trod the earth in a biblical Golden Age, walking and talking with God face to face."

"People are so hungry to believe. I'm working on this, and even I feel robbed of something."

"Of certainty, perhaps. We haven't come all that far from the cave dwellers' superstitions. But, that's unsettling. How will others react when we spring this on them?"

***

At that moment Pastor Steward paced the floor of his den. He must do something, but what? He needed help powerful help. Satan might well be in this, the Tablets smoldering evil. Whatever they contained could only be assessed if the right people possessed them. Get the Tablets to America. To pull it off was the trick. After all, the Tablets must be weighty and maneuvering to get them out beyond him. The more the Pastor pondered the more he realized only one person could do it. The Pastor looked up a number in his address book.

***

In Washington D.C. a tastefully groomed secretary picked up. For over six years Mrs. Hedgerow had been answering President Straihorn's private line. She took messages flawlessly, delivered them personally, and, according to recent court testimony, forgot their contents immediately.

Like hundreds in D.C. circles, she counted the days this outlandish President had left in office. Meanwhile she hand carried the message to a side door of the Oval Office and tapped. The President opened it and took the note, closing the door in her face. Returning to his desk he frowned. In spite of her efficiency perhaps this icy Mrs. Hedgerow had outlived her usefulness. He would give that more thought. Now he read the note with interest.

The President leaned back, rereading. Puzzling. Pastor Steward of recent acquaintance requested a meeting in person on a matter of national importance. What could this religious do-gooder have? Smiling, Straihorn touched his cigar end to the small note and watched it burn in his metal ash tray. Watching cameras would pick up the gesture. Hands behind his head, he leaned back rolling the data through his steel trap mind. His private phone line was secure at least part of the time. After all, he'd spent some time by means of money and blackmail gathering a core of agents loyal only to him. Each hour these compromised agents checked his line. Steward's message may have slid through the wiretaps during a lull of spy vs. spy activity.

President Straihorn had first met Pastor Steward in the days following disclosure of his most audacious caper, the peccadillo with the aide. The President played the role of repentant sinner, gathering distinguished clergy to witness his confession. Pastor Steward alone among the distinguished church leaders said that judging wasn't the province of mortals. That amazed Cliff Straihorn who had no religious leanings. Life in the present interested him so he never allowed himself to waste time thinking about life after death.

The President conferred privately with this southerner several times. Pastor Steward understood how strong the sexual drive really was. His sincerity and candor intrigued the cynical President who opened to this modest man more than with anyone else in years. Pastor Steward's concern impressed the President. Besides, Straihorn genuinely enjoyed nonjudgmental company. He told the good pastor to call his private line if he ever needed anything.

Remembering all this, President Straihorn had to satisfy his gnawing curiosity. Within minutes Steward's phone rang. The brief message was to be at Hartsfield-Jackson Airport in one hour to meet a man wearing a light blue suit and gold framed sun glasses at terminal eighteen. Steward called his puzzled wife saying he'd be gone a few days on church business and would explain later. At the airport, the escort steered him to a Boeing 747. He was its sole passenger except for two quiet men at either end of the compartment, no doubt armed guards.

The Pastor considered the difference between money and power. The former brings material comforts, but the latter controls life and death. These guards would kill him on command, and all his millions wouldn't buy him one more second. Word of the Jesus Tablets, now outside the world of academia, entered one devoid of morality.

Despite Steward's worries the engine sounds lulled him until the plane touched down on a long runway in a forest, empty of human habitation. One of the guards frisked Pastor Steward before they deplaned. A black limo waited, rear door open. A man with close-cropped white hair sat at the far side of the back seat. As the limo started moving, curtains closed automatically on all sides of the rear seat. The older man, wearing regulation sun glasses, drew the Pastor into conversation about the comfort of his trip and how much they appreciated his acceptance with such short notice. Pastor Steward tried to relax. After all, if these men wanted to harm him they could have. However, he had no idea where he was or who he was to meet. All he'd brought were his wallet and Michael's letter. His companion chatted inanely about Georgia State football team's prospects as the limo descended into an underground tunnel.

They stopped. Another dark-suited man with the universal sunglasses opened the car door, asking Steward to follow to an elevator. After at least thirty seconds it settled to a cushioned rest. The air had that coolness even strong central heating can't overcome. When the elevator door opened, the man led the Pastor down a short hallway. They entered a small room where, next to yet another guard, a second elevator door confronted Steward whose guide indicated he step in alone.

Sweating, Steward pushed the sole button. After another long ride the elevator halted and opened soundlessly on a brightly lit hallway. A voice over a sound system instructed him to walk until told to halt. After he walked for at least fifty meters the sound system instructed him to halt and enter the single door. Entering, the Pastor stood in an ornate room paneled in glistening mahogany, the floor carpeted in white wool that felt like a wall to wall pillow, the ceiling aglow with crystal chandeliers. Greek statuary stood in solid marble niches. Water trickled melodiously over river rocks.

The Pastor seemed the sole visitor in a private museum. That sensation vanished when a familiar male voice invited him to be seated in a plush leather chair to his left. He sat, facing a fifteen-foot-tall copy of Rodin's *The Kiss* made of glowing glass, the lovers so perfectly molded they might disentangle and speak.

"Do you approve of our version of *The Kiss*?"

"It's a beautiful rendering," Steward answered.

"It should be. It's the world's largest one piece Zircon, extremely difficult to work. It took the artist nearly five years to complete. Sadly, he was killed in a car wreck within a week of finishing."

Silence hung heavily until, amazing to Steward, the twenty foot pedestal ascended into the ceiling, replaced by a darkened glass cylinder in which the Pastor could barely make out a man seated behind a desk.

The shadowy figure asked, "What do you have for President Straihorn?"

"What I have is for his eyes alone," Steward said, trying to sound firm.

The figure barked a short laugh. "Don't you know where you are?"

Steward shook his head

"You're in Virginia at a site built at the dawn of the nuclear age. A number of underground sites were built to ensure the government could function in the event of nuclear war. I shouldn't fault you. Few know about these old bases secretly funded and maintained by the CIA." In that moment the man in the cylinder struck a match, the open flame applied to the end of a Cuban cigar. President Cliff Straihorn sent up a cloud of smoke, then rose and placed his hand against the seemingly solid glass tube. A section opened along invisible seams and he stepped out. The tube disappeared through the floor, replaced by the Rodin statue.

The President extended his hand in greeting. "One can't be too careful in my line of work," he said. "Follow me?" The President led Pastor Steward to a niche, carefully removing two objects like motorcycle helmets, one face shield clear, and the other tinted. The President donned the tinted helmet and gestured for Steward to wear the other, a final security to ensure their conversation would be private. "My own men sweep the room, but this is added security."

The Pastor found the phrase "my own men" strange having thought the government belonged to no one individual. Nevertheless, he felt relieved to finally explain the Sepphoris discovery. He emphasized the need to rush the Tablets to America for analysis. He also read aloud from Michael's letter.

President Straihorn was wise to have worn the helmet with the tinted visor. Even after a lifetime of dissimulation he couldn't have masked his amazement. Had Steward read his mind, he might have stopped. The President saw the dominance the Tablets might give their possessor. Behind the tinted shield a smile formed. Here was the ultimate revenge on religious self-righteousness; here the opportunity to rein in the Jewish lobby's influence over the media. Besides that, what would the Arabs pay to have these Tablets? After all, they were floating on wealth and would be delighted to prove the Jews incorrect in their claims to Palestine while also protecting their own origins, depending on what might be revealed. Nor could it be forgotten that Israel threatened nuclear war. Straihorn's hubris chafed having to endure smug Israeli politicians who had the United States by the balls because of the Jewish lobby. These Tablets could tip the world to the President's advantage.

If the Old Testament were proven a fraud, would the Jews' chagrin drive them to political silence? Israelis had, after all, even been caught spying on American soil! Better yet, the moral majority would be exposed as having no real base, everything they deemed right and wrong nothing more than a self-serving myth invented to hoodwink a backward desert tribe. Democrats could quite possibly hold the majority for the next forty years. He would go down in history as the President who told the truth, for generations a hero to educated liberals. This would more than wipe the impeachment stain from his legacy. It would insure his immortality.

The succulent taste of this revenge was more than the President ever dreamed. Using these Tablets would provide the sweetest pleasure. Compared to the possibilities of this international game his dalliance in front of Oval Office cameras was teenage petting at the drive-in. His exhilaration grew. What might people do to quash them? With a smirk he reminded himself that work came before pleasure.

"Pastor Steward, may I keep this remarkable letter for reference?"

"Yes, of course. I didn't make a copy. No one but you knows about it in the States."

The President considered eliminating Pastor Steward, but he liked the man. Besides, the Pastor's moral standing and national reputation might come in handy before this was over.

Cliff Straihorn ratcheted up his charisma and gripped Pastor Steward's hand in both his. "Thank you for your patriotism, Robert. The United States Government will obtain the Tablets for proper analysis. Please, tell no one about our meeting until I send you the okay."

With a smile and a tightening of the handshake, Steward was released, then led to another elevator by the older man with the ever-present sunglasses. Steward missed the questioning look his escort shot the silent guard who glanced at his desk top of many panels and buttons out of view of the other two. He pushed a button marked inquire. In seconds the no button lit and the guard shook his head. The Pastor left alive.

In a surprisingly short time he landed in Atlanta, his brush with power like an unnerving dream. The lush Georgia air had never felt so good. Shaken, he couldn't wait to get home. He hadn't eaten since morning and could easily eat three dinners at once. With thoughts of fried chicken in mind he strode eagerly through the lot to his cherished Cadillac.

**

Two people with two different intents watched as Steward located his car in long-term parking, the first a federal agent who'd barely made it to the Atlanta airport before the subject was expected to land. The second was Abdul Mohammed, a Palestinian physics major at Georgia State, by far the most nervous. Although a fervent nationalist, he'd never killed; yet he held a transmitter to detonate a car bomb with the push of a button.

Abdul, an unlikely choice for this operation, was the only resource Hamas could reach on short notice. Like many Palestinians, Abdul's family had suffered. Zionists had confiscated everything his parents owned and two of his brothers had been killed in the Palestinian underground. Worst, his sixteen-year-old sister Tami had died after three days of Israeli interrogation, her body dumped in the Arab quarter of Jerusalem. The family doctor stated cause of death as hemorrhage from rape. Abdul, nearly insane with grief and hate, joined Hamas. Bright and willing, he became part of the long range Palestinian plans to train bright young men in physics in hope that eventually these deep plants could build an atomic bomb in the cause of Allah. Hamas sent him to America.

Abdul approached his studies with a passion, but heard nothing from his handlers in all seven years at Georgia State. Then a Federal Express package arrived at his efficiency apartment. Opening it, he found an object the size of a small loaf of bread. Instructions identified it as ten pounds of plastic explosive complete with a radio detonator. Pastor Steward's address, and phone numbers, photos of the target, his home, and car clarified the assignment. Abdul had heard of Pastor Steward, a prominent Atlanta citizen often featured in local newspapers. Abdul called the Church from a downtown pay phone and learned from the secretary that the pastor had left town for several days. A call to Pastor Steward's home under the guise of a needy person confirmed it.

Resourceful, Abdul knew men of Steward's means usually traveled by air. Therefore, Hartsfield-Jackson International was a likely place to search for the Pastor's distinctive Cadillac. Dressed in an American suit and sporting the sunglasses favored in the South, Abdul looked like one of hundreds of young professionals who frequent the air terminal daily. The long-term parking lot holds over four thousand cars. Abdul cruised parking lanes for Pastor Steward's car. An hour later, he found it and parked his modest compact within fifty feet. Terrified, he remained determined to avenge Tami. Whatever Hamas wanted must lead to that end.

He had to place the bomb, to be held in place by the metal plate made strongly magnetic by the flip of a stiff lever, under the driver's seat. Activating the magnet also armed the device. Pushing buttons in sequence on the transmitter would detonate the bomb. The instructions dictated Abdul must recognize his victim and set the device off only when the Pastor sat in his car. Challenging because Abdul had no idea where the Pastor had gone or when he would return. Nevertheless, Abdul would follow orders and leave the outcome to Allah.

Abdul walked to Steward's Cadillac and knelt momentarily out of sight, lifting the bomb from his briefcase. Parking was tight. Two Lincolns flanked the Cadillac which left little room to maneuver his arm and the package under the car. Nerves taut, sweat pouring, Abdul reached his limit as an untrained, novice terrorist. However, he did arm the device under the driver's seat. The magnet grabbed the undercarriage. He just had time to close his briefcase and dust himself off when a cheerful couple in animated conversation passed. Shaking, he strode back to his Toyota.

The next five hours were the longest of his life. When would Steward show up? Risking notice, Abdul sat in his car, reducing exposure by placing sunshield blockers in both the front and rear windows. He had his Wall Street Journal memorized before he finally saw a man with focused stride nearing the Cadillac. Pastor Steward. Removing his sunshields, Abdul backed out. He cruised past the Cadillac down an adjacent lane as Pastor Steward unlocked it. It bothered Abdul that the Pastor seemed so happy, wearing a look of youthful excitement that struck at Abdul's basically tender heart. But Abdul pushed tenderness away as he made sure his radio transmitter was at the ready.

He wasn't far past the Cadillac when it backed out, heading for an exit. Abdul's finger was beginning to push the final button when the Cadillac paused to allow a happy couple and their children cross in front of it. Abdul also hesitated. One of them, a girl around sixteen, bore a haunting resemblance to Tami. That galvanized him. The time for death had arrived. When the Cadillac moved, Abdul muttered a brief prayer to Allah and pushed the button.

Ten pounds of C-4 plastic explosive went off, the pressure wave traveling at speed faster than sound. A camera would have recorded the driver's side door being ripped off before the recording the sound. The force lifted the Cadillac two feet before the wreck lit on the passenger side. Every window in the deforming car shattered. Solid steel flowed like taffy and those parts that couldn't bend fast enough ripped. The blast's epicenter was beneath the driver's seat.

By the time the explosion's force reached one hundred fifty thousand pounds of pressure, the car bottom was nearly to the roof. The Pastor's body blew through the steering column into that roof at the windshield, first crushed, then dismembered. Smoking body parts landed on pavement thirty-five feet away.

The Tablets had their first victim.

Nearly in shock, Abdul drove out and onto the Atlanta beltway as the federal agent ran toward the Cadillac before its pieces came to rest. During these chaotic seconds he called every source of enforcement from his radio. They responded from all levels, sirens blaring, converging before the wreckage quit burning. Abdul escaped closure by almost three minutes, his last good fortune.

* * *

Enraged, President Straihorn went into a cursing tantrum that sent White House personal scrambling. After thirty minutes the chief executive calmed enough to call the Governor of Georgia to assure her of full federal cooperation in finding the criminal behind this act of infamy. When the Governor took the phone from her burning ear she had no doubt of President Straihorn's sincerity.

Hartsfield-Jackson International Airport's fixed cameras covered terminals as well as parking lots to record every vehicle entering or leaving. Review found Abdul's car and license plate. He joined forty-seven suspects picked up within four hours, one of only three without a clear reason for being at the airport, and the only one not recorded entering the main terminal. His suit clothes showed fragments of grease, dirt, and gravel. Investigators bearing rapidly issued warrants to search his apartment found a Federal Express package in the garbage showing minute traces of C-4 embedded in the wrappings.

Abdul exercised his right to remain silent, his only hope to plead innocent and trust his fate to the unpredictability of an American jury. State and federal agencies congratulated themselves, certain they had their terrorist. Confident that Abdul would talk, they would soon find the motive and others involved. Strangely, when the President learned of the arrest of a Palestinian national he appeared neither satisfied nor relieved. Cliff Straihorn was in a white-hot rage knowing he wasn't the only serious player to know about the Jesus Tablets. Some powerful person or nation wanted to prevent the President of the United States from acquiring them. Cliff Straihorn had never wanted anything as badly as he wanted the Tablets. Could he obtain them? How should he respond to this attempt to deprive him of them? When he asked to be left undisturbed for fifteen minutes, his staff complied with alacrity.

Chapter Twenty-two

The President pushed anger aside long enough to think. In addition to the Steward family, he'd ordered dossiers on Stein and the Cross couple in Sepphoris. A top secret meeting was set for that evening for him and heads of the CIA and the FBI. The bomber's intent had to be to silence the Pastor. The man who placed the bomb, just a person assigned to the job, would know nothing. His brain could be rung like a wet rag, but there would be no useful information from it.

The killer lacked professionalism, signs of a hasty, somewhat desperate job. That could only mean Hamas, or whoever, didn't feel in complete control. Lacking access to the Tablets, they were trying to delay the flow of information until they developed a plan, but were both late and unlucky. Even more revealing, they had to know their amateur killer had little chance of escape. That meant that his handler decided to spend a life to stop the Pastor from passing on his letter.

Obviously it wasn't in any Jewish, Christian, or perhaps even Muslim groups' interests that such damning information be revealed. On the other hand, President Straihorn realized with a frown that the Catholic Church was the only western religion with experience and money to obtain and destroy the Tablets. No doubt the ancient corruption known as Catholicism was more than capable of murder to protect its empire. After all, President Straihorn thought, who could blame them?

The Israeli government must be unaware of the Tablets or they would have acted by now. Unusual that the famed Mossad would be last to know, but that could end momentarily. President Straihorn smiled. How complicated this game was, how high the stakes. To play and win at this table his greatest challenge, he would spare nothing to sweep in the mountain of chips represented by the Jesus Tablets.

The President thoughtfully lit a cigar, considering the unknown terrorists. Perhaps it would be useful to send a clear message that knowledge of the Jesus Tablets had reached seats of power in the United States. If it were Hamas this might force their withdrawal, allowing the President to operate unhindered by small fry opponents. By the time he ground his cigar into his heavy ash tray he knew his next step. As emperors put it at Roman circuses, President Straihorn decided to "Let the bloody games begin." It was time to assign an operation to those the President used for personal operations.

So it was that major powers were drawn like iron filings toward the irresistible pull of the Tablets.

***

Stein in Israel believed no one except him, Henry, and Alice knew of the Tablets. He valued knowledge of antiquity for its own sake, for the satisfaction and the pleasure of discovering the truth. Indeed, to find a truth was a measurable forward step in the long march of civilization. Stein gloried in the brief account by Samuel.

***

"Both David and Solomon hungered to establish dynasties. Both used propaganda. Palace historians and a servile priestly class supported the crown. Their unabashed fraudulent writings claimed bloody King David was 'a man after God's heart' and a 'favorite Son of God' as if to claim the God of the heavens favored his murderous career. Avaricious Solomon in turn produced drivel touting him 'the wisest man ever born.' As my father told me, whoever holds power has the means to write history. No government can be trusted to tell the truth."

Samuel also recorded that King David's family and the elite lived in Jerusalem. He wrote of how the people were forced to worship in Jerusalem, paying for the removal of sins.

"Payment took the form of sacrifices at the Holy Temple in Jerusalem. God had to be appeased with blood by killing animals although the very poor could give grain. The upper classes owned nearly all lodging, food, and sacrificial animals. The invented image of a violent and bloodthirsty Yahweh brought us to this.

"Certain sins could only be forgiven by the sacrifice of a specific animal such as a goat. Since the traveler was unlikely to have one, he had to purchase it at an inflated price from the Temple. Often the animal had to be a specific color or type which drove its price even higher. If the worshipper had money or goods different from those required by Yahweh, the priests had moneychangers and commodity traders who charged for converting one value into another. Every requirement cost. The priests wallowed in wealth. Jerusalem was named the City of God by the government priesthood in collusion with the upper classes to maintain that myth.

"The opportunity for Northern tribes to rebel came when King Solomon died." Civil war, Samuel wrote, occurred when ten Northern tribes in Northern Israel seceded. Samuel ended his narrative by expressing dark foreboding for his peoples' future. Skeptical, but still hopeful, he wrote, "Perhaps the only faith that a man can have is that some wise God has His own plan. Who are we as mere men to claim to know the mind and will of such an Almighty Creator?"

***

Stein rubbed his nose vigorously, an old habit when stressed. Solomon was a tyrant, no holier than a thousand other murderers and exploiters. Biblical accounts supplied the same basic data. Samuel merely recorded his times in a way seldom discussed.

In fact, current biblical scholars would see their theories confirmed in this ancient document. They long suspected that biblical accounts had been invented to support palace interests. After all, no evidence showed that either free speech or free press existed in Samuel's time or for centuries after. Even in America, free press is often not so free. Of course, ancient kings had absolute power. Didn't the Bible have many examples where the king controlled life and death by command? No body of law controlled kings. The checks and balance system didn't exist. King Solomon, like Adolph Hitler, held absolute sway including historical manipulation. In ancient times religion married to government did likewise. Catholic Church history reveals it as the de facto government for centuries, at times declining into corruption. Nevertheless, religious faithful believed there had been an era when God spoke directly to His followers. They so wanted the Bible to be God's word.

***

Stein's theological musings soon became irrelevant thanks to a meeting in Washington, D.C. The man in charge, President Cliff Straihorn, didn't care about theology. The meeting addressed other questions. How should the United States proceed in regard to the Jesus Tablets? What message should be sent? Who should know that the United States held an exclusive claim to something felt to be of vital national interest? In this Pentagon conference room, a handful of men and women discussed the Tablets' implications. On President Straihorn's right sat trim and alert Brigadier General Blake, Chairman of the Military Joint Command, then former Senator Albright, cool head of the Central Intelligence Agency. Continuing around the table were Bill Homes, thoughtful section chief of the CIA in charge of the Near Middle East, then Garrett Black, head of the Federal Bureau of Investigation in charge of Domestic Intelligence and finally, warmly inquisitive Mrs. Sarah Morgenstern, United States Ambassador to Israel. Senator Albright was the only party with advance notice of the classified subject at hand. The CIA furnished all information on the Jesus Tablets and the Sepphoris site. Black of the FBI brought all information on the Pastor Steward bombing.

The President briefed those present, emphasizing the Jesus Tablets' potential for the United States. Obviously, control of the situation meant their physical possession. They could be used as a political lever or demolished if a threat to vital United States interests. The real issue was to seize them first.

"We all know," the President said firmly, "religion is a tidal force. Populations in the grip of religious fervor have brought down governments. The Catholic Church even harnessed and used this to control and crush monarchies. For that reason, and my apologies to you of that persuasion for my bluntness, the

Church is a viperous enemy to the international political elite. If we control the Jesus Tablets we just might control the Catholic Church. That, my friends, is a goal worth nearly any price."

There was no discussion of right or wrong. The only issue was how to possess the Tablets. "A military operation to seize them in Israel, well, that country would view such a move as an act of war. We lack the forces in place to succeed," the general cautioned.

The Ambassador added, "Absent some unimaginable factor, Israel would move immediately into Sepphoris if they learned of the Jesus Tablets."

Albright, CIA, emphasized the extreme difficulty in secreting such a big cargo out of Israel. "The Israeli forces guarding Sepphoris keep close tabs on site activity. In our agency's opinion Mossad will know of these Tablets at any time, miraculous they don't already."

Homes, really the flunky at this meeting, left the talking to his boss, Senator Albright. His only purpose was to answer specific questions about Mideast issues. The FBI's Garrett Black had no significant resources in Israel, but could provide information on any stateside situation.

The President, a lawyer before entering politics, observed, "By virtue of its contract with Israel, Harvard legally owns anything discovered at Sepphoris."

The idea that legality might factor into the discussion surprised his listeners. He asked, "Doesn't our Government have the legal right to seize any national resource on United States soil if vital to national interests?" All heads nodded, but how did this address the problem of getting the Tablets out of Israel? "Our first step must be to leak to the top reporters that they should fly to Sepphoris, Israel, pronto. Tell them I'll be releasing history-busting news about the site from the Oval Office within twenty-four hours. Include a caveat if word gets out ahead of time they'll be cast into tip outer darkness forever. Don't tell them why they're going." The President went into detail, his plan imaginative, ingenious, or nuts depending on the listener. In this instance his listeners struggled to muster their thoughts.

Former Senator Albright said, "Mr. President, the CIA has no plan which leaves us unable to guarantee the United States time to find alternatives."

"Israel, as you know, is beyond my jurisdiction," the FBI head said, not without some evident relief.

The general contributed, "This involves a policy question, not a military one, although the Armed Forces stand by to perform whatever duties our Commander in Chief requires."

The Ambassador to Israel said, "Israel can be depended on to act in her own interests. I do agree that with the eye of the world on this issue it would be difficult for the Israelis to renege on the contract. Israel needs U.S. support. Anything adversely affecting public opinion toward her threatens the Israeli State."

The belief in finder's keepers seemed distinctly American. Homes said, "Something like these Jesus Tablets is so threatening I'm not sure we can make any predictions. So many extremists dwell in that part of the world God knows what'll happen."

On that sobering note President Straihorn adjourned the meeting for one hour. A decision then had to be made because there was no guarantee the U. S. had time to act successfully. After centuries of stillness, the Jesus Tablets possessed a schedule of their very own.

Reconvening briefly, all present pledged full cooperation to the plan with the exception of the CIA's Albright. "Mr. President, I see this plan as too hasty. It will place untrained American civilians in a line of danger not sufficiently assessed. Having said this, I must add that the CIA will support our President's decision, whatever it might be, with all resources." When finished, Albright exhaled with the sense of having told the whole truth for the first time in a long while.

All eyes turned toward the President. "As always, I thank you for your input and acknowledge the CIA's concerns. However, in spite of any hazards I'm convinced that honesty must be shown to the global community. I have confidence in Americans' support of administration efforts to be forthright. Israel will see it in their best interests to comply." He closed by asking everyone to remember him and the country in their prayers as he implemented his plan. History didn't record the dread chilling the hearts of everyone there -- all except one. That heart, President Straihorn's, pounded to the joy of victory. The game of his life about to begin.

***

When Father Tobenhien landed in Rome he proceeded to the Vatican, so deep in thought he barely heard his driver's request for prayers for his ailing mother. Rushing into his office Father Tobenhien hardly acknowledged his staff's greetings. Scribbling a few words on Jesuit stationary he sealed the note and instructed a secretary to hand carry it to the Pope. Father Tobenhien missed the young Jesuit's quizzical expression. Requests for an immediate audience to His Holiness were rare.

***

A soft knock disturbed Pope Jerome' audience with an Austrian diplomat. The Pope graciously apologized to his guest, masking his irritation. His audiences should never be interrupted. It was a curse of being the Holy Father that everyone thought their petty problem achieved the level of exception. He took the note from the bowing young priest, annoyance flowering as he noted the Jesuit letterhead. The last thing he needed was a reminder from these fifth column traitors that the Pope didn't have power even over his own time. He scanned the message, astonished. He should be outraged, but shuddered instead. It read:

Your Holiness:
If we are to save the Roman Catholic Church you must send for me immediately. We haven't a moment to spare. The body of Christ is in mortal danger.
Father Tobenhien
Secretary General of the Brotherhood of Jesus

Pope Jerome's blue-veined hands trembled. Could this explain the oppressive dread plaguing him for weeks, fears so strong yet vague they'd frightened him awake in night's empty hours? Even after prayer and self-examination the fears hadn't abated, but blossomed like poison plants. He finally spoke of them in confession to his Father Confidante. He'd intuited the Church was in danger, Satan lurking in shadowy corners. Now, he composed himself to close his meeting with tact and grace.

The experienced Austrian diplomat noticed a slight sheen of sweat on the Pope's high forehead and would report it to his country's intelligence services. A small thing, he thought to himself as he departed, but small things have a way of ballooning. As calmly as possible the Pope requested Father Tobenhien be summoned. The secretary considered for the millionth time the privilege of working for a man who beckoned and the world attended. The subordinate didn't know his Pope didn't feel powerful. A worried pontiff bowed his head in prayer.

Father Tobenhien picked up on the first ring. The Pope's prideful secretary relayed in a crisp voice that His Holiness required his presence. Within twenty minutes the smug secretary led him into the Pope's private chambers. Father Tobenhien picked a chair facing the seated Pope. A pendulum clock counted off seconds as the two adversaries studied each other, the room humming with mutual distrust. Finally, the Jesuit coldly suggested this problem was dire enough to transcend their differences. The Pope nodded as if even speaking to Tobenhien were distasteful.

The Jesuit succinctly covered the Tablets' discovery. The Papal heart thumped. His anxiety finally acquired its definition. Angels of God had been preparing him for Satan's latest weapon against the Bride of Christ!

After concluding, the Jesuit asked Pope Jerome if these sacred chambers contained anything that would pass for drinking wine. Despite his dislike for the upstart Jesuit, the Pope opened a black walnut cabinet, extracting an ornate bottle and two crystal goblets. He poured the ruby-red wine with an experienced hand. The two took strong draughts. Finally the Pope observed this was much larger than their mutual resentments. The Roman Catholic Church was now a beach shack facing a tidal wave. In moments it could be gone without a trace. Not a board, not a nail, and not a sign of its former existence. The day of deposing kings was gone.

Today the Church morphed into a ritual performing organization that blessed trinkets. Pope Jerome didn't want to go down in history as the Last Pope.

Using that as a springboard the old Jesuit suggested to the even older Pope that they serve the Church best by joining forces. Here again the Church's ancient wisdom: Be willing to deal with the enemy to serve her greater needs.

The aging Pope never fretted over his own needs, having devoted his life only to the Church and her faithful. Nor did it cross his mind that the Jesus Tablets bore the truth, that his lifelong faith had been based on myth or misinterpretation. For him, nothing changed. God's being different from Catholicism's concept inconceivable. To his undoing, Pope Jerome couldn't sever the Church's needs from the truth.

These adversaries traded ideas, forgetting time, only weighing the most effective application of their influence. Scarred politicians, they foresaw that what couldn't be controlled must be destroyed. The two faced the same problem as others. How does one extract a ton of material from a guarded camp in a foreign country, especially a country like Israel in which the Church had few friends? If the Church couldn't have the Tablets, she must demolish them.

For the first time the Catholics and Israelis should be in agreement, these Tablets a mortal danger to both. Israeli forces already at the site could seize the Tablets on some pretext and destroy them. The academicians would be powerless, and before the United States could formally protest, the Tablets would be reduced to desert dust. The appropriate apologies could then be made, scapegoats blamed for the egregious error. A few careers destroyed, a few bodies thrown to the wolves, but all would be well.

Smooth Israeli Prime Minister Roth would be the voice of authority. An American-style politician, Roth could talk for hours not once making a definite statement. Roth, with openly close ties to extreme orthodox factions in Israel, was a long-time member of the Likud Party whose right wing beliefs made the Ku Klux Klan look like Boy Scouts. His hatred of the Palestinian resistance was such he had been known to turn a blind eye to

Mossad excesses. Furthermore, Roth was not squeaky clean, almost indicted for corruption in 1991. He barely avoided a no-confidence vote of the Israeli parliament. Rumors of slush fund money buying key votes circled like vultures. The Vatican could deal with Roth.

Nevertheless, Roth had to take care with Israel's diverse citizenry, fierce nationalists as well as the most tolerant people. With survival under daily threat, the gap between hawks and the doves was unbridgeable.

***

A smug President Straihorn had no more returned to the Oval Office from the Pentagon meeting than he summoned those necessary. His plan in effect, he inhaled a cigar, reflecting on death's handiness. Soon another enemy would learn a damned good lesson. As he flicked the ash, he chuckled. Power was such a delight, in its own way better than sex. Puzzling how the two tangled in his mind.

Chapter Twenty-three

Deep within Gaza slums, another mind pondered new intelligence. Pebbles frowned into the flickering candlelight. Pastor Steward had successfully relayed the message of the Jesus Tablets to someone high in the United States Government, perhaps President Straihorn, an unpredictable maverick. If so, a clear message had now been conveyed to Pebbles. Abdul had been found in his cell, his throat slashed. Baffled Atlanta police had no suspects. That murder was only the introduction. Nine Palestinian students attending various Georgia colleges had also been murdered by a single shot to the temple, their only connection being Palestinians. Georgia police surmised the crimes were part of a hate crime network. Pebbles grimaced. None of the dead had ties to Hamas. They'd been killed to make a statement. President Straihorn was an infidel, a loose cannon. The commander prayed for these martyred Palestinian children, then returned to deep thought. He would make the United States weep one day for her own children. The vulnerable crowds, the high buildings... But for now, possession of the Tablets took priority. The candle melted to its tarnished holder's base. Dawn had advanced when Pebbles' frown relaxed. He had his plan. Allah was truly great.

***

John Martin of the *New York Times* viewed the clouds from thirty thousand feet as he flew from Paris to Tel Aviv. In twenty-seven years he'd reported on every disaster inflicted by nature or humanity: riots, murders, wars, and political corruption. It had been a long time since anything surprised John Martin.

Like all investigative reporters, he depended on informants and leaks. A provocative story took insider information. He had to cultivate and then protect contacts. Police, even intelligence agencies, hungry to identify leaks embarrassing to those in power had grilled Martin who never revealed a name even though he

once spent seven weeks in a dirty jail cell for contempt of court.
When a higher court overturned his imprisonment, Martin
emerged a hero. His network of informants grew. Already a
nationally-known journalist, his reputation became international
as he broke ever larger stories. News readers in nearly every
civilized country knew his name.

His present cluelessness as to why he was going to Sepphoris,
Israel, intrigued him. He didn't know nine other top journalists
also flew there: two from the States, two from Europe, one from
Japan, one from the Middle East, one from the Philippines, one
from Latin America, and an Australian. A master moved these
pawns.

***

The Head of the CIA, a political veteran, perseverated.
President Straihorn's plan felt wrong, that Pentagon meeting a
sham. The President led them all down a garden path to a
preconceived conclusion. Telling the world about the Jesus
Tablets before the United States possessed them seemed insane.
Albright smiled bitterly. That word kept popping up in
connection to Straihorn. Yet what did the CIA really have on the
President? He was careless, sometimes incompetent, and strange.
But was he insane? Mad? The murdered Palestinian troubled
Albright, so clearly done by professionals. Someone powerful
had to have ordered them. A ranking politician? Could a rogue
element exist within the CIA or FBI taking orders from the
President? Was Straihorn smart or crazy?

However, he never dreamed he'd stand helpless in the wake of
a President running wild. Right or wrong the Ten
Commandments were America's foundation. Institutions of faith
and learning would lose financial support. Duped people often
reacted violently. Marriages and families held together by the
glue of religion might fly apart. Many would conclude there was
no right and wrong.

Latin America might burst into class warfare if the poor were
stripped of their Catholic yoke. Europe, still class structured,
wouldn't be immune. Labor unions constantly fought against

religion's justification of private property. After all, Karl Marx called religion the "opiate of the masses,", too much for the majority which, however, could still go communist.

China would win the propaganda sweepstakes. The world's most unified people would be unscathed, left standing tall as having been right all along. Turmoil in the West might tempt China to expand its holdings by absorbing the Koreas, Vietnam, and parts of Southeast Asia. China could seize Taiwan overnight. Even Japan, dependent on healthy western nations to keep her economy running, would be weakened, and might find it difficult to keep China at bay.

Islam might strengthen. Political momentum would shift to Arab nations. Israel's support for her occupation of Palestine could evaporate like morning dew. Displaced Palestinians would finally have their day before oil hungry nations. Israel would be left to stand alone with her nuclear bombs. CIA Director Albright grimly made the first of several calls.

***

In spite of his elation, Stein felt flustered. He normally would have shared a site discovery with Israeli academics. However, Israeli archaeologists were also Israeli citizens. Anything that threatened the Jews might be rejected as too dangerous for public revelation. Looking with open eyes at a discovery that threatened their country might very well force Israeli scholars to destroy the Tablets. More than anything, though, the Tablets themselves kept Stein's attention.

Amos, Samuel's son, recorded the next entry. He wrote of Jeroboam's attempts to "insure the freedom of the Northern tribes from Judah's greed. Among these efforts was reestablishment of the ancient religious shrine at Dan as alternative to Jerusalem. Although many longed forJerusalem many more were relieved to be released from taxation by the Temple elite. Finally, Northerners were free to worship as they desired. Most gladly returned to their fertility gods; once again ancient phallic symbols topped the hills."

Jeroboam was succeeded by Omri who "brought Israel greater strength by wisely developing trade relations with Phoenicia. He sealed friendship between the two by marrying his son, Ahab, to Jezebel, daughter of the king of Sidon. Ahab saved both the Northern and Southern kingdoms from the Assyrians at the battle of Qarqar by forming a coalition of small states to hold back this ruthless giant. Ahab fell in battle years later against the Arameans."

Amos ended on a pessimistic note fearing his weakened country's destruction.

***

Stein ruffled his thinning hair as he pondered this brief account, the only list of kings ever found outside the Bible. Scholars had only recently recognized both Omri's and Ahab's greatness. The difference between the biblical account of them and the newly discovered re-assessment would be a matter of great debate between scholars and biblical defenders.

The tired Chairman had to stretch his legs. Rising, he noticed Alice sleeping in an exhausted heap on the couch. Slightly abashed at this intimate view of the woman he'd always had a slight crush on, he pulled a throw over her, not waking her as he would have done his Esther. He needed sleep, too.

He walked to the window to gaze upon the brooding hill of Sepphoris. Dawn was hours away. Clouds scudded across the moon's dappled face so its light raced over the broken ground. For a moment it seemed the hill lived and moved. Stein sensed he watched an eerie corpse struggling to dig its way out of an ancient grave. His skin crawled as the moonlight flickering across the hillside became an enormous hand wriggling to free itself.

Stein was coping with this when mournful howls of a baying dog from Sepphoris' summit pierced the night. At that moment the moon broke free and Stein saw two dogs. Even in the dark he could easily see one was much larger than the other. The smaller dog was silent. Stein remembered childhood stories that a howling dog at night signified death hovered near.

Fear gripped him. He closed his eyes to shut out these portents, but every time the dog bayed something died in the rapidly aging chairman. Just as it seemed the slow steady keening would never end, silence fell. When he opened his eyes the dogs had vanished. It was as if a Sepphoris spirit had given a final warning. With a sense of doom Stein returned to his desk. Something horrible was happening, and he could only read.

Chapter Twenty-four

Prime Minister Roth's day began early in his Jerusalem office. Typically the energetic forty-nine-year-old's day began at 3:00 a.m. and often ran all night. Just keeping up with various ministries' status reports took time, and he liked seclusion. He sipped strong black coffee. Although an Israeli native, he was as much at home in the United States as in this troubled land. Only fourteen when his family moved to Philadelphia where his father taught mathematics, he'd learned English and adopted American mannerisms. A brilliant student, he gained popularity with American peers who shortened David to the more playful Davey.

Handsome David graduated fourth in his senior class at Phillips Exeter Academy, one of the most competitive private schools in the United States. He sought uninhibited girls, a freewheeling habit which later tried his marriage and political career.

He missed his Phillips Exeter Academy graduation, instead flying to Israel to fight in the 1967 war. He well remembered the day the Arabs attacked: June 5, 1967. He learned the horror of war while his American friends were fledglings in parental nests. With luck, guts, and skill David rose to rank of captain in a secret branch of the fighting intelligence. He'd looked on the face of death, once when wounded leading a rescue of a hijacked plane and once swimming in the Suez Canal under Egyptian fire. He'd refused to drop the heavy machine gun pulling him under the water's surface. Israel needed that gun. He survived and ended his five year military career as a respected soldier and patriot at twenty-three.

Returning to the States, he entered Columbia University where he did six and a half years' work in less than half that time. At the end of that marathon he'd earned a Masters of Business Administration, a feat never done before or since.

War broke out again in 1973. David flew home, leading men in combat within hours. In America once more, he became a fervent Zionist. Marie Brunel, Israeli consul to Boston, noted his organizational abilities. Brunel placed him on a political track by arranging a debate between David and a PLO activist, Professor George Zait. On television David proved both photogenic and intellectually agile. The CIA and Mossad began to track his rising star.

The Prime Minister might have continued as a vocal Zionist, but for the death of his beloved brother Johnathon. Johnathon was the commando leader who engineered the rescue of a planeload of hijacked Jewish citizens from Ethiopia. As always Johnathon led from the front and was the only casualty. Even now Roth anguished over that loss. A picture of Johnathon sat on his desk. Roth formed the Johnathon Institute, committed to abolishing terrorism; an expert, he authored three major books on the subject. Rising in Israeli politics, David organized an anti-terrorism conference. Now he served as Prime Minister of a troubled nation.

Problematically, Israel's standard of living was based on deficit spending, the United States picking up the slack. Survival meant matching the military might of five surrounding enemy governments. More worrisome, sooner or later America's declining infrastructure would have to be reclaimed at a cost of billions. Foreign aid would shrivel. To gain votes he promised what Israel couldn't afford. Holding off the inevitable, he endured charges of reneging on promises.

Roth felt further restrained by predecessors' acts. Prime Minister Guzemann had nearly given Israel away to the Palestinians with his foolish peace plans. For Roth every inch seized by Israeli forces belonged to Israel forever. Nevertheless, pressure built from a United States chafing at the cost of keeping Israel afloat, to trade land for peace with the Palestinians. Although Roth had long worked with the CIA, he was by no means the pawn its people thought him. America needed a secure military foothold to protect its vital interests in Middle East oil. It invested in Roth to move peace talks forward, yet remain a dependable ally. Once in power, Roth complied less with U.S. orders. Israeli policy was to continue seizing and settling land for acknowledgement that Israel owned Palestine. He smiled sardonically. Every day he stalled was another day Jewish settlers could dig deeper into recently seized territory.

Roth scanned his weekly economic report. No changes. He picked up a much thicker manila folder, Mossad's report. During the next two hours, the Prime Minister frowned as he read that Hamas had assassinated four more leading citizens. In spite of tongue-lashings, pleading, money, and more over the past eighteen months, Mossad continued ineffective in identifying the master mind plotting increased losses. Roth himself survived three assassination attempts in seven years, and he was Israel's most guarded citizen. Prominent citizens were leaving Israel until security was restored. Highlighting these sad facts the Prime Minister wrote in his meticulous hand, "Find and kill this Hamas leader at all costs." He'd been writing similar orders every week for over a year.

The last entry puzzled Roth. President Straihorn was scheduled for an international statement at 7:00 p.m. Eastern Standard time, less than two hours away. Mossad had been unable to ascertain its subject.

The next item, hand delivered by a Vatican diplomat, handwritten and signed by Pope Jerome himself, requested a meeting concerning Israeli survival. It would involve one emissary of the Vatican and Roth, this despite the fact that relations between the Vatican and Israel had been icy since WWII. Roth sipped the bitter dregs of his coffee.

Chapter Twenty-five

Train up a child in the way he should go and when he is old he will not depart from it.
Proverbs 22:6

Give me a child for the first five years of his life and he will be mine forever.
Vladimir Lenin

President Straihorn checked his tie (burgundy for credibility) just minutes away from the speech of his life. Of course, his advisors protested his saying anything without group analysis for political impact. Nevertheless, the smirking President insisted this address would be received with good will, his message really just good news to all people. Of course, the President knew full well the Jesus Tablets would be anything but good news to the Establishment. How ironic that the Bible had been written by hacks penning the type of speeches he'd given while clawing to the top. Even more delicious, he'd deliver this death blow under the banner of freedom of information. Everyone near the Oval Office noticed the President's good cheer. However, more than a few skeptics worried. No one but President Straihorn had any idea what the statement might be.

President Straihorn felt buoyant, joking with his make-up crew and chuckling as he listened to a rumor that one of his opposing Republican senators might indeed have been gay all along, delectable news since this particular Senator ran on the platform of family values.

The thirty second countdown began.

***

In Israel, Stein jerked awake to insistent knocking on the study door. He looked around, confused. He'd dozed off reading the Amos section. Alice still slept on the couch while dawn tinted the room pink and gold. He cleared his throat to say he was coming. When he opened the door he faced John Martin, celebrated New York Times reporter.

"Dr. Cross?" the pug-faced journalist asked.

"No. Samuel Stein, Harvard Archaeology Chair," the befuddled academic answered. He heard Alice pulling herself together behind him and wondered what the reporter might assume. "Come in, please."

"John Martin, New York Times." The newcomer extended his beefy hand which Stein half expected to be ink stained. "What's so special in this dusty dig?" Martin continued.

Stein hesitated.

Martin checked his watch. "Well, it must be something because the President's making a speech about it in fifty minutes."

Stein's heart plummeted. He gathered his wits and inhaled. "Well, this is the first we've heard of a speech, but Dr. Henry Cross and his wife Alice here behind me have unearthed a potentially significant discovery."

Alice gasped. News of the Jesus Tablets had escaped.

Alice Cross excused herself to locate Henry. She found him supervising further excavation of the area that yielded the Jesus Tablets. When Henry saw her face he knew what they feared had arrived. Still, how could the secret have spread from his locked study?

Henry and Alice entered the study, stunned to see not one, but four reporters, each pressing Stein for information which he stoutly refused. Alice defused the verbal onslaught by suggesting that everyone sit down while she sent for iced tea. Her hospitable gesture reduced the scene from verbal chaos to one of civilized questioning. The journalists knew each other as competitors in a business chary of rewards to second place scoops. Henry avoided the sharp questions by setting up the boxy television set normally wrapped in dust proof covers. Questions flew wildly. Clearly, the reporters knew nothing yet.

Each journalist soon figured out that no one had an exclusive story regardless of sources. By the time Henry hooked up the television and tuned to channel nine, reporters snapped pictures, talked on cell phones, or took notes. The boisterous group quieted only when Henry brusquely called attention to the television screen, the mystery about to be revealed.

***

With practiced charisma President Straihorn smiled, captivating the cameras, and began to speak. "My fellow Americans and citizens of the world, it gives me the greatest pleasure to relay good news to our often pressed and worried planet. It is all too seldom that world leaders can report positive news to nations so racked with war, trials, and despair. During my administration it has been my lot to come to the American people with the dispiriting news that force was necessary to stop evil, that we would hear the clash of war once again. Many times I've prayed with my family that the men and women of our armed forces would return home safely after being placed in harm's way. Many times I have wept over the coffins of those who paid the ultimate price for the freedoms that each of us often take for granted.

"Tonight, however, is a time of celebration and discovery. Tonight I speak of young Americans serving peacefully as members of the historical army of truth seekers of all nations, searchers for truth that benefits each of us and our children. America guarantees freedom of speech and thought so truth can be found and protected. We are privileged to live in a country where freedom and truth are equally valued. The greatest tyrants of the world used lies to bind their people. Truth alone is the ultimate standard of meaningful existence.

"Sometimes we focus so hard on the gangs and on the violence that we forget to praise the hundreds of thousands of young men and women who are not violent, not senseless, and definitely not mindless. These are our all too often forgotten youth. Sometimes our government is working so hard to solve our nation's problems we forget to celebrate those doing everything right. It is in celebration of those honorable young people that I make this very special report.

"At this hour in Sepphoris, Israel, are two hundred American students working on an archaeology dig under the tutelage of Harvard University. With backbreaking labor under the broiling Middle Eastern sun they seek knowledge of our human past. They toil unpaid at a little known site to unearth the truth. They know the odds of finding anything significant are almost nil. Palestine, the Holy Land, has yielded little hard evidence of its elusive past. However it is God's will that they have found something staggering: a treasure trove of truth.

"A library of baked clay tablets has been discovered at Sepphoris that may well rewrite our knowledge of ancient Palestine. This library, nearly one ton of ancient tablets, may enlighten us about our religious heritage and fill in broad gaps of history. It appears authentic, representing a complete history in the form of a family diary spanning generations. In fact, this is by far the most complete body of data on the religious and political history of Palestine ever found. Its spiritual and academic value become even greater since it appears to record none other than the biblical Moses and his descendants. Not only does this library give the complete Moses account, it covers Palestinian history to and through the time of Jesus. The most amazing details are writings from the actual hand of Jesus himself and the hand of Mary his mother.

"I have decided this is news for all humankind. Secrecy would be dishonest to humanity and God alike. Even the President of the United States has no right to withhold information God has allowed us to find. Therefore, after hours of prayer with my wife I decided to make the knowledge of this discovery every person's property. No leader should stand between others' relationships with God. There have been moral lapses during my presidency, and I openly asked for my fellow citizens' forgiveness. Hopefully by this honest disclosure I can regain your trust.

"I have told you this without consulting Congress or the international community. Responsible leaders of every nation will agree that knowledge must be freely sought and none has the right to withhold such vital information. If I am wrong, the fault is mine alone. I take responsibility.

"By legal contract with the government of Israel everything found at the Sepphoris site belongs to Harvard University. I have no doubt Israel will honor that contract. Plans will be made with Israel to transport the library and the students to America. After a parade in Washington D.C. the students and their teachers will be honored at a state dinner at the White House. I am also assured that Harvard will provide translations to the scholarly community as well as the world at large just as soon as the Tablets can be thoroughly studied by the appropriate experts. It is Harvard's and the American Government's wish that nothing stand in the way of the quest for knowledge. The name given to the library by Sepphoris archaeologists is the Jesus Tablets. I speak for knowledge seekers everywhere when I say that we all look forward to the near future when the Jesus Tablets will land safely in the United States. It will then be the privilege of our government and people to convey their contents to the international community. In honor of the students and staff of the Sepphoris dig, I wish each inhabitant on this earth the benefits of peace, goodwill, and a cheerful goodnight. God bless America."

President Straihorn said nothing as he left the podium, his thoughts conflicting. On one hand he felt the thrill of this new game, on the other discomfort at a steady and growing sexual tension. It would be hours before his new lover could join him in the Oval Office.

***

The post-speech media, like everyone else, was flummoxed, religion not common subject matter for hardened journalists or worldly pundits. Nevertheless, the media knew a hot story when they saw it, and had no trouble seeing the possibilities of this ancient library. The President's decision to reveal the Tablets directly to the people was hotly debated. A quick poll showed most voters commended it as morally correct making it difficult for any politician to publicly object, but key figures felt slighted at being left out of the decision. Nearly all, however, said they would have supported the President's revelation.

Secular liberals smelled blood. These Tablets could change the perception of Jesus. The conservative right found itself debating the worth of further disclosures about the Jesus story. The religious establishment who'd formerly pushed the need to know and accept Jesus now found themselves saying that perhaps we knew as much about Jesus as we need to. Many insisted they had the Bible; therefore, they didn't need to know more. Of course, the educated likened this to someone claiming to love, but not wanting better acquaintance with the beloved. Without knowledge of Jesus there would be no Jesus story. There were open questions as to whether the New Testament wasn't just a story after all. Avid fundamentalists thundered this was a satanic plot to destroy the inalterable word of God. Many clergy and believers continued to have faith that their understanding of God and Jesus would withstand anything new.

A strange state of affairs developed. The public, formerly unengaged in debates on the canon and infallibility of the Bible, were now intrigued. Theologians teaching in cloistered ivory towers awoke to find themselves in demand on television and print interviews. Psychologists sat across from talk show hosts discussing the merit of public confession. Other psychologists explained the dozens of cases of mentally ill people who claimed to be God or servants of God. Obviously, Jesus' claims would put a modern speaker in treatment. Barely literate preachers from obscure fundamental sects found themselves on television explaining how and why they knew the will of God, finding themselves in strange water. Outside their isolated groups they stumbled. Educated interrogators asking pointed questions were never allowed in the local churches where people already agreed with each other.

Established church leaders acknowledged little was known about the historical Jesus. The Christian Church precariously balanced on only a few nuggets of hard information. Clearly, there was barely enough evidence to argue that Jesus lived much less was God of the Universe. Indeed, original writings claimed to be written by the Apostles were long lost. Only copies of copies that might never have had a valid original existed. They wouldn't be admitted in a court of law, just stories that could've been written by anyone. Even worse it was now emphasized on national television that many biblical accounts contradicted each other. Having to prove their precarious position rather than merely state it challenged religious leaders, inflaming the imaginations of all ends of the political and faith based spectrum. Part of the world viewed the Jesus Tablets as a key to unlock a room of mystery while another wanted to destroy them.

In short, the Jesus Tablets caused a revival in philosophical and theological discussion. Questions that formerly interested small numbers of specialized thinkers now intruded on kitchen table talk. "Could God really die?" became a hot question.

This turmoil slammed into the Catholic Church like a tsunami. Publicly the Mother Church appeared unworried. Priests and bureaucrats reminded followers that Catholics were guided as much by Church decisions as by the Bible. However, the Church couldn't control what parishioners saw and heard.

Television transmission and radio placed the issue of the Jesus Tablets before most of the earth. Since Jesus and Mary worship is the heart of the Catholic religion, the Church could hardly deny the need and desire to know more about these two deified figures. As the Catholic laity turned to the parish priest, so did the priests turn to their bishops for help. The bishops in turn appealed in growing desperation to their cardinals. It was like a resurrection of the men of the Renaissance who'd torn the Catholic Church to pieces at the close of the Middle Ages. Pope Jerome summoned key cardinals. Powerful, ruthless, and ambitious, they prepared to fly to Italy. The war to survive the Jesus Tablets must be fought from Rome.

Barely twenty-six hours had passed since Straihorn's speech, and Pope Jerome, bombarded with appeals for statements, clarifications, and explanations, hadn't slept. The Holy Father could only present a calm outward appearance assuring all that the Church was secure within Jesus' arms. Privately, the Pope suffered.

Father Tobenhien had acted on their agreement to convince Israel of their mutual danger. The erratic President Straihorn had effectively compromised that plan's effectiveness. Even if they'd suspected the President knew about the Tablets, his acting independently was unbelievable. Kings and presidents are assumed to be figureheads controlled by financial and military powers.

President Straihorn's actions remained baffling. Unpredictability is a trait world leaders fear, and he had been unpredictable. For the first time Pope Jerome was grateful for the shrewd Father Tobenhien. Tobenhien pointed out President Straihorn had actually said nothing about the Tablets' contents. Tobenhien added that Straihorn's popular speech notwithstanding, the United States still didn't possess them. The Jesuit urged the Church to press on with plans to convince Israel to seize and destroy them. Once destroyed, there would be no proof as to what they contained. The Jesuit also urged the secret emergency session with the key cardinals.

Pope Jerome wasn't one for the dark deeds that might become necessary. Other popes had been experts in murder, blackmail, and shady dealings, but modern popes were public relation agents, blessing trinkets and being photogenic. In addition, he was aging, unable to keep the hours of years past. Pope Jerome turned to prayer, sincere prayers that rose to heaven not from the ego, station, or status. Quite the contrary, these prayers came from a frightened Polish boy who had the misfortune to become Pope Jerome.

Father Tobenhien concentrated in his own Spartan living quarters, furnished only with a cot, small study desk, and chair, convinced there would be plenty of time to give God prayers of thanksgiving once the Tablets were under control. He'd learned that great danger often bears great opportunity. With thought, luck, and God's will these Jesus Tablets might change the Church for the better.

President Straihorn's speech had caught Tobenhien by surprise just as it had all others. He concluded the wily President Straihorn knew exactly what he was doing. Tobenhien perused Straihorn's dossier, aware of the American system for monitoring their President's stability. One of the doctors on that panel, a devout Catholic, had been supplying the Jesuits information for years. No doubt the perversely deviant President's activities on camera in the Oval Office were intentional. Madness comes in many flavors. Many had become millionaires because obsessions drove them to acquire material things without limit or rest. In modern culture such behavior wouldn't be considered insanity, but it seemed to Father Tobenhien that such obsessions were a type of madness. Perhaps madness would compel a man to desire on camera fellatio. In addition there were the implications that he'd had personal enemies killed. Straihorn might be mad, but keen of mind. Straihorn's murderous psyche, capable of meticulous planning, showed characteristics of an evil genius. He must have good reason for exposing the Jesus Tablets. If Tobenhien found that reason, he'd have a vital key.

President Straihorn must be aware that knowledge of the Tablets had escaped Sepphoris. What if he felt someone might try to destroy them before the United States could secret them out? Without this public announcement the Jesus Tablets would have been dust by now. Realistically speaking, only Jewish forces could seize and destroy the Tablets under some pretense. President Straihorn might have decided it didn't matter who else knew of them because only the Jews could do that job. The only flaw in this line of reasoning was that obviously the Jews had not yet destroyed the Tablets; therefore, they couldn't have known about them. That could only leave two possibilities. First, the President might have figured Israel would be informed of the Tablets before the United States took them. Second, he might have wanted the Jews to know of the Tablets for the perverse challenge of seizing them in spite of the odds.

There had to be a missing string tying both strands together. Major news agencies had journalists on site. Of course! The bastards were already in place before the President spoke! The clever Straihorn had pre-positioned reporters so the Tablets couldn't be destroyed. Tobenhien smiled, appreciating the sheer genius of it.

That had to be the string. This fumbling Pope would grant him full powers of negotiation. Tomorrow he'd convince Prime Minister Roth to move immediately for his country's survival.

With this the Black Pope of the Jesuits bowed his head in gratitude to the God of the heavens.

**

Ever since President Straihorn's bombshell speech, the media had inundated Roth, requesting specific answers to questions for which he had no responses. When he called on agency heads they knew nothing either. One of his first calls was to Heinz, head of Mossad, who promised a complete report in twenty-four hours. He asked the Prime Minister if the military should seize Sepphoris and confiscate all onsite materials. Roth rejected that as premature and provoking United States' fury. No one knew better than he how Americans revered property rights and college kids. Storming the camp would be a public relations disaster.

A show of cooperation in protecting and transferring the Jesus Tablets would make for good press. Still, people were so emotional about religion. Roth had little use for it himself. Israel's religious heritage meant less to him than a division of good soldiers. Yet, Roth wasn't without compassion and had always been respectful of religious feelings.

However, the very title Jesus Tablets made him nervous. Jewish circles seldom spoke of Jesus. Jews had been persecuted for centuries by people who claimed to be obeying this semi-mythical person whose very name was seldom spoken in his childhood. After being called "Jesus killer" at school, Roth spoke to his father who explained that Jesus might have been a Jew of very early history although evidence was scanty. Nevertheless, a story of this Jesus did survive. The child David listened, amazed as his father related the New Testament story. He asked his father, "Do people really buy this?"

His father nodded. " They not only buy it, they're often willing to kill those who don't."

His father went on to say that most people fear the unknown and will believe anything that makes them feel special to God. Unfortunately, they often use this special relationship to justify persecuting others. His father cautioned David that Jews are not immune to this blindness, believing tales just as silly in their own texts. The Moses story had similar features to the Jesus tale.

The more young David studied, the more it appeared Jesus was only one of dozens of Jewish social and religious critics of the era. Jesus appeared to run afoul of religious authorities desperately trying to avoid provoking the Roman government. Romans executed Jesus for being a threat to stability. Blaming the entire Jewish race for the death of one man seemed crazy, Jesus being God seemed extremely unlikely, and God being three beings made no sense at all.

At last an evening came when David and his scholarly father discussed his findings. His father told David how proud he was of his inquiry. He went on to comment, "Yet God exists and we all seek him. You travel the correct path. Remember, the heart often desires in error. God gave us minds to judge evidence. If the evidence is insufficient to determine what is true, then we must live with that. Apparently God in his wisdom knows few can endure the blinding light of truth. You have chosen the hardest path. I hope God values such honest thinking."

From that day forth David tried to make choices pleasing to a just God. He made compromises with truth only when it served the greater good. He liked to believe that God would forgive his weakness for willing women.

Now, he sought information from a reticent United States. His calls to President Straihorn floundered. All Roth got were assurances that President Straihorn would call him shortly. More troubling were reports that part of America's Seventh Fleet was sailing toward Israel and would be within carrier range in a day. To show his displeasure Roth placed several coastal Israeli Air Wings on high alert, also sending crack Israeli airborne soldiers to the Sepphoris site on the pretense of adding security. He frowned. What games to play with soldiers' lives.

Father Tobenhien would arrive that afternoon. It made Roth squirm to deal with the Catholics. Nevertheless, the practical Prime Minister would work with anyone to clarify the present situation. Religious people were more and more a part of international politics. The more science advanced the more the masses sought the caves. He needed a religion expert. Fortunately he had one, Professor Gold of the Israeli Institute of Hebrew Antiquities in Tel Aviv.

***

Other eyes studied intelligence reports from a different viewpoint. Straihorn's actions hadn't surprised the reclusive Pebbles, now certain that the Palestinian students' killers in America acted under the President's orders. Pebbles' dispensable young Hamas agent, Abdul, must have died in the Atlanta jail on orders from the same source. This Straihorn was a crazy infidel. His obsession with earthly pleasures showed a man with no respect for God or God's tender creations. The President was using world attention to protect the Tablets from Israeli destruction. What a shame that cunning mind wasn't in the service of the only God, Allah.

The Arabs couldn't depend on the American President's public promise to share these Tablets. Also the longer the Tablets were in Sepphoris, the tighter the security. The longer they remained in Israel the easier for the Jews to come up with means to annihilate them. If the Tablets made it to America, the Jews' chances dropped to zero. The window would be when the Tablets were in transit to the airport or airborne. Therefore, something had to force the Tablets into transport phase. When the sun went down Pebbles had his plan.

History would reveal him more right than wrong about the American President, but this game had many players.

***

One major player was Albright, head of the CIA. President Straihorn's speech ignited a fireball of inquiries from other countries' intelligence agencies. Much intelligence is traded between such agencies as favors among those acquainted for entire careers.

The pressured Heinz informed Albright this withholding of information wasn't viewed as friendly. Pleas, hints, deals, and even slightly veiled threats from Mossad bombarded Albright. He explained he had orders to leave all decisions to the President, also mentioning the President's speech could have been worse. Mossad took the hint. The Jesus Tablets posed a threat to Israel. After the briefest of pauses Heinz changed his tone, asking about the health of Albright's wife and how well his son was doing in journalism at Florida State. After a couple more minutes of casual conversation Heinz attempted to bid goodbye to Albright who delayed the farewell by asking the head of Mossad how his daughter was doing in her psychology studies in Jerusalem. There was a split second before Heinz answered she was doing very well indeed. After the conversation, Albright rubbed his tired eyes and ran his fingers through his thinning hair. What lunacy, he thought, where fathers make small talk after threatening the lives of each other's children.

***

A few hours brought changes to Sepphoris. Airborne soldiers arrived; camp security tightened. Stein called the students together at the dining tent, saying he hadn't yet completed his primary review of The Tablets, but they did appear to be as the President represented. He apologized for not sharing all this sooner; however, he reiterated that he'd not yet finished. He would do his best to keep them informed as to any developments at least as far as Harvard and the United States Government would permit.

The idea of international press on site and a being honored in Washington, D.C., made up for being uninformed. The students basked in anticipated career-enhancing fame. They looked forward to press interviews where remembered hunches would be soberly discussed.

Alice and Henry stayed with the Tablets. Stein had ordered that journalists be allowed any pictures of the Tablets in situ they wanted, but were not to photograph the writing on any individual tablet. Of course, enterprising photographers managed photos of a few exposed corners. These ultimately made their way to the public and were studied by eager scholars.

Stein contacted Harvard's president who told him to cooperate fully with his government. Harvard received and needed the tens of millions in research funds allocated annually. Stein was encouraged to continue his work as a Harvard scholar. Mossad, more interested in the Tablets' destruction than in scholarly translation, recorded their discussion.

Chapter Twenty-six

Hamas left Amal alone for many months. When not at work, she walked the hills gathering flowers and watching for message drops. The arrangement of a few stones or disappearance of a branch might be her signal. Her affair with General Kessler, this aging man who represented a deadly enemy, had matured into a something surprisingly tender. She learned even the life of an Israeli general isn't easy. The general showed her as much kindness as his position allowed, even finding her mother hard-to-come-by employment with another officer. Amal now had freedom to set her schedule. Her paperwork ensured immunity from roving Israeli patrols.

She lay nude on her rude covers late at night and wondered what it would be like to make love to her own man, never having known mutual pleasure. She wept after rare self-gratification because she deserved a husband. Amal sometimes dreamed peace had come, that she had not only a husband, but barefoot children playing outside their own home. Then reality woke her. A member of Hamas has no future but the grave.

One early fall day after completing her tasks, she went walking. The general had been gone for days. She knew nothing of President Straihorn or the Jesus Tablets, only that this evening had a velvet feel. Cool air wafted across the scorched hills. As always, she carried her documentation and a flower basket.

She automatically glanced over the first three drop sites. At the last, thirty paces from the trail, a message rock was missing. Amal, heart slamming into her ribs, approached the site as if picking flowers. She dropped a rock into her basket. A message folded and taped on its underside gave instructions for her next mission, a map, and two photographs. Her assignment targeted two people at Sepphoris. Her war would soon be over. To kill one at such a guarded site would be difficult. To kill two meant at least two shots, one too many. Escape would be impossible. A tear dampened the rock. The Fawn had been reactivated.

***

Doctor Stein sipped water, a pause before rereading the previous two translated sections, each brief but rich with new information. How little these ancient authors felt compelled to write during their turbulent times. Clearly Israel and Judea were little islands in the much larger Middle East Ocean, contrary to the prominent image the Old Testament ascribed to them. The real power brokers were Egypt, Assyria, and rising Babylon. Only the fertile coastal areas and vast river drainages of the Nile and Tigris supported large populations. Israel and Judea were poorer hill country with an erratic climate. With this in mind, Stein started to re-read. Jeroham, Amos' son, added his "grain of sand to the anthill of history." That history was of a people in decline, of murderous rulers and Machiavellian priests, of the poor suffering while only the elite prospered.

Then came Jeroham's son Nathan's account.

***

"When any nation suffered a setback or ruin its neighbors called it punishment from the Lord. Thus it was when Israel fell to the Assyrian Empire. The story has spread that Assyrians stripped Israel and led its population off to the hinterlands wailing and gnashing their teeth. Only the governing elite were exiled to Assyria. The rest stayed where they had always been, farming. The lot of the Israeli farmer did not change. He merely had new masters. What was left of the Israeli army merged into that of Assyria. Our new Assyrian overlords intermarried with Israeli women."

Nathan wrote of "Hezekiah who plotted constantly to overthrown Assyrian rule. His plot discovered, the Assyrian army vanquished fifty Judean cities before besieging Jerusalem where Hezekiah hid." Sieges claimed the lives of thousands before both sides went to the peace table.

In the end, Jerusalem became an Assyrian vassal. As with his predecessors, Nathan wrote with humility, believing in some sort of God.

***

Stein stood and worked his tired shoulders. The Jesus Tablets would scour academia like a desert storm. If the religious world tried to ignore first person evidence, its credibility would be annihilated.

Alice walked over to see where he'd left off. "Isn't it true," she asked, "That those thousands died partly because poor sanitation, bad diets, vermin, and rotting corpses caused siege disease?"

"Sure. The height of biblical medical knowledge was that demons and witches caused disease. Thousands of eccentric women and harmless children burned as a result. Not Moses, Jesus, or any of the rest spoke a word about virus, bacteria, mental illness, or modern anatomy. Not a word about antibiotics, anesthesiology, sanitation, or medical sterilization. These had to be discovered by those who didn't believe in unproved causes."

"Religious figures couldn't pass on what they didn't know," Alice said.

"Worshipers transformed human beings into deities. The sham must eventually be shown up." Shaking his head, Stein returned to his reading.

Jabez, Nathan's son, wrote of life in the reigns of Josiah through that of Nebuchadnezzar. At the end of his writing, Babylon claimed Judah, oppressing its long-suffering people.

Stein pressed on to the next account, written by Jahath, son of Jabez, the tenth generation to carry on the family records. Sold to a priest after the destruction of the temple in Jerusalem and the exile of upper classes to Babylonia, Jahath learned the great secret known as the Yahweh Promise.

***

He wrote: "I was assigned modest quarters in the home of my new master, a fanatic who believed he knew the will of God. The fates granted that I witness a strange labor.

"The exiles in Babylon had been wealthy in Judea, and longed to recapture that status. Like all who suffer misfortune, they sought reasons. Yahweh priests provided them, promising a future return of the exiles when wealth and status would be restored by divine promise. For now, they were being punished for not being obedient enough to the priests.

"However, the priests saw the return to Canaan might take time. Something had to keep them yearning for Canaan. That became known as the Yahweh Promise. Although secret, I witnessed its unfolding.

"My master believed any measures acceptable if the Jewish exiles could eventually reclaim Judah. Their difficulty was that hundreds of stories passed down through generations made up the Yahweh tradition. Various versions of the Moses story made it difficult to claim any one absolutely true. Also the basic legends of Moses and the settling of Canaan did not answer all emotional needs. People wanted to know how the world was created, and how God decided to act through the Jews. Creation of a believable story was the task.

"Six leaders became the force behind the Yahweh Promise, meant to turn all the Moses legends into one record designed to give a sacred promise between God and the Jews. In Babylon there was no one to contradict this new version. The priests were wise enough to know that the second generation of exiles would grow up believing this story of Yahweh's revelation. These six were not only fanatics, but also geniuses.

"The Yahweh Promise took three years to complete. I was responsible for actually writing the story. Its exact details are so lengthy I will describe it broadly. The general idea was a series of books the priests claimed were written by Moses. They did, in fact, have a basis in the original tales Moses told during evening storytelling sessions, according to our family's secret Eli accounts. The priests, of course, only picked and chose or added to the many versions handed down. Using Moses, the six created a cohesive story. These priests fit the creation of the world into the seven day cycle the Jews were familiar with already. Countless details went along similar lines. Flood stories were popular with all the nearby countries, so the priests had a flood tale in their saga. Everything was linked to obeying God's laws, subject to priestly interpretation. It all hung on a covenant between God and Moses. We would return to Palestine if we obeyed God.

"What a thorny task to weave all the tales into one. The Priests invented characters and an idyllic plot. Since palace gardens were treasured in Babylon, they invented a garden of Paradise for the first man and woman, Adam and Eve. The Priests had the God of the heavens stroll there in human form. God had to be good, so something had to be bad, and it was now they redefined Satan. Improbably, God both created this enemy and permitted him to live. The first couple did not obey God and were cast out of the garden as punishment. The original sin was to disobey God. Because of this all future generations must suffer. One was guilty on birth. This was the illogical basis of the invented story.

"The tale was woven with strands of Cain, Abel, and Abraham. Moses discovered in the river by the kind princess was a modification of a child's tale common to many peoples, told and retold for generations. Tales of escaped slaves who became kings and heroes were a common part of Mideast folklore. When the impossible had to be overcome, the priests created miracles. Nearly all these tales were given by God or angels to the most unlikely people in the form of trances, dreams, or visions.

"Since the priests wanted obedience, Yahweh was murderous, acting in fits of rage. He gave life to people he must have known would displease him, and then murdered them by flooding, burning, and burying alive. He ordered murder by the sword down to the last unthinking animal and innocent infant. Actions that would warrant justice in any court were committed with impunity by Yahweh. Jealousy, rage, revenge, genocide, and spite were his traits. A more petty and fickle deity would be difficult to imagine.

"To reinforce that Palestine belonged to the Jews, these plotters had Yahweh order the murder of every inhabitant in Canaan. The worst ruler never made a greater swath of murder, pillage, burning, and rape than their imagined Yahweh inflicted on the first dwellers of Canaan.

There had never been a conquest of Canaan. Our family records clearly showed a peaceful merging of two outcast peoples. These priests did not want to promise peace. I decided no one could believe them, but I was wrong. This blood-drenched god attracted many.

"Blood, blood and more blood flowed through their myth. Only obedience could satisfy this god. These priests invented countless laws. Many demanded bloodshed, the death of doves, sheep, goats, and cattle required for a list of infractions too numerous to remember. The only way to be right with god was to obey and pay the priests. The priests were careful not to exclude money as payment for alleged offenses.

"These priests needed the Temple system. This House of God was a centralized location that made it simple for them to extract money from worshipers. People were required to come to God's House so priests had an orderly schedule of income. Why a true god of the heavens would need money and blood was never clear to me. Why the creator of all life would take pleasure in destroying life so illogical I did not believe the Yahweh myth would survive. As it happens, people will believe anything.

"The priests were careful not to name the pharaoh who drowned with his army in the Red Sea. Yet, the names of all the pharaohs had been known for hundreds of years. I was certain future thinkers would note other inconsistencies."

The writer wrote of how the priests touted their new version as a clarification of older stories from the oral tradition, how over time this convinced believers that it was the only true version of Yahweh, the infallible Word of God. When the Persian King Cyrus defeated the Babylonians, the priests were allowed to return with the rest of the elite to reclaim their holdings. The poor lost their land to the returned exploiters. The priests turned to rebuilding the Temple.

***

Stein leaned forward, his face in his hands. "This handful of pages tears the heart out of Judeo-Christian beliefs. The Torah, the Old Testament, is so influential to Western Civilization. Islam is seriously threatened. Moses and Jesus are critical to the divine chain of prophets toward Mohammed's vision of Allah."

"I know," Alice said, pouring him a glass of ice water. "German scholars sifted through the Old Testament and found flaws. Henry and I took undergraduate courses on the multiple story lines woven together. This is hard evidence of the original fabrication."

Stein rose from his desk and walked to the large window overlooking Sepphoris hill where work still progressed. Hundreds dug and sifted. He felt the hill was only enduring this indignity. Fingers of dust slid across the site as the wind ebbed and flowed across the hillside. The wind seemed harsher, its lulls shorter and the blowing spans longer and stronger. Henry told them at dinner how some workers were nervous, and rumors spread that evil was afoot. Stein pondered how strong the fear of the unknown is. Yet, those lacking knowledge were worst affected. He picked up the next translation.

***

Amnon recorded the Temple's completion and that, "Priests have dropped a curtain around Palestine and control every facet of life. Ruthlessly, they ordered all marriages between Jews and other races void. Husbands and wives married for decades were separated by force. Their children paid the greatest price, but the priests insisted on purification. Love or family well-being did not stop them. Everything revolves around the Temple. Every transaction has a fee and all money goes to this theological class. Every sin has a fine the priests collect. Most resent this, but are helpless. Palestine has lost hope."

Next Amnon's son Ezra wrote of continuing hardship and that, "The hands of the priests still rest heavily upon Palestine. A mythical figure is being created during the evening hours by storytellers who describe a holy man who will overthrow the elite. The poor turn frustrations into a dream of rescue. There is talk of a future kingdom when justice will reign and lands be returned to peasants."

***

The three Sepphoris scholars pondered the short passages over a midnight snack of goat cheese and olives. "Greece was a rising power by then," Henry said. "The ancient conflict between that prime sea power and Persia made war inevitable. Amnon lived during the time of Darius I, the great king of Persia."

Stein picked up the thread. "And Darius crossed the sea with six hundred ships and one hundred thousand men. At Marathon, twenty thousand disciplined Greeks defeated this Asian horde which set the stage for a war between the two great civilizations. In 485 B.C. Darius I died, succeeded by Xerxes I also mentioned by Amnon. Xerxes raised the largest army ever known. Over twelve hundred ships ferried two and a half million men to the mainland of the Northern Mediterranean. Here Leonidas and his three hundred Spartans faced the Persians at Thermopylae. The Spartans died to the last man but bought the Greeks time to muster a survival strategy. They eventually prevailed, giving birth to the European world."

Alice chimed in. "Ezra might have lived through Greece's' Golden Age, 480 B.C. to around 400 B.C. The world didn't center on Palestine. It never really did. Well, an early start tomorrow. Time for bed."

Later, Stein reflected how little the world had changed since Amnon and Ezra. Palestine was still a chip floating toward the East or the West depending on international currents. Oil and nuclear power changed the playing table. How typical to dream of being saved by a kind leader reigning over a happy land. Thoughts of heaven were just the next step. Jesus spoke of a coming kingdom where justice would prevail. Alice and Henry had bid Stein good night, but haunted by a sense of time slipping away, he pressed on.

Ezra's youngest son Aram continued the Messiah theme, describing Israel dominated by troubled Persia. "The Messiah myth grows. Hope for a savior crops up everywhere and nowhere. The priestly elite crush hopes of this savior, because the idea threatens their power. They use capital punishment against claimants to this savior title. The common people long so for a savior that every wandering social critic is assigned that title whether he wants it or not."

***

Stein considered. Most religious beliefs were so old they were lost in mists of unmeasured time. When Jesus referred to himself as "the light," he used a common religious term. Drinking blood for religious purposes predated modern communion by eons. Ideas of a heavenly king, paradise after death, divine justice, endless punishment, and the cosmic combat myth were used by civilizations without number. Of course the Persian demonology was adopted later, nearly intact by the Christian faith. The Persian Satan, Ahriman, would be known as a Prince of Darkness and he, too, led demons. By the same token the Jewish faith borrowed the Persian system of sacrifice of nearly every form of edible flesh or plant. Persians believed in a great Last Judgment. The cynical writer of Ecclesiastes stated, "All is vanity. There is nothing new under the sun." With that thought the weary archaeologist pressed on.

***

Aram's son Gad recorded living through the Greco-Persian Wars. In the end, after the division of the Greek Empire, Palestine went to Alexander's successor Ptolemy. Gad wrote, "The common people of Palestine still work the soil and hope for a messiah, a Jewish king. Yahweh priests now claim the messiah will come as a direct descendant of King David. They try to use the messiah myth to bind Jews closer. The people yearn for a savior to release them from oppression, but the priests want a messiah for a king to maintain the status quo.

"There is tension among Jews. Always and forever it has been a mixed land. Thousands of Palestinians still worship Baal and the ancient gods of fertility. Yahweh worship is now in power, but others smolder under the oppressed surface. It is doubtful whether factions of the Jewish people can coexist. Intelligent Jews are content to become Greeks, but revolutionary Jewish nationalists oppose them. The poor envy the rich and the rich fear the poor. The world will ever be so.

"I have lived under Greek rule for fifteen years. Priests and their extortion remain; however, the Yahweh cult is uneasy. The Greeks have brought their habits of questioning all ideas, such questioning dangerous for the priests' Torah. Questions demand answers. Myths demand blind faith. Many are adopting Greek analysis as well as democratic ideas of equality. Tolerance is anathema to the priests, but Greek manners, ethics, and even their language attract our people.

"I, too, am drawn to them. Their search for truth using logic, proofs, and argumentation strongly appeals. Their love of mathematics, learning, and knowledge has a refreshing vitality. I am most impressed with their concept of science; a new method to search for facts which the Greeks claim will change everything. The priests try, but Greek ideas are impossible to kill. The power of logic may burst the chains of superstition."

Edom, Gad's third son, wrote of a growing middle class who, under Greek influence, began to act on their own ideas. The Yahweh priests fought this tide of Greek independence using two weapons to resist the Hellenists. First, the myth that the Jews had the absolute word of God contained in the Torah; second, the myth that the Messiah of the David line was returning soon to cleanse and lead the Jews. He wrote, too, of wars among Greek city states where, "Palestine, as always, is just one of many small bones that the wolves of power fight over."

***

Next morning, Alice found Stein still at work. She saw that he'd progressed to the writings of Eliphaz, the last son of Edom after Eli. Eliphaz wrote of Palestine under the Seleucid Empire.

***

"Educated Jewish Hellenists placed Jason in the post of Jewish High Priest of the Temple. He opened it to many Greek practices. The ranks of the Jewish Yahweh party grew overnight eventually causing war among us. I learned a truth, that religious fanatics will murder anyone not sharing their vision. The more a man claims to know absolute truth the more likely he is to become an intolerant killer.

"Antiochus then forbade circumcision and Sabbath, probably saving the Yahweh extremists. When he attempted to enforce these radical decrees a national war of resistance broke out, the Maccabean War, which lasted twenty-five years of my life pitting nearly every Jew against Antiochus and his reign. After years of raiding and attrition, we Jews drove the followers of Antiochus from the land. I was in my seventies when the Jews recaptured Jerusalem.

"The Jewish war effort was supported by all sectors. Yahweh extremists claimed it was a war about true religion. In fact, a growing sense of nationalism was the strongest motivation. Finally, Antiochus died. His successor, Lysias, negotiates terms with us. Unfortunately, the Jews have formed a treaty with the growing power of Rome to bring Lysias to the peace table. Rome is of frightening strength, unlikely to wait by the roadside. The Jews have again divided into political parties tearing the Jewish nation apart. Extremists gleefully kill moderates. The priests have shrewdly bound themselves to the nationalists, the priests more severe rulers than the Seleucids."

Stein reread the account. Eliphaz showed the Jews not of one mind, but fractured. Being a Jew was no insurance of being spared by another Jew. But, time for reflection would have to come later. For now Stein had to keep reading.

***

"I am Amos, last surviving son of Eliphaz. My life has been rent by strife, war, and fear. Jews killed Jews for the slightest of reasons. Murder was rampant on the throne, in the street, and in the countryside, plotting as intense in the Temple as in the palace. After the Maccabean War Israel split along economic, educational, religious, and political lines.

"Israel divided into three major political parties, the Pharisees, the Essenes, and the Sadducees, and many minor ones. The

Pharisees originated a new oral law, a constant revision of the Laws of Moses. Pharisees favored local religious gathering places called synagogues where people could worship locally and have a place to send their children for religious education. Pharisees competed with the Temple priesthood in Jerusalem.

"Essenes were zealots who believed withdrawing from the world the only way to serve God. They formed self-sustaining communities and few could match the asceticism of Essenes who did not believe in marriage and strongly supported the Messiah myth. Essenes were constantly telling everyone that the world was coming to an end, a last judgment and the coming kingdom of God at hand.

"The Sadducees were the upper classes who accepted the Greeks and religious tolerance. They avoided strife, favoring Temple worship which placed them in direct conflict with both Essenes and Pharisees. Sadducees were a peace party, committed to the status quo because they were in a favored social position.

"Yahweh priests could not see which way to jump. They could not be Sadducees because they could not accept Hellenism. Nor could they be Pharisees because they could not support synagogues with the resulting reduction of power of the main Temple. They could not be Essenes because they could not give up worldly power and wealth. Yahweh priests had no choice but to align themselves with the hated governing powers.

"Rome saw its chance to gain influence, and Pompey marched into Israel. Our country passed into Roman hands. The Romans appointed Hyrcanus High Priest of the Temple. After thousands of Jews killed each other no Jew was fit to lead. The chosen people decimated our own population. Without tolerance, we withered.

"I am old. My seasons exceed eighty. I enter the unknown valley of death, having seen more than enough blood and tears. Romans are cruel taskmasters, but keep us from each others' throats. If there is a kind God, I yearn to meet him. I have kept the family records throughout this turbulent period. I have done my duty. I, Amos bid the world farewell."

***

"My name is Tahath, last surviving son of Amos. Like a boiling kettle filled with vile things, Israel continues to build pressure. The Romans are ruthless. Jews burst the Roman bonds periodically with deadly results. Religious and political Jewish factions are an endless whirl wind of merging, separations, and murder. No man of any race or belief is safe in Judea today.

"When Pompey seized Israel, the Roman Empire faced its own civil war, its rough democracy destroyed. Julius Caesar was a rising star with Rome so corrupt the Empire barely stood. Their descendants lost the love of country held by sturdy Roman farmers. Pompey seized Israel in his name, not that of Rome. I was thirty before Julius Caesar defeated him at Pharsala which placed Judea under the control of a stabilized Roman State. Julius Caesar became Emperor of Rome's holdings.

"Judea at this time was ruled indirectly by Antipater. His son, Herod, clawed to power when I was forty. Shrewd, he sought official appointment over Judea. He anticipated that Octavian, adopted son of Julius Caesar, would gain Rome following the assassination of Julius Caesar. His judgment correct, Herod was appointed King of the Jews.

"However, nothing was simple in the cesspool of Judea. One son of the old Maccabean line still lived: Antigonus. Antigonus appealed to Parthia, a resurgent state of Persia, for help in resisting Rome. Backed by Parthia, he held off the Romans and Herod for nearly three years. Then Antigonus fell and Herod took power. Herod killed anyone perceived as a threat. A shameless vassal of Rome and a scourge of the Jews, he also worked tirelessly to beautify Jerusalem and restore order. In poor harvest years he forgave taxes, an unknown concession. Above all, King Herod built the shining Temple in Jerusalem where Jews could worship their fierce Yahweh.

"The Temple showed Greek influence: seven hundred fifty feet square on a side, with bronze doors seventy five feet high, twenty four feet wide, with surrounding marble columns. Wealth and craftsmanship beyond measure were spent; still, Jewish people hated Herod for being a gentile and even worse, a great admirer of Greece. Jews rejoiced at his death, but our future was black. We remained divided. Each party claimed to hold the truth, murdering to gain advantage. I will not repeat the major schisms fracturing our tiny country. I merely add that another major party has formed: Zealots, extreme nationalists desiring Jewish independence.

"The common Judean people suffered under taxes for the Temple, local government, the local king, and the Roman state. Laws penetrated daily life: what a man ate, where he lived, whom he married, how far he could travel, and hundreds more took his liberty. No matter how hard he worked he was barely allowed to live. If he fell behind, he and his family were sold into slavery, as likely to end up bought by a Jew as a Roman. Desperate peoples' dream of a Savior was strong.

"In the main, Romans practice religious tolerance, allowing their conquered freedom of worship. Intolerance offends them. Romans are pragmatic, their feet solidly on the earth, hands solidly on their famous short swords. Rome strives to keep us from killing each other, to achieve the Pax Romana.

"Rome has additional reasons to worry about Judea. To the East lies Parthia which Romans have met in battle many times, always failing to vanquish it. Jews have been willing to join the Parthions. Thus Judea is a gateway for Parthia to threaten the larger Roman Empire. The growing idea of a Jewish "Savior" smacks of revolution to Romans on the lookout for dangerous figures. Judea presents a problem to Rome. I sense a coming bloodbath. Rome feels the same.

"I have been a merchant, able to travel and prosper. I fear for my four children by my faithful wife Shara. I gave them a good Jewish and Greek education, and all were informed of our family records. I also gave them wealth. Soon I shall pass the way of all flesh. Farewell from Tahath."

Stein sat back for his usual post section rumination. Then he gasped. His eye had fallen on the following words shimmering in the lamplight:

Mary of the tribe of Moses
The mother of Jesus known as the Christ

Stein shook. He'd come to Mary, believed by millions to be the mother of God made flesh. Tides of awe chilled the archaeologist, even as sweat glistened on his forehead.

Chapter Twenty-seven

David Roth cursed. He'd been on the phone for hours to learn more about these Jesus Tablets without learning much. Finally, he'd been assured the President would call shortly, the first positive news since the "Jesus Speech." The President supported Israel so Roth remained his ally. Even Israeli experts couldn't agree as to why Straihorn did what he did. Mossad knew nothing about the Jesus Tablets. The Prime Minister ordered a full report by day's end. At that moment his intercom delivered the message that Father Tobenhien from the Vatican had arrived.

As Tobenhien strode in Roth sized up the big, black-garbed man. He stood, offered his hand, and motioned for the rawboned Jesuit to take a seat. The two looked at each other. Roth felt he confronted a military veteran, one who'd been in hard places and survived. Yet there was a smart, humorous glint in the priest's eye.

Tobenhien opened the conversation. "Prime Minister, I'm not here to waste time. I'm here to tell you Israel faces great danger because of these Jesus Tablets. I have full authority from the Vatican. Please, we mustn't indulge in games. We've already read each other's files. Shall we agree to concentrate on the Jesus Tablets?"

The Prime Minister asked him to proceed.

"Thank you. We know about their contents, an eye witness history of Israel from Moses through Jesus. As a primary source, they show Jewish and Christian religions as based on myths alone. This will not only convince scholars, but most everybody else. It will prove Moses was a runaway slave who deceived a tribe of savages who evolved into the Jewish Nation. There are no miracles, no talks with God, no special divine promises. Moses will be revealed as a beneficent charlatan. There was no Exodus or Conquest of the Promised Land. Jews will be revealed to first be victims of, then perpetuators of, lies. This will destroy your Israel's moral base. America will slowly withdraw support. The Palestinian underground will gain power.

"The Jesus Tablets also contain writing by the hands of Jesus and Mary. Jesus will be revealed as pathetic, suffering mental illness, no longer to be seen as the resurrected Son of God. The Vatican is prepared to do anything to help you destroy these Tablets. President Straihorn knows this. We are convinced he's mad enough to do anything and will base our actions accordingly."

Roth listened with the demeanor of a seasoned commander. Father Tobenhien was telling the truth. The Prime Minister leaned forward and asked, "Do you have confirming information besides your source?"

"Our informant is reliable."

"How can Israel be sure of this threat?"

"Authorize a Judaic scholar to evaluate the Tablets on site and report back. Your government can assess its risk and plan to demolish the Tablets without implicating Israel or the Vatican."

The Prime Minister pondered. "Would the Vatican agree to leave all operational decisions to us?"

"The Vatican prefers to be an active consultant with me representing it. Operational details would remain with you as long as the Tablets are on your soil. The danger to the Vatican is too great to allow a less active position."

"That's reasonable. If you're correct my government will agree."

Tobenhien felt a frisson of victory. Israel would ally with the Vatican.

The Prime Minister said, "President Straihorn will call me within hours. We'll see what importance he gives these Jesus Tablets."

Tobenhien felt this a good time to add, "We are well aware of your country's dependence on American support. Perhaps blame for the Tablet's loss can be assigned to other parties."

This intrigued Roth. Perhaps it could be done. "Do you know Dr. Isaac Gold of the Israeli Institute of Antiquities?"

Father Tobenhien brightened. "Of course, Gold is highly respected in academic circles. Eminently suitable. Adopt a slow-down strategy to serve two goals. First, to reduce public attention on Sepphoris. The longer actual movement of the Tablets can be delayed the less interest in them. Second, provide your people time to plan. Israel should have legal means this foot dragging can be accomplished."

Prime Minister Roth had to admire the Jesuit's canniness. A questionable ally, but the two shared a mutual enemy. Isaac Gold would appraise the Tablets objectively. The Prime Minister coolly considered his options. "Perhaps, you would dine with me this evening? Allow me time to talk to our friend Straihorn, then we can review our choices."

Tobenhien took the pawn. "Delighted. Does 7:00 p.m. suit you?"

The Prime Minister rose, extending his large hand. "A driver will pick you up."

***

Nearly three hours had passed. The man in the Oval Office had savored every minute. Being so elevated that dozens studied his every action twenty-four hours a day overjoyed him. Night was absolute best. He checked his watch, almost time to call Roth. He reviewed his latest intelligence report. So the Catholic Church knew more than he'd thought. Well, the Vatican was an old adversary with a long reach. *What a game! 'How much does the Church think I know? Do they know I know it all? How would they react if they knew I hold the verbatim discussion held between the Prime Minister and Father Tobenhien?* For two million dollars an Israeli citizen betrayed her country. He smiled, so little for a country, yet so much for an individual. Every organization had its Judases. One only has to ferret them out.

He liked the wandering Israeli Prime Minister, a worthy opponent. Pressing his intercom, he instructed his aide to get Roth on the line. While he waited for the call he took a long draw on his cigar, clouding the air around him. He slid into that mellow mood he often experienced when the game picked up, everything proceeding perfectly.

President Straihorn spoke smoothly as the two initially exchanged pleasantries. The Israeli got down to business first.

"Can you tell me about these Jesus Tablets? My people know next to nothing about them."

Straihorn grinned. "Basically, what I know was in my speech. Of course, I haven't read the translations yet because we don't have them. These Tablets have created quite a stir. Overwhelming, really. Pressure to bring the kids and Tablets home is staggering."

"Mr. President, we are apprehensive that the Tablets might affect religious beliefs among us and others. What are your views?"

The President voiced appropriate surprise and concern. "Frankly, I don't think too much on religious stories. We'd like to transport the kids with the Tablets in two to three weeks with Israel providing security. This should give time for the arrangements."

"Israel will assist you, of course, but you must see the pressure on me to be sure these Tablets pose no threat to Israel."

"How can we relieve you of some of that?"

"Allow an Israeli scholar, Isaac Gold, access to the Tablets to validate their authenticity and contents. This would let me knowledgeably address my government. Of course, Israel will provide security during transport of the Tablets. After all, they're on our soil."

"No problem with you sending Gold to inspect on site. But, no Tablets leave Sepphoris under any circumstances. Once the Tablets are in the United States, international scholars will have access to them. It's nearly impossible for me to delay their movement for more than three weeks. Assign your scholar now. He'll have full access. However, no entry into the camp by Israeli forces. The site is leased to Harvard. Everything found there is Harvard's property. The United States Ambassador is going to Sepphoris with a Marine guard assigned to her, more than capable of protecting internal site security. We'll work fully with your government. We expect quid pro quo."

Roth spoke with deliberation, "Of course, I reiterate Israel's goal is to cooperate in protecting and transporting the Tablets. I do ask for assurance that I can communicate directly with you if questions arise?"

"Call at any time. I didn't mean to sound hard-nosed, but you understand what I'm up against. Our two countries have mutual interests and we certainly want nothing to jeopardize that."

A politician for too many years not to understand the standard threat before a kiss, Roth replied, "I'll need to avail myself of your time and information to ensure my government understands."

"Understood, Prime Minister, and please be so kind as to send my regards to your wife."

"I'll do that, Mr. President, and mine to the First Lady."

Nothing felt right to Roth. The President knew more than he was telling. The Prime Minister pressed a button and said, "Tell intelligence I want an analysis with video and audio of this conversation within one hour."

In a short time he had it. All agreed the President had lied concerning the Jesus Tablets. On the other hand, analysis of Father Tobenhien had come up clear. Experts quickly added that the proposed alliance with Israel was only a matter of convenience. Distasteful for Israel to ally herself with the Catholic Church, hazardous to contest the United States.

Israel couldn't afford a weak position. The Tablets must be assessed soon, access to them exploited to the maximum. Ike Gold was also a longtime friend. Roth sighed. Time to call him.

***

By now Stein waxed nostalgic for the simple pressures of chairing his department at Harvard. At Sepphoris, interruptions slowed his reading. Persistent reporters and resourceful international news corporations had contacted Harvard requesting more on site cooperation. Stein received directives to be available to journalists. Harvard needed research grants. The Harvard president archly mentioned that the Archaeology Department would, of course, be the leading candidate for any funds raised. During daylight hours Stein studied, then made himself accessible for interviews. Sepphoris put reporters up as guests with cots in the student and laborer quarters.

On top of this mess of claims, theories, and fears, an Israeli scholar might be coming to inspect the Tablets. When Stein protested that he hadn't been given adequate time to study them in peace, he was told the order came from the President. Stein lost control over Sepphoris, infuriated that while he studied the most important discovery of modern times, he also had to play host and storyteller. He snapped at Alice when she interrupted to say the United States Ambassador to Israel had arrived.

A distinguished, if slightly disheveled woman glided into the office just ahead of Alice. "Dr. Stein. I've heard so much about you and your remarkable discovery!"

"I'm pleased to meet you, Ambassador, even though it's under such hectic circumstances. How may we serve you?"

"I have a letter from your Harvard president setting it all out. I look forward to working with you and the Doctors Cross." The Ambassador smiled, extending a one page letter on Harvard letterhead.

The letter instructed Stein to house the Ambassador and answer all questions she might have. Marines assigned as the Ambassador's security would guard the Tablets twenty-four hours a day. The United States wanted American troops guarding the Tablets, and that was only possible under laws granting protection of the Ambassador. Stein should expect an Israeli scholar soon, to be allowed access to the Tablets with all cooperation. Under no circumstances were the Tablets to be removed from Sepphoris. Stunned, Stein sank into his chair.

The perceptive ambassador spoke in almost maternal tones. "I know this is unexpected, but I assure you the Tablets and your protection is all President Straihorn wants. I'm here to serve and see no mistakes are made in communication. I have no expertise in archaeology. I'll try to stay out of your way. Nevertheless, I am authorized to ask questions and receive answers based on our country's needs."

Stein studied her earnest face. "Please sit down, Madam Ambassador. I haven't finished the Tablets, but I'll answer what I can."

"I have only a question or two right now. President Straihorn wants to know whether in your opinion the Tablets are valid, and will have serious effects on religion in America."

Stein appreciated how this graceful woman went straight to the critical heart of the matter. "I'm not ready to give any final impressions, but I will say all indications are that these Tablets are legitimate. As matters now stand, they'll have a devastating impact on organized religion and individual faith."

The Ambassador absorbed this. "You may be under the impression that diplomats dislike direct answers, but we appreciate frankness since we hear so little of it. Are you saying the Jesus Tablets support the view that Jewish and Christian belief systems are myth based?"

"Yes. For better or worse these Jesus Tablets have the potential to change our world."

"I was afraid that's what you'd say." She sighed. "Alice tells me I'll have a room here. My officer in charge will handle security. The United States government will protect you, your people, and the Tablets."

Stein said, "Thank you."

Chapter Twenty-eight

Not many miles to the East, Amal the Fawn perused new maps and orders. This wasn't a suicide mission or it would have ended with Islamic prayers of encouragement. Nevertheless, her life would be spent sooner or later. She prayed to be up to the sacrifice.

No longer eager to die in the Palestinian cause, she knew that killing has little romance. Her Palestinians used bullets and bombs because they lacked cruise missiles, bombers, artillery, or fighter jets. However, nothing could be more dangerous than a trained killer ready to die to succeed. This was a three day mission. Amal had the time because General Kessler was at staff meetings in Tel Aviv for the next nine days. However, she would have to traverse twenty heavily patrolled miles, set up her hide, and then make two difficult shots. A single shot is often lost in the surprise attack. Two shots give away the sniper's general location. Fortunately, Amal carried both a special device and a survival plan.

She would travel at night crossing rolling hills and narrow valleys. The long-barreled Russian Dragunov was hard to conceal. Night travel had its own perils. Patrols assumed anyone out after dark was an enemy. Her liberty papers would be worthless if she were captured then. No one picks flowers in darkness.

Sepphoris sat on a hill. Normally snipers like to be above their targets, the sun behind their backs, using the last half hour of light for their shot. That's when winds are calmest and hit probability highest. Israeli commanders would search toward the west, expecting the killer to want just that. Amal wouldn't be there. Commanders might also suspect a northern position because Nazareth, a Palestinian village permitted by the Israelis to survive for propaganda reasons, was only five miles from Sepphoris. However, she picked a southern position. That decided, Amal bent, frowning with intense concentration over her maps.

***

Cardinals from disparate countries had been in closed session in the Vatican for two days, the Pope unable to brief them on Father Tobenhien's clandestine mission to Israel. If this collusion between the Church and Jews were known, scandal would erupt. The Pope did inform the Cardinals that the Jesus Tablets could endanger all they held dear. All the Pope could say was that the Church was doing everything possible and now the matter must remain in God's hands. This was poor consolation to Cardinals used to assuming active roles.

Jesuits were well represented among them, but so were members of Opus Dei, a conservative faction with two thousand ordained and eighty thousand fanatic lay members. With control over the Church's finances, Opus Dei was no puppet force. Deadly enemies of Jesuits, whom they deemed traitors, Opus Dei members followed a strict chain of command, most little more than robots. Opus Dei's power lay in recruiting politicians and entrepreneurs. Any action that protected the Church was justified. Opus Dei had killed before, and would again.

***

In a heavily guarded Jerusalem suburb, Prime Minister Roth and the Jesuit General spent a pleasant evening in fruitful conversation. Israel readied to act as soon as the dependably objective Isaac Gold validated the Tablets. Tobenhien assured his host that the Church would leave all operational matters to Israel. However, he reiterated that the Vatican felt released from that commitment if Israelis failed to destroy the Tablets in Israel. Exact details of the mission would be left to Mossad. Political deniability was essential for both parties.

***

North of Jerusalem a grizzled Isaac Gold smoked a cigarette, gazing out over a dusty dig covering nearly thirty acres known as the Et-Tell, formerly Ai. In the book of Joshua 8:28, Joshua "burnt Ai and made it a heap forever." He grimaced. Forever is a long time. The past has its way of intruding. Gold sucked in another drag. A jackal barked from the far end of the site. He smiled; jackals would outlive humanity. Humans were too aggressive to survive long.

Isaac Gold shared much with that jackal. He, too, had survived many trials. Born in 1916 near Salzburg, Germany, to a middle-class Jewish mother, he never knew his father who was killed during the Great War. He did know his father was awarded the Iron Cross for bravery in the Kaiser's army. His mother hated wars and believed another would break out. While Hitler slithered his way to power, her anxiety rose as orchestrated anti-Semitism menaced Jews.

So brilliant that despite his being Jewish instructors gave him high marks, Isaac Gold possessed the rigorous analytical mind German scholarship was famous for. But with Hitler's rise his mother perceived her bright son would never finish a higher education. She sold everything to send him to an aunt in Norway. Penniless, she and his sister fled to a cousin's farm in Lithuania.

In 1941, he lost contact with them. After the war he learned the Jewish community was murdered along with two thousand five hundred others by Einsatzkommando 3 at Zarasai. His Norwegian aunt died in 1942. With some Norwegians, he reached England in a small boat. Hearing no word from his family, he volunteered to fight Nazis. Gifted in languages and rapidly fluent in English, he analyzed intercepted intelligence reports. Untangled countless cryptic German memos finally explained the meaning of the unthinkable Final Solution. He flicked one cigarette away, and his hands shook slightly as he lit another smoke, never able to kick the chain smoking habit developed in those days.

His British superiors wouldn't believe the systematic slaughter of hundreds of thousands in Eastern Europe. He failed to convince them for months. Finally, Russian armies pushed across Poland and confirmed the unbelievable. The world learned a new German word, Vernichtungslager, extermination camps. Polish towns such as Treblinka, Belsec, Sibibor, Chelmno, and Auschwitz became infamous. He hadn't been accurate enough.

Convinced Jews would never be safe without their own homeland, he became a secret agent for Zionists, transferred to British-controlled Palestine. There he transmitted secret intelligence to various underground Jewish nationalists fighting the British, but in the Zionist intelligence division his Jewish nationalism began to crack.

He learned of plans to displace Arabs in Palestine. These horrors seemed too similar to German tactics to rest easily on his conscience. Leaving the underground service, he became personal secretary to a refugee scholar who specialized in ancient Semitic languages. The old scholar dedicated his life to writing a dictionary of the Old Akkadian language. In under a year his employee mastered Akkadian. In less than two he reached proficiency in Hebrew and Aramaic. Within three years young Gold made original contributions to studies of these ancient languages. In record time the aged scholar's dream project reached publication. Grateful, he contacted those who could see his protégé granted a formal education. Sponsored by a wealthy Swiss Jew, Ike Gold found himself at Cambridge.

Within a year of his arrival he authored seminal works in prestigious journals of ancient language studies, the first undergraduate ever published in them. His star rose so blindingly Orientists the world over noted it. Within three years he earned his Ph.D. in ancient Middle East languages. He'd just started. He obtained his doctorate in Mid-Eastern archaeology. Interest in religious belief led to another Ph.D. in clinical psychology. The young Jew nicknamed Ike was now the internationally respected Dr. Isaac Gold. In Israel, he found employment with the growing Department of Jewish Antiquities. He was one of the first to openly doubt the official line of biblical history, an unwelcome position in Israel. Dr. Gold never insulted or offended, only posed difficult questions. The lack of reasonable answers began to chip away at belief structures. His inquiries affected archaeology.

Gold's questions stimulated a young undergraduate student at Harvard, Sam Stein, to also question established order. Gold cautiously backed young Stein who laid his ax to sacred trees of Palestinian archaeology. They become close friends. Gold's suppression drove Stein harder to expose myths of biblical archaeology.

No amount of humility could conceal Gold's brilliance. Awarded international and Israeli honors, he befriended David Roth. Occasionally the two spent an evening in lively discussions over local wine. The old man smiled at how much they had in common, each often taking a circular route to arrive safely where he wished.

The world was aflame over these Jesus Tablets. He knew the Israeli government would soon call him. Stein must be sitting on a bomb. Who would've dreamed the young firebrand would now be chairman of Harvard archaeology? The distant jackal barked again, a high, desperate sound. Gold would know soon enough.

His thin jacket protected him poorly in evening air so near Jerusalem, high and cool. How ignorant the world was about this area. Gold sauntered toward his old sedan. He felt the Jesus Tablets might be his most compelling subject. His glowing cigarette arced in the night sky as he flicked it away. The jackal and the earth fell silent.

Chapter Twenty-nine

The earth is flat, and anyone who disputes this claim is an atheist who deserves to be punished.
Sheik Abdel-Aziz ibn Baaz, Saudi Arabia's supreme religious authority, 1993-1999

The doctrine of the double motion of the earth about its axis and about the sun is false, and entirely contrary to Holy Scripture.
Congregation of the Index (of Prohibited Books), 1616 under Pope Paul V

Prime Minister Roth worked through copious paperwork. Besides the Jesus

Tablets, innocuous matters also needed attention. Glancing at the clock, he noted Heinz was due in ten minutes. Mossad's long arm could provide more information. He frowned. How little glamour lay in nation leading. He'd worked so hard to reach this position, imagining all he had to say was, "Do it," and the task would be finished. Not the reality. Often he had to base life and death decisions on blurred facts. Weapons, armies, and even nations could be hamstrung because of failure to have intelligence agents in right places at right times. Without accurate knowledge of an enemy's intent, billions in equipment was rendered blind and useless.

Mr. Heinz was announced, "Mr. Heinz" the agreed title for the head of Mossad. A wiry olive-skinned man wearing sunglasses entered. "Have a seat, Heinz." Roth gestured to a leather chair.

"Thank you, Prime Minister." The man's voice registered metallic. Efficient, seldom seen by anyone in politics, Roth's head of intelligence preferred to receive orders and send assessments by courier. The Prime Minister only asked that information be good with no acts traceable to the government. Ever courteous, Heinz never raised his voice, and never removed the sunglasses. Although Roth was an experienced soldier, this dark little man unsettled him... like chatting with a cobra.

To snap himself out of this discomfort the Prime Minister asked, "What do we have on the Sepphoris situation?"

Heinz opened a black briefcase, removing one sheet of paper. "Would you prefer to read it yourself or should I read it to you? It's all we have at the moment."

"You read. I'll concentrate," the Prime Minister answered.

Heinz began, "We have agents throughout the United States, Europe, and Israel working on the Sepphoris case. An archaeological discovery there was covered up by a Dr. Henry Cross, the site superintendant. His wife Alice also knew of the discovery, being the translator. Samuel Stein, Chair of the archaeology Department of Harvard University was informed of the discovery by an elementary cryptic phrase in open international fax. Our agents were able to get a copy of the fax without compromising Stein's secretary. We have an agent at Harvard close to Stein's secretary who recalled the date Stein flew to Israel.

"We suspect, but have yet to confirm, that President Straihorn was told of the Jesus Tablets by a Pastor Steward of Atlanta, Georgia. Our agents traced Steward to an unscheduled private flight. To date we've not determined its destination. An Arab student whose family was eliminated for anti-Israeli activities killed Steward in a car bombing. We suspect on orders from Hamas. Interrogation of Palestinian suspects has convinced us they know nothing. Pastor Steward's son, Michael, undoubtedly informed him of the situation. Michael is the homosexual lover of a fellow student, André, nephew of a Baltimore priest. Secretary General Father Tobenhien of the Catholic Jesuits recently visited this uncle. Tobenhien followed that visit with a Papal audience. Therefore, we believe the Catholic Church knew of the Jesus Tablets before President Straihorn's announcement. Of course, Tobenhien also sought his meeting with you.

"The Sepphoris camp is guarded externally by Israeli forces. The Marines assigned to the United States Ambassador are guarding the Cross home with full battle equipment. Penetration is impossible without a major military operation, and the Marines would respond with force. It is, therefore, Mossad's position that the Tablets are extremely dangerous and that President Straihorn understands their value. The Tablets do contain content harmful to Judaism. This cannot be a psychological asset to our nation. Much of Israeli support both internally and externally is based on the concept of the Jews being chosen people. This idea is crucial to our long-term interests. Without it, our political strength will be severely weakened. President Straihorn grows increasingly unpredictable. We suggest we pick up this Michael or this Andre for questioning. Since they're American citizens, we haven't done so without your orders.

"We might destroy the Tablets via a missile or artillery attack blamed on Arab terrorists. It would be easy to supply dead Arabs around the over-run guns. Mossad suggests we also shell our own troops, incurring Israeli sacrifice, but worth it to annihilate the Tablets. Dr. Gold will merely confirm the danger posed by the Tablets. We await your orders."

Prime Minister Roth pondered. This would mean the deaths of American students, Harvard staff, and Israeli soldiers. He took no joy in ordering military action. There were no such things as surgical strikes. Furthermore, there was no guarantee such a strike would destroy the target. Sepphoris was too far inside Israeli borders to be shelled from outside. Thankfully, he had logical reasons to reject this proposal.

"For the present, refrain. Detain no American students or staff. Come up with alternate plans to destroy the Tablets with no fatalities. It's possible they can be held for legal and security reasons without antagonizing America. We need time to plan. Ideally the Tablets could be destroyed after leaving Israel, useful if blamed on Arabs. There'll be no ceiling on funds and manpower for this. I'll contact you after Gold examines the Tablets and talks to me."

Heinz betrayed no emotion. "Very well, Prime Minister. Of course, it's unlikely we can accomplish destruction of such highly guarded items without fatalities, but Mossad will do our best." With a nod of his close-cropped head, he rose and departed.

Roth was reflecting when his intercom announced Dr. Gold. Smiling, the Prime Minister stood to take the elderly man's extended hand as Gold entered. "Good of you to come at such short notice, Isaac."

"It's my great pleasure. I've been expecting your call. This meeting has to concern these Jesus Tablets everyone finds so fascinating?"

"It does indeed. Since time is vital I'll get to the point. You're the most qualified man to evaluate the Tablets. We need to know their impact on Israel. We won't ask you to make policy decisions. That's in other hands. Would you undertake this for Israel and as a favor to me? "

Dr. Gold paused. "How much time would I have? You may be expecting more than anyone can deliver."

"As I understand it, you're a friend of Harvard's Stein. Do you feel comfortable with his opinions?"

"Certainly. I've known Sam Stein for years. His integrity is beyond question. I wouldn't hesitate to accept his basic findings."

"Israel needs to know the Tablets' contents and your predictions as to their effect. Dr. Stein is undoubtedly studying those same questions. We hope your relationship will speed your evaluation. While we realize the value the discovery undoubtedly has for the scholastic community, our concern is political. Will you help us?"

"David, I can tell you right now, if these writings are a history of ancient Israel, they will affect Judeo-Christians. Religion is emotionally loaded, thriving without proof. The basic Jewish and Christian stories carry spiritual value, but aren't history. This has been no secret among modern scholars.

"Religion correctly understood is only a hope. Unfortunately many assert they possess absolute certainty, and this can drive the believer into dangerous behavior. Martyrdom, for example. People deprived of their foundational belief system typically display despair which can lead to suicide or antisocial behavior. The social fabrics of entire civilizations can unravel. Economies crumble. History records many such cases. I assume these are the government's concerns?"

"Exactly. We need you. Will you take a look at these Tablets, consult with Stein, and give us your honest opinion?"

"I will. But leave me out of the politics. No paperwork and bureaucratic nonsense. I'm too old for hassles."

The Prime Minister grinned. "Everything will be taken care of. Call me if you have any problems."

The old man stood. They shook hands again, and Ike Gold turned to begin his journey.

Chapter Thirty

Stein sat in the study having just completed the Mary and Jesus writings. His heart pounded. He'd never dreamed of anything this stupendous. However, his role was limited. He sent for the Ambassador who joined him in fifteen minutes.

"Ambassador, you said you prefer frank discussions. I've finished my preliminary study. The Tablets are historically valid, presenting no problems of translation. Potentially, they're the most important archaeological discovery found to date. The basic contents are a history of ancient Palestine, written and preserved by one family continuously for over eleven hundred years. They include a firsthand account from Mary the mother of Jesus and a brief section from the hand of Jesus. They also describe the early Christian movement.

He described the Mary revelations, then said to the astounded Ambassador Morgenstern, "The political arena is yours, but the quicker these Tablets are in the United States the better for everyone."

The Ambassador paused. Her voice shook slightly when she said, "Dr. Stein, thank you. I'll convey your information immediately. The President has promised safe transport of the Tablets. Unless ordered to do otherwise, I'll stay with them; my presence is the only way to validate the Marine guards. Technically, they're guarding me, but since I'm with the Tablets, it's one and the same. Time is critical, so I'll get to the communication part now." In minutes the Ambassador rejoined him reporting that the President expressed delight. Every effort would be made to speed the process. Stein's instinct told him danger still encircled them.

***

President Straihorn sat in the midnight darkness of the Oval Office, pleased with the Israeli situation, the news better than hoped for. Possessing the Jesus Tablets crowned all his dreams.

He would finally crush the smug Christians with their so-called "family values." He would finally control the Jews with their grasp on the mass media. Gradually the United States could distance itself from Israel and grow closer to the Arab nations who controlled needed oil. Without U. S. support, Israel would have to negotiate with the displaced Palestinians.

The Catholic Church would be crippled when the world realized Mary was just another woman. Hypocritical Bible thumpers would find their Jesus wasn't the God of middle class dreams. What a game! He pressed a button on his desk. In a few moments the door opened and closed behind a buxom young woman. She approached the desk with a stiff smile, her first time to service him. With a wave of impatience he signaled her to come closer.

***

In Israel, Stein opened the study door to greet Isaac Gold. The old friends embraced, laughing in joy at their reunion. "Tell me, Sam, what is it you Harvard brains have discovered? It seems to have created quite a stir!" Isaac Gold said, finding a seat on the couch.

Stein sobered. "It's astounding. A bigger discovery I can't imagine, so big the ramifications scare me."

"Sam, let's get a couple of things on the table. The Tablets' fate is not in our hands. You're in the hands of your government, while I'm in the hands of mine. We're scholars, old friends. We must be sane even if all around us go mad."

"You're right, Isaac. The Tablets are authentic firsthand writings for over eleven hundred years. I've made every effort to cross-check the Tablets to Alice Cross's translations and I'm satisfied with them, but the truth may kill us all."

An odd smile broke out on Dr. Gold's face. "Everybody dies, Sam. Not everyone gets to die after working on such a discovery. Who doesn't hold hopes, fears, and dreams of a life after death? Unfortunately, these are only fears, dreams, and hopes. When people confuse the unproved with the proved bad things happen. Maybe it's time the human race lets go of fairy tales, implausible stories. Maybe it's time for us scholars to actually talk to those outside our world. We have to allow politicians their games. After all, they have the guns. Yet, we're responsible to the truth. I've avoided that responsibility. Maybe the old man in the sky is giving us another chance. What do you think, Sam?"

Stein looked at his old mentor. True enough. Scholars had withdrawn into their ivory towers, invented their own vocabulary, and established private publications. Safe behind walls, they advanced knowledge but failed in the greater task of sharing it, like neglectful parents who never bothered to educate their children. Science had advanced, but the masses were still steeped in superstition. Could they go to their graves knowing they negated the efforts of centuries?

"You're right, of course. We'll do our duty. As citizens we'll let our elected leaders do their jobs. If they fail, we'll do ours as best we can. Start with Alice's translation and examine the Tablets. I'll assist any way I can. Can I get you anything?"

"Not a thing, Sam. Let me get right to it."

Thus a pair of scholars made that timeless and dangerous commitment to tell the truth. In a world that values profit, comfort, and power over veracity, such a commitment is no minor thing. It is also true that the story of the Jesus Tablets reveals the price of courage is often tragedy.

Chapter Thirty-one

Twenty miles east, Amal hoisted her heavy backpack and rifle. Her fears faced, having planned and prayed well, she now focused on her mission. She'd memorized the unnamed faces. Next time she saw them, they'd be within her sniper scope's field of view. Hopefully, their deaths would bring Palestinian victory closer. Her targets and destiny waited at Sepphoris.

She must cover twenty miles before first light, penetrate the Israeli stronghold to within six hundred meters of her kill zone, and by dawn prepare a hide good enough to escape detection all day by several hundred Israeli soldiers. If all went well she'd kill her targets thirty minutes before dark, then escape. If her targets didn't appear, she'd wait another twenty-four hours. She needed food. Most of the weight she carried was water, camouflage, folding shovel, and binoculars. She also carried an electrical device that might give her the edge needed to escape.

Mile after mile slid under her nearly soundless strides. She made compass readings, taking bearings off lights from villages and highways. Every sense was alive to a sound or movement. Lessened concentration could mean death.

Stealthily, she crossed highways and secondary roads. Finally the lights of Iksal appeared on her right, those of Nazareth to the north. Amal knew nothing of Nazareth's historical importance. She knew little about Jesus except that he was important to Christians. All she knew of Christians was they were infidels who worshipped three gods, a mixture of father, son, and some sort of Holy Ghost. How could people believe that three beings could be one being? The Christian story that their God had impregnated a mortal woman who gave birth to another God horrified Amal. There was only one God, Allah, indivisible.

To believe God would copulate with a woman was blasphemy; worshipping Jesus, the result of this infamous union beyond understanding. Allah, who gave wisdom even to uneducated peasant girls, would punish such fools. Amal shifted the pack on her weary shoulders and murmured a prayer before continuing her murderous path.

By the stars, she had fewer than three hours until dawn. She would soon see the lights of Sepphoris. In one hour she must find a place to lie up. In twenty minutes she spotted the camp a mile away. Carefully she skirted south to be on a finger ridge that gave her a level shot across a small valley to the Sepphoris camp plateau. After traversing several hundred meters she heard voices above on the crest of the ridge, Israeli soldiers complacently waiting for daylight. Amal quietly moved on. Stars in the eastern sky winked out. She had to find her hiding place soon. Amal crawled into dense cover on the finger ridge's north side. Finally, creeping under the low cover of her netting, she placed her pack and rifle in a stable location. Sepphoris lay six hundred meters north. Having accomplished the first step, she drank deep of her water. No need to carry that heavy pack again. Sepphoris slept. Death could wait a little longer.

***

Dr. Gold leaned back in the sturdy old wooden chair after a long night. He snuffed out another cigarette, the ashtray loaded with crumpled butts. Lighting another he reflected his reading.

Not devout, to Gold faith was just a popular word for lack of evidence. Although the idea of God was useful as a first cause there were logic issues. The child's question as to who made God remained a valid stumbling point for the astute. Even assuming God's existence didn't solve major questions such as was God interested in individuals? God could be a remote creator, not the guardian angel many imagined. The God so many called personal kept silent. So many religious themes resulted from dreams, visions, or bodiless voices. Could these emerge from the subconscious? Much religious literature was written by people fasting or who'd experienced long periods of hardship. Modern science proved visions, trances, and hidden voices could be induced by lack of sleep, food, or sensory deprivation. Could this explain the fasting Jesus' so-called temptations in the desert?

It was so human to believe ourselves God's highest creation. Only vanity? Misfortune struck with an even hand across social, racial, age, and economic classes. Blind chance described reality. Perhaps God did exist, but placed no higher value on a cancer cell than on a human child. Perhaps God didn't take a personal interest in any creation. Such a truth might be uncomfortable, but a lifetime of study had shown Gold many uncomfortable truisms. God had permitted millions to die of diseases in ages past who could be treated by modern medicine today. Wasn't that evidence God refused to act in those cases?

Eli's Moses rang truer than the biblical one. Moses of the Jesus Tablets was a great leader who formed a great people and led them out of a wilderness. Unfortunately, he had to use deceit, superstition, and raw force to civilize his followers. Gold took another long draw on his cigarette. Leaders today used similar tools. Perhaps realists are always rare, but clearer vision enables their rise to leadership. Most place higher value on comfort than on seeking often painful truth. It takes special courage to face the void of limitless mystery. Moses of the Jesus Tablets had that courage.

Isaac Gold rested his cigarette on the ashtray's rim. Clearly the Torah and the Old Testament would be discredited, full ramifications unpredictable. Only the extent of the damage remained in question.

***

Amal watched the sky lighten, Sepphoris coming to life. Laborers and students going to their various digging and sifting sites covered the hill. Amal studied the camp layout against her map. Nothing out of place. She focused her seven-power German Zeiss binoculars on the Cross home where her targets lived and worked. At six hundred meters the building was crystal clear. She studied the soldiers guarding it, puzzled they weren't Israeli. Could these alert men be American? Israelis were above and behind her, unable to see below the lip of hill. Easy to hear their voices when the wind was right. Studying the Cross home, she noted one main door. The strange soldiers were watchful.

Amal slid her sniper rifle into position and extended its bipod. She placed her face behind the rifle scope and focused its optics on the door. With professional attention she adjusted the 10X sniper scope to exactly six hundred meters, her point of aim now the point of the bullet's impact. In a steady prone position, her left hand supported the weapon's rear with a sand-filled sock that allowed raising or lowering her cross hairs with steady control. She went over the essential list of her trade. Her weapon was loaded, the safety on.

She bracketed the door with her rifle scope. At six hundred meters she could easily bisect the door knob in her cross hairs. She closed her eyes for ten seconds, then opened them to see if her body was in a strained position revealed by a new location of the cross hairs. No. The cross hairs still held a natural, relaxed position on the doorknob.

The door swung open. Five people walked onto the patio. Through her scope Amal could easily see the faces of three men and two women. One man was younger, tall, and in working clothes; the first woman, middle- aged, wore an expensive pants suit. The soldiers seemed to pay closer attention to her. The other two men were older, the oldest, with white hair, smoked. Beside him was a stocky male of upper middle age whose thinning hair still contained a great deal of brown. A tall slender woman wore khaki shorts and a sleeveless shirt. Amal compared faces through her rifle scope. As the cross hairs rested on each in turn, Amal studied their features. Yes, she found her two targets. How strange that neither sensed death so very close. Just a slow squeeze of the trigger, and each would spin lifelessly to ground.

This group had no military training at all. They stood without the experienced movements of people who knew danger could appear in a second. Their eyes lacked the hunted look that searched for possible threats and places to take cover. What must it be like, a life so pleasant? Civilians could easily be killed in pairs. Lack of military training typically froze them in shock when a person beside them was killed. This allowed time to kill the stationary second target. Trained soldiers would dive for cover in a millisecond.

The group broke up. The younger man and woman walked out to join workers at the dig. The middle-aged man and the well-dressed woman remained on the porch speaking earnestly. The old man with the white hair flicked his cigarette off the porch and reentered the main office door. Now came the waiting. She prayed and felt Allah's reassuring hand on her shoulder.

***

Dr. Gold reentered the study after some early morning sun with the others. He pressed on. Hour after hour passed as the ashtray filled with crumpled butts. He read all the translations that told of the generations between Eli and Mary. He carefully spot checked the clay tablets themselves finding nothing in error. The writings' plain meanings could not be misunderstood. Here after centuries were Judaic writings not by the upper classes, but loaded with the undeniable ring of integrity. The world at large could easily understand them, a separate objective history of the formation of the Jewish people and religion. He had to remind himself that the Tablets were the problem of American and Israeli governments. Nevertheless, a gnawing presentiment warned that these governments might prove untrustworthy.

Gold had been particularly impressed reading Jahath, a ghost writer of the Torah, who apparently placed contradictions in the first five books of the Bible to signal its fraudulent origin. In one account of the creation the order was plants, animals, then man and woman, in another man, plants, animals, and then woman. In one the number of animals taken on the ark was seven pairs of clean and one pair of unclean animals. However, in another there was only two of each. There were simply too many of these problems to believe one person had written the entire Torah. For example, in Genesis 6:3 God limited the lifespan of humans to one hundred twenty years, yet later in the Torah many lived longer. The Ten Commandments in Deuteronomy had differences from the Ten Commandments in Exodus 20. Most apparent was an entirely different reason for the Sabbath commandment.

The deity was referred to by different names. With painstaking analysis scholars separated the passages by the referent name of the deity and discovered at least three and maybe four stories that could stand alone. These had been skillfully merged to appear written by one author. This discovery was known as the "Documentary Hypothesis." Jahath's efforts to enclose evidence proving the Torah was not by Moses didn't escape scholarly revelation. Many Moses referrals were in third person. Of course, Jahath was right about the improbability of Moses recounting his own death.

The letter J was used for the author who referred to the deity as Yahweh, The letter E for the author who referred to the deity as Elohim or El. The letter P referred to an author safeguarding the interests of the priestly class. The last author, suspected to have written nearly all of Deuteronomy was named D. D used a different terminology from the first three. Using this hypothesis, scholars found patterns and traits establishing at least three authors. The author J, for example, never used the word God with but one exception. The author P used singular words for deity hundreds of times. Likewise the author E showed the same type of pattern.

Seldom did the suspected authors cross over and use the other author names for God. Scholars also noticed the authors' favorite phrases. Individuals had easily identifiable writing styles. P liked the phrase "tribal leader" which he used sixty-seven times while J and E used it only once. D was partial to the phrase "lengthen your days in the land" which he used eleven out of the twelve occurrences in the Torah. Both J and E preferred anthropomorphisms such as God walking, smelling, wrestling and being physically seen by Moses on Sinai. All such descriptions of deity weren't in the more refined priestly concepts of P. Dr. Gold smiled, remembering that the priestly version P never used the words mercy or grace. Perhaps clergy then, like many now, liked to instill fear.

Undoubtedly P was interested in the tabernacle which he mentioned over two hundred times but which was never mentioned by J or D. P didn't like the idea of a person being able to communicate privately with God. P never used angels, talking animals, or dreams. P's purpose lay in persuasion that a priest was required to deal with God. It occurred to Gold that P was the sole source of hierarchical divisions among the clergy. P was probably a member of the Aaron family line since P established that only descendants of Aaron could be priests whereas other suspected authors were clear that all Levites were qualified priests. P reduced other Levites to a lower class clergy. When J, E, P, and D were separated from the Torah each lettered author formed a book that stood alone. This couldn't happen by chance.

The Bible claimed Moses wrote the Torah and if that were wrong, anything else in the Bible was open to question. If not God's word then the Bible was flawed man's. Extreme believers objected that there were no original copies of J, E, P, or D. True, but such believers conveniently overlooked the absence of original copies of their own Bible. They retreated into private church clubs safe from scholastic questions and evidence.

Yet scholarship didn't cease. After the philosophers Hobbes and Spinoza came Reuss, Graf, Vatke, and Wellhausen. Unfortunately the religious didn't welcome light shed on sacred literature, already possessing what they wanted: comfort against the unknown. Faith became a virtue as believers clung to their dogma, truth seeking associated with Satanism. God's silence became license to talk for him.

The Jesus Tablets, a valid archaeological discovery containing writings by one who claimed to be an Old Testament writer, would change everything being by far the best information ever discovered. The authors had no reason to fabricate, and their accounts had been documented by other bits of ancient evidence. The Tablets would be welcomed by scholars and reasonable people. For once the religious detractors would face critical evidence written at the time. Some could close their eyes to the Jesus Tablets, but others would read with theirs wide open.

Dr. Gold had a difficult time understanding religious emotionalism. After all, believers and scholars both professed to respect the truth. Most believed that God would respect the truth and that, in fact, God was the truth. Gold smiled as he remembered what a professor had told him many years ago, "Wisdom is the knowledge of how little one knows." How very true, he thought, taking another draw on his cigarette.

Gold snuffed it out as he moved on to the final translations. His chest tightened as he picked up the narrative.

Chapter Thirty-two

Mary of the tribe of Moses
The mother of Jesus known as the Christ

"My name is Mary, last surviving child of Tahath. I am old and my eyes have cried many tears. My story is long and I do not know how my family history can be continued. All of my children are dead. The Jewish people are conquered, dispersed, and despised. Many Jews openly curse me because I am the mother of Jesus who many believed to be the Messiah. The Greeks called my disturbed son the Christ. I will describe to you the events of my time.

"I write this in my seventy-seventh year, having lost everything I held precious. I cannot understand why I am still in this suffering world. Perhaps that is a foolish sentiment, and no reason exists for anything. The fool and the wise man both face the grave. The young have hopes and dreams while the old face loneliness and death. I am the last of the Eli line, keeper of the family history. War, disease, and death have taken all the rest. Some fought for Israel, and the Romans murdered them. Some fled the land in hopes other countries would give them peace. Many died of diseases the priests and peasants believe are caused by demons. I am alone, an old woman with a quill living in an empty house haunted by memories.

"I write memoirs read by no one. I have only my duty, a cold companion. There is no one to entrust with the family library of twenty long lifetimes. Within the Tablets are the true history of Israel and the Jewish religion. How strange that no one wants the truth. How odd that so many will believe the strangest of fables in the name of God, but not the truth. Perhaps it is because the truth does not always comfort, but is in fact, painful. Sadly, the few who seek truth are often killed. If the authorities knew of these Tablets and their contents, they would kill me. Truth is seldom helpful to governments or religions. I have heard that no man is so hated as he who speaks the truth. As a girl I laughed at this. Now I see its wisdom and weep. Nevertheless, I will tell my story. I make no apology for its length. I hope my ancestors can forgive me for not passing on the library, but I have done my best. It is left to me to tell my story and die.

"I was born in Sepphoris in Galilee to an educated, wealthy merchant and his wife, a kindly woman who lived for him. I have many memories of her devotion to our family, and beautiful singing around the house. I lived an idyllic life until the age of fourteen when, in a three-week period, I lost my father, mother, and three siblings to a sudden disease. I alone recovered.

During that time my mother's sister, who loved me, moved into the family home to care for me. My estate being considerable, I, an eager student received an education. My aunt employed Greek and Hebrew tutors, although Galilean girls rarely even became literate. Judaism is biased against women, apparent in our religious literature. The Greeks and the Romans are much more enlightened and grant women far more rights and freedoms. Their tyrannical God chose not to grant equality to Jewish women, forbidden to take active roles in religious ceremonies. Jewish men often divorced their wives for the slightest of offenses. As a headstrong girl I rebelled against such attitudes by excelling in philosophy, history, and writing. I found great joy in discovering the thoughts of other peoples. By the age of fifteen I was well-read, my education not inferior to any of my age in Sepphoris.

"Romans ruled Galilee as the iron fist inside a Jewish glove of collaborators and proxies. Not intellectual, Romans' love of order stood them in good stead. We Jews, boisterous to govern, constantly divided into intolerant sects. The more a country claims to be religious the less tolerance exists. The all-too-common belief that God is offended by different modes of worship is extensive. Perceived heretics could not survive in Israel. In the name of God, one group would kill another with a ruthlessness that made the most hardened pagan shudder. Community stoning was the most common execution. Even the bloodthirsty Romans disapproved of such a savage death for the trivial offense of religious disagreement.

"The pragmatic Romans insisted their subjects obey the laws, or suffer severe punishments. Those who disapproved of Roman rule often faced death. As God's chosen, Jews justified rebellion against Rome. After all, we alone had the right to rule not only our small country, but the world. Rome called this treason. Jews were a fatal combination of religious fanaticism and single-minded nationalism. I watched it destroy our nation.

"I learned of the family Tablets at the age of twelve. My father believed in maturity gained through adult responsibilities. Under his instruction I read and absorbed the writings my ancestors had preserved for centuries. Young as I was, I recognized the danger posed by this library. Religion was the base of power, our nation built on the belief that God had made a covenant with the Israelites. If that were proved false, the priests would be threatened. Next to agriculture, religion was the largest business in Israel. For their profits from it, the Priests murdered challengers to their authority. Religion gave meaning to being a Jew, a drug that dulled the pain of peasant existence.

"The Jewish religion being based on myth and deception did not surprise me. Impressed since childhood by the practical Romans with their casual disregard of the gods, I had always been a skeptic. Not Jewish, Rome yet ruled the world. My Greek tutors with their cosmopolitan understanding of many religions as well as their rich history of Greek mythology gave me reasons to doubt. I learned that dreams become myths, and when myths are full grown they become religions. However, the Tablets were different. It is one thing to suspect, but quite another to actually know, the truth. Deeply moved, I used to spend days in my father's study carefully reading my ancestors' accounts. To know that the blood of Eli, the escaped slave from Egypt flowed in my veins filled me with wonder. I could never escape feeling these Tablets would somehow move the known world. Even today I feel their power. I am helpless as to what to do. I have prayed for an answer. All is silence. I add my mite and leave fate to the gods whose existence I doubt.

"My life began to change as I approached sixteen, maturing into a strong-willed young woman. My aunt was wise enough to allow me the privileges of adulthood. It became apparent I did not fit the Jewish mold of a subservient woman. I did not accept male authority and particularly rejected community religious authorities. Because of my wealth and social standing elders and rabbis left me to my own devices, no doubt hoping I would later reform.

"My sense of adventure led me in other directions. Beautiful, I found myself drawn to men, associating mostly with well-educated Hellenistic Jews. The orthodox Jewish community with their stifling bigotry held no appeal for me. I rejected their simplistic values. It was not long before my virginity was a thing of the past and I accepted all pleasures of love. Soon, my boldness was used as an example of sinful behavior to other Jewish girls. What hypocrisy. Many sons of leading families wanted access to my bed. Even several leaders whispered that they yearned for my company, much more interested in my physical charms than in giving me religious instruction. Surprisingly, women sometimes sought me, murmuring how they wished they had the courage to change their lives.

"I enjoyed my freedom, wanting no marriage. The only group I avoided was Roman with their oppression of conquered peoples and harsh treatment of Israel. I would have been content to continue so, but, to my own astonishment, I fell in love with Amos, an emotional nineteen-year-old Jew from a well-to-do Hellenistic family. In the beginning he showed no interest in me seeming to think of serious matters at all times. I flirted as young women are wont to do, but he ignored me, undeterred from his mission. In time I learned what that mission was, nothing less than the overthrow of Roman rule in Israel. A nationalist of the highest order, Amos rejected Rome with passion and despised Judaism which he saw as a drug dulling the masses. It took me long to win him. Then I learned what being a true revolutionary meant.

"The most intense, thoughtful person I had known, his loves and hates lay poles apart. On some days his joy knew no bounds, yet other times his dejection blackened beyond the deepest cave. He cherished truth and freedom. A pragmatic planner of violent action, he led a loose web of like-minded Galileans. They met in secret to strategize, thorns in Roman paws. Roman patrols were ambushed, supply depots burned, and influential Jewish collaborators killed. This Jewish resistance caused a steady flow of blood in Galilee, and the Romans placed no limits on efforts to stamp out resisters.

"Amos killed men, yet I saw him weep before a plucked flower doomed to die. Sophisticated, well-read, he could not see that his imagined world could never be maintained. Frighteningly devoted to duty, he was fully prepared to die for Israel's freedom, blind to the fact that the Jews, divided into countless factions, were incapable of self-government.

"Still, he was the bravest, most dedicated man I have ever known, his God far beyond the human God figure normally imagined. To Amos, God was not a man writ large nor did God have the passions with which we embellish our deities. To Amos, God was in the laws of nature and reason. The God of Amos could never be contained in any book or parchment. His God set honesty above piety. Amos believed that God could only be worshiped by seeking truth. Freedom was his Temple, and truth the only thing he bowed to. Amos did not just talk about freedom, but killed and ultimately died for it. Many evenings I listened to him speak passionately of a time when men could think and speak their opinions without fear. Many times I held his hand and tried to temper the heat of his mental flames, but to no avail. Not for him the ability to be moderate. He could not be lulled by worldly pleasures, convinced it was the duty of the intelligent to lead and protect. Amos was a great man, also a paradox too large for us. He dreamed of peace, but waged war. He lived and died for a world that never was nor ever could be. In time Amos became my lover though I knew he could never be a normal husband. However, love is not rational. As long as he lived, I loved and held him.

"Amos was the father of my son Jesus who later in his own troubled life would be known as the Christ.

"My pregnancy scandalized Sepphoris. I became even more of an object lesson to orthodox maidens. I cared not, honored to bear a child for such a man. I supported Amos' decision not to marry until Israel swept the Romans away. It was standard Roman policy to confiscate all property of a known revolutionary and sell his family into slavery. Amos would not put me and his child at risk. He could fight with peace of mind with no formal connection between us.

"Eventually the name of Amos as a freedom fighter became known to both Romans and Israelis alike. Because of his notoriety we met infrequently at secret locations.

"As my pregnancy advanced, community leaders inquired as to the child's father. Righteous matrons feared their husbands might have dallied in my bed. Irony strained the tolerance I extended to my interrogators, two priests and six elders. Out of these eight men, three had approached me in the past, one of my would-be lovers a priest. How amusing to watch these busybodies work up their courage to come to the point. Of course, I could not name Amos as the father. On the other hand I had no intention of crawling before the eyes of these hypocrites.

"I decided to play with my assembled questioners. In solemn awe I explained that I had been in my room when a radiant angel appeared and announced my selection by God to give birth to a son. This son would be named Jesus and be given the throne of David. This beatific angel said Jesus would reign forever. The shock and consternation of my questioners gratified me. Of course, they were collaborators with Rome who made money keeping the Jews tranquil in their synagogues. My tale presented a serious problem. This was the old messiah myth which the credulous masses deeply believed. This mythical messiah would be an earthly king destined to overthrow our oppressors and place the lower class in a favored position. Common people clung to this theme tenaciously.

"Recovering a bit, one of my questioners asked if I expected him to believe that a woman could become pregnant without lying with a man. I expanded my outrageous tale by explaining that the angel, Gabriel, said I would be impregnated by a Holy Spirit. Then I closed by innocently asking that surely as men of religion they believed all things possible with God? Furthermore, was it not obvious that I was with child and was not God the father of all life? If God wanted me to have a child by his spirit who was I, his simple Jewish handmaiden, to object? Of course, the idea of conception without carnal knowledge was silly, but religion spins webs of such complex fantasies. My ruffled questioners needed to discuss this in private. I graciously consented to leave and told them to fetch me from the family garden after their discussion. Little did I realize as I strolled smugly beneath the cypress, that my little joke would burgeon beyond my simple humor? The joke was on me.

"In a short while they summoned me. I confronted much friendlier priests and elders. My pregnancy had been declared God's mystery. The leader asked that I remain quiet about my angelic vision and allow God to work in his ways. I replied that I would do my best to remain silent, but if directly asked, who was I to muzzle God's Word? The Priests' eyes glittered as they realized they had been trapped. Several of the elders' (who had wished to bed me) eyes twinkled as they acknowledged a girl who had tricked them. As the dignified group rose to leave, the last old man in the solemn line patted my bottom and winked. I could not help but smile back. At least he was a man with a man's healthy interests.

"Unfortunately, the tale of my divine conception swept Sepphoris by sundown. Certain elders could not resist sharing such a good story over brews with companions. Within hours even Roman soldiers on watch and street merchants knew of the angel Gabriel. The priesthood seethed, but would not risk the Messiah emotion so did their best to stifle the story. Elements of Jewish society did not like priests and made a laughingstock of their bureaucracy. Even Amos, when we met in the field weeks later heard the story with amusement, complaining with a smile that it would be difficult to compete with God. I took the time to show him it was not all that difficult. Unfortunately, like many Jewish tales, mine did become part of my son's future reputation. I had not foreseen the ramifications of my divine conception tale.

"Contrary to religious fantasy, Jesus was born according to natural laws, a beautiful child with large luminous eyes, olive skin, and a full head of black hair. Like any infatuated mother I was certain Jesus was the most beautiful baby ever born. He looked exactly like his father.

"Jesus differed from any baby I had known. He almost never cried. His eyes studied everything. I read to Jesus for hours as I cradled him. I had the uncanny feeling he understood. I spent nearly all my hours with my son. I formed the habit of talking and reading to Jesus as to an adult. He listened intently. I read Greek classics as well as Hebrew legends and folktales. At times I fretted that he was too serious, never smiling or playing with toys. His first two years passed.

"Amos met his son only three times. The war against Rome was intense and leadership demands absorbed Amos. The last time we met he said he could die in peace because in his son he had seen his hope for a free Israel. Dread flooded my heart. My last memory of Amos as a free man was him smiling, saying he had nothing to fear from a rational god. He lived for freedom and truth, prepared to lay his life's work before any bar of justice.

"An informer betrayed Amos and a band of freedom fighters two months later. Two hundred-fifty Roman legionnaires surrounded Amos' small command of thirty. When the Roman commander called on him to surrender, he refused. All the freedom fighters were killed in the bloody melee except Amos and two hardened veterans. They fought fiercely, backed against a large rock. The commander, reluctant to lose more soldiers to these fanatics, ordered the rebels to be stoned from a distance by Roman slingers. Rocks they could not defend against struck the three senseless. Romans bound them and dragged them to Sepphoris.

"A strong man takes long to die of crucifixion. My beloved suffered four days to die an indescribable death. At some moments during his torment, he recognized me. He never revealed our love, referring to me several times with the neutral word, woman. The rest of the time Amos fell mercifully unconscious or mumbled in random delusions. Safe from suspicion, I watched helplessly. Crucifixions attracted crowds. Many viewed these horrors as cheap entertainment while morbid curiosity drew others. Mourners grieved the loss of courageous, patriotic young Jews, but disgusting businessmen profited by selling spectators food and drink. Even prostitutes worked the crowds reminding men of the shortness of life. Pickpockets had a good day stealing purses of those avidly watching tortured men die in blood, vomit, and excrement.

"How hard I prayed. I sent pitiable petitions to any god or gods who might exist. I prayed only for a quick death for my Amos. I bargained with any deity, promising anything if only my Amos were released from merciless suffering. I received no answer. My pleas, sent with full conviction and sincerity, only melted into black silence. I offered my life if only Amos would die quickly. I received nothing: no comfort, no answers, no compassion, and no quick death for my suffering Amos. I offered everything, even the life of my son. I received more silence. God, if there is a God, chose not to answer. Amos was a good, sincere man who believed he gave his life for freedom and truth. As one who wept at the foot of his cross, I knew Amos died for nothing. While it may be human to hope Amos lives again in some pleasant setting, I saw no evidence of a caring deity. On the fourth day of Amos' suffering I carried Jesus to the crucifixion site. I felt an overpowering compulsion for Amos to see his son before he died. By this time the other two Jewish fighters had died. Amos was a fly-eaten mass of twitching flesh.

"The sun and wind had burned Amos so that large sections of his body blackened. I could barely tell that his ravished body still lived. Jesus, just two, stared with wide, attentive eyes. Then an amazing thing happened. Tears formed in Jesus' eyes, then poured down his face. My son who never cried sobbed loudly-- pathetically. I started to turn to take him home when Amos lifted his head and looked at Jesus. The baby ceased crying. Amos tried to smile and murmured, "God is now your father. Your father and God are one." Then Amos said to me, "It is finished." His head dropped to his lifeless chest.

"They threw his body to scavengers in the community dump. Romans watched for anyone trying to claim the body of a rebel. I conceded. How ironic that a man likes Amos would feed birds of the sky while lesser men lived fat lives of collaboration with Rome, eventually buried in honored family tombs. However, for the safety of our child I appeared to live as always. General mourning was accepted but excessive mourning attracted notice of informers. I carried on for Jesus' sake, alert in perilous days. My few friends and acquaintances drifted away. My world contracted until I had only Jesus and memories of Amos. Others noticed my change of lifestyle. I was unaware of the rumors about me and my son, but later events clarified them. Uneducated sectors began to believe me a witch or evil because of my solitary life. They interpreted my habit of talking to Jesus as an adult on our long evening walks as satanic communication between an infant and adult. Stories spread that demonic forces centered on my household. Memories of the tall tale I told the prying elders expanded with vicious gossips adding morbid details. Rumors spread that Jesus resulted from an inhuman relationship between me and a demon. What few people I met by chance looked away or would actually cross a road to avoid us. I noticed faces peering from windows as I took Jesus on our outings.

"In my mourning for Amos and my concentration on Jesus I did not realize my growing danger, not appreciating how the dark side of religion is superstition, fear, and cruelty. The priesthood had not forgotten or forgiven their drubbing over the divine incarnation story. They sought revenge. My solitary habits with Jesus provided their opportunity. The priests contributed to the theory of me a witch, my son possessed. I learned later they connived to have me condemned as a witch to execute me.

"The priests might have succeeded. In those days, I placed little importance on activity around me. A respected old friend of my father saved us. Joseph, a pillar of the religious community and a just man, held high standing in Sepphoris. His worship was regular, but not excessive. Jews throughout the city knew Joseph, twenty years my elder, as a man who would help any worthy person in need. After my family perished, Joseph visited my aunt and me occasionally. He never judged me during my carefree days, and during my period of most severe mourning Joseph kept his visits short. I received his message requesting an audience with me and responded that his visit would be an honor.

"That evening, after sharing a meal with us, Joseph explained my growing danger. I felt chagrin to have overlooked something so predictable.

"The Priests steadily maneuvered to destroy me. I knew not what to do. Sepphoris was home. Furthermore, I still bore responsibility for the family library, my duty to my ancestors clear. Yet Jesus meant everything to me. I had to protect him.

"Joseph suggested an amazing solution. He said he had been interested in my welfare since I was a child. He had promised my father he would protect me. Joseph proposed to marry me with certain conditions. He loved, but only wanted to protect me. So much older, he would not expect us to live as man and wife. It was acceptable that I take a discreet lover from among his employees. Joseph would fulfill his responsibilities as a father to Jesus, and our marriage was certain to stop the priests and most gossip. His position would provide high status; the priests would not openly criticize us for fear of jeopardizing Joseph's support.

"I told this good man I was flattered and grateful for his offer of protection, but did not share his religious beliefs. I despised priests and had strong reasons not to adhere to Judaism. I felt certain he would be appalled. However, Joseph chuckled and said, 'Mary, my child. I have never believed there was fact behind the tales people call their true religion. Men and women need hope and security which religion provides. Since I want to help my community, I give money to religious centers. If there is a God, perhaps my efforts please him. I share many of your beliefs and those I do not share do not matter. I am a tolerant man who accepts human folly. I hope a life of helping others pleases any deity. Mary, fear not, I am with you. Perhaps in time your feelings for me will grow. Regardless, I will provide a harbor for you and your son.'

"I asked Joseph if he could accept that I might never love him or lay with him. He chuckled and said he had loved me for years without the slightest hope that I even knew his feelings. Furthermore, his serving woman had long met his carnal needs. He had mastered the art of living alone, but preferred to share life with me. Moved by his benevolence, I placed my hand on the hand of Joseph and accepted his marriage proposal."

Chapter Thirty-three

"All went as Joseph said. He felt a country rabbi would suit our modest ceremony. Rabbis, not officially associated with the priesthood, tended to serve poor rural folk. Priests served affluent urban centers. Our marriage took the priests aback, and the assault upon us ceased immediately. The financial support Joseph gave guaranteed immunity. True to his word, Joseph made no demands on my person and made my home his domicile. His gentle consideration of Jesus, me, and our entire community impressed me more and more.

"Three peaceful years passed. However, Jesus was not a normal child. My son would stare at an unknown word or a vexing problem for hours as if his mind could not let go. He seldom sought help. By the age of five Jesus read scrolls that should have been beyond him. However, he never played with other children, often avoiding them. He spoke only when he chose. When he did, he formed complete sentences. We hoped Jesus would outgrow such strangeness.

"However, in his sixth year we began to hear him talking and responding to invisible voices. Children often have pretend companions, but this was drastically different. Jesus spoke directly to God, becoming agitated when Joseph or I explained we heard nothing. Jesus would point at a rock and say, 'God stands right there.' If I said I could not see anyone, Jesus became so upset he would not speak for days.

"Like most upper class children, Jesus was educated by tutors, but his behavior made retaining them difficult. Finally we found a Greek physician willing to instruct in Hellenistic philosophy, classics, mathematics and language. He concluded Jesus suffered from an illness of the brain, claiming to have seen several of these cases during his practice. He said Jesus saw images and heard voices, but these existed only in his mind. The physician knew no cure. We hoped our child's condition would improve as he grew.

"Jesus had a second tutor, an old rabbi retained to teach both Hebrew and Aramaic languages. From him we learned that long-told Israeli folktales fascinated Jesus. He could sit for hours listening to them, the calmest he ever seemed. To Jesus the stories were literally instructions from God. Jesus' memory astonished us. The child recalled story plots and quoted characters in minute detail. Nevertheless, Jesus was not stable. On days he gave his instructors unnaturally intense attention, his learning was prodigious. Or Jesus might ignore them. Trying for them, but the well-paid tutors stayed.

"To say Jesus was sensitive does not begin to explain. He dwelt in a place of a tangible God, angels, and spirits. He spoke intimately and often to beings who existed only for him. Unfortunately, he had a violent self-destructive trait. He spoke often of dying and rejoining his father. Jesus would describe the need to suffer for God. Our son sometimes flayed himself with thorns until blood ran. Such behavior frightened us. We feared he would kill himself in some delusion that his death was God's will. Jesus became fascinated with Judaic apocalyptic legends. The idea of God returning to scourge the earth with fire and blood intoxicated him. He found a judgment by God that resulted in elevating the few and damning many exciting. Jesus never tired of the Messiah legend, believing a Jewish kingdom would arise momentarily.

"By the time Jesus reached the age of twelve much had changed. He now had younger brothers and sisters. I had long ago welcomed the kind Joseph into my bed and with patience brought him to desire. I conceived easily. Thankfully, none of these children showed the traits of our troubled Jesus.

"Jesus spent days perusing writings in Joseph's study, usually folklore and religious thought. Several times I broached that these were not history which brought violent reactions. Truth, logic, and evidence meant nothing. To Jesus things were true because God told him face to face. Jesus often wept that God was angry, judging him guilty of some monstrous crime he could only atone for by dying. He announced he was born a sinner. During bad bouts my son wept that only his death could save all of us. Sometimes Jesus ranted his father God would destroy the world unless Jesus died for everyone. I held him until he finally slept the sleep of exhaustion.

"His behavior could not be hidden. Many remembered the tale of my so-called immaculate conception and believed Jesus to be divine, not an unusual concept in either Greek or Jewish thought. Many believed deities could impregnate humans. For example, many political leaders claimed to be sons of gods. Kings commonly claimed divine parentage. How easy for the superstitious to believe Jesus had divine blood. Many expected God to do great things through him. Others argued Jesus was the offspring of demonic beings; therefore, evil. Tension between community awe and fear fed our unease.

"There was also the never ending anticipation of the Jewish Messiah born to free the Jews from oppression. Pious poor saw signs of the coming kingdom everywhere. Rumors flew from one end of the country to the other that the Messiah had been born or that the Messiah was seen in this or that setting. Any event would be turned into a sign by desperate hopeful. A riot, floods, wars, earthquakes, stars, any numbers of things were argued to be a sign by this or that group. Many Jews in Sepphoris hoped Jesus might be the young Messiah. `

"Our handsome son's behavior did not change in his stripling years. His aloof behavior attracted women. He ignored them, instead loving his realm of heroic figures and learning everything in our religious lore. Jesus quoted pages of ancient scripture from memory. He loved to amass and quote folk proverbs, parables and catchy stories from our heritage, generations old and long forgotten by most. (Most peasants were young and uneducated, living less than thirty-five years. Only the elite had been exposed to Judaic folklore and literature. A story or parable seemed newly created to the toiling peasants.

"Jesus sought lonely places to pretend to be this or that religious figure, assuming the identity of Moses, Jeremiah, or Elisha with great conviction and authority. His rhetoric formidable, he favored the role of religious teacher. He loved to lecture using ambiguous, cryptic statements. He loved to speak for God and often believed he was God made flesh. These shocking statements contributed later to his death, but before that black hour he practiced his skills day after day with abnormal intensity. My beloved son was rehearsing for death.

"Jesus would stand for hours talking to entities no one else saw or heard. People tried to persuade him to come out of the sun, to sit in the shade during his endless prayers. Often we had to lead him, entranced and unaware of his actions, away by the hand. Such fervor naturally excited imaginations of the religious, but raised the fear of the ignorant that Jesus was possessed by evil. Belief in ghosts, evil spirits, and the evil eye were so strong. His extreme behavior excited extreme people. People tended to either love or hate him, a tendency which followed him throughout his short life.

"Traveling preachers or storytellers who earned meager livings by preaching, giving prophecy, public healing, and social criticism enthralled Jesus. They preached and prophesied standard themes that rural folk yearned to hear: the poor would inherit the earth and their oppressors would suffer. Healings were usually of excitable poor whose ills were often more imagined than real. Is there some connection between the emotional and the physical in illness?

"Because of their poverty and fatalism these nomadic entertainers, openly criticizing and poking fun at their betters, lived immune from the rich and powerful. It was standard fare that the wealthy would choke on their riches and suffer eternally in hell. The poor really wanted the exact material things they criticized the wealthy for having.

"These wandering speakers were wise enough not to encourage theft or revolution, so governing authorities left them alone. Experience and cunning rendered these traveling beggars clever. Any upper-class member who contested their simple pretensions often came out on the losing end. Crowd sympathies always went against the well-to-do. These travelers mustered a meal or two, then trekked on to other towns or villages. Jesus listened to them by the hour.

"As our son moved into manhood, we discerned more changes. Jesus became convinced God had a mission for him. He spoke endlessly of awaiting a call. Jesus began to take an increasing interest in priesthood corruption and collusion. He spoke more of the coming kingdom when the Messiah would make everything right.

"Jesus had a genius for speaking and acting. Credible since he actually believed he spoke for God, Jesus never hinted that he wanted food, money or material gain, breeching their last wall of resistance by making no claims on what little his poor listeners had. Lives of the poor were tedious. They remembered and repeated anything interesting. Also, Jesus' sincerity warmed them. His heart did bleed for the needy. His obsessive religious studies placed his knowledge far beyond even priests.

"Jesus spoke with lively authority. He hesitated not in claiming to speak for God. Other traveling speakers avoided crossing this line. Jesus crossed it openly because his mental condition did not permit comprehension of his vulnerability. Other speakers downplayed this coming kingdom because Roman authorities saw such talk as treason. Jesus spoke fearlessly, ignorant of his mortal danger. To the crowds, such bravery could only come from God.

"His budding fame was also driven by his healing. Uneducated folk of my time had to have a cause for everything. A run of bad luck would seldom be accepted as the cause of a peasant's hardships. The reason must be evil spirits or an enemy's curse. Poor people make up for their lack of education with excess emotion. All these add up to a heightened sensitivity to suggestion. Jesus built a reputation as an exorcist. The excitement of the moment, the faith of the patient, and the intensity of Jesus' speaking actually caused many a cure. Imaginary ills are susceptible to imaginary cures. Exorcisms were public drama. The exorcist's part consisted of pompous authoritative statements. The victim's part usually consisted of irrational behavior before his cure and amazingly sane behavior after the miracle. Of course, the crowd played their part of awe, amazement, and religious renewal. They expected a happy ending. The major difference with Jesus was raising the enactment to new levels of excitement and accomplishment, greatly appreciated by the crowds. I trembled as his fame grew.

"By this time Joseph was elderly and in ill health. The years had brought true love to my heart for Joseph, a man of compassion. Joseph quietly went to the governing authorities and explained Jesus and his mental health. The pragmatic Romans were courteous. Nevertheless, they responded that unbalanced people could be dangerous. The authorities' primary duty was public safety. Constant retelling of feats Jesus allegedly performed enhanced interest in him. The illiterate poor passed information by talking. Storytelling skills were prized and every listener had license to expand a good story, not placing high value on truth. Rumors and embellishment abounded. Ordinary events could be and often were transformed into miracles. For awhile Joseph and I kept Jesus' activities from boiling over, encouraging him to refrain from speaking. When Jesus felt moved by one of his voices, we urged him to speak only to small groups in rural areas.

"Then the inevitable happened. My beloved Joseph died.

"Jesus took Joseph's passing hard. Like most sons, he had taken his father for granted, never fully expressing his love. He withdrew even more, spending much time wandering the hills. He spent days in remote places. I worried constantly as the land held many dangers for a man alone after dark. Often I searched those hills calling his name. Sometimes I found Jesus seated on a rock, mumbling. Sometimes I could rouse him to rational talk, sometimes not. Often I led him home like a child. Eventually these nocturnal wanderings became so frequent I had no choice but to leave his fate to God.

"This went on for several years. Since Jesus no longer spoke publicly, authorities ignored him. However, speculation about him did not cease among the common people. Without Joseph, my son was at risk from the priests. The Romans were reasonable, albeit cruel, but the priesthood was different. The priests considered Jesus a potential threat. It became painfully clear my money alone could not keep Jesus safe from religious persecution. It was possible, but dangerous, to play the Romans against the priests. I played the part of a modest, reformed Jewish woman in order to protect Jesus, not a strong defense. In the end nothing I could say or do would save him.

"Jesus never did become a mature adult. He never married depended solely on me. When Jesus entered his twenty-sixth year, new abnormalities arose. He addressed the people again which brought him to the attention of the authorities. The beginning of the end arrived in the spring of my son's twenty-seventh year, a beautiful spring with nothing to suggest this year would be different. His behavior continued with periodic wanderings and occasional speaking to the curious.

"What happened to us cannot be understood without explaining the state of Israel. The Jewish underground Amos served grew stronger. Romans responded by killing anyone suspected of threatening their rule. A mad cycle of raids, retaliations, and crucifixions gripped the country. The cycle of action to reaction increased in size and frequency. Military conflicts involved many, crucifixion of Jewish rebels by the hundred common. The Romans placed tremendous pressure on the Jewish elite to control the common people. Revolution against Rome reared imminent. War with Rome would be our end. Israel could not resist the might of the Roman Empire. Unfortunately many wanted war, believing they could defeat the Roman Eagle. Rank and file militant Jews were so repressed they had nothing to lose. Leaders of these uneducated fighters were usually disaffected members of the elite.

"These underground leaders used any tactic to make war inevitable. The single most powerful belief was in the coming Messiah, a fantasy so galvanizing the Jewish underground longed for anyone to actually claim this title. If they could find this Messiah the Jewish freedom fighters could push Jewish society into war. Whether this person actually was the Messiah mattered not. They needed an identified Messiah to ignite the flame of Israel. Once afire, Jewish nationalists were confident the Romans could not survive the inferno. Unfortunately, Jewish nationalists' needs matched the delusions of my son. Had Jesus lived at any other time the authorities would have given little heed to his strangeness, but in a country verging on self-destruction, the exasperated Romans had no tolerance.

"My nightmare began when Jesus failed to return from one of his sojourns in the hills. Frantic, I kept assuring myself he would be back in another day. After five days I could stand the strain no longer and began searching the hills and hollows for miles around

Sepphoris. I sought him alone for three days until despair overwhelmed me. I enlisted the help of the community and many good hearted people searched. After two weeks I feared the worst, paid off my searchers, and thanked the community for their help. It appeared my son's illness had been his end.

"Jesus had been missing for twenty-three days when news reached me that a shepherd herding his goats had found him by a spring between Sepphoris and the Sea of Galilee. The boy figured out my starving son was from Sepphoris. On his own incentive he took Jesus by the hand and led him back to our city. A neighbor ran to tell me that Jesus was found, and was at that moment speaking to a crowd in the marketplace. I rushed to the heart of Sepphoris and found my son addressing a curious throng of over five hundred. I made my way through the suffocating horde and tried to embrace Jesus, but he did not know me.

"The crowd was astonished that my son could not recognize his own mother, but Jesus said, 'Anyone who loves his father or mother more than me is not worthy of me; anyone who loves his son or daughter more than me is not worthy of me; and anyone who does not take his cross and follow me is not worthy of me.' Astonished, they thought Jesus a prophet. Crowds always excited my son, making him unpredictable. I gently grasped his hand and said 'Son, please come home with your mother and let there be peace in the community.'

"Jesus raised his arms high and shouted to the enthralled crowd, 'Do not suppose that I have come to bring peace to the earth. I did not come to bring peace, but a sword. For I have come to turn a man against his father, a daughter against her mother, a daughter-in-law against her mother-in-law. A man's enemies will be the members of his own household.'

"Many began to shout that surely this was a prophet! Others violently disagreed because the Jews had the holy Temple. Men began to push each other. Jesus again raised his hands over his head and shouted in a resonant voice, 'I tell you that one greater than the Temple is here.' That froze them into shock because that statement was known by all to be the expected words of the long-dreamed-for Messiah. I stood paralyzed with fear. This would provoke the Romans and the Priests. I yanked Jesus' hand and started leading him away through the crowd. He followed like a stunned child.

"Then someone shouted. 'Are you the Son of God?' I tried to distract Jesus because the question really asked if he were the Messiah. My poor fevered son grasped his head with both hands and shouted in anguish, 'All things have been committed to me by my Father. No one knows the Son except the Father, and no one knows the Father except the Son and those to whom the Son chooses to reveal him.' The crowd was in tremendous turmoil arguing about such statements when Jesus pulled out of my grasp and faced them. 'Come to me, all you who are weary and heavy laden, and I will give you rest. Take my yoke upon you and learn from me, for I am gentle and humble in heart, and you will find rest for your souls. For my yoke is easy and my burden is light.' I dragged him away. Sick with fear, I heard the multitude behind us shouting and fighting. This rioting would not be overlooked by Romans or priests.

"At last I got my poor son into the safety of our home, appalled at his gaunt appearance. For hours I bathed his fevered head and overheated body. Jesus claimed a spirit told him to go into the desert. He claimed to have been tempted by a devil for forty days. This devil had apparently tried to convince Jesus to make rocks into bread. Jesus was convinced that this story really happened even though I knew full well he had been gone only twenty-three terrible days. Later I remembered that the number forty was a common device of early Jewish storytellers. In the flood myth it rained forty days and forty nights. Jesus confused such fables with reality.

"Jesus said the devil took him to the top of the Temple in Jerusalem. The point of this strange transportation was to tempt Jesus into jumping to his death. Jesus said quite proudly that he had replied, 'Do not put the Lord your God to the test.' Jesus told me this persistent devil next transported him to a high mountain where they could magically see all the kingdoms of the world which this spirit offered to give Jesus in exchange for his worshipping this devil. Jesus claimed that he refused and that this spirit left him. Jesus said good spirits arrived and fed him.

"Of course, this was the product of a number of ancient Judaic folktales all mixed together in my son's fevered mind. This story was told and retold in many different versions after his death, known as the 'desert temptation' of the Messiah. He drifted in and out of sanity over the hours I nursed him. I spoke to several physicians later about my son's strange story, and they assured me that anyone might report vivid sights and sounds if deprived of food, drink, or even normal surroundings. In time, I rewarded the goatherd and his parents so richly they were no longer debtors. Looking back, it would have been a mercy had Jesus perished in the wilderness.

Chapter Thirty-four

"It took ten days for Jesus to recover bodily. Sadly, from that day forth he believed himself selected for some great mission. I hoped this period of intense instability would pass like the others. Jesus was not the only member of our family so troubled. His cousin called John the Baptist, a break-away member of the Essenes, was also enthralled with preaching the coming of the Messiah. Like many wandering charismatic preachers, John was extreme. The Essenes, a Jewish sect, lived a communal existence, gave up personal property, and shunned women. These bizarre people believed in the immortality of the soul and described our bodies as prisons to escape by death. They disdained carnal knowledge as evil and espoused ritual baths in their concept of being right with God. John, like the rest of his strange associates, believed in baptism in water for the remission of sins, and eternal burning hell for anyone who differed from their views. Fascinated by the concept of the Messiah, whom they called the teacher of light, Essenes also expected and welcomed the end of the world in an immense conflagration. They labeled those who disagreed 'sons of darkness' to be punished in everlasting fire. Being poor, Essenes hated the rich, and being uneducated, hated the learned.

"Jesus adored his cousin. When he heard John was baptizing at the Jordan River I could not restrain him. After a long, uncomfortable trek we reached John, who stood in the Jordan raving at some Pharisees and Sadducees observing those being baptized for imagined sins. 'Produce fruit in keeping with repentance. And do not think you can say to yourselves, `We have Abraham as our father.' I tell you that out of these stones God can raise up children for Abraham. The ax is already at the root of the trees, and every tree that does not produce good fruit will be cut down and thrown into the fire.' He spouted standard Essene doctrine, but Jesus shook with excitement. John again shouted the strange Essene beliefs. 'I baptize you with water for repentance. But after me will come one who is more powerful than I, whose sandals I am not fit to carry. He will baptize you with the Holy Spirit and with fire. His winnowing fork is in his hand, and he will clear his threshing floor, gathering his wheat into the barn and burning up the chaff with unquenchable fire.' This was the extreme view of an extreme group.

"Jesus insisted he must be baptized for his terrible sins. I saw no harm in a simple dunk in the river. John was amazed to see his cousin, Jesus, request to be baptized because harmless Jesus had never hurt anyone. John said, 'There is no need for your baptism. It would make as much sense if you baptized me!' Jesus was so swept away by emotion that he solemnly said, 'Let it be so now. It is proper for us to do this to fulfill all righteousness.'

"John looked at me, and I shrugged. John then shook his head and immersed Jesus. Much later, I wondered at the stories that grew out of this simple act. My son's exuberant followers later claimed to see the sky open and the spirit of a dove descend upon Jesus. Some even claimed to hear a voice from heaven claiming that Jesus was the son of God. All I saw was a harmless event to pacify a disturbed young man.

"After our return to Sepphoris, Jesus began speaking in nearby villages, his passion and eloquence higher than ever. Expressing intense conviction of the coming Kingdom of God, he attracted growing crowds. Everyone knew that the Kingdom of God meant the Messiah would soon arrive. With pathetic need, the oppressed turned out in hundreds to hear the message they craved. Jesus affirmed and spoke to their dreamed-of hopes. The difference between my son and other itinerant preachers was that Jesus was charismatic, an effective speaker after years of obsessive perusal of religious writings in Joseph's study. The endless hours spent speaking to imaginary crowds now drew real ones. From muddy hamlets to larger villages like Nazareth, they flocked to hear him. There was no doubting his power. Mental illness made his conviction total, his compassion for the downtrodden boundless. One could not compare my son to the wandering charlatans who preceded him.

"My handsome Jesus taught in the Israeli parable tradition. A parable is a short story with a double meaning, the first a moral or religious lesson, the second concealed with a deeper, hidden meaning. Jesus showed his understanding of parables when he told his disciples, 'The knowledge of the secrets of the kingdom of God has been given to you, but not to them. That is why I speak to them in parables.' The purpose of a parable was to make a point, the story itself seldom true, just a vehicle to reach the goal. Parables often spoke in clichés such as, 'A worker is worthy of his hire.' Often the parable would be cryptic, 'No one puts new wine into old wineskins.' This readies the listener to hear the answer the speaker wants to implant.

"Jesus modified or combined old parables to make them sound new or offer new meaning. Parables came from Jewish history, but the unlettered country Jews had never heard them and thought Jesus a prophet. I heard many say things like, 'No man has ever spoke like this before!' Generations of storytellers had told those ancient tales.

"Parables were short, easily remembered, and retold. Others rearranged and expanded those told by Jesus. A storyteller, not a theologian nor a philosopher, Jesus never used long theological dialogues attributed to him later. After his death, followers invented long dialogues he never used. Jesus related pithy sayings and clever short stories. I doubt my son could have given a complicated dialogue. Parables did often have barbs aimed at the rich. Roman rulers suspected wandering story tellers because underneath many of their parables lay messages of revolution and hatred.

"Since the poor could not bear the costs of physicians, they approached anyone who might heal without pay. The ill, the maimed, and the deranged sought Jesus. The energy of the crowd and their faith in my son's divine connection made 'healings' a foregone conclusion. It would have been almost impossible for the sick person not to play his part in the drama. Some occurrences puzzled me, but much remains to be learned about what may connect illness of body and power of mind. Jesus gathered strength from the crowds, feeding off them and their deep emotional need. He never hinted or asked for money, a Godly sign. Jesus, obviously in his speeches, did not comprehend the value or need of money. Anyone willing to tend without charge appeared a novelty in the peasant's experience. Seeing one who really cared for them left these needy poor predisposed to accept any story about him, contributing to the myths and legends that grew around my odd son.

"Crowds grew daily alongside the fame of Jesus. I wanted to stay near him at all times. Of course, I met his financial needs. His unreasonable attitude toward money cropped up frequently in his speeches. The crowds believed his lack of concern about food and daily needs derived from Jesus as a man of God, a clear sign of God's approval.

"I did my best to appease the priests and Roman overlords watching these crowds by explaining my son as just another traveling preacher, no more dangerous than any other. Due to size of the crowds, Romans feared another Jewish riot or rebellion. Authorities urged me to control my exuberant son. I bribed anyone with power and pled my son's instability. Their fears were reasonable, with many in the Jewish crowd hoping for rebellion to begin.

"Jesus criticized state religion. I implored the priests for time, arguing that his condition would peak and subside. Most Pharisees and Sadducees reacted reasonably. War with Rome would mean tragedy for the Jews. I implored Jesus to curtail his speaking, but talk and tears availed nothing. The authorities promised to arrest Jesus if he did not leave their area. When Jesus announced God was calling him to Capernaum, I leaped at the chance to depart Sepphoris environs.

"His spreading fame reached Capernaum before we arrived on the northern shore of the Sea of Galilee. Ridiculous tales of Jesus' power preceded us. Each time a story left another person's lips it created another sign or miracle, blatant expansion constant in my poor son's life. Curious crowds followed us wherever Jesus spoke. I began to notice quiet Jewish men with hard eyes measuring the size of the crowds. These men had no interest in parables. They had that determined look I remembered in the eyes of my beloved Amos. Jesus had the potential to influence multitudes and to a revolutionary that is over half way to war. These fighters would use Jesus to ignite a rebellion against Rome.

"Tension soared, war possible at any time. Many sects claimed the world was coming to an end. The Messiah would appear to recreate our world free of illness, poverty, or problems. The idea of the Messiah was complex. The poor liked the idea of being the 'new rich,' avenged against the former upper classes. Others wanted a warrior to destroy Romans and rid Israel of non-Jews.

"Tens of thousands lived in despair, ready to leave home to try anything new. Sons chafed, unhappy with inherited occupations, and husbands considered abandoning family for adventure. In the Capernaum vicinity, Jesus began to collect disciples. Teachers or religious figures often gathered followers, an ancient custom in the East. Since the Messiah would lead a new Kingdom of Jews, there were benefits in finding and joining him. The original disciples hoped to share in his power.

"By the Sea of Galilee Jesus invited two fishermen, Peter and Andrew, to join him. They had heard of Jesus and were willing to walk with him for awhile. In less than a mile, two more young fishermen, John and James, accepted the smiling invitation to join Jesus for a short distance to hear him talk on a nearby hill. They abandoned their father Zebedee, fuming next to the family fishing boat. Jesus was in excellent form. He enjoyed playing the great religious leader. He searched for a mountain where he could reenact his childhood dream of Moses speaking to the Israelites. A nearby hill had to do.

"Jesus walked up the gentle slope with stately strides, a perfect combination of hauteur and humility. He made his way to address the crowd whose numbers exceeded several thousand. Jesus raised his hands over his head and slowly wheeled to silence the surging throngs, motioning them to sit. Nearly all destitute, they looked upon Jesus as their Savior from a life of misery.

"With consummate timing my son suddenly threw his hands skyward shouting, 'Blessed are the poor for theirs is the kingdom of God!' The crowd roared back approval. This inflamed Jesus who cried, 'Blessed are those who mourn for they will be comforted!' 'Yes! Yes!' the crowd shouted back. Nearly everyone present mourned for loved ones who had either died at the hands of Romans or been sold into slavery to pay taxes to the rich. Jesus lowered his hands, his eyes downcast for some moments. Tension in the crowd palpable, Jesus looked up in tears. He pronounced, 'Blessed are the meek for they will inherit the earth.' The very thing they dreamed of! The crowd started to chant, 'Now! Now! Now!'

"Terror struck me. The crowd had gone insane. At some distance I saw Roman soldiers nervously finger their swords and officers send messengers off in great haste. I prayed there would not be a riot. In long minutes the crowd's passion subsided. Finally, they responded to my son's motions for silence. An ominous stillness covered the assembly. I thought the crowd could no longer be restrained. Jesus raised his arms and intoned, 'Blessed are those who hunger and thirst for righteousness!' The crowd again shouted praise and approval. They had no doubt Jesus spoke to them as the poorest in the land, their idea of righteousness to kill their oppressors. Again my son shouted, 'Blessed are you who hunger now for you will be satisfied!' This vast throng of impoverished people knew all about hunger and dreamed of their day of revenge. 'Blessed are you who weep now for you will laugh!'

"The crowd, near hysteria, became an open-mouthed roar. Jesus, with dignity, turned his palms down for silence. With a rich tremulous voice he intoned, 'Blessed are you when people insult you, persecute you and falsely say all kinds of evil against you because of me.' The people often endured insults and persecution because they hoped for the Messiah. They believed Jesus was the Messiah and were eager to spring at his command.

"Even as they roared approval Jesus shouted again, 'You are the salt of the earth! You are the light of the world!' Jesus said, 'Remember my brothers, a city on a hill cannot be hidden.' Some impassioned men stood up screaming agreement. Jerusalem was the city on the hill that could not be hidden and many inflamed listeners dreamed of cleansing her of political and religious tyrants. Jesus pointed to some Pharisees and Sadducees gesticulating to Roman commanders a discreet distance from the mob. 'But, woe to you who are rich, for you have already received your comfort. Woe to you who are well fed now for you will go hungry. Woe to you who laugh now, for you will mourn and weep!'

"I buried my face in my hands, certain my foolish son had started a war. The crowd rose, screaming rage at the Romans and Pharisees. I saw the hate in the crowd as they picked up stones to hurl. The Roman commander ordered his men to arms. Fewer than one hundred Roman soldiers snapped to attention, ready to face certain death if the mob charged. How alone they looked compared to this inflamed host. Yet they did not run. They would never run. For a moment the only sound was the snapping of the Roman flag as the wind worried it. The standing crowd prepared to charge the Romans when my son spoke in a firm voice, 'Blessed are the peacemakers for they shall be called Sons of God.' Jesus began descending the hill away from the Roman command.

"The crowd wavered. Some men tried to take command and storm the Romans, but the will left the throng the moment my son started to walk away. Finally the crowd broke in knots, questioning each other. What did Jesus mean? Surely this was the Messiah? Surely the poor Jews were the Sons of God? Finally, they began making their separate ways home.

"I had witnessed a miracle. I scrambled to catch up with Jesus. To my amazement he sauntered along reciting children's rhymes learned in my arms. I gripped his hand and told him we had to leave. Years later I read a fiction of our brush with disaster. The benighted writer called this near riot 'The Sermon on the Mount.'

"From that day the disciples from the Sea of Galilee accompanied us. Jesus enjoyed their company. They were in a quandary about whether Jesus was the Messiah. He spoke several times a day to burgeoning crowds. His basic message always, 'The time has come and the Kingdom of God is near. Repent and believe the good news.' Everyone understood that to mean the arrival of the Messiah.

Chapter Thirty-five

The church at the time was much more faithful to reason than Galileo himself, and also took into consideration the ethical and social consequences of Galileo's doctrine. Its verdict against Galileo was rational and just.
Paul Feyerabend quoted in 1990 by Cardinal Ratzinger. Ratzinger became the Pope in 2005

If we lose Genesis as a legitimate scientific and historical explanation for man, then we lose the validity of Christianity. Period
G. Thomas Sharp, Chairman of the Creation Truth Foundation

"My son considered himself a Jew with a Jewish ministry. Proud of his race, he had little to do with others. Jesus was born a Jew, lived a Jew, and died believing himself the Jewish Messiah. For example, he said, 'Do not go among the Gentiles or enter any town of the Samaritans. Go rather to the lost sheep of Israel.' Jesus first refused the pleas of a Canaanite pagan to heal her sick daughter. He plainly said, 'I was sent only to the lost sheep of Israel and it is not right to take the children's bread and toss it to dogs.' Jesus also told his disciples, 'Do not cast your pearls before swine.' Jews considered swine and dogs unclean. This meant avoidance of gentiles.

"He made strong statements on the Jewish Torah; for example, 'Do not think that I have come to abolish the Law or the Prophets; I have not come to abolish them but to fulfill them. I tell you the truth, until heaven and earth disappear, not the smallest letter, not the least stroke of a pen will by any means disappear from the Law until everything is accomplished. Anyone who breaks one of the least of these commandments and teaches others to do the same will be called least in the Kingdom of God, but whoever practices and teaches these commands will be called great in the Kingdom of God. For I tell you that unless your righteousness surpasses that of the Pharisees and the teachers of the law, you will certainly not enter the kingdom of God.' Jesus never preached that the Jewish Law was void.

"Once a learned Jew asked which was the greatest commandment. Jesus answered like the Jew he was, 'Love the Lord your God with all your heart and with all your soul, and with all your mind.' This is the first and greatest commandment. And the second is like it: 'Love your neighbor as yourself.' All the Law and the Prophets hang on these two commandments.' It would be difficult to express more Jewish thoughts, steeped in Jewish tradition.

"How is it that Jesus became the foundation of a faith so different from Judaism? His every example was from Judaic tradition. To fulfill the law was always to explain the fullness of the law. The 'till all things are accomplished' meant the coming of the Messiah. Only then would 'heaven and earth disappear.' To Jesus, like other rural preachers, the Law of Moses itself was untouchable. His views were Jewish beliefs rewrapped in his own fertile mind. Jesus did not travel to other lands because to him, he could lawfully associate only with fellow Jews. Strangely, few note my son never cared to save non-Jews. Nor did Jesus baptize anyone.

"Jesus, like nearly all the itinerant preachers, was for the poor. Little in his messages encouraged the wealthy. Jesus never said 'Blessed are the rich.' What he did say was 'Blessed are the poor.' Later manipulators tried to soften his attack on the rich by saying things like 'Blessed are the poor in Spirit.' This made it easier to appeal to rich people and get at their purses. Jesus asked the rich to become poor to please God. After his death, falsifiers of my son's story turned his message from an earthly Jewish kingdom into some sort of heavenly one for all races after death. If Jesus had preached of heaven after death, the elite would not have feared and killed him. Neither would the poor have adored him.

"Jesus attacks were upon the rich. 'Again I tell you, it is easier for a camel to go through the eye of a needle than for a rich man to enter the kingdom of God.' Later writers softened it. One clumsy attempt was to have my son say, 'With God all things are possible.' Rarely, a wealthy person consulted Jesus about becoming acceptable to God. He would respond, 'Obey the commandments, sell everything, and give your money to the poor. Then take up your cross and follow me,' not a welcome message to one of property. On many occasions my son cast 'woes' upon the upper religious class and the wealthy.

"Jesus had no concept of earning a living, common to those reared in affluence. Outlandish utterances only heightened his mystique. For example, 'Do not store up for yourselves treasures on earth, where moth and rust destroy, and where thieves break in and steal.' Confusing since prudent savings seemed much like storing up treasures. He said, 'You cannot serve both God and money.' However, normal people earn money and support religions.

"This also seemed odd. 'Therefore, I tell you, do not worry about your life. Look at the birds of the air; they do not sow or reap or store away in barns, and yet your heavenly Father feeds them. Are you not much more valuable than they? Who of you by worrying can add a single hour to his life?' A literal adoption of this would be the ruin of family and nation. Jesus said many impractical things because he never assumed adult responsibilities.

"Jesus made many bizarre statements such as, 'I tell you the truth. If anyone says to this mountain, 'Go, throw yourself into the sea,' and does not doubt in his heart, but believes that what he says will happen, it will be done for him. Therefore, I tell you, whatever you ask for in prayer, believe that you have received it, and it will be yours.' No one has been able to cast mountains into the sea by mere command and many prayers go unanswered.

"I never witnessed miracles. Christian converts later invented myths of Jesus curing lepers, restoring sight to the blind, calming storms, and walking on water to convert the gullible. Miracles have always existed in Jewish folklore: the staff of Moses turning into a snake, axes floating on water, rivers turning to blood, and water flowing from stones. Common people wanted to believe the unbelievable because it gave their lives hope. Christians created stories where Jesus raised the dead and turned water into wine. Of course, he never did such things. Only those who want to believe in the impossible can accept such silliness.

"This desire to believe expanded after my son's death. He performed no miracles before the Sanhedrin or Pilate. Had Jesus gone to the Temple after his death or appeared to government leaders in public places that would have been persuasive. If Jesus wanted the world to see him risen from the dead he could have appeared before large crowds, talked to leaders and legal authorities. Nothing of the sort happened. Jesus supposedly appeared to small groups of unimportant people. That defies common sense. I was his mother, and Jesus never appeared to me after his death.

"Jesus felt everyone should be as obsessed with God as he, never comprehending that most have to labor to live. A young man was following Jesus when the man received word his father had died. When he asked Jesus to release him temporarily to perform the duties of a Jewish son at the death of his father Jesus replied, 'Follow me, and let the dead bury their dead.' Such callous requirements could only be made by an unstable person.

"These subjugated people would have killed Jesus if he openly asked them to submit to Romans and elite Jews. 'Love your enemies,' would have meant instant death if spoken to those bled dry by those enemies. Rural masses dwelt in semi-starvation, their children sold into slavery to pay crushing taxes. Falsifiers who profited by my son's story long after his death created such stories.

"My son had no concept of heaven. Jewish ideas of life after death were vague. Traditionally, salvation meant collective salvation. However, to the later Christian leaders the idea of a heaven for the individual provided tranquil citizens, easy to exploit. Jesus taught that the promised Messiah would rule an earthly Jewish kingdom. Later exploiters changed my son's belief in an earthly kingdom into a heavenly one. Christians invented heaven to cover for Jesus not returning to establish his kingdom in his generation, something he promised many times.

"Much of the bombast Jesus supposedly aimed at religious leaders is the product of later Jew-hating Christian writers. The Pharisees and Jesus all favored relaxation of rigid legalism. The

Roman bias of later Christian writers is plain. For example, in one later account the Pharisees allegedly tried to trap Jesus into saying that paying taxes to the Romans was not correct. Christians had Jesus dodge the trap by saying, 'Give to Caesar what is Caesar's and to God what is God's,' Romans believed this and wanted their subjects to, also. Christians wrote this to tunnel into Rome's good graces. If Jesus had preached a Roman viewpoint, Rome would have spared him.

"Jesus was no asset to Rome. 'You strain out a gnat to swallow a camel.' 'You travel over land and sea to win a single convert, and when he becomes one, you make him twice as much a son of hell as you are.' 'You snakes! You brood of vipers! How will you escape being condemned to hell?' It is most unlikely my Jewish son would have called any Jew a 'son of hell.' Hell is undeveloped in Judaism. Hell is elaborated and populated by Christians. Later Christian sayings are, 'You blind fools! You blind guides, you hypocrites. Full of hypocrisy and wickedness! Fill up, then, the measure of the sin of your forefathers!' How easy to detect hatred for Jews these writers imagine killed God. Romans killed my son who was not God. The Jews are innocent.

Chapter Thirty-six

"After the Sermon on the Mount speech Roman authorities increased their vigilance. Commanders kept troops on full alert whenever Jesus appeared in their districts. By this time Jesus had added eight disciples to the original four from Capernaum, so there were now Peter, Andrew his brother, James and his brother John, Philip, Bartholomew, Thomas, Matthew, James son of Alphaeus, Thaddaeus, Simon, and Judas Iscariot. Idealistic, they yearned for a new Israel. They also anticipated high positions in the coming Kingdom of God, often asking what their positions would be in this new regime. Some advocated violence to advance their cause and punish their enemies. James and his brother John were nicknamed Sons of Thunder for their willingness to use force. John and Peter were especially headstrong, impulsive, and imaginative. After Jesus' death however most drifted away.

"Following my deluded son saddened me. No persuasion could alter the map of his life. A turning point occurred with the death of his beloved cousin, John the Baptist, who made the mistake of criticizing the wife of King Herod on religious grounds. The furious woman persuaded her new husband to get rid of this gadfly. King Herod needed little persuading.

"Jesus mourned and withdrew from the multitudes. At this time he was on the east shore of the Sea of Galilee. After four solitary days, he took a boat to the other side. A huge throng waited on the west shore when we tried to land. Jesus spoke from the boat. Not until dark could we land and slip away to a quiet campsite.

"At daylight he greeted the crowds, more confident than ever, insisting that John the Baptist had been a great prophet. 'I tell you the truth: Among those born of women there has not risen anyone greater than John the Baptist.' Then Jesus told the crowds that John was the dead prophet, Elijah, sending a great shock through them. According to ancient Israeli tradition, Elijah had to return before the Messiah could arrive to take his throne. My deluded son said, 'Elijah has already come and they did not recognize him, but have done to him everything they wished.' Jesus further elaborated, 'I tell you the truth: Among those born of women there has not risen anyone greater than John the Baptist; yet he who is least in the kingdom of God is greater than he. From the days of John the Baptist until now, the kingdom of God has been forcefully advancing, and forceful men lay hold of it. For all the Prophets and the Law prophesied until John. If you are willing to accept it, he is the Elijah who was to come. He who has ears let him hear.' Everyone in the crowd understood what Jesus claimed. Yet John the Baptist had clearly stated he was not Elijah or a prophet.

"Jesus rested on a rock, his disciples close around him. Jesus asked Peter, the impulsive romantic, who did he think that Jesus was? Peter answered from his hopes and dreams, 'You are the Christ, the Son of the living God.' The throng held its breath, waiting to hear if Jesus assented. Then Jesus took that final fatal step, 'Blessed are you, Simon son of Jonah, for this was not revealed to you by man, but by my father in heaven.' This affirmation coursed through the multitude like a wind blast. People ran to spread the news. I knew then Jesus was a dead man. The authorities would murder him.

"Next day was the Sabbath, and Jesus spoke in the nearest synagogue as he often did. He read a passage from Isaiah interpreted to predict the Messiah. 'The Spirit of the Lord is on me, because he has anointed me to preach good news to the poor. He has sent me to proclaim freedom for the prisoners and recovery of sight for the blind, to release the oppressed, to proclaim the year of the Lord's favor.' Worshippers froze, waiting. Jesus poised as on a cliff's edge. He finally rolled up the scroll, handed it to the attendant, and sat. The eyes of everyone in the synagogue were on him. He said, 'Today this scripture is fulfilled in your hearing.' The crowd could not be restrained. Many rushed to spread the news that Jesus was the Messiah. Fear like lead crushed my heart.

"Jesus' announcement swept the country. Adoring crowds followed us from village to village, delirious at the prospect of a new Israel. Jesus spoke to throngs of five thousand. Farmers abandoned their fields to see the new Messiah, radiant with excitement. Jesus lost reality. Convinced he was the Messiah, he merged his identity with God's.

"Step by step my poor Jesus strode toward death. Pontius Pilate, Roman governor of Judea, ordered that informants as well as soldiers keep Jesus and the crowds under observation. Pilate was a typical Roman leader: cynical, intelligent, ruthless, and head of the judicial system with power to execute which he used freely. Given the turbulent times and constant Jewish resistance, Pilate was probably no better or worse than any other Roman leader. Typical of Roman rulers, he slaughtered anyone deemed dangerous and called the result peace. Later Christian writers would portray Pilate as a defender of my son's innocence. Pilate would kill anyone, innocent or guilty, just for a good night's sleep. He preferred to remain in Caesarea on the coast with his comforts and mistresses more than Jerusalem.

"The Jews in that overheated city often petitioned Pilate to judge their disputes. He refused. Pilate had some Roman legionnaires but mostly auxiliary units of infantry and cavalry, inferior to regular Roman soldiers. This contributed to his chafing insecurity. Rome's strength lay in Syria with four legions at the Syrian legate's disposal, too distant to help Pilate bear tremendous responsibility in an unstable area. Jewish nationalists weakened his ability to keep peace. Anyone might ignite the tinderbox of Israel into war with Rome.

"The disciples angled for position and power. Even the mother of John and James appealed to Jesus on the behalf of her sons. Worse, the disciples encouraged Jesus to go to Jerusalem during the upcoming Passover, sensing it the perfect time to announce his kingship. I tried to dissuade him. Passover, a celebration that gathered Jews from all over the civilized world to Temple observations, also raised tension highest between Romans and religious fanatics. Riots commonly broke out. Such violence had every possibility of breaking into full-fledged revolution. Jesus could not have picked a more dangerous time to be in Jerusalem.

"The Sadducee party, working closely with Roman overlords, had charge of the Temple. Any threat to it incurred Sadducee wrath. They did not believe in the Messiah myth, but realized that dream had potential to start a revolution. Tiny Israel could never prevail over trained legions of the Roman Empire. Jesus entering Jerusalem during the volatile season of the Passover would make him a rabbit entering a lion's den.

"Jesus in his madness seemed compelled to make this trip. Strong religious beliefs coupled with ambition motivated the twelve disciples. Peter and John believed utterly that Jesus was the Messiah and anticipated rewards in the new kingdom. There was also a strong militant thread, Thaddaeus, Judas Iscariot, and especially Simon the Zealot being good examples. I did not learn until after my son's death how the Jewish underground had been in constant communication with them, wishing to use Jesus to incite revolution.

"With only three weeks until Passover, I steadily lost what little influence I had over him. The crowds intoxicated my crazed son who rode upon a crest of joy. The Kingdom of the Messiah captivated him. Fourteen days before Passover Jesus announced he would enter the Holy City of the Jews. In agony, I sent mounted messengers to Sepphoris to muster his brothers and sisters, hoping his family could persuade him to return home. They arrived after great expense and effort. Jesus addressed a large crowd as we approached and tearfully begged him to return home because he was ill. Jesus asked his listeners a callous question, 'Who is my mother, and who are my brothers?' Then he pointed at his fawning disciples. 'Here are my mother and my brothers. For whoever does the will of my Father in heaven is my brother and sister, and mother.' Jesus was lost. I am not sure he even recognized us. We had done everything. Sobbing, his brothers and sisters went back to Sepphoris. I did not want them to see the end.

"The few days passed swiftly as we neared Jerusalem. The crowds never left us, and at every crossroads Jesus stopped to speak. I would shudder to hear someone shout, 'The Messiah goes to Jerusalem to claim the throne.' We approached Bethany on the road to Jerusalem. There, Jesus and the disciples spent both Friday and Saturday the Sabbath with our old family friends Mary, Martha, and Lazarus. Each tried to dissuade Jesus from going on. He did not sense his own hazard. He believed the entire city would welcome him to the throne of David.

"Sunday morning dawned sunny and calm. Jesus awakened eager to enter the city. The disciples, with an instinct for the theatrical, found a donkey for Jesus to ride through Jerusalem's gates. Some said this had been prophesized in ancient Scripture. Frenzied peasants lined both sides of the road. Some called my son the Messiah. Others welcomed the King of the Jews, and still others shouted 'Hosanna,' an ancient shout of joy from the times of King David. Undermanned Roman sentries observed the procession closely.

"Pilate was in Jerusalem, available if there were trouble. There had already been small riots in the city which he squelched. Pilate had learned that talk of a Messiah always meant bloodshed. Contrary to the legends of holiness, elements holding scant regard for the law amply populated Jerusalem. Pimps paraded their harlots. Farmers exchanged money for the sweaty arms of well-used women. Thieves and pickpockets worked the crowds as they have done since the first cities. Vendors hawked varieties of goods. Food, drink, and lodging were available, all at inflated prices that seem to go along with any religious activity. Anything and everything could be bought for a price. Even street beggars did well with increased numbers of religiously inclined making their way to and from the Temple.

"Jesus made his way through hundreds trying to see or touch him, the din deafening. Some shouted his name. Others announced the new Messiah. Some argued over whether Jesus was a prophet or a simple country teacher. Many hailed the new King of the Jews; others boldly denounced Rome, calling on Jesus to announce the revolution. There was hysteria because these dreamer's eyes had finally seen their Messiah. Through this chaos my son smiled and waved at the multitudes. The polished poise of a king combined with the practiced humility of a common man. A superb image. When this throng reached the Temple grounds I stood, again amazed at the immense structure King Herod had erected. However, I trembled, not knowing what would happen next.

"Jesus slid off his donkey and mounted the long flight of stairs to the Temple grounds proper. The boisterous crowds brought sanctuary guards running to meet Jesus on the steps. Jewish guards pleaded with him to maintain order among his riotous followers. Pilate lived only several hundred meters away in the Antonia Fortress. But when the crowd roared its disapproval, Jesus lost control.

"Pushing the hapless guards aside, he strode the corridors of the Temple grounds where religious pilgrims bought their sacrifices, their foreign currency exchanged for local coin. For generations Jews accepted such business. Every religious building of every nation had some financial transactions conducted on its grounds for the convenience of worshipers. With a huge shout Jesus said, 'My house will be called a house of prayer. But you are making it a den of robbers!'

"After this my deranged son overturned all the business tables, scattering money everywhere as well as releasing all the doves and sacrificial animals. He grabbed ropes and began to beat the currency handlers. I cannot describe the violence and chaos. No one had ever behaved so on this holy ground.

"When the guards recovered from their shock they drew their swords, running toward my son. I was certain Jesus would be cut down, but a Temple Priest stepped beside him, signaling the guards to pause. In soothing tones, the Priest calmed the crisis. Talking to my son, he guided him from the Temple proper, advising Jesus to go and rest. Occasionally Jesus nodded in agreement, but at other times stared blankly into the distance.

"When the Priest reached the top of the Temple grounds steps he announced, 'Here is your teacher. He needs rest for the day.' Jesus seemed to forget his wild few minutes as he waved to his admiring followers. The Priest had temporarily saved my son's life. Jesus serenely descended the steps.

"I tearfully thanked the Priest, now known to me as Benjamin. I explained Jesus was ill and had been since childhood. Benjamin asked if this were the country preacher known as Jesus. I affirmed it, explaining my son's history. He listened, and then informed me the Temple Priesthood was divided over how to handle this Jesus situation. Now Pilate would surely hear of this violence. Pilate vowed to kill randomly for any civil disturbances. The kind Priest said he would represent my case to his superiors, but also warned that Jesus lived in mortal danger.

"We arranged a time and place to communicate that evening. I assured the tolerant man I would not forget his kindness and would reward him financially for saving Jesus. Benjamin smiled saying, 'Give to the poor,' and walked away.

"Word of Jesus in the Temple corridors spread. Everyone speculated about the outcome. His violence outraged some, but others declared Jesus a righteous prophet for demanding change. Roman soldiers with hard, determined eyes converged outside the crowd, hands resting on their sword grips.

"Jesus walked wearily, almost in a trance. Finally the crowd reached Lazarus' dwelling. I led Jesus, who seemed oblivious, into a private room. I begged him to cease all this and return home to Sepphoris. He apologized for causing me trouble. I stroked his brow, telling him how much I loved him. Fleeting moments of sanity faded from his eyes; my son returned to a jumbled world of angels and voices. Toward evening he plunged into a deep sleep. I felt it safe to return to the Temple grounds, anxious to find out from my new friend the Jewish leadership consensus.

"I covered myself with a hooded cloak as the narrow streets of Jerusalem were perilous after dark. Several times Roman soldiers stopped me, sharply criticizing my unattended movements, but I convinced them I was a religious woman who only wanted to pray at the Temple. The poor lived in the alleys like animals, feeding themselves through criminal activities. Finally, I reached the safety of the highly secured Temple grounds.

"I waited, fearing Benjamin would not come. Finally, I heard his voice advising me to step deeper into the columns' shadows. With genuine concern he asked about Jesus. I said he rested, but I worried about his future actions. The priest said the Temple leadership and elders of Jerusalem had been meeting for hours because of Jesus and the Temple disturbances. He told them Jesus was ill, not to be held accountable regardless of the crowds.

"The Romans were furious because the Jewish community did not turn Jesus over for proper punishment, which meant crucifixion. Benjamin reassured me that most Jews were unwilling to turn over one of their own. The leadership of the Jewish community endeavored to downplay the incident to the Romans, but they remained unconvinced Jesus was harmless. Pilates' representatives made clear that anyone claiming to be a king of the Jews would promptly be sentenced to death. Pilate verified the Jewish community would be held responsible for any riots Jesus might cause.

"Many revolutionaries fomented in Jerusalem. If fighting started during Passover, innocents caught in battles would die by the cartloads. Benjamin suggested we meet every evening to discuss strategies for keeping Jesus alive. The priest would talk to his superiors and perhaps devise some means to legally restrain my son during Passover week, convinced the Romans would kill an uncontrolled Jesus. I agreed to anything to preserve my son's life. The priest smiled, saying perhaps he had a plan to cool the hot heads. He then assigned two guards to accompany me back.

"Next morning Jesus rose late, his need for sleep always greater after one of these bizarre episodes. As always, a large crowd eager to see this Jesus surrounded the house. Many brought sick and injured loved ones for him to heal. Their presence imbued him with vigor. The disciples and crowds yearned to see Jesus return to Jerusalem.

"I noticed several men approaching who bore that carriage suggesting learning and wealth. They engaged Jesus with questions. Whenever it seemed that Jesus prepared to proceed to Jerusalem a learned Jew would respectfully ask another religious query. Everyone showed interest in his answers to complex questions. Inevitably he responded in parables. The scholars remained reasonable, never saying anything disturbing. Yet Jesus grew caustic. I gradually understood. These men were here to be foils for my son to fence against so he did not proceed to Jerusalem. The Jewish leadership was doing everything to save my son and the community. They absorbed his insults. This generous display of humility astonished me.

"For two days the scholars strung along on subjects like adultery, divorce, oaths, fasting, and giving to the poor. On and on these patient men gave Jesus time-killing topics. Jesus loved to play the traveling teacher able to surpass learned city scholars. Speculation on worrying, life after death, and judging others formed springboards letting Jesus dip into his store of ancient stories and sayings.

"In the evenings I slipped away to the Temple to talk to the Priest, Benjamin, who confirmed the use of the scholars, hoping it would work through Passover. The Jewish community attempted to convince Pilate that Jesus was a harmless eccentric. Tension eased.

"After two days most of the curious crowds drifted away. The disciples pressured Jesus to return to the Temple and proclaim his kingship, arguing that only in this way could the Romans be expelled and the new Kingdom of the Jews established. Jesus was always susceptible to playing the leading role. Nothing could erase his self-image of being King of the Jews. The exhausted scholars could not defeat the combined efforts of the disciples who alone convinced him to return to the Temple. Jesus dropped the persona of teacher and assumed the role of a king entering his adoring kingdom. As Jesus began walking toward Jerusalem, I knew he would never leave it alive.

"When Jesus reached the Temple columns he turned and addressed the gathering crowd. He criticized the rich, the educated, and the elite. The enraptured poor listened. Soon my son began to talk about the coming 'Kingdom' and the 'Messiah.' Priests and teachers tried to resolve the danger, gently asking Jesus by what authority he made these statements. Jesus refused to answer.

"The scholars asked him for a sign of his divine authority. Ancient scriptures demanded signs from authentic prophets. The scholars asked when all he described would come to pass. My son responded with growing excitement, 'I tell you the truth, this generation will certainly not pass away until all these things have happened.' Then he said, 'I tell you the truth, some who are standing here will not taste death before they see the Son of Man coming in his Kingdom.' My delusional son could not have spoken more plainly. The people had no interest in life after death. Jesus spoke to real people with problems crushing them in the here and now. Non-Jewish religions promised a blissful afterlife in the land of sweet someday. However, Jews had rejected such childish concepts for centuries.

"The mob grew. Men roving among us shouted that this was the Messiah, the new king of Israel, urging the crowd to claim their new king and overthrow the Roman oppressors. My son shone ecstatic at the idea of finally being a king. When containing the turmoil seemed impossible, a burly man ran up to Jesus and boomed out, 'Are you the Messiah, the Son of the Blessed One? Are you the blessed King of the Jews?'

"Hushed, all waited to hear the fateful answer. There was no hope. Clever agitators, especially this burly man, had played the crowd and my sick son like a lyre. Jesus threw his arms to the sky, shouting to the crowd, 'I am, and you will see the Son of Man sitting at the right hand of the Mighty One!'

"With that the crowd could not be contained. Strategically-placed men urged them to attack the Romans and follow their Messiah King. Roaring zealous assent, they reached for stones. Rocks rained down on the soldiers who counter-attacked with drawn swords. The tumult turned into a major battle as outnumbered Romans went for their attackers. Then armed Jewish men swarmed out of buildings. The Jewish underground had planned and executed this ambush. I saw dozens, Jew and Roman alike, die in seconds. Roman trumpets called a signal for reinforcements. I will never forget the screams and terror of the innocent. Then the Jewish fighters melted into the warren of streets and alleys, their job done. They had caused a battle based on belief in a new Messiah. Jesus was doomed.

"He stood dazed by the reality before him. Benjamin took his arm to hasten him from the Temple grounds. The disciples followed. I had no idea where the priest led us. Jesus was now a wanted man. Pilate would avenge himself upon the Jews for these losses. Once again the idea of the Messiah, mythical King of the Jews, caused bloodshed. Pilate would not rest until he saw my son executed.

"Benjamin led us to a large garden. After a hurried discussion, we entered the house of a prominent Jerusalem Jew, Joseph of Arimathea. Everyone tried to make sense of what had happened. Jesus leaned against the wall, pallid and stunned. The utterly bewildered disciples had expected angels to descend from clouds to combat the hated Romans. Unfortunately, no angels came down. We knew ourselves to be in mortal danger.

"I asked one of the servants for a bowl of water to cool my troubled son. I dreaded what Pilate would do in his towering wrath. Repercussions were certain. As I bathed Jesus' face, he drifted in and out of sanity, repeating that people were supposed to be happy with their new king and God would bless them if they just obeyed the commandments. I hushed him as if he were a small, troubled child. The disciples still believed Jesus their Messiah. How blind worshipers can be.

"One of the disciples said he now knew how Jonah must have felt in the belly of the whale. Overhearing that chance comment, Jesus brightened. The Jonah fable had been one of his childhood favorites. I tried to get him to relax, but too late. Jesus straightened and announced in his dramatic voice, 'A wicked and adulterous generation asks for a miraculous sign! But none will be given it except the sign of the prophet Jonah. For as Jonah was three days and three nights in the belly of a huge fish, so the Son of Man will be three days and three nights in the heart of the earth. The men of Nineveh will stand up at the judgment with this generation and condemn it; for they repented at the preaching of Jonah, and now one greater than Jonah is here.' Confused, the disciples debated frantically over what this could mean. I tried to calm my irrational son, but he announced, 'Remember the third day. God will save us on the third day!'

"With this my poor son smiled cheerfully. The frightened believers regained confidence that God had a plan. Jesus was personified anew, now the suffering prophet in the belly of a whale, to be cast ashore after three days, again a hero of Israel. Some disciples would remember this sudden identification of Jesus with the fictional Jonah after his death. Who could imagine this crazy thought of being entombed for three days would form the basis of a new cult who believed my poor son was God? Yet, that is exactly what blossomed.

"Benjamin returned and reported forty-six Roman troops dead and over one hundred Jews, among them sixty women and children, slaughtered. Pilate arrested ninety-two Jewish males at random who hung from crosses this very moment, two for every dead Roman soldier. Pilate, enraged over the battle, offered a reward for Jesus.

"The divided Jewish community leadership met in emergency session. Some wanted to protect Jesus from Rome. Others wanted him apprehended for a fair trial. A few denounced Jesus as a common criminal who should be delivered to Pilate. Rumor flooded Jerusalem. Reputed to be drinking heavily, Pilate refused to meet with Jewish leaders. Hundreds of common folk spread a rumor of having seen Jesus vanish into the sky. Many wished Jesus had never been born and locked their doors, praying Pilate would soon recover from his rages. The religious community was horrified that the crucified Jews might be alive during the holy Passover. Zealots encouraged everyone to military action, claiming Jesus the Messiah. Roman soldiers patrolled the streets, keen to avenge their comrades.

"Joseph of Arimathea sought to confer with Pilate whom he knew well. Thanks to his gambling, Pilate owed Joseph a large sum. Perhaps Joseph could reason with this fierce Roman governor. My first instinct was to flee with Jesus. But with the city gates under guard we surely would fail. Jerusalem was a walled fortress. The reward posted for Jesus added to my terror.

"It amazed me to see the disciples in earnest discussion as to how they were going to prepare the Passover meal, and how God was going to place Jesus on the Jewish throne. I had never seen such religious intoxication. Some of the lesser-known disciples slipped out to purchase food, among them Judas Iscariot.

"Many have chosen to misuse my son's memory and many have misused the memory of Judas as well. Judas was no different from the other disciples. Young, idealistic, he believed Jesus the Messiah. Then, too, Judas was impatient, restless, and hoped for a reward in the coming kingdom under Jesus' rule. Like the others, Judas nursed extreme hopes and passions. He hated the Romans and kept solid faith that the Messiah would sweep the foreign oppressors into the sea.

"Judas, a religious fanatic, differed little from the extreme views of Jesus. Jesus' erratic behavior confused Judas as it did the other impatient disciples. Why didn't Jesus strike the enemies of Israel to the ground and assume the Jewish throne? Exactly like the others, Judas believed the legendary history of the Jewish people and the Messiah myth.

"Judas believed Jesus could call legions of angels to destroy the Romans with a wave of his divine hand. Judas, like all the rest, wanted to help craft the moment of Jesus ascending the royal throne. Judas had the fatal flaw of religious certainty, confusing hope and faith with reality.

"Judas visited the elders gathered at the home of the high priest Caiaphas. Like any evangelist, Judas believed God would convince each elder that Jesus was the Messiah. They asked why Jesus was not there himself to present his case as Judaic tradition required. Judas assured them Jesus would be more than willing to talk to them. After all, Jesus had said many times he had come to save the sheep of Israel, and these men were part of the flock. Judas agreed to take them to Jesus after the Passover meal. He believed himself part of God's plan.

"That Judas went to the Jewish leadership to betray Jesus for thirty pieces of silver is a silly falsehood. Like other fanatics, Judas had little concept of money. He reached for the Coming Kingdom. Concerned that Passover would end with Jesus missing his chance to speak to the multitudes, Judas did not see Jesus in danger from Jews, but from Romans. There was no betrayal. This fable was written by Christians for Christians long after the death of my son. Christians invented it to make the Jews villains and imply that Christians only wanted to be good Roman citizens. Such was the fawning strategy of that falsifier Paul.

"Judas told the leaders he would take them to his master on the Mount of Olives after the Passover meal. Jesus had indicated he wished to go there to pray and have fellowship after the sacred meal.

"When evening came the fugitives partook of the supper, their mood surprisingly light. They did not comprehend their danger. Nor did my son make any grim predictions of his own death. There were no romantic details of a latent betrayer or a dramatic promise by Jesus to rise from the dead, fictions spun much later. After supper, the disciples and my exuberant son walked to the small garden called the Mount of Olives. Unaware of the meeting between Judas and the elders, I found what happened next confusing.

"I noticed men approaching, all older prominent Jews, but sensed no particular danger. Judas rose from his seat near Jesus and introduced my son to the leader of the group with the simple pronouncement, 'Here is my teacher Jesus, the promised Messiah of the Jewish people.' Later embellishments of a kiss of betrayal are pure fantasy. The elders asked Jesus if he would explain his position to the Sanhedrin, the highest Judaic court. Jesus wanted to speak to that prestigious body. Other disciples appeared uneasy. The delegation did not arrest Jesus or use force. They told him he was wanted by Roman authorities, but they would try to keep the Sanhedrin session secret from them. Jesus accepted.

"As we walked down the gentle slope, my heart sank lower with every step. Jesus was in custody.

"We went to the house of Caiaphas, the High Priest. Caiaphas asked Jesus if he came voluntarily, and did he further agree to testify to the gathered Sanhedrin the following morning. Jesus affirmed both. With that Caiaphas said we would go to the Sanhedrin in the predawn hours to avoid Roman soldiers.

"Christian legends maintain court was held that night at the home of Caiaphas, but such a thing did not happen. The Sanhedrin, an esteemed group of seventy-one men, did not lower themselves to allow sessions or trials in the dark of night. Furthermore, the Sanhedrin only met in the Chamber of Hewn Stones. The Sanhedrin itself could not even make an arrest, but only hear charges made by citizens against an accused. Prosecutors made charges. The court cross-examined the accusers, the accused, and any witnesses. In short, the most cursory knowledge of Jewish law would show that a nighttime trial by the Sanhedrin in a private home was impossible.

"We dozed until the appointed time, then reached the Sanhedrin Chamber without drawing Roman attention. Once in the chamber, I trembled. The Sanhedrin consisted of men of education, experience, and travel. They would ask Jesus difficult questions, and he would not survive their scrutiny. Procedure and protocol slowed the process. A roll call of members was taken, then double checked. The judges quizzed the several court reporters as to their readiness. Members of the court took oaths separately and collectively, then in totality.

"Finally, the inquiry began. Jesus was asked if he had appeared voluntarily and was prepared to answer the questions of the court. My son answered, 'Yes.' The High Priest asked the audience if there were any accusers against Jesus. No shortage existed. Many accused Jesus of starting a riot in which loved ones were lost, others of his claiming to be the Messiah. Still others alleged Jesus claimed to be God. A few said Jesus had threatened to destroy the Temple. The High Priest then ruled there was the necessary number of accusers to permit court to proceed.

"The High Priest asked if there were any willing to speak on behalf of the accused. Many were. Some testified to miraculous cures for family members or themselves. Several claimed Jesus cured them of blindness, and two people recounted being raised from the dead because of my son's powers. Others described visions or hearing voices after seeing or praying about my son. Others professed their convictions that Jesus was the Messiah, come to save Israel.

"The Sanhedrin examined each of Jesus' accusers and supporters one by one. Never once was a voice raised or a witness demeaned. Once the accusers and the supporters testified, the Sanhedrin turned to my confused Jesus. The charges were read back to him and he was asked if he understood them. I could see clear signs of his irrationality. Jesus said he understood the charges, but they did not apply to him because he was a king. The clerks recorded that response. The court ignored it. Jesus was asked his age, background, education, and past activities.

"Sometimes Jesus answered rationally. On other points he made absurd responses that had nothing to do with the question. One of the Sanhedrin questioners asked if he were a descendent of King David, critical since according to legend the Messiah must be. To this Jesus answered in his illogical way, 'The Lord said to my Lord; 'Sit at my right hand until I put your enemies under your feet.' If then David calls him 'Lord' how can he be his son?' The entire room was silent except for the scratching sound of clerks recording the answer.

"A member of the court then asked if Jesus could give a sign to validate his claim of being the Messiah. I watched my son's eyes as he drifted away into his imaginary world. Finally, he replied, 'When evening comes, you say, "It will be fair weather, for the sky is red,' and in the morning, "Today it will be stormy, for the sky is red and overcast." You know how to interpret the appearance of the sky, but you cannot interpret the signs of the times. A wicked and adulterous generation looks for a miraculous sign, but none will be given it except the sign of Jonah.'

"When the questioner asked Jesus to explain, Jesus did not reply. Finally, the scribe recorded the defendant did not answer. Another questioner picked up the thread, asking if Jesus had made the following statement, 'If you have faith as small as a mustard seed, you can say to this mountain, 'move from here to there' and it will move.'

"Jesus replied that he had. The questioner then asked whether Jesus had ever moved a mountain by command. Jesus refused to answer. Another questioner asked Jesus if it were true he had stated, 'Woe to you, Korazin! Woe to you, Bethsaida! If the miracles that were performed in you had been performed in Tyre and Sidon, they would have repented long ago in sackcloth and ashes. But I tell you, it will be more bearable for Tyre and Sidon on the Day of Judgment than for you. And you, Capernaum, will you be lifted up to the skies? No, you will go down to the depths. If the miracles that were performed in you had been performed in Sodom, it would have remained to this day. But I tell you that it will be more bearable for Sodom on the Day of Judgment than for you.' Jesus replied that he had made such a statement. The questioner asked if Jesus felt it reasonable for entire cities to be condemned because some doubted the existence of miracles. Jesus refused to answer.

"Another asked Jesus whether he said, 'For by your words you will be acquitted, and by your words you will be condemned.' Jesus affirmed saying so. The questioner pressed harder. 'If that is true, how can you remain silent on these critical questions of the court? How can you expect to be acquitted?' To this reasonable question my son remained silent.

"A white-bearded member of the Sanhedrin asked Jesus if he had said, 'If your hand or your foot causes you to sin, cut it off and throw it away?' Jesus replied that he had made that statement. The questioner asked did he mean that literally, and did not such a statement run the risk of foolish people maiming themselves? Jesus refused to answer. The questioner asked Jesus if he understood the question. Once again, no answer.

"Another questioner raised his hand for permission to query the defendant. He asked my son, 'If you are the Messiah why do you refuse to show the necessary signs to this court? Are we not all waiting for the Messiah?' To this my son remained silent. The questioner pressed even harder, 'If you are a singular son of God, why have you not appeared to the authorities of Israel or Rome to state your case and to prove your authority?' Silence.

"The crowd grew restless seeing that Jesus was not going to prove his Messiah claim. One by one the disciples abandoned Jesus by slipping through crowded doorways. Only Peter stayed in the hallway. The Sanhedrin's patient but relentless questioning distressed Judas. Jesus would not answer most questions, at times giving obscure sayings in place of logical responses.

"Finally, the Sanhedrin concluded their questions. The High Priest turned to Jesus and reminded him of all the critical questions he had refused to answer. Did Jesus now choose to answer any of them? Jesus, confused and aloof at the same time, made no response. Finally the high priest in a gentle tone asked, 'Are you not going to speak? What is this testimony that these men are bringing against you?' But Jesus remained silent and gave no answer.

"With deep patience the high priest quietly asked my son the critical question. 'Are you the Christ, the Son of the Blessed one?'

"To that my excited son shouted, 'I am, and you will see the Son of Man sitting at the right hand of the Mighty One and coming on the clouds of heaven.' That sudden outburst seemed terribly out of place in the stately courtroom. At last the high priest asked the Sanhedrin and audience if anyone bearing more information wished to speak.

"Benjamin the Priest stood. He explained his experience with Jesus and his conviction that Jesus was an unbalanced person not responsible for his actions. Benjamin argued that Jesus needed medical care, not punishment, adding there was much about illness God had yet to reveal.

"I raised my hand. Although a woman, I was allowed to speak. I explained the history of my son's illness and behaviors I witnessed as his mother. It is a credit to Jewish law that I was granted a respectful audience. After my testimony I answered a number of tactful questions from the Sanhedrin. With no more witnesses, the Sanhedrin withdrew to deliberate.

"Later Christian accounts completely changed the circumstances of the Sanhedrin trial. They claimed the highest Jewish court of the nation demeaned my son and even physically abused him. Ridiculous. Would the elite of the Roman Senate physically attack a witness before their body? The Sanhedrin gave Jesus every opportunity to prove his claims. Of course, my son was neither the Messiah nor God. It did not take the court long to reach a verdict. The High Priest read the five charges against Jesus: Jesus claimed to be the Messiah; Jesus claimed to be God; Jesus was responsible for a riot; Jesus threatened to destroy the Temple; Jesus claimed to be King of the Jews. A hush filled the chamber.

"The High Priest read, 'On the first charge of claiming to be the Messiah, the Sanhedrin finds the defendant guilty based on the defendant's own claim and the testimony of other witnesses. The defendant's silence on key questions and his unwillingness to show reasonable proof to the court left no alternative but to rule that the defendant is a false Messiah. On the second charge of claiming to be God, the Sanhedrin finds the defendant not guilty based on the vagueness of the statements he uttered and the vagueness of witness testimony. On the third charge of being responsible for a riot, the Sanhedrin finds the defendant not guilty due to the fact that the defendant neither called for nor participated in the riot after it began. The court does find the defendant guilty of the misdemeanor of contributing to a public disturbance. On the fourth charge of threatening to destroy the Temple, the court finds the defendant not guilty for lack of evidence. On the fifth charge of claiming to be a King of the Jews, the Sanhedrin finds the defendant guilty based on his own confession.'

"I trembled. All that remained was the sentencing. Two of the guilty charges could be punished by death. Then the High Priest spoke, 'This case was particularly difficult. The court is convinced this defendant has given spiritual and medical help to many. This was mitigating. While many of his statements were irresponsible, the court must weigh whether he was in control of his senses when making them. After listening to and questioning the defendant, as well as weighing the testimony of many, the court is convinced that the defendant was not and is not in control of his mind. Therefore, it is the opinion of this body that justice would be served if the defendant would be held in the protective custody of the Jewish authorities until the Passover festivities end. At that time he will be turned over to his mother's care with the injunction that she control her son and see that he receives a physician's treatment. The Sanhedrin reserves the right to intervene if the defendant cannot be controlled and thus endangers himself or his community. This case is terminated. This court is now in recess.'

"I had underestimated Sanhedrin pragmatism. Such mercy only enhanced their prestige. Jesus would burn out his credibility and fade into obscurity. The men of the Sanhedrin knew that great beliefs and great causes often demand martyrs, and martyrs grow reputations. The last thing they needed was a martyr turned legend. It is sad that in spite of their wisdom and cunning they still became saddled with a legend that accused them of great wrongdoing. How long this legend will last I cannot say. The Sanhedrin did everything right and all still turned out tragically wrong.

"All the disciples had abandoned Jesus except for Peter and Judas. Both crushed, Peter still hung near the door while Judas hovered near Jesus. Several court guards spoke to Jesus, persuading him into coming with them peacefully. When Jesus looked for me I reassured him I would accompany him. With that Jesus walked with the guards out to a street.

Chapter Thirty-seven

"A sizable crowd waited for Jesus, many still shouting and calling him Messiah. Jesus smiled and waved. He accompanied his guards without hesitation, to be held under house arrest at one of the homes of Joseph of Arimathea.

"Much that happens in life is capricious chance. Romantic personalities call it destiny. All I know is that hope was ripped from me in the next few minutes. Results of the next hours have grieved me for over thirty years.

"It began with a woman's scream somewhere ahead, then more both before and behind us. I heard the clatter of iron-shod feet and saw mounted Roman officers. Roman foot soldiers blocked every escape route, brutally grabbing people, demanding to know if anyone knew Jesus. Nearly all denied knowing him. Two big soldiers nabbed Peter and asked if he knew Jesus. He grunted, 'I don't know the man!'

"The soldiers readied to cast Peter out of the circle when a Roman officer rode up and growled, 'Surely you are one of them, for your accent gives you away.' Then Peter cursed and swore, 'I don't know the man!' With that the officer waved his imperial hand and the soldiers cast Peter outside the milling crowd. Peter wept as he staggered off.

"Next, a Roman soldier grabbed my son's arm and asked if he knew Jesus. Jesus responded with amazing calm. 'Friend, do what you came for.' A brave Jew drew a sword from under his cloak to defend Jesus who raised his palm toward the defender. 'Replace your weapon, for all who draw the sword will die by the sword.' Everything paused when Jesus shouted, 'Do you think I cannot call on my Father, and he will at once put at my disposal more than twelve legions of angels? But how then would the Scriptures be fulfilled?' The superstitious soldiers fell back.

"The Roman officer wheeled his horse. 'Are you Jesus?' Jesus assumed his all-too-familiar prophet persona, saying in a polished voice, 'Yes it is as you say. Am I leading a rebellion that you have come out with swords and clubs to capture me? I have sat in the Temple courts teaching, and you did not arrest me.'

"The officer turned to his soldiers. 'Seize him. Take him to Pilate at the Praetorium.' The Romans took my Jesus away.

"I heard him shout as they led him along, 'For if men do these things when the tree is green, what will happen when it is dry?' The last thing he shouted was a passage related to Leviticus, 'I have come to bring fire on the earth, and how I wish it were already kindled! But I have a baptism to undergo, and how distressed I am until it is completed!' That was probably the most prophetic thing my poor son ever said.

"The Romans seizing a Jew already ruled upon by the Jews and in protective custody outraged the Sanhedrin. They sent a formal delegation to seek an audience with Pilate and petition the release of Jesus into their custody. All happened so fast. My beloved son hung from that bloodstained cross less than three hours after his arrest. Later Christian writers tried to make his case long and convoluted as if Pilate had nothing better to do than talk to an accused Jewish revolutionary. These writers gave a word for word account of interrogation between my son and the Roman governor. No Jew or Christian was there. Pilate gave little time to any simple Jew charged with crimes against Rome. My money bought me the details afterwards.

"In an hour Pilate, in a foul mood and drinking heavily, learned that the accused revolutionary Jesus had been seized outside the Hall of Hewn Stones. Pilate lounged in his judgment seat as guards brought Jesus into the chamber.

"Pilate asked one question, 'Are you the King of the Jews?' Jesus replied, 'Yes, it is as you say.' All Pilate needed. His verdict: 'It is a capital crime to claim to be a king without authorization by the Roman State. You are found guilty by your own admission, and are condemned to death by the cross. Guard, see to it that the prisoner is flogged and executed by normal procedure.' The trial was over, Jesus pushed roughly to the courtyard of the Praetorium.

"The Sanhedrin arrived. Pilate received them, but denied their petition on grounds that the Sanhedrin had no jurisdiction on capital charges against Rome. The Sanhedrin appealed for mercy since the prisoner was not sane, and his death would be an injustice. Pilate snapped that these were not times when anyone sane or insane could claim to be a King of the Jews. Dismissing them with a haughty wave, he returned to his wine.

"Later Christian writers tried to make Jesus' trial complicated. Not true. A confessed Jew and one more crucifixion mattered little to a Roman like Pilate. The Christian fable that Pilate tried to release Jesus from the bloodthirsty Jews is false and impossible. Pilate was a murderer with Roman authority, and the thought that such a man would literally wash his hands in front of a provincial mob to cleanse himself of guilt in my son's murder is absurd.

"A confessed 'King of the Jews' would be guilty of a capital offense. The Christian claims that Pilate released the murderer Barabbas when he, Pilate, would have been willing to release my poor son instead is also silly. Anyone who knew Pilate or the Roman justice system would know better. There was no custom to release a murderer on the Passover. The Roman legal system did not permit such light handling of justice. Roman governors, legal representatives of Rome, did not consult mobs and Rome did not release murderers for local custom. The tale is even more farfetched as Barabbas was supposedly a revolutionary. Rome would never release a threat to itself. Pilate would have killed both Jesus and Barabbas. Once again, these later Christian fables were to flatter Rome while tarring the Jews with the broad brush of infamy.

"Devastated, despairing, I remembered how long Amos suffered on a Roman cross. I wandered toward the Temple where Benjamin and Joseph of Arimathea found me on the steps. Both tried to comfort me, but they, too, knew Roman justice. Pilate had never released a capital case. Everyone knew of Roman flogging and torture on a Roman cross. Joseph said he was on his way to Pilate's court to see if anything could be done to lessen my son's fate.

"Further tragic news reached us through a Temple guard. Judas, in his final despair, hung himself. I mourned the waste of this young life. Religious fervor had claimed another victim in our troubled land. Events were outrunning my ability to comprehend. Perhaps God provided me that mercy.

"Joseph returned from pleading mercy for Jesus. Pilate would not release Jesus for any reason or sum, grumbling Rome already had him under scrutiny. Any deviation from official policy would end his governorship. However Pilate did bend the law on one issue. He allowed Joseph's personal physician to give Jesus a potion to numb his pain and end his life fairly quickly. Joseph watched Jesus swallow the drink in the Praetorium. In a few hours my son would die. Much later I learned that this act of kindness on the part of Joseph of Arimathea released Pilate from all his gambling debts. Then I heard Roman trumpets announcing yet another victim being led to crucifixion. It must be Jesus.

"The route to the execution site was well known. The victim had to carry his own crossbeam the half mile from the Praetorium to the ghastly location, "the Place of the Skulls." I saw my poor child lurch with that weighty beam along the dusty street, blood-covered from his flogging, the skin on his back flayed to the bone, so weak he could barely carry his heavy load. Every step took forever, an endless nightmare, but Jesus never cried out. His eyes glazed. He made no sound under the blows.

"The potent drug Joseph had provided, a massive dose of opium mixed with hemlock, killed gradually. For his mercy I will be forever grateful to Joseph of Arimathea.

"How can I describe the blood, dust, and flies that swarmed over my son's torn body? How do I explain the horror as my son stumbled under his burden? How many times did the lash tear his flesh, and how many times did I see my poor son struggle back to his feet? I will never know because everything blurred in pain and horror. Foot by foot I watched Jesus stumble up the dusty street in fits and jerks without pattern. Many in the crowd wept at the suffering of yet another Jewish son.

"All roads end, and finally Jesus collapsed with his beam next to a hole dug to receive this instrument of indescribable death. At midday the heat burned stifling. Two other condemned Jews, zealots captured fighting Roman occupiers, shared his day of death, their war over. I closed my eyes to shut out the spikes being driven into my son's hands and feet. I heard screams of the victims as cruel iron drove through twisting flesh. Efficient soldiers performed their dark task and erected the crosses. I saw Jesus hanging in the center of the three crosses, looking deep into the sky. He seemed to find what he sought. His chin sank to his chest.

"Crucifixion is a slow death, finally finished by thirst, general exhaustion, and exposure. The victim is intended to linger for days in agony as an example to the community. Victims often lived for forty-eight hours on the cross and strong men suffered for three or four days. In rare cases where death was desired sooner, the victim's legs were broken so they could no longer support the body's weight. This led to rapid exhaustion and suffocation. My poor son dying quickly on the cross without having his legs broken should have signaled something unusual. By crucifixion standards he did not suffer long, thankfully only half a day.

"The large crowd swelled. Many believed Jesus would use divine strength to save himself and destroy all enemies of the Jews. Others were sympathetic Jews who did not want these three to die alone. Sadly, a few perverted people taunted them on their crosses. Jewish men warned the hecklers to remain silent if they wished to live. Those who persisted were stabbed. No one ever saw the righteous killer.

"I read later Christian accountings that my poor son made prophetic statements on the road to his crucifixion and conversed with various individuals. By the time the flogging ended, the victim, often incoherent, could barely stand much less talk. Christians, so intent on smearing Jews, claim Jewish leaders taunted Jesus about his claim to be the Messiah. This did not occur. Upper-class Jews, like others, were sympathetic with those dying at the hands of hated Romans.

"Every horrific image runs into others. Swarms of flies fed on the blood of the victims, crawling over open wounds, entering ears, mouths, and noses. The victim could do nothing to alleviate this torture. Although the suffering of the other two was visible, Jesus seemed calm, eyes closed, chin upon his chest. Time stopped on that appalling knoll. Thirst is a demon of those on the cross. Sometimes victims pled for mercy and other times cursed their captors. Often they called for their mothers or begged the soldiers to kill them. I was no different. I begged the Romans to kill Jesus. They ignored me. I begged God to kill my son. God ignored me.

"Jesus never cried out or seemed lucid, and never raised his head. The opium and hemlock spared him. He drifted toward an easier death. Gradually the space between his breaths lengthened, his breathing shallower and shallower. How surprised I was when death finally took him. I turned to Joseph and asked if he had seen Jesus breathe. Joseph's massive gray head shook side to side, and tears ran down his wrinkled face. The flies sensed all resistance was gone. They flew in and out of my son's mouth with no hesitation.

"Images overwhelmed me, images of my son as a baby, a stripling, and a troubled man. It did not seem possible we would never speak again. Never again would he spellbind listeners with his fervor and compassion. Never again give hope to the masses and tell them the dreams they so wanted to believe. How could I know how wrong I was? All that came later, but at the time I was just another suffering Jewish mother who had lost her son to a Roman Cross.

"Since Passover would begin at sundown, the elders approached Pilate requesting that the victims' legs be broken so the end would come quickly. He agreed. When the soldier came to Jesus, Joseph cried, 'Soldier! Spare the body. That man is already dead!'

"The Roman officer remarked, 'I never saw a criminal die of crucifixion in less than twelve hours!' He stood in front of my son's body studying it for signs of life. Finally, he turned to Joseph saying, 'Surely this was a righteous man to escape so easily.' With a cold eye for duty the officer called a soldier over and told him to pierce Jesus' heart to be certain of death. With a quick thrust that cut me to the depths, the spear head disappeared in my son's chest. Blood and clear liquid seeped slowly from the wound. There was no sign of a pulsing blood flow, only the sluggish seeping of blood draining by gravity.

"Jesus was gone.

"Joseph then left saying, 'Perhaps there is something I can still do.'

"Typically the bodies of victims were not given to the family. To maximize the horror of the punishment the Romans would throw the broken body onto the burning trash heap of the city dump. Precluding a decent burial was another way to punish the victim by punishing his family. Much amazed, Joseph returned with a signed document from Pilate permitting Jesus' body to be turned over to our care. The officer sharply ordered soldiers to lower the cross and remove the body. Benjamin and Joseph wrapped it in blankets and servants carried it. Joseph knew where to bury Jesus with full Jewish rites. I followed, weeping.

"Later Christians wrote of odd things said to have happened that endless day. Some claimed the Temple curtain tore from top to bottom. Others claimed the sun disappeared for hours, that there were earthquakes. Still others depicted many dead rising from their graves to wander the city. Needless to say, none of that happened. Jesus was another tragic victim destroyed by Roman occupiers. There were no voices from heaven, no miraculous signs, and no divine intervention. Many versions of events were written by people infatuated by dreams of Jesus' imaginary Kingdom. None are true.

"We did not walk far to reach the burial site, a shallow cave hewn from soft rock. Joseph's servants prepared the body by washing, then wrapping it in burial shrouds with spices customary for burial of the wealthy. They shelved the body in its final resting place. After Benjamin intoned the Jewish prayers for the dead, we withdrew. Five men sealed the tomb's mouth by rolling an immense boulder, designed to be removed only with difficulty, into the entry portal.

"It was nearly sundown on Friday when the burial was finished, the tomb sealed. As I lingered at the mouth of the sealed tomb I had no idea this was not the end of the story of my troubled son. Fate decreed his memory did not end with his entombment, but extended far beyond. Events between the crucifixion on Friday and the Sunday morning following Passover have been so misunderstood. I now tell you what happened.

"One of my overriding memories of my son's final hours was the rapidity of the events. Even after years of reflection I can barely put them in right order. I do remember that after the stone was rolled into place the sun set, making it officially Passover when Jerusalem would be in religious celebration. Heartbroken, I returned to the city in deep mourning.

"Joseph and Benjamin escorted me through quietly tense streets. I did not notice the increased activity of Roman soldiers. More attentive, I would have noticed our avoidance of main streets in the poorer neighborhoods. At Joseph's home, he advised it was not safe for me to leave. I approached Benjamin with questions, but he told me to wait until Joseph returned with information. When I asked if this had to do with Jesus, Benjamin reluctantly nodded. I was at a loss. Jesus was dead and far beyond further turmoil.

"A worried Joseph returned after two hours. Finally, Joseph and Benjamin led me into a private room. Joseph explained that large sections of Jerusalem were rioting in the name of Jesus. Fighting might soon spread over the entire city. Zealots were claiming Jesus had risen from the dead to command the Jews to overthrow the Roman oppressor. Many claimed to have seen Jesus alive. These rumors swept through the religious hopeful like desert wind. Even some disciples proclaimed they had seen the 'risen Lord' and thrown their influence behind this delusion.

"I was speechless. How could such a thing be believed? Hundreds watched the soldier plunge his spear in my poor son's heart. Hundreds had seen Jesus' body removed from the cross and borne to his grave. What sane person would believe the dead could rise from the tomb? Such tales might entertain children, but surely no rational adult would accept them! When I brought up these objections, Joseph insisted this hysteria was real. I objected that no one had ever seen anyone rise from the grave. Who could produce an example? Finally, I gained self control and asked what could be done.

"Joseph reported Pilate was in a sodden fury. Joseph had sought an audience with him, and Pilate raged against the Jews, Jesus in particular, threatening to have Jesus' body removed from the grave and dragged through Jerusalem's streets. Pilate even threatened to feed the scraps of his body to swine.

"Could I have done anything differently? I had just buried Jesus with no time even to mourn. All I could think of was how important it was that he rest in peace. The thought of Romans dragging his poor body through the streets and feeding its remnants to swine terrified me. Joseph rose to fill a wine glass for me. Finally he turned and said, 'The body must be moved to avoid its desecration. However, moving a body without official permission is a capital offense even for a man of my standing.' Both the Romans and the Jews had strong laws against moving bodies. If anything was to be done it had to be done quickly. I implored Joseph to save my son from this unbearable humiliation. We had to move his body.

Chapter Thirty-eight

"Joseph smiled grimly. 'I will help you, but time is short. I must find the men for this dangerous task. In a short while one will come to your window. 'You must slip out of it to follow him with no questions. Do you understand?' With no idea of what this would do to history, I embraced my honorable friend saying I would take any risk to spare the body of Jesus.

"I dreaded every minute until I heard a low voice below my window. A black man motioned me to slide out into his arms. In moments I followed him through dark alleyways. I made out the solid outline of the city walls. My guide motioned me to duck into a dim room and closed the small door behind us. Joseph stepped beside me saying we were in a grain warehouse and must be lowered by rope through a ventilation window thirty feet to the ground outside the city walls. Several men slipped out and slid down the long rope in seconds. They lowered Joseph on a loop. In that manner, praying, I slipped over the edge into the dark unknown. Rough hands halted my descent and my feet touched the hard ground outside Jerusalem.

"We stealthily moved off. Joseph and I struggled to keep up with these hard men. Fortunately, the distance was not far. Even in the dark I could tell we had arrived at the burial grounds. In minutes we stood before the boulder that sealed the entrance of my son's grave. A thin moon hung in the sky. Its pale light cast sheen over the chalk-white stone. I shivered, although I had no idea moving that stone would move the civilized world. I had no time to reflect with dawn only a few hours away.

"These brawny men pressed against the stone's mass, muscles bulging. For a second it seemed nothing would move that boulder. Then I saw the slightest movement. The stone began to inch left. Huge hands took new holds and I heard these muscular titans inhale to renew their assault. Slowly, steadily, the stone moved to the left until it reached its center of gravity and rolled over. The men glistened with sweat. They gasped, gripping their knees. I looked at that huge stone, now moved, and could not escape feeling this would never be forgotten. A muscular black man entered the tomb and emerged carrying Jesus like a baby in his huge arms. Joseph placed a steadying hand on my shoulder, whispering that we must leave this place quickly. No one resealed the tomb. The men had neither time nor energy to replace that huge stone.

"The story of Jesus and the empty tomb would grow far beyond the sad truth of our desperate mission. Jesus' missing body shored up the foundation of a religious cult whose impact I still do not fully understand.

"Jerusalem and everything in it terrified me as we moved northwest. The speed these men could travel with their heavy burden amazed me. I pushed myself to keep up. Fear of Romans and the coming dawn kept me going. I have no idea how far we traversed in those dark hours, but I estimate over ten miles.

"Finally, stars in the east flickered out. Joseph conferred with the brawny leader. We stood on a shale ridge. The dark leader made the final decision. We were near a depression about eight feet deep, a rock slide above and below. The upper section appeared to be held back by key boulders. They placed their dear burden in the hollow. This was the end. Jesus would rest safe from wild beasts and the greater savagery of men. Our companions pried the key boulders. The leader nodded to Joseph to indicate that the slide was poised to go. Joseph suggested I turn my back to the scene, but I had to see this last sight of my son's body. Joseph nodded to the leader, and at least fifty feet of rock swept over Jesus. No sign of the depression remained, covered now by one of countless rock slides.

"Joseph took my hand and said a prayer for the dead. I thanked each of the black men. It seemed somehow fitting that people despised by both Jews and Romans laid Jesus to rest.

"A great weariness clouded me as we left my son's burial site. I had no idea where I was, and in truth, was too exhausted to care. I staggered on. I do not know how far we traveled, at least another hour before dawn. By then we trekked on a goat path.

"We finally came to a hamlet of six tents in a saddle between two hills. The inhabitants were nomads staying one wary step ahead of the tax collector. Joseph purchased rough bread, crude wine, and bitter cheese. How delicious that food tasted. We washed at a small spring, shedding our former appearance of dirty fugitives. We kept north on the goat trail until it merged with a small road which by midmorning flowed into a large one. Our pace now normal, we looked like any party of a wealthy, traveling Jew. I could easily pass as mistress of a well-to-do merchant and the six dark men were rugged servants charged with protecting their master.

"We reached Antipatris where we rested for a day in another of Joseph's home. We determined to continue from Antipatris to Caesarea where both Joseph and I had property and financial resources. From Caesarea I planned to go home to Sepphoris and my family. Joseph would resume life as a merchant.

"In Antipatris we first heard rumors from those returning from Jerusalem. Fighting there between Romans and Jewish nationalists raged through Passover night. People convinced that Jesus was the promised Messiah swelled the ranks of fighting Jews. Pilate committed every military resource he had, then decided on desecration of the tomb at first light. He would discredit the belief in Jesus as the Messiah by ordering his body dragged through the streets. Of course, the soldiers found the stone rolled aside, the body missing. We had beaten them by five or six hours. The soldiers informed Pilate, and the story of the abandoned tomb swept the city.

"Many Jews accepted the vacant tomb as proof Jesus had risen from the dead. Reports of imaginary sightings and conversations with my dead son followed. Some distraught women claimed to have gone to the tomb Sunday morning and seen angels roll the stone away. Others claimed conversations with a strange man dressed in white. Others claimed to mistake Jesus for a gardener. Apparently such emotionalism overtook the more unstable disciples. Peter and John announced they entered the empty tomb and saw proof that Jesus had been raised from the dead.

"Sightings began to accumulate as people's imaginations scrambled their senses. Jesus supposedly appeared on city streets, country roads, and even behind closed doors. No stories matched. Pilate blamed the Jewish community for the body's disappearance and beset leaders could only respond that perhaps the disciples had absconded with it. Most of the disciples disavowed any connection with Jesus. The few who still clung to their illusion of my son as the Messiah were in hiding. Years later I read stories about the tomb being allegedly guarded by Roman soldiers overcome by an angel sent to retrieve Jesus.

"I believed these fantastic tales would blow over. They had no logical basis. What an incredible leap from an empty grave to the dead coming back to life. There is an even greater leap between the crazy idea of a resurrected person and the even crazier idea that the dead returned as God of the universe. Of all the possibilities to explain an empty grave, surely a physical resurrection has to be least likely! Why would a resurrected god only show himself to insignificant people in obscure locations? Surely, a god who defeated death would have no problem facing a petty tyrant like Pilate? Why would he not speak in public? Surely, the Sanhedrin and even the Roman Senate would wish to gain favor with the God of the Universe. Would Jesus rise from the dead and simply disappear? It did not seem possible that such nonsense could last. I greatly underestimated the power of blind emotion. At the time, Roman authorities concerned me more. Joseph and I would be prime suspects to have taken the body. Joseph assured me he left messages to tell anyone who inquired that he left at first light to escort me to Sepphoris. That was credible, so no harm should befall us.

"From Antipatris we proceeded to the coast of the Mediterranean Sea near Apollonia. Each now carried papers from Joseph stating he was being sent to distant ports on business. Each would board at Joppa. They were runaway slaves with no motive to reveal the past, and Joseph rewarded them heavily. I embraced them and wished them God's blessing. Six of the eight knowing the true story of the empty tomb vanished into North Africa. Within two years fate would reduce our number to one.

"We reached Caesarea and stayed at another of Joseph's homes. Rumors reached us that the Jerusalem rioters had been crushed and Pilate would soon be returning to Caesarea himself. Joseph said it would be best to be there when Pilate returned. Within the week Pilate arrived and summoned Joseph who easily survived Pilate's interview. Pilate had no evidence of involvement or unusual flight. He did not lower himself to speak with me. The crisis appeared to be over. Pilate assumed the Jesus myth would disappear into local history.

"Of course, it did not.

"All parties were relieved to put the tragedy behind them. At last, I could mourn like any bereaved mother. Joseph resumed his normal life, and I tried to get on with mine. I never told my children the true story of the missing Jesus. That would endanger their lives.

"As Sepphoris was a major community, I could keep track of the country at large and followed the so-called Jesus Movement, so surprisingly durable. The main groups of resurrection believers lived in Jerusalem. The message seemed to be that Jesus was the Messiah and faith in this idea saved the believer. Central to this, Jesus would return from heaven very soon to establish his kingdom and elevate the faithful. Since the believer assumed this heavenly return to be imminent, many forsook daily work, selling their property and means of making a livelihood. These fanatic Christians said this proved their faith. Since the Christians believed in close fellowship, many lived together leading to speculation of immorality.

"The first Christians considered themselves Jews following the ancient practices of Judaism. Christians worshipped at the Temple and adhered to standard Jewish commandments. The larger community saw the Christians as one more Judaic sect. In time divisive Christians would rupture this view.

"Bewildered, I watched this movement grow. The initial body of Christians was the so-called Jerusalem Church. Peter and John, the most emotional disciples, led them. The sincerity and enthusiasm of the original Christians was contagious. Their other world view and willingness to accept any fellow believer as a brother or sister attracted many. Christianity drew elements of society who had never known love or even friendship. Thus, the poor and the powerless found in Christianity a family many had never known. This odd movement continued to expand. It had the advantage of novelty. Converts thrilled at being the new faith's cutting edge. The story appealed to people's imaginations, a god born of a virgin siding with the oppressed. I expected all this to gradually collapse, its foundation that Jesus would return soon to claim his kingdom.

"Years passed, and Jesus did not return. Many disillusioned left the Jesus movement. Nevertheless, Christian numbers continued to swell. Many dispossessed willingly tried this new system. The average Christian converted for support, love, and fellowship rather than as the result of objective study. At times, extreme Christians were disruptive. They would be arrested, tried, and punished. For example, John and Peter were called before the Sanhedrin for excessive proselytizing and given corporal punishment, not unusual for any Jewish sect.

"Christianity would have continued as a Jewish sect except for Paul, who entered when problems beset the movement. Jesus had not returned to found his kingdom. Nearly ten years had passed, and the faithful found their patience tested. Many of the original believers had died and there was questioning as to what their reward could be. In my own circle of friends, Joseph of Arimathea and Benjamin died of disease. Joseph bequeathed me a large portion of his estate, and now my resources were very large.

"I alone remember the details of my son's true story.

"Christians accepted gentiles into their ranks and the question of Jewish laws loomed. Divisions between Christians grew. Natural leaders and strong personalities appeared. Christianity was at a critical point when Paul arrived.

"A short man with one bad eye and the build of a back-alley wrestler, his good eye gleamed with intensity common to an unhealthy personality. He was obsessive, argumentative, and filled with latent violence. He suffered from epileptic seizures. Everywhere he went he brought strife, intolerance his most notable characteristic. With his keen mind, sharp tongue, and fierce demeanor Paul manipulated others, bending facts and inventing history as needed. His behavior oscillated from honeyed terms of love to the sword edge of violence. Occasionally Paul threatened his followers with a whip.

"He said he heard heavenly voices, saw visions, had divine powers, and authority from God. Paul transformed a local Jewish vision of Jesus into an international religion that embraced all comers. I met him on a trip to Jerusalem. Paul had little use for women and none for me. Since I was supposedly the mother of God, I found this odd.

"Paul had arrived from Tarsus, the main city on the plain of East Cilicia in Southwest Asia Minor, claiming to be a Roman citizen from a strictly Jewish family. Like many of his claims this was not entirely so. He converted to Judaism from gentile parents who showed a modest interest in it. Rome granted his father citizenship for business services toward the Roman army making Paul, too, a Roman citizen, rare for a Jew. His adopted Judaism filled his spiritual needs for a time, but Paul embraced a conviction that the world's future depended on him. Paul felt the Jews of Tarsus were bad Jews, so he moved to Jerusalem anticipating a pure city of God, filled with the pious. Instead, Jerusalem was a city like any other filled with the tastes and vices of normal people wanting to make money, seek pleasure, and live comfortable lives. In his disappointment, Paul concluded his God-appointed task was to save Judaism from such debasement.

"For years Paul, supported by his gentile parents, studied under various rabbis. His native tongue was Greek, so this education in Hebrew and the Torah served him well in years ahead. Rabbis who attempted to teach this intense man were appalled at his impatience. In Paul's muddled thinking, God told him what was right. Anyone who disagreed was evil.

"Eventually Paul refused the teaching of his patient rabbis. Laborious daily study seemed unnecessary since God spoke to him. Paul announced only the great Jewish teacher Gamaliel worthy of his time. Unfortunately, Gamaliel only accepted advanced students. Gamaliel gently encouraged Paul to advance his qualifications which Paul took as an insult. The Pharisees rejected him so he would reject them.

"Rigid Paul saw the Pharisees' tendencies to reexamine the Torah with changing societal needs to be the gravest of sins. Paul found comfort and employment with the Temple party, the Sadducees who declared the Torah unchangeable. He threw his lot in with them with fanatical fury.

"The Sadducees found uses for this extremist. The Temple party used the crime of apostasy to harass those annoying to them. These witch hunts involved minor affairs with modest punishments imposed to discourage dissent. Many critics were Pharisees, and Paul relished the chance to harm them. Over time the high Priest found more use for Paul. This symbiotic relationship might have lasted but for the High Priest's attractive niece. It is a mystery how the pure emotion of love can change so quickly to hate.

"The niece was actually exquisite. Paul fell in love, burning with unhealthy intensity. He convinced himself she loved him deeply. His single minded pursuit of her soon transcended acceptable standards. The girl could not convince Paul she found him wanting.

"Paul also exceeded instructions from the High Priest as to degrees of punishment inflicted on minor dissenters. Paul entered private homes to make unauthorized arrests, doling out punishments far more extreme than the Temple Sadducees ever intended. Evangelistic Christians attracted his attention, and he bore down on them. The High Priest reprimanded Paul. The High Priest's niece suspected Paul could become dangerous and took her fears to her uncle.

"Matters came to a head when Paul, without authorization, arrested a young Hellenistic Christian, Stephen, and ordered him stoned to death for apostasy. Only Romans could enforce a death sentence. The High Sadducee Priest summoned Paul, relieved him of all official power, and warned him to leave the niece in peace. Finally, Paul was banished. He hated Jews, the Torah, and all women from then on. Humiliated, escorted to the gates of Jerusalem and expelled from the city, Paul felt Jews had betrayed him. Humiliated, angry, and disturbed, Paul resolved to go to Damascus in search of a more receptive audience. On this ill-fated trip, international Christianity was born.

Chapter Thirty-nine

"What did Paul think he saw on the road to Damascus? Paul carried a heavy history of extremism. My experiences with Jesus taught me that unbalanced people often claim to converse with God. Perhaps Paul's conscience chafed about Stephen's death. Given his tormented mind, convoluted past, and painful present Paul might have imagined anything.

"Paul claimed to see a godlike risen Jesus who assigned him the mission of telling gentiles Jesus was the key to personal salvation. However, Paul never told the story the same way. In one version he went directly to Damascus after his vision struck him blind. At Damascus, Paul was given back his sight after he talked to a Jew named Ananias. On other occasions, Paul claimed he went into Arabia to reflect on his vision at length, apparently not blind during that detour.

"Themes of blood, sacrifice, and rebirth so prevalent to pagan religions never left Paul. Paul never dwelt on my son's moral sayings or reported miracles. He saw only the brutal cross, morbidly fascinating to his overheated mind. Not for Paul the sweet tale of a virgin birth. All Paul could see was his blinding vision of a cross, and anyone who did not share this was a devil's agent.

"Paul boasted he would be all things to all people to press home his views. All too often he slandered Jews. Pagan gentiles were easy prey, knowing nothing of Jesus' Jewish past or Judaic beliefs. While the Jews embraced many sects, Paul lacked such tolerance. He never told his followers that Jesus was an observant, broadminded Jew, or that all the disciples continued to worship at the Temple after his death. Nor did Paul remind his followers that Jesus believed in an earthly kingdom to transpire within his listeners' lives. Paul changed references of an earthly kingdom into a heavenly kingdom. This sleight of hand fooled few Jews, but many gentiles.

"Paul claimed salvation followed death. Jews knew salvation as the arrival of the Messiah and the coming Kingdom of the

Jews. Pagans knew little or nothing about the Messiah, but knew a great deal about half-divine kings and resurrections. The dialogues where Peter renounced Judaism were fabrications. Even within them one can read that Peter never allowed unclean food to cross his lips. Jesus' disciples were law-abiding Jews.

"Accounts of early years of the Jesus movement in Israel must include my son James. Much younger than Jesus, James studied religion and grew concerned over Jesus' impact on impressionable people. As I have written, many sold their personal goods and property anticipating Jesus' return. Spiritually, many believers showed signs of drifting from Judaism. This bothered idealistic James. With extremists like Paul coming forth, James went to Jerusalem.

"There, he assumed leadership of the Christian body. It made perfect sense that the closest relative to Jesus would lead until Jesus' return to establish his kingdom. Disciples like Peter and John simply could not displace Jewish tradition. James decided to repulse Paul as one who warped the Jesus message. In his writings James exhorted that faith without works was dead, a strictly Jewish idea opposing the very heart of Paul's theological position of faith alone. James secretly intended to gradually return Christians to the Orthodox Judaic fold.

"I spent funds to see to it the more needy Christians did not starve because of their deluded beliefs. I hoped to ameliorate the worst effects of my sick Jesus. Tragically, my beloved James lost his life in the treacherous quicksand of Israeli politics. I never mourned for him. James was a rational man who entered into his cause fully aware, although his real purposes for the Jesus Movement did die with him.

"Thus the Jesus Movement swelled. Rationality is rare. People love a romantic story threaded with mystery. Most seek easy answers to impossible questions. We cannot know the how and why of life and death. The Jesus cult met emotional needs, offering certainty in the face of the unknown, and hope to the hopeless. Converts like Peter and John and adventurers like Luke, and later, Mark extended this illusion. Fanatics like Paul damned to hell those he could not dominate. Slaves, poor farmers, and the dispossessed joined the movement. By land and by sea this story of the Good News seemed to move under a power of its own.

"It has taken me years to understand that the strength of Christianity is not in facts because it is neither factual nor logical. The strength of Christianity lies where reason cannot touch it. Christianity is only a state of mind and heart.

"The Roman Empire itself waxed ripe for new religions, forgetting the old Roman gods. Roman conquest had destroyed the gods of many cultures, and new ideas could easily flow due to the unprecedented construction of the Roman road system and security. Ideas raced across hundreds of leagues thanks to them. While Judaism was admired, becoming Jewish was difficult, the host of Jewish laws and the requirement for circumcision formidable barriers. Conversely, acceptance of Jesus as savior was the sole requirement to be Christian. The early church offered unmatched material and emotional support. Under Christianity rich and poor were equal. Master and slave broke bread together. Christianity was a bargain, Paul an adroit trader.

"Already there have been martyrs. Christianity is divided. Some abandon all earthly goods and follow Jesus on a hard road of poverty. Others admire the moral precepts while holding on to earthly possessions. Still others seek martyrdom. Many more accept salvation with little outward change in their lives. But there are those who abandon family, work, and earthly involvement to become cave dwellers meditating on divine visions.

"A bloody debate clashes as to whether Jesus was human, divine, or both. Grave confrontations rage as to whether Jesus was God or created by God. Some sought a solution by claiming Jesus and God the same yet different. I see division, hate, and even killing ahead. Most Christians hate Jews even though Rome crucified Jesus.

"Already I see collected sayings attributed to him, most products of fraud or unbridled creativity. Contradictory accounts claim to be gospels of my son's life. Neither I nor most of the disciples ever wrote a word of support for Jesus being the basis for a new religion. Paul never knew him. The disciples were unlettered peasants, except for Matthew, a low-level tax collector. They saw the error in their hopes and returned to normal lives. None of Jesus' brothers and sisters wrote a word to support Christian claims, except James who took a Jewish viewpoint. Although many Christians begged me to become a vocal Mother of God I refused. Some of the more deluded even suggest worshipping me. Outlandish.

"I am at the end of my life. Here ends my account. I write as the last of a long line which began with Eli and Moses in Egypt and finishes in Sepphoris in Galilee. It is fitting that I close with a small writing penned by Jesus. There were other of his writings, but everything was of the same tone. Perhaps you can understand them. I cannot."

***

"I am Jesus the Son of God. Voices speak to me. I see that which I cannot touch. Sometimes I am happy, but today I am afraid. My head hurts. I shout, but no one hears. I am shouting now. Thank God my mother has heard me. I fly many places. Where am I now? The water feels good. Mother why are you crying? Mother, can't you see the angel? Mother, don't be afraid. Mother, please stop crying. Don't worry. I will bring peace to the earth. The kingdom is coming soon. Mother, please don't cry. Someday I will get better. Then I will come back. Goodbye. Goodbye. Now I am gone."

Chapter Forty

Liberalism and Western-style democracy have not been able to help realize the ideals of humanity. Today, these two concepts have failed. Those with insight can already hear the sounds of the shattering and fall of the ideology and thoughts of liberal democratic systems...Whether we like it or not, the world is gravitating towards faith in the Almighty and justice and the will of God will prevail over all things.

President Mahmoud Ahmadinejad of Iran, in a 2007 open letter to President George W. Bush

I believe it's a lot easier to change the Constitution than it would be to change the word of the living God, and that's what we need to do is to amend the Constitution so it's God's standards rather than try to change God's standards.

Mike Huckabee, Republican presidential candidate, 1/14/2008

Isaac Gold shivered, automatically reaching with a tremulous hand for a cigarette. He lit the new cigarette and drew the acrid smoke deep, welcoming the burning assault of this lifelong poison. He needed the steadying influence of a bad habit.

The Tablets were authentic. Only God could have any real idea of their impact. It hadn't taken long to read the translations. The sun still hovered high. Yet for him the world might as well have turned flat that afternoon. Academic reaction would be astonishment, then skepticism, then cautious examination of the evidence, and finally overwhelming confirmation of the Tablets' authenticity followed by academic exhilaration and countless serious books, but no danger. Among professionals, Jesus was a liberal Jew with common apocalyptic expectations. How would the faithful react? His training in psychology raised a caveat: possible denial, released emotional repression, sudden shifts in personal values with a possibility of deviant behavior.

Gold reflected. As Paul's early Christian numbers grew, so went politics. Personalities rose through the ranks and gathered followers. Charges and countercharges of heresy swooped like falcons. Theologically ambitious used fraud and force as often as prayer and persuasion to achieve power. Finally, one group clawed to dominance: the Roman Catholics. As the Empire's center, Rome's voice was loudest, justifying Mary's concern about being worshipped.

Some books attributed to Paul were authored by others. No Gospel was written by its claimed author. Many well-accepted Christian Gospels didn't survive selection for the New Testament. Winners wrote the New Testament nearly four hundred years after Jesus death, its books voted upon by fallible, prejudice-driven men. Typically pastors knew this, yet told their congregations nothing. Enter the Jesus Tablets.

Gold inhaled. Why did the New Testament, compiled into one rough body nearly three hundred years after Jesus lived, trigger such emotion? Before that believers just had sayings, rituals, and memories of Jesus. Thousands of Christians lived and died without the New Testament. Now fundamentalists bicker over obscure passages. The Greek Orthodox, the Roman Catholics, and the Protestants read significantly different Bibles. How many translations does each version have with passages shaded toward particular theological beliefs? The idea of one correct biblical interpretation or one version was laughable. Dr. Gold drew smoke deep into his lungs as he pondered on human folly.

Jesus probably suffered from schizophrenia, viewed then as demonic possession. Or, Gold considered, bipolar affective disorder. Sometimes Jesus functioned normally, the euthymic state. During manic stages he displayed a command presence, able to inspire a following.

Paul's writings swung from rapture to teeth-gritting hate, symptoms of manic depression. Recently researchers found areas of the brain could be electrically stimulated to induce visions. Fifty million worldwide suffered from schizophrenia. Why not millions of Jesus' time also?

Gold paced, thinking hard.

He glanced at pale early evening Sepphoris light. A chill of dread gripped him. Annoyed, he shrugged it off. It made sense to stay the night and leave to report to Roth first thing tomorrow. He wanted time with Sam Stein, Alice, and Henry to compare findings.

***

"Well," he told the other three over stuffed eggplant that evening, "my findings match yours. The Tablets are authentic."

The fellowship of minds nodded as one. "I almost hoped you'd find some error. I feel like we're racing toward a cliff's edge," Alice responded.

"Unfortunately, we're each so meticulous and brilliant that wasn't likely," said Stein, trying to inject humor into the situation. It fell flat.

A solemn group drifted out to watch the setting of the blood red Galilean sun. They leaned back contemplatively in battered camp chairs, enjoying the cool drift of evening air as crimson light sank beneath the horizon. Brooding Sepphoris loomed in dusky shadows as the Ambassador joined them.

Six hundred meters away, Amal lay motionless, watching. An American woman joined them. Amal's sniper scope picked up and amplified the fading light as she studied each face. Both targets present, although not beside each other. Now her fate would be in Allah's hands. She would fire at the last moment of daylight to increase chances of escape. She placed the cross hairs on her priority target's heart, ready to turn on the radio transmitter switch near her right hand before shooting. The programmed device would jam every radio signal in a two mile radius. Blended with meaningless static were words in Hebrew about remaining at your post because there have been accidental discharges. Without orders an officer or soldier is loath to act. There was a chance in their confusion they wouldn't respond to her shots. Amal's only hope.

Light softened as Amal turned on the transmitter switch. Twenty seconds of static before the garbled orders, time for two aimed shots to shatter Sepphoris' quiet. Amal placed the cross hairs on her primary target. She evaluated the elements. She squeezed the trigger. Perfectly aimed, her bullet tumbled through the body, destroying the victim's heart. Professor Samuel Stein of Harvard University spun out of his chair, dead. The recoil pulled Amal off target, but in a moment the second bullet stuck center mass on its second target, Ambassador Morgenstern.

Amal abandoned her rifle and gear. She settled into a ground-eating pace with no effort to be silent, depending on the soldiers'being swamped with conflicting stimuli.

Radio operators tried frantically to make their radios function as commanders cursed over their shoulders. The garbled Hebrew telling soldiers to hold their positions worked perfectly. Junior commanders grasped at seemingly legitimate orders. In seventeen minutes commanders realized a sniper made the kills and the hunt began. In thirty-two minutes soldiers discovered the transmitter and weapon. Amal ran in absolute darkness three miles away.

The Marine guards allowed no one on site, their first responsibility to protect the Tablets. They snatched the surviving scholars, dragging them into the study. The Crosses and Gold took cover while a few Marines stood guard. Others secured the main gate. This small but determined force persuaded the Israeli Major not to try to enter the base if he wanted to live to collect his retirement. The Marine lieutenant in charge suspected Israelis of making the kills. After all, they surrounded the site.

The Israeli command finally ascertained that two high profile Americans had been killed. The search for the sniper expanded. Israeli helicopters from a dozen military commands rose airborne to search for the shooter who had defeated the security of over three hundred Israeli soldiers and made two kills mortifying to Israel.

***

Prime Minister Roth understood that these American deaths changed everything. He ordered all resources thrown into the hunt with a full investigation to start forthwith. These murders would inflame America. Hopes of the Jesus Tablets cooling off died with the victims.

Onsite journalists grasped the situation. Overhead satellites already downloaded the facts to international newspapers. News that the site of the highly controversial Jesus Tablets was now the scene of two ruthless murders bombarded the air. President Straihorn canceled all appointments. Within minutes advisors arrived at the White House. President Straihorn was on a secure line calling the Israeli Prime Minister. In seconds a nervous aide knocked on the Prime Minister's door to tell him President Straihorn was on the line. Never a man to avoid his duty, Roth picked up the phone and greeted his caller.

"Prime Minister we've been informed of two Americans murdered on the Sepphoris site. We're short on facts. What can you tell us?"

Roth kept his voice level. "Mr. President, all I know at the moment is that Ambassador Morgenstern and Dr. Stein of Harvard have been assassinated by sniper fire. I've authorized all resources toward capturing the killer. My people are studying the evidence. Apparently the investigation is hindered by your Marines unwillingness to allow anyone to enter the base. What is your position?"

President Straihorn answered smoothly, "I advise you to make no efforts to enter the base. Obviously the shooter operated from outside Sepphoris. There are already rumors that the Israelis are trying to destroy the Tablets. A surprising percent of Americans are predisposed to believe in conspiracies. We must prevent damage to Israeli and American interests."

Prime Minster Roth pondered this. "It's incredible that anyone could accuse Israel, a faithful ally of the United States. We Israelis share a common religious heritage with many Americans. Israel has no reason to destroy the Jesus Tablets. We'll share any information we have in solving these murders."

"Prime Minister, I never doubt the honesty and loyalty of your government. It's just important to keep such rumors in mind as we address this emergency. Let's double-check our facts. Your Dr. Gold was there at the shooting. Is that correct?"

"Dr. Gold was there, but unharmed. He's to brief me concerning the Tablets tomorrow morning. If possible we'd like to remove him from the camp for his assessment of the Tablets as well as any help he might be about the murders."

"I'll order the Marines to admit an Israeli ambulance to remove the bodies and provide Dr. Gold with a secure means to leave. This might help dispel the notion our two countries are at odds. Reflect the cooperation of our governments!"

Prime Minister Roth clutched this pawn. "Excellent. I'll have an ambulance standing by outside Sepphoris. The bodies will be delivered to U.S. authorities with all due care and, of course, Israel's sympathy."

***

The object of the manhunt made it five miles from Sepphoris. Adrenaline fueled, her feet flew over the rocky ground. She would stay in the rough hill country continuing southeast toward En Harod before crossing the main highway, then switching back toward Ya 'bad in the southwest. Amal gambled the Israelis would assume she'd head north into Nazareth or bypass it to reach Lebanon by sea or land. On the other hand, if pursuers detected her general route toward the southeast, it would look like she was attempting to reach Syria by crossing the Jordan. The Israelis might assume she wanted to reach the ghetto slum called Ya Bad. With luck she could make it back to the general and the fragile safety of her employee identity. Still, she'd planned well and had resources. She heard the chopping of helicopters increasing in absolute numbers. Most still seemed near Sepphoris.

Helicopters rose from all over Northern Israel. Nearly twenty lifted from the two large military complexes north of Ummel Fahm. Fifteen came from the north from the large base near Beit Jann. Fifteen more flew directly toward the Ya-Bad sector from their home base near Baqa el Gharblya. Eight hundred soldiers scurried to contain all major highways around Sepphoris. Amal's only real advantage, the dark of night, could no longer conquer technology. Thermo-imaging devices capable of detecting a human by body heat alone rode on every helicopter. Amal wagered her life against modern equipment.

Now, in early evening the devices would have difficulty separating her body heat from the countless stones and boulders that absorbed heat all day. As night wore on, the stones would cool, and heat-detecting devices' accuracy increased dramatically. In parts of the terrain a human would be the hottest object within the sensor's range. The closest helicopter, a mile away, swung in her direction. Watching its approach, Amal cuddled against a boulder formation. As the chopper neared, Amal prayed to Allah. In seconds she'd know her fate.

The helicopter technician distinguished no thermo signature except the terrain's ambient temperature. Amal, spared for the moment, exhaled as the helicopter continued on its hunt. Every minute of night meant cooler terrain. Amal hunched and ran as fast as she could without making noise, far enough from Sepphoris that her danger now lay in troops stationed near roads. Israelis would be unlikely to send patrols out into the night. Amal had twelve more miles of hard ground to cover and several major highways. With luck she would make General Kessler's property by dawn. If still in open country at sunrise, she would be unlikely to live to see it set. She pushed on.

***

The murders traumatized Alice and Henry. Sam Stein had been like a father to Henry through his student days, his mentor after Henry obtained his teaching position. Everyone had admired, if not loved, this kindly scholar, now gone.

Henry and Alice lay on their bed in dimmed light, trying to make sense of the violence. An Israeli ambulance under heavy Marine guard had finally taken the bodies and the stunned Dr. Gold. Then Marines confined everyone to quarters. Not only was the house surrounded, but four somber young men stood within ten feet of the blanket-covered Tablets. Henry couldn't escape the impression of the Tablets as another shrouded corpse. "Ambassador Morgenstern's murder bewilders me the most," Alice murmured. "I'm so devastated about Sam that I'm embarrassed to admit I'm relieved we barely knew her."

Henry nodded. "I think people learn in war how to ignore the deaths of strangers. Friends or family dying, that's different. Always personal."

"The Tablets must have caused all this," Alice ventured, feeling idiotic for pointing out the obvious. "But I'm lost as to what purpose murdering those two served."

Henry shifted and sat up a little. "I've been going over it. Mrs. Morgenstern was a politician, but not an important one. Dr. Stein had no political clout. Even more confusing, the killer shot Sam first. Why would Sam Stein be a mad sniper's first priority?"

"Do you think Dr. Gold…"

"No. He's as devastated by Sam Stein's murder as we are. Their friendship was known all through the archaeology community. And how do these deaths help Israel? Even if they wanted to destroy the Tablets, this wouldn't do it. After all, security around the Tablets is higher than ever."

"Well, somebody murdered because of them," Alice said. "Since the Marines won't talk to us about it, we have to wait and watch. It's funny. It's like the other shoe dropped. My instincts were right. The Tablets brought evil to our door." She turned, but didn't push Henry away when he sighed and spooned against her. The night seemed very large.

***

John Martin, still at Sepphoris, intuited this might be the scoop of his career. Interest in the Tablets had been high world-wide. His headlines capped the front page since he'd received his mysterious tip to go to Sepphoris. News chiefs screamed for more on the murders. Fortunately, Martin gave his editors shattering information even though he couldn't name his sources. That night, while Henry and Alice talked softly in their room, Martin, about to rest his head, instead found a note pinned to his pillow. It read, "Go to the men's room. Remove the lid on the second toilet." He looked around. Assured no one watched he restrained himself from sprinting to the men's room. He lifted the lid and found a letter.

Astounded, he read names, dates, and times implicating Israel in the murders. It mentioned the conspiratorial meeting between Prime Minister Roth and Jesuit Father General Tobenhien. Even more damning: it listed a time and date when Heinz met with Roth to implement plans for the Tablets' annihilation. The anonymous writer further alleged that the Israelis had intentions to storm the camp during the murders, but the Marine lieutenant in charge foiled them. Enclosed were pictures of Roth shaking hands with Tobenhien and for the first time ever of Roth shaking hands with a short dark man in sunglasses said to head Mossad. Last was a shot of the Marine Lieutenant, jaw set. John Martin scanned the photos and sent his article. The *New York Times* had its story.

* * *

Deep in the Gaza strip, Pebbles read the report on the Fawn's successful kills at Sepphoris. She survived the shooting and was now the object of a relentless manhunt in Northern Israel. Helicopters hunted his young agent. Israeli troops covered every road. Pebbles' assets were expendable, but he was unusually impressed with this sniper's performance. He had long plans requiring someone with her nerve. He glanced at his cheap timepiece. Four hours since the shootings. The Fawn must be in the rugged hill country southeast of Sepphoris by now. In eighteen minutes the next stage would begin. He'd been lucky, cunning, his distraction plan flawless. He smiled, baring his teeth. This should take some pressure off his valuable Fawn.

* * *

Hidden in the hills west of Nazareth the young fighter, Sabry al-Banni, a nineteen-year-old veteran of the wars against Zionists, watched as the Israeli military operation unfolded. Not an educated man, he could still trace his Arab ancestry by memory for nearly a thousand years in Palestine. The Jews hadn't been in the majority for all that time. His family farmed, toiling over the same soil for centuries, surviving the long list of conquerors. All that changed in 1948 when a new breed walked the Arabs' ancient land. The Zionists didn't wish to merely tax the Arabs. Quite the contrary, they wanted to eradicate them and take their ancient lands. Sabry was the last male of a family of seven, simple farmers no more. For five decades they'd been Palestinian terrorists and freedom fighters. At nineteen, Sabry nursed no illusions as to his own longevity.

Nevertheless, he found the current mission distasteful. A bound and gagged girl about eighteen sat beside him. Sabry didn't know her name, but had been given a picture and told her route. This was not his first kidnapping, part of warfare in Israel involved hostages as pawns to free imprisoned Palestinian fighters or raise money for operations. Sabry lived in the Arab town of Nazareth. Nazareth was allowed to exist to appease Christians. A poor Arab community survived there as petty traders with hands in each other's pocket, poverty, prostitution, and despair all too common in this revered town where Sabry kidnapped his victim. Nazareth, known as the home of Jesus the so-called Savior of the World, now bred Palestinian fighters.

Sabry knew this area better than his own gloved hands. He filed every hill, road, and trail in his hardened mind. If anyone could survive, he could. As his night-adjusted eyes studied the rapid build-up of Israeli troops, Sabry wondered what had happened to justify such military action. His present assignment could only be a small part of something bigger, and he might never know what it would accomplish. However, he had his orders and must fulfill them.

Sabry studied his target objective, a two-man listening post beside a narrow two-lane road. An Israeli truck deposited two soldiers every one hundred fifty meters along it. Now that Sabry understood the layout, he waited. The night dragged. Sabry glanced at his watch for the tenth time, grateful that the appointed hour finally limped near. It should be quick. He would be glad to fulfill this mission and be on his way.

He tugged on the loose end of the rope binding his victim, a pretty girl, even with her gagged face streaked with tears, caked with dust. Sabry had warned her to follow without a sound or he would cut her throat. She'd nodded with wide, horrified eyes.

Moving carefully down a dry ravine, Sabry approached to within three hundred meters of the first Jewish listening post. The sound of helicopters pervaded the dark sky, concerning him most, but he knew his routes. From a slight rise, he scouted the location of the nearest listening post.

He motioned the girl to sit on a rock while he held the muzzle of his captured M-16 against the base of her head. He untied her hands and ungagged her. She nodded rapidly when he held his finger to his lips. Offering a clean rag, he motioned for her to wipe her tear-stained face. Sabry kept the muzzle of his rifle on her as he handed her a light pack he'd been carrying. He motioned for her to slip it onto her back. Terrified, she scrambled to obey. He handed her a pair of light gloves and motioned for her to slip them on. She was surprisingly well-dressed. He motioned her to straighten her hair and indicated several places on her face where she'd missed smudges.

She seemed to interpret these orders hopefully. She shook her hair and moistened her lips, trying to smile seductively as she pointed at Sabry's groin and motioned for him to come to her. Sabry shook his head slowly, leaving the woman more confused and terrified than ever. She smiled at her captor again, an awful, desperate grimace of a smile, as she undid her top button. Sabry smiled slowly as the young woman unbuttoned the second button revealing lovely breasts. She reached for the third.

Sabry's .223 bullet struck her chest, centered exactly between those perfect mounds. The bullet exploded her young heart, taking out a two- inch section of spine when it exited. She fell in a heap on the rocky ground, her life's blood draining into the hard soil. Sabry swung around, sending a burst of bullets over the heads of the nearest Jewish listening post. It took the startled soldiers some seconds to return frightened bursts. A second listening post joined the first in returning fire. Sabry heard bullets fly wildly wide of his position. He left the rifle next to the body and raced down his predetermined escape route. In less than thirty seconds, the sky filled with helicopters converging on the site of the gunfire. Sabry was only about a mile from Nazareth cross-country.

In less than two confused minutes, helicopters dropped Israeli soldiers to reinforce the listening posts. They found Sabry's victim, the M-16 at her side. Meanwhile, helicopters picked up Israeli officers and investigators. Once again, confusing turmoil saved a Palestinian fighter. Sabry sighed in relief as he reentered Nazareth through its dump. He shook his head. This was too close for even his hardened blood. Giving a quick thanks to Allah for his salvation, Sabry faded into the warren of antique streets.

***

Amal the Fawn, still slightly west of En Harod, worried. She'd crossed several small highways undetected. If she could just cross this last major one, she'd be on home ground. Daunting, because listening posts with roving soldiers between them were less than fifty meters apart here. The night air cooled. Rocks chilled. Helicopter's thermo devices could detect her body heat. Machine gunners would kill her. The helicopters searched systematically, concentrating close to highways. These airborne hunters knew the killer would be waiting for a chance to cross.

Amal heard a helicopter coming from the west about a mile away, flying slowly to give its thermo operator the best chance at good readings.

Saul, a young Israeli technician bent over his screens trying to pick up anomalies hotter than surrounding rocks. Dropping night temperature increased his instruments' reliability. He'd never been on a night operation this big. Rumor had it that whoever found the killer would be instantly promoted. Extra money would be welcome, but Saul really wanted his active enlistment to expire so he could go back to school to become an electrical engineer.

Amal watched the helicopter coming. This was at least the seventh or eighth time she had tried to fool these sensitive devices, and felt in her heart she couldn't escape another close fly by. She huddled next to boulders. The stones lacked that comforting warmth of a few hours ago. As the helicopter flew toward her, Amal prayed hard to Allah.

Saul saw a possible spike of heat growing out of the signals from rocks. It wavered, receded, and then grew again. As they continued east, Saul watched the signal grow slightly stronger. It lacked the clear pattern of a human being, but the signal seemed hotter than the rocks. Sometimes a piece of scrap steel gave off this type of pattern. Saul debated whether to tell his officer in charge. He'd already called out six false readings. As the helicopter bore slightly to the north, Saul watched the signal start to fade. That decided it. Saul called out "Sir, I have a possible reading toward the southwest about one hundred meters."

"How hot, soldier?" asked the bored copilot.

"Not hot, sir, just a wavering low signal."

"Let's go on to our pattern's north end. We'll check it out on the return pass. It'll be cooler then. You can get a better reading," said the officer who'd missed a hot date for this nocturnal fly around.

Saul didn't bother to respond. Officers were idiots. He watched the signal fade as the helicopter took four minutes to reach the end of its assigned pattern. Irritating that his superior would leave a transit reading to follow a preset pattern. As the helicopter returned to the location of the former reading, the heat signature was gone. It had been a living thing, not just a random piece of metal. He felt the building excitement every hunter feels close to his quarry. He asked if they could go into an expanding circular search pattern. The bored officer started their turn.

Amal had only managed to move about three hundred meters before the helicopter's return. She slid into a shallow cave formed by boulders, not sure of concealing her body heat.

About half-way in the second circle Saul picked up a transit hot spot on his screen, the same type of signal about three hundred meters further out, not a clear human signature. Yet he was sure it was something living.

On the ground, a terrified Amal knew heat undoubtedly spilled out between the boulders. Saul was about to alert his superior that he thought he had a target spotted when the helicopter radio emitted a dispatcher's cool tones. All helicopters were being given coordinates toward various bases to pick up medical and legal specialists. The detached voice reported that the Sepphoris killer had been engaged and killed near Nazareth. Saul's chopper banked sharply and accelerated. Saul thought about objecting because he was sure something alive was near their former position. Then he decided to hell with it. What was the military after all except one big stupid ride? Saul turned off his thermo unit in disgust, closed his eyes, and leaned back in his barely-padded chair to get some rest.

Amazed, Amal watched the helicopter bank sharply from her direction and speed northwest. Thanking Allah for her life, she waited for a chance to clear the highway.

She studied the listening posts for another half hour. Something had happened. A convoy of trucks stopped by each group. In moments the soldiers mounted into the backs of the trucks that continued lumbering west. To Amal's astonishment, the highway emptied in minutes. Not a living thing saw her slip across and continue toward the general's house.

A thankful young woman slipped into her quarters with an hour to spare before the sun billowed up on the land of her ancestors. Allah had saved her unworthy life. Amal never learned that another young woman lost hers on Pebbles' orders so Amal could see the sunrise. Ignorance is war's reality.

***

In the United States, President Straihorn met with advisors. The Jesus Tablets had been front page news since their discovery, America captivated by their implications. Now news of the gory murders flooded American households.

Most of his advisors urged the President to take a low key approach, along the lines that the United States and Israel were working closely to investigate, and until more facts emerged there was little to add. President Straihorn listened with patience and respect, even asking penetrating questions. Finally he thanked everyone kindly, adding he would consult with intelligence agencies before reaching final decisions.

Those meetings took a different tone. The FBI noted a sharp rise in anti-Semitism. Crazies were claiming an international Jewish plot was behind the murders, fundamentalists that Jews and the Christians couldn't co-exist since Jews murdered Jesus. Hate groups' presses couldn't keep up with demands. Anything related to the Jesus Tablets was snapped up, and a surprising number of Americans didn't believe their government was telling the whole story.

The CIA reported on Israel's cooperation with the investigation. There were no fingerprints on the murder weapon, but it appeared the Sepphoris sniper had been in place for at least twenty-four hours. Evidence indicated a person of slight stature, probably a woman. Israel predicted she would be found shortly. The U. S. had few CIA assets in Israel because of its being a trusted ally. Even using all its resources, it had nothing yet to report. The President thanked his advisors, adding that American citizens needed to know their government was providing them with honest information. After the President dismissed them more than a few advisors worried as to what "honest information" meant in this unpredictable situation.

To everyone's surprise, President Straihorn made a nationwide television announcement within hours. Americans from coast to coast heard his brief statement. "My fellow citizens, we have all heard of the tragic shootings at the Sepphoris site in Israel a short while ago. This is the site where a major and very intriguing archaeology discovery, the Jesus Tablets, has been found. Helen Morgenstern, our Ambassador to Israel, and Dr. Samuel Stein, Head of the archaeology Department at Harvard University were killed by a sniper yet unfound. The United States and Israel are cooperating fully to find and bring the perpetrator to justice.

"Unfortunately, some believe the State of Israel is conspiring to destroy the Tablets, and even more incredibly, that Israel is behind these murders. I assure you there is not one shred of evidence to support such an outrageous claim. Israel is and has been a valued ally of the United States since its inception. I have just gotten off the telephone with my long time friend Prime Minister Roth and have his assurance that all Israel's resources are being poured into a manhunt of unprecedented size to apprehend those who committed this heinous crime. I have his assurance that Israel is cooperating fully with the United States and will continue to do so.

"I pledge that I will keep you completely abreast of the facts as this investigation proceeds. Thousands of you are exercising your right to urge Congress to see to it that the Tablets and students are returned safely to the United States. Your requests are being weighed respectfully. The safety of the students and the Tablets is America's top priority. Prime Minister Roth concurs. Israel is acutely aware that these murders occurred despite the Sepphoris site being guarded by three hundred dedicated Israeli soldiers. These forces have been increased, and security is now impenetrable. We gain nothing by haste or fear. Therefore, the Sepphoris site will not be closed down by executive action. However, the United States will offer free, immediate transportation to any American citizen at the site who feels it is in his or her best interest to return home.

"As your President, let me assure you I will not hesitate to use America's full influence and power to protect United States citizens at Sepphoris. In closing, I promise that as long as I am President I will place nothing higher than the safety of all Americans at home and abroad. God Bless America. Thank you and good night."

***

A sober Prime Minister Roth joined millions of viewers, a politician for too many years not to realize he'd been neatly boxed into a corner. President Straihorn had announced positions Israel never agreed to including making the United States a full and equal investigative partner in the shootings. Nor had Israel declared its highest priority the safety of the students and Tablets. No, Israel had clearly said she needed to evaluate their effect before expressing any opinion. National security always trumped other issues. Roth fumed.

No word of success yet on the hunt for the Sepphoris killer. Even though the President denied Israel was part of a plot to destroy the Jesus Tablets, he'd neatly brought such a concept to America's (and anyone else's) attention. Roth now walked a knife's edge. He frowned when his intercom buzzed, and his secretary announced Isaac Gold. Perhaps at last he would know what danger, if any, the Jesus Tablets posed for Israel. "Send him in," he said.

A drawn Ike Gold entered. Roth felt a pang of concern as he took his old friend's extended hand. "Isaac, I'm so very sorry you had to endure such a thing. Be assured, I wouldn't ask to see you so soon if I didn't need your information so urgently."

"I understand." Gold had aged years since their earlier meeting.

"Please sit down. Losing a friend in such a senseless crime is a terrible thing. I know how close you were to Dr. Stein." The Prime Minister offered Gold a comfortable chair. The old scholar took it gratefully.

As the Prime Minister took his own chair, Isaac Gold gazed at him with bloodshot, but steady eyes. Roth braced himself.

"David, Sam Stein was like my own son. He never injured anyone. If the government had anything to do with his death, I will never forgive you."

Roth leaned forward, his gaze as direct as Gold's. "It's not always possible for me to answer as completely as I can now. In this case I can give a wholly honest answer. I swear to you as a man and as the Prime Minister of this country that neither Israel nor I had anything to do with these murders. That said, I must ask you never to ask me such a question again."

"I believe you, David, and am sorry I had to ask. You can't imagine what Samuel's loss means." Isaac Gold's voice broke.

Roth watched the older man brush tears away. "I do understand. I've lost too many in battle, including my own brother."

Gold straightened. "Of course. I haven't forgotten Johnathon. Let us turn to our current business."

Roth sensed it best to press on. Perhaps the older man would be calmer with his mind on other matters. "Tell me about the Jesus Tablets. I assume you had an opportunity draw conclusions?"

"I had time to read Alice Cross' translations. Sam Stein had already reviewed them. I concur with Alice, Sam, and Henry Cross. The Tablets are authentic, the most remarkable find in ancient Near East archaeology. From a religious standpoint, the

Jesus Tablets will wreak havoc. They prove the Torah was a fraudulent political expediency. The Tablets tell a complete history of Israel through the first hand observations of one family. They're entirely credible, and I believe scholars will accept them as real, primary evidence.

"The Tablets contain first hand writings from Mary the mother of Jesus that depict him as mentally ill, possibly schizophrenic. The resurrection was a desperate mother moving her son's body to avoid its desecration by Romans. She describes early Christianity as a study in power, politics, and psychology. The Tablets even contain a brief writing from the hand of Jesus which would be a textbook example of schizophrenia in any medical school. That, David, is it in a nutshell. Religious foundations of Christianity, Judaism, and to some extent Islam will be shaken."

Roth rubbed his eyes, suddenly exhausted. "That's some nutshell, Ike."

"None could know that better than I," replied Dr. Gold, "and I don't envy you."

"Would you stay as special advisor on this if and when I need you?"

"Of course. It is my honor."

Prime Minister Roth rose to bid his visitor goodbye. A lonely man weighed his options for fifteen minutes, then concluded he had none. Pushing his intercom button, he gave his secretary the succinct order, "Send for Heinz."

In minutes the wiry Mossad director sat across from the Prime Minister, appearing to be sitting on something that pleased him. "What do you have for me on the Sepphoris situation? Good news would be welcome," said Roth.

"I do have good news. The investigation is incomplete, but reports say an Arab woman approximately eighteen years of age, carrying a light pack with pictures of the victims and a map of the Sepphoris site was eliminated near Nazareth. She had no identification, but our people are working on it. It seems probable she was heading for Arab Nazareth. Apparently she got careless within one mile of the city limits. There were no Israeli casualties. The hunt is over."

The Prime Minister's shoulders sagged in relief. "Good news, Heinz. With pressure off this Sepphoris mess we can take time to study our options. You've heard Straihorn's latest speech?"

"Yes, I keep abreast of his activities, not to say anybody can predict what he'll do next. He confided in no advisors about addressing the American people. He's a loose cannon. His actions may be random or cunningly calculated. A president not controlled by handlers is dangerous. Why he didn't use the Sepphoris murders as reason to evacuate the students and Tablets immediately confounds us. Now we've found the sniper, perhaps the wind will be taken out of the sails of world interest."

Roth considered, puzzled that Straihorn didn't evacuate the students and Tablets. Haste would have made it difficult for Mossad to destroy the Tablets. The Prime Minister weighed his next words. "I've spoken to Isaac Gold. The Tablets pose a fatal danger to Israel. Do you have a plan to annihilate them?"

"Our people are working every hour, but we need time. Israel must stall to let world scrutiny die down. With United States Marines guarding the Tablets, there's no way our forces can penetrate Sepphoris without high losses."

Roth explained his intentions for an upcoming conversation with President Straihorn.

"I'll attend to your orders. We'll send troops to Sepphoris. Intelligence will find a way to neutralize the Tablets," the Mossad head replied.

As the Prime Minister watched the intense little man leave, he couldn't help but wonder whether the Jesus Tablets might be bigger than both of them.

Now for President Straihorn. In less than ten minutes the President of the United States picked up. "Good to hear from you, Dave. What do you have for me about the situation on your side of the world?"

"A break in the case, Mr. President. The Sepphoris assassin was killed near Nazareth. Soldiers found pictures of the victims, a detailed map of the site on her."

"Excellent. That will take some of the heat off."

"Yes. Please understand, the investigation is incomplete, but I want to keep you up- to- date. I've recalled our eight hundred troops dispatched to find the killer. They'll soon be at Sepphoris, surely enough to assure security."

"This will go a long way toward calming American citizens. I'd started to doubt our ability to contain this thing," Straihorn said.

"Israel appreciates your loyalty and faith in us. We'll do all we can to maintain our friendship. I don't need to tell you we need time to evaluate the Jesus Tablets."

"I understand, but how much time? Americans want the students and Tablets on our soil. These killings strained my ability to control the popular will. Pressure on me and members of Congress is greater than even you can fathom."

"Israel is also a democracy and needs time to discuss this in open forum. If we have two to three weeks to go through the political process, everything should go smoothly," offered the Prime Minister.

"I can't absolutely promise that time frame, but if nothing rocks the boat I don't see any real obstacle. If anything unforeseen does crop up, I'll have to cope with it."

"I understand. However, Israel feels we've earned some time through our efforts to track down this sniper. Surely America can accept that."

"These are emotional days. The Jesus Tablets have struck a chord with American citizens that nothing undermines. If things aren't stirred up again, I don't think we'll have problems with a reasonable delay for a fair review by Israel," the President said.

"I appreciate your understanding. Your words in defense of Israel won't be forgotten."

"It's a dangerous world and friends must be appreciated. By the way, what did your scholar find out when he reviewed the Tablets?"

"That's part of our challenge. Dr. Gold says the Tablets are authentic and cast grave doubts on the validity of Judeo-Christian religions. The effect on our citizens must be taken into consideration," Roth said.

"I can't imagine what the problem could be. Any intelligent person has doubted or outright rejected supernatural tales long ago. Same with the Muslims. Heck, same with the Hindus. Surely the world is mature enough to look objectively at scientific data without all the emotion."

"I'm not certain the world is all that mature. Religion goes beyond rationality in all countries," answered the Prime Minister.

"You might be right. America seems filled with Bible thumpers who have nothing better to do than steal books they don't like from public libraries. I know you can see that these Tablets belong to America and the world. A find of this nature can't be buried. Such a thing would mean humanity is taking a step back to the caves. Modern leaders such as you and I can't condone book burning or suppression of science."

"I couldn't agree more," said the Prime Minister, "Knowledge must go forward and if that means some are uncomfortable, so be it."

"Keep me abreast, Prime Minister. Your news is heartening. If you have nothing more, I have a busy day ahead," said the President in an upbeat voice.

"As do I. Thank you again for your support." When Roth placed the phone in its receiver he felt ashamed. His words might be necessary, but were lies none the less. Politics remained such dirty business. He felt a nostalgic pang for the business world where profit was so much cleaner.

President Straihorn felt no shame. In fact he grinned, again reminded that politics, especially the Jesus Tablets, was the best game he'd ever played. It should get even better.

Chapter Forty-one

President Straihorn wasted no time briefing the media on his conversation with the Israeli Prime Minister. News that Israeli forces had found and dispatched the Sepphoris killer interrupted television and radio across the United States, bringing sighs of relief. However, vocal cynics harbored suspicions. The Jesus Tablets remained a focus of attention for millions, including a few world leaders. The latter pulled strings and wove threads that made the story of the Jesus Tablets such a complex saga.

The Monday edition of the *New York Times* shattered complacency. The front page reported Israel and the Roman Catholic Church had joined in a conspiracy to destroy the Jesus Tablets, thus changing everything.

It hit the United States like a tsunami. The story flashed around the globe, spelling out in detail the threat the Jesus Tablets posed to the conspirators. For the first time many Americans learned how much U.S. taxpayers paid to keep Israel afloat, and of the fragile nature of the contemporary Catholic Church. The article spelled out Father Tobenhien's trail to the United States where he received the original warning from an obscure Baltimore priest. It recounted the Vatican meeting between Father Tobenhien and Pope John when they resolved to destroy the Tablets. It traced Tobenhien to Israel and his meetings with Prime Minister Roth, asserting that in Israel Tobenhien and the Prime Minister entered into a pact to destroy the Tablets at all costs, then covered a meeting between the secretive head of Mossad and Roth where Prime Minister Roth gave orders to devise a plan to destroy the Tablets by storming the camp during the assassination of Samuel Stein and the American ambassador. The *New York Times* also cast grave suspicion on Israeli claims of engaging and shooting the actual Sepphoris killer. In all a devastating collection of times, dates, accounts of meetings, and original pictures.

Chaos hit. Voters demanded everything from immediate withdrawal of the students in Israel to termination of all foreign aid. Congress, both parties, floundered. Many called for immediate investigation. Others appealed for calm. Some felt that the *New York Times* should be sued for libel while others threatened an injunction to shut it down. Anti-government groups waxed triumphant. Conspiracy buffs and extremist groups went wild with self-congratulation. Their printing presses worked around the clock to fill the hands of the curious. Anti-Semitism reared up. Questions as to Israeli's loyalty and dependability hit mainline television and newspapers. A growing chorus of queries and suspicions drowned out moderates. The world waited for Israel, the Vatican, and most importantly, for President Straihorn to respond.

The President urged restraint, acknowledging the gravity of the charges, but reiterating that the Tablets belonged to the United States, the students American citizens. Their safety was his highest priority. The Tablets had the full protection of United States law.

He would soon be in contact with both Israel and the Vatican. He reminded voters that the *New York Times* had not revealed its sources. He then restated the government's offer to fly anyone immediately from Sepphoris back to the States. President Straihorn closed by promising to keep the American people fully informed. Opinion polls showed his popularity at the highest level of his tenure. The world didn't know his inner thoughts. For President Straihorn, things were going very well indeed.

In Israel things weren't going well. The story caught Mossad off guard with its exact details and pictures of Prime Minister Roth, Jesuit Tobenhien, and the head of the Israel Secret Service. Mossad searched the Prime Minister's office and found a hidden camera complete with recorder in the exact location the pictures suggested. The tape was missing. Even worse, the Prime Minister's long-time private secretary had vanished. A search disclosed she'd taken an overnight flight to Paris.

Prime Minister Roth had never known such disarray. Heinz was in a white fury. Never in his long and distinguished career had his reputation or that of his agency plummeted so far.

Heinz entered Roth's temporary office with diffidence. "So it appears the Prime Minister cannot be assured a secure private office in the nation of Israel," snapped Roth, glaring.

"So it appears for the time being," the small dark man admitted.

"As you are aware, I don't have time to replace you even though I am inclined to."

"I would gladly step down if it would serve Israel, but the timing is wrong. We have to salvage our reputation, proceed to destroy the Tablets, and then deal with the traitors."

The Prime Minister considered. Perhaps a bitter, unscrupulous man was exactly what he needed. "You can save your career. You've got one chance to rectify this debacle. You won't see another. I have just one condition. I make the final call on how the Jesus Tablets are destroyed."

"Understood."

The Prime Minster leaned forward. "How do we deflect the current danger?"

"The best course, Mr. Prime Minister, is to deny any conspiracy to destroy the Jesus Tablets. Don't deny your meeting with Father Tobenhien. Explain it as an effort to better relationships between Jews and Catholics. Maintain that your secretary was a deeply troubled woman you befriended years ago. No matter what the pictures and tapes reveal, maintain they're fraudulent, fabricated via digital technology. As far as pictures of me, insist that it's Israeli policy never to discuss security issues publicly. Appear willing to cooperate with the United States. Stall for time, but be ready to expend lives to get at the Tablets. If you do this, Israel won't be pulled into the undertow. Furthermore, pull out all the stops. Say allegations of a Jewish conspiracy are nothing less than anti-Semitism. That will make publishers and leaders think twice. As long as we deny accusations, we'll at least be innocent to many. If we admit them, we're guilty before everyone. Although he appears supportive, Straihorn may be our most serious adversary."

It made sense. "We have no choice but to follow the path you described. It's the accursed Tablets or Zionism. I'll call Straihorn and buy time to find a path through this labyrinth."

Heinz stood. "It shall be done." With that he walked out the door, and the world became even more dangerous.

***

The Vatican, awash with journalists, struck the position that charges of conspiracy involving the Pope were ridiculous. Pope Jerome declined to even discuss an issue so far beneath his dignity. The media searched history for easily found examples where a pope did, in fact, lie, along with papal orders for assassinations and mass murder. Such attention affronted a Church doing its best to downplay dirty linen. No one knew better than reporters that the Pope couldn't avoid the issue forever. Sooner or later they'd pin His Holiness down to a quotable statement.

The Pope secluded himself in his private quarters. He would rather die than place the Holy Church in a bad light. Nevertheless, if the Jesus Tablets survived, they would fatally wound the Catholic Church. Fortunately, Jesuit Father General Tobenhien was en route from Israel. Perhaps the canny Jesuit would bring a clear strategy.

Even worse was news from Boston where Father Charles, his old Jesuit adversary, had been found dead in his study. The media already reported rumors of foul play. Father Tobenhien also digested news of his colleague's unexpected demise. Had Father Charles been murdered?

Father Tobenhien looked out his airplane window on earth so many thousands of feet below. Determined people seeking to end human life rendered a person so vulnerable. Father Tobenhien pondered on how few seconds he would live if his airplane were to suddenly plunge, quickly rejecting such negative thoughts. He was not likely to be on any hit list. The Church and Israel needed his talent more than his death. Still, he felt better once on the tarmac in Rome.

At the Vatican, a pale Pope Jerome received him asking, "The situation is quite grim, would you not agree?"

This Pope, Father Tobenhien observed, was not up to the stress this business created. "Serious, but by no means out of hand. Surely you didn't think such a task as destroying the Jesus Tablets could be performed without problems?"

"Undoubtedly true, but it is only human that I ask God to spare me unnecessary complications," said the Pope in a quavering voice.

"Fortunately, we have the State of Israel as well as God on our side in this complicated matter," said the worldly Jesuit with a touch of kindness.

"God's purpose will be served in the end," said Pope Jerome sharply.

"Without question. However, wouldn't it be gratifying if His will matched ours in this case? Perhaps it would be a better use of our time to try to map out our options since we agree God is capable of planning his own."

"What do you propose we tell the world?"

What a child this pope is, thought the hardened Jesuit. Nothing at all like the popes who ruled in centuries gone by. "We only have to fear ourselves. If we hold firm to our convictions, the Church will be saved. We both know her salvation depends on obliterating the Tablets."

"Is Israel with us?"

"Israel has no choice. Israel will do her best to destroy the Tablets."

"Successfully?"

"The Church of the living God has more tools than Israel, and I'm ensuring they'll be where they can be most useful. We can't afford mistakes." Father Tobenhien talked earnestly for the next twenty minutes.

At the end of the one-sided conversation, the Pope mustered his troubled thoughts. Finally he said, "The Church can have no part in your plan. It would be nothing less than the murder of innocents."

Silence ensued while Father Tobenhien walked to the far corner of the room, then turned. "Which of us is innocent, and whose lives are worth more than the preservation of the Holy Roman Catholic Church?" he asked. "Do not the innocent go directly to heaven to live forever within God the Father's gaze? What is a saint if not the innocent who died for God and Church?

If it is God's will that a handful die, what is that compared to the millions sheltered by the Roman Church from their cradle to their grave? If the Church is destroyed, who will protect the weak and powerless? How will those helpless ones live if we allow the Jesus Tablets to destroy their hope and their faith? What of the thousands of laborers in the Roman Catholic Church who forsook hearth, home, and loved ones to serve God? What is life but a handful of days? What difference does it really make to God and eternity whether a man lives twenty years or a hundred? Have we not always preached that the destiny of man is death and the rightful home of the faithful is in heaven with God? Is not the entire Christian religion based on the idea that innocent Jesus died for our salvation?"

The aging Jesuit finally stopped his passion for the Church outweighing his energy to defend it. The room's heavy furniture seemed to wait for discussion to begin again. Pope Jerome sat, eyes downcast, his head in both hands. Father Tobenhien tried a different approach. "Your Holiness, if you can see any other way from your exulted position, then I stand ready to listen."

The room was silent. The Pope prayed. He ended his prayer with words of Jesus in the New Testament, "Father if it could be your will, take this bitter cup from me, but not my will, but Thine be done." Finally the Pope looked up at the Jesuit. "I see no other way. I will live out my life in agony."

Father Tobenhien returned the sad gaze. "Many a Godly man has lied for the greater good. A lie is often more merciful than the bitter truth. Would God's cause be better served by telling millions of faithful that their Jesus was a lunatic? Would God's people be better able to survive life's trials without their spiritual protector the Church? In the name of truth do we have the right to annihilate their only hope? We have no choice if the Church is to survive. That, too, is honest. Truth is sometimes bitter."

The Pope rose and slowly paced, weighing his choices. The age-darkened clock ticked.

Finally, he stopped, turned to Father Tobenhien and said, "We will go with your plan and leave fate in God's hands. I petition for mercy for what I must do to save the Church. God will decide whether Israel is successful or whether we must implement our own strategy. May God forgive us. I place the power of the Church behind you. Please, leave me now."

Father Tobenhien placed his hand on his old adversary's shoulder. "Pray for Israel's success that this cup not be handed to us. Holiness, I ask you to pray for me as well." With that he left for South America.

Within an hour of Father Tobenhien's departure, Pope Jerome called a press conference. He announced there was no truth to the preposterous theory that the Catholic Church and the Israeli government had joined in a conspiracy to destroy the Jesus Tablets. Catholics exhaled in relief that the Church had been spared the shame of an admission. For them, the Pope's unequivocal denial equaled the voice of God.

However, there were cynics, men and women without the slightest doubt the Pope brazenly lied. How dangerous the Jesus Tablets must be, they thought, if the Pope himself was willing to prevaricate. Journalists smelled blood.

***

Elaine DuBois, junior reporter at the *Paris Times*, stroked the furry chest of Henri Menchant, an executive of the French State Department. She loved the way that fairly made him purr. They'd made love and lay languorously in the afterglow. "Ah," Henri murmured, "how nice this is after the craziness with the Jewish Prime Minister's rogue secretary."

Elaine's hand paused imperceptibly as she made little curls on Henri's chest. "Have the Israeli's had some trouble?"

"Enough. The woman is seeking political asylum here in France. But, I should not speak of such things to you."

Elaine curled a finger around a few chest hairs and yanked. He yelped. "Henri, Mon Amour, what would your long suffering wife do if she were to learn of our little afternoons? Your powers are surely not so great that she would not mind sharing you?"

"Ma Cherie!" Henri protested. His dexterous amour was not joking. He spilled the story. The defecting secretary, seeking French protection and citizenship, possessed recordings of all conversations between the Israeli Prime Minister and the Roman

Church, as well as the head of Mossad. The French government weighed this even as Mossad promised payment and favors upon return of both tapes and secretary to Israel.

Elaine knew gold when she saw it. She gave Henri the ride of his life, then dashed off to the *Paris Times*. In hours, Elaine and the former secretary connected. The tapes were published, complete and unabridged, first in the *Paris Times,* then in every major paper everywhere.

The French had been on the verge of returning the defector to Mossad. The French had no choice in the glare of international attention but to offer protection, citizenship, and asylum to one claiming to be a person of conscience with information for the world.

***

Public curiosity about the Jesus Tablets peaked in America after the Pope's statements. Twenty-five students in Sepphoris accepted the President's offer of free transportation home only to be met at the Reagan International and whisked off to waiting television stations. These students had wild speculations as to the Tablets' contents. In this atmosphere, President Straihorn called Prime Minister Roth.

"How are you doing, Prime Minister?"

"Frankly, I've had better days. All I can tell you is this conspiracy accusation is false. I apologize, but I'll have to wait for time to pass to calm the situation."

"I'll do all I can. I've never varied from supporting you. However, I'm under pressure to remove all remaining students and the Tablets by executive order. Your willingness to give United States investigators access to your investigative agencies helped. I need your cooperation, and in return I'll give you time to review the Tablets."

"Your support is greatly appreciated," answered the Prime Minister. "Israel has done everything to insure the safety of American students still in Israel with the Tablets. We have twelve hundred soldiers protecting the site and your investigators are working side by side with our counterparts. We believe the sniper was a Palestinian terrorist whose primary objective was to disrupt United States and Israeli relationships."

"I'm sure you're right on that. No rift can be allowed between our two nations," the President interjected. "I'm ashamed to admit anti-Semitism as well as anti-Catholicism seems alive and well here. This Jesus Tablet situation has highlighted details of our foreign aid to your country that I prefer at a quieter level. Don't fear. American support will continue."

"Your support and friendship have never been in question, or forgotten. I'm sure we can work through this if we encourage calm."

"Of course, but if anything else happens I'm not sure I can control the political reaction. Surely, you understand," said President Straihorn.

"Surely, but the worst is over. Time will allow this storm to pass," said the Prime Minister.

No one saw the Prime Minister remove his handkerchief to dab sweat from his forehead following the conversation.

***

Pope Jerome reflected on his own conversation with President Straihorn. Lying about the Jesus Tablets to this smooth politician had been nearly unendurable. Yet, President Straihorn was reasonable, expressing gratitude that the Church had addressed her critics. He stressed he never doubted the Pope's credibility. Although the words were polite, Pope Jerome intuited the odd President was laughing at him and the Church. There was something frightening about a leader who communicated with his citizens on such a prompt and open basis. The Church usually dealt with world leaders behind closed doors, amiable to secret arrangements. Pope Jerome certainly preferred that the past remain locked away. He'd never imagined himself contributing to that dark history of murder and deception. It tortured him to not only be lying, but agreeing to murder. The Pope never considered that opposing truth might well be opposing God, that hiding truth might be the ultimate sin.

Chapter Forty-two

In a gracious house in a gated Los Angeles community, Becky Fadlallah's mother worried. She hadn't heard from Becky for days, not surprising since the strong-willed eighteen year old had chafed for her independence.

The formal spelling of Becky's first name was Bekaa. The Fadlallahs, second generation Americans, had prospered in retailing. Fadlallah elders had immigrated, wealth intact, as an extended family before Zionists seized their homelands in 1948. Becky's now-American family, bi-lingual and versed in Arab-Jewish relations, kept ties to the "old country." Her father found America's politics similar to the guarded corruption of Palestine's. Money crossing hands as "gifts" was standard, and he swam well in American political waters. He rose in California politics, elected a senator of that great state of mixed races and cultures.

Becky's father knew the realities of being a Muslim senator in a legislature influenced by Jewish and Christian interests. He served with dignity, reminding colleagues of the need for fairness and justice toward minorities. After all, Arab states had the oil the United States needed. However, devoted to keeping California afloat amid conflicting demands, the Senator was neither radical nor exclusively focused on Arab problems.

He hadn't been too concerned at not hearing often from Becky, an independent girl with money. She'd decided to tour Europe, Egypt, and Israel before starting UCLA, promising to call every two days. But, days slide together when one is young and adventurous. Becky wanted to see the locales of her family heritage. She'd last called from Tel Aviv. Her strong Arab appearance subjected her to special attention from the Israeli forces, and for the first time Becky felt the full force of racial profiling. In every case her American citizenship brought forth belated apologies. It was important she see such behavior was a part of the Middle East. It was also a busy time for the Senator. The furor of the Jesus Tablets high, he was swamped with pressure to get the students still at Sepphoris and the Jesus Tablets home.

Finally, Senator Fadlallah succumbed to his worried wife, contacting a CIA official whose daughter he'd recommended for appointment to Annapolis. This official called in favors from field officers in Israel who checked Becky's whereabouts. Most predicted she'd partied a few days and shacked up with some hot young national. Under the pressure of the Jesus Tablets many wished they could do the same.

A random thought tied two questions to one agent, Leo Christon. The twenty-four-year paunchy veteran bore a perpetually questioning expression. Eligible for retirement, he enjoyed overseas duty, currently as liaison between Americans investigating the Sepphoris murders and the CIA station at Tel Aviv. The joint investigation dragged. Over beers with one of the Americans it became clear to Christon the Israelis weren't trying hard to identify the woman known as the Sepphoris Assassin, but in fact, discouraged American efforts to interview natives in the Nazareth area.

The American investigator insisted there were things about the body that didn't add up. It showed signs of being shot at close range, not one hundred meters from the Israeli soldiers. Powder burns showed on the girl's clothes and body that wouldn't exist if she'd been shot from a distance; the body had none of the calluses or scrapes on the knees and elbows you'd expect on a trained sniper. She seemed too clean, too well-dressed for a terrorist, no sweat stains or dirt under her fingernails. After Christon bought the investigator a few more beers, he added evidence that proved the girl was no local terrorist. Apparently, the body had the faintest scent of Channel No.5 which the American knew well because his wife wore it. "Why'd a terrorist wear American perfume to kill Americans?" asked the tipsy investigator.

Why indeed? Christon asked whether the investigator still had access to the body, and could take finger and palm prints. The body remained in the morgue. The American investigator agreed to make copies of the girl's photographs and meet Christon at this same bar the next evening.

Meanwhile, Christon called in a favor from a retired CIA friend who'd taken a part-time job with the California Department of Driving Records. A quick scan and international fax later, Christon held a good copy of the index finger's print. When the investigator arrived, the two compared prints. They matched. The killer of Sepphoris' identity had been solved. Christon left after giving the bartender a hundred dollar bill, telling him to give the other American as many drinks and munchies as he wanted.

Christon's head ached. This would blow the ceiling off the Jesus Tablets situation. Another cover-up would be possible, but the morgue pictures haunted Christon. The girl looked so much like his daughter at that age. What a nightmare for her parents for her to be missing and not know if she were dead or alive. Opening a pack of gum, he pondered. Flicking the wrapper into the street, he decided. He faxed his superiors his doubts that the so-called Sepphoris killer was the right one. Then he scanned and faxed the prints, photographs, and possible conclusions in a letter to his retired CIA friend also announcing his own retirement.

Within the hour the friend studied the fax. In less than twenty minutes he had Senator Fadlallah on the telephone. Two hours later he faced Senator Fadlallah. Before handing over the packet, he explained that careers would be destroyed if this evidence were correct.

The Senator gravely accepted the paperwork and photographs and studied them. Tears began. It was Becky. The retired agent gave his condolences, then told him the story of evidence covered-up by Israeli services. Such failure to disclose would not be attempted by lower echelons. The Senator slowly rose from his desk and stared out onto Pennsylvania Avenue. Several minutes passed before the bereaved father composed himself enough to speak. When Senator Fadlallah finally turned to face him, the agent looked into the eyes of a dangerous man.

"Tell the agents who solved this case to retire soon and be prepared to testify. You do nothing. The Senate reconvenes in an hour. Justice will be done for my child and Palestine. Now I must prepare myself, and see to it that someone is with my wife when this outrage is disclosed." With a silent nod and a handshake the messenger of grief left the deadly stillness of the Senator's office.

When Senator Fadlallah placed calls, people listened. In minutes the *Washington Post* sent reporters to hear him address the issue of the Jesus Tablets and Israel. Television stations acted on tips. Junior Senators gladly yielded time slots in order to give the senior Senator from California time to make his remarks. If Senator Fadlallah had something to say, it was important. His staff prepared the requested media package, but with no idea what the material represented. When the Senator's speech writers offered assistance, he declined.

A packed Senate watched Senator Fadlallah stride down the aisle. Gone the handshaking and trading of polite comments. Gone the beaming smile. There was stiffness unlike the personable Senator. Veteran colleagues exchanged glances. When the leader of the Senate offered the honorable Senator Fadlallah the podium, everyone leaned forward.

When he finally stood behind the lectern, his eyes swept the chamber. "I ask for forbearance. My subject is complicated. It is the Jesus Tablets in Israel. To understand the Jesus Tablets one must understand Israel's relations with the United States and Palestine. In 1945 my family had lived continuously in Palestine for over twelve hundred years, farming the land from father to son. My father could identify the graves of nine hundred of my ancestors. During this time Jews also lived in Palestine as a minority. Arabs never sought to crush or displace them. Trade, intermarriage, and religious cross-conversion were possible. Both peoples lived in peace. There were isolated outbreaks of violence between them, but nothing changed the fact that they coexisted in peace and general interaction.

"In 1946, World War II ended and the exhausted world learned the horrors of the Holocaust. One Jewish faction saw political opportunity in the global reaction. Zionists, using violence to advance their cause by fighting the British who governed Palestine, had long striven toward a homeland for the Jewish people. The British had seen enough death. My father was astute as well as successful. He saw trouble ahead for Arabs.

"In 1948, Israel was proclaimed a state by the United Nations at the expense of the Arabs whom no one consulted because they were poor and powerless. The Arabs fought for their land and lost. Israelis induced panic in the Arab population and caused them to flee their ancient homes. The West did nothing when Zionists refused to allow the Arabs to return to their homes and farms. Jews claimed the land was abandoned, and the United States made no objections. Since then nearly four generations of Palestinians have lived and died in refugee camps. We did not speak out in outrage, indeed we did not speak at all.

"Supported by the United States, Israel defeated Palestinians in several wars, continually seizing land. We've all heard that Israel repelled the Arabs because God was on the side of his chosen remnant. What of Arabs who died in a futile attempt to regain their farms and homes? Were they not brave, and did they not have justice on their side? However, justice is not enough. Palestinians lacked the billions in aid the United States has given Israel.

"The Jews seized rich Palestinian farmlands and coastal cities on the Mediterranean Sea, forcing Arabs into refugee camps and the marginal lands of the dry and eroded hills. Arabs could not earn a living. Arabs have been subjected to targeted killings and torture, They had to become laborers and de facto serfs for the ruling Jews.

"Israel has segregated roads and villages. A Jew cannot legally marry an Arab in Israel. Most importantly Arabs who fled for their lives during the wars have not been allowed to return to their homes. Nor have they received compensation. Even an Arab-Israeli citizen cannot serve in the Israeli military. To be deported from the workplace of Israel proper is to starve. A single Arab job might be barely supporting eight to ten dependents.

"Arabs never sentenced for a crime suffer in Israeli prisons. Even the word settlers, used to describe those who live in our former homes, imply this was empty land. Jews have bulldozed Arab homes and villages under such thin guises as zoning law violations. Arabs in the occupied territories have few rights. I say these things because I want you to face the real Israel when you consider the Jesus Tablets situation. Israel is ruled by a government willing to do anything to maintain domination of Palestine.

"We have all heard of the ancient library found in Sepphoris, Israel. We know the site was granted to Harvard University and all finds are United States property. What we don't know is the contents of the Tablets. Why aren't they in the United States? A noted American scholar was killed there. Our Ambassador to Israel was also assassinated during that same attack. We've all heard assurances that Israel was working hard to solve the murders and to protect our students.

"We relaxed somewhat when Israel claimed to have found the murderer of our citizens at Sepphoris. Most of us believed Israel's declaration of the case closed. They even opened the investigation to our criminal experts. We gave Israel time to study the Tablets. We forgot past actions and current policies of this government of oppression. God has reminded me in the most terrible way. I make my charges before you.

"Before God, I accuse Israel of plotting to destroy the Jesus Tablets. I accuse Israel of murdering the Americans at Sepphoris and of killing an innocent girl near Nazareth to make it appear Palestinians committed the murders. I accuse Israel of being a mortal threat to every American life there. My evidence will prove part of my case and open court will prove the rest. Israel has not only lied, but murdered in cold blood to cover that lie.

"Now you will see proof of Israel's murder and deception." With the click of a button an overhead image of a large hill came into focus on the twenty-foot-square screen. "This is the Sepphoris site," said the Senator. Students and laborers were excavating the hill. The Senator continued, "These are some of the Americans who discovered the Jesus Tablets." Another click brought the smiling face of a middle-aged man. "This is Dr. Samuel Stein, murdered at Sepphoris." Another click brought the image of a distinguished older woman. "This is Mrs. Morgenstern, United States Ambassador to Israel, also murdered during the same attack." The next showed an aerial view. "This is the Sepphoris camp with Israeli military forces surrounding it, allegedly guarding students and personnel." Enlarging the image in selected spots the Senator showed entrenched Israeli soldiers. "The Israeli government would have us believe a single young woman eluded these hundreds of trained soldiers, killed two Americans from over six hundred meters and escaped those same alerted troops." The Senator paused. "To convince America, Israel claimed to have killed the assassin near Nazareth hours after the attack."

Another click produced revealed body of a girl, a striking beauty even dead, on a steel table. "This is who the Israelis claim is the Palestinian sniper. They tell us she ran into an Israeli blocking force and died under Israeli fire at approximately one hundred meters." The next click brought the corpse into focus, body drape drawn down below her breast line, thin gauze covering her nipples. With the push of a button the Senator zoomed in until her face and chest filled the screen. "Notice the bullet hole slightly off-center." A tiny arrow pointed to the bluish-purple hole. "I'll zoom in on the chest area for a closer look." The image grew until only eight inches of the chest with its ugly bullet hole filled the twenty foot screen. "Notice numerous black spots around the bullet hole. These specks, powder burns caused by a shot at very close range, extend as far as seven inches from the wound. Such marks don't appear on a person shot from over ten meters. One American expert broke ranks to tell the truth. This girl was murdered at close range, not at the hundred meters the Israelis claim. The Israelis murdered her to buy time to destroy the Jesus Tablets."

Reporters ran for phones. The Senator raised his hands, palms out. "Please wait, the brutal truth is not over yet." With the click of his button he showed a beaming girl holding school books in her arms. "This is the living young woman the Israelis claim was the sniper of Sepphoris, the girl we saw lying in a morgue. They call her a terrorist who defeated over three hundred Israeli soldiers at Sepphoris and met her death near Nazareth. No, this girl is a victim. Israel needed a body to throw the Americans off-track. They failed to destroy the Jesus Tablets during the confusion of the Sepphoris murders thanks to our on-site Marines. Needing more time to try again, they killed this girl to cover their evil deeds.

"This is a copy of the index fingerprint taken from her whom the Israelis say was the sniper at Sepphoris." With another click the Senator split the screen to make room for a second finger print. "The print on the right is a California girl's, taken from her driver's license records. Watch carefully as I superimpose the right print on the left." It formed a perfect match. The Senator continued, "Investigation will prove that this girl was an American citizen from California who'd never been out of the United States. Further, she hated violence, had never fired a gun, and had no connections with any political organization. The investigation will prove she had just graduated from high school with honors and was vacationing in the land of her ancestors before enrolling at UCLA. It will prove she was unlucky enough to be kidnapped near Nazareth because of her Arab appearance. One was as good as another for the murdering Israelis."

The Senator paused to collect himself. "How do I know all this? Two honest Americans smuggled information out of Israel. God sends a message to all in power. I pass this simple message on. If we ignore Palestinian needs there will come a day of reckoning. I can never forget these pictures. I will never cease my efforts to bring her Israeli murderers to justice. We forget victims of violence have a name. This wonderful girl's name was Becky. Becky had a last name that I swear the Israelis will never forget. That name was Fadlallah." The Senator paused in the stunned silence, then continued with dignity. "The Zionists have murdered my lovely daughter who never hurt a soul. May God forgive them. I cannot." A grieving father left the podium.

The stunned Senate chamber froze, then flamed into bedlam as hundreds were on their feet. Dozens shouted into phones to the media, their families, and anyone else who struck them. The Senate leader pounded his gavel. Finally, he set it down and joined those comforting the weeping Senator Fadlallah as they escorted him back to his office.

Senator Fadlallah's speech beamed to stunned coast to coast audiences. Radio played the speech so drivers and mass transit riders heard it in an hour. Millions gathered in shocked groups. Switchboards in Washington D.C. were swamped by demands for immediate removal of the students and the Jesus Tablets. Some parents told media they would file tort claims against the Federal government for willful endangerment of their children. Not since the Japanese bombing of Pearl Harbor had there been such a collective sense of outrage in the United States. Some called for a declaration of war and even conservative congresspersons spoke of curtailing Israeli foreign aid. Many in congress saw political opportunity and began to attack the President's past tolerance and patience. Right-wing groups renewed conspiracy theories, the President even more deeply enmeshed in their hatred.

Voices originating in Israel urged American and European Jews to raise the flag of anti-Semitism, but now that couldn't be credited. Some still insisted the evidence was fraudulent, meant to destroy Zionism. Others, more cautious, called for reviewing the evidence. The Nazi image of the conspiring Jew was exactly what they dreaded to see again. This false image had led to hate and ultimately to the gas chambers for millions of innocents. Many in the Jewish community felt smoldering resentment that Israel would expose them to such danger.

President Straihorn called his advisors into emergency session, the discussions short, heated, and ultimately grim for Israel. With unprecedented speed, the President addressed the nation two hours after Senator Fadlallah's revelation. President Straihorn told America the Senator's charges were under investigation, the outcome to be disclosed as soon as possible. The President assured the American people that no action threatening the safety of the students or the Tablets would be tolerated. He promised to make the appropriate response to what the truth revealed.

***

Stunned, Prime Minister Roth called in Heinz who insisted Israel had not killed Becky Fadlallah. He admitted suppressing the discovery she'd been shot at close range pending verification of her identity. Clearly the girl was, in fact, the powerful Senator's daughter, kidnapped and murdered by unknown enemies to discredit Israel. Repercussions would be immense. There was no time to replace Heinz, no choice but to deny all efforts to destroy the damned Tablets, operating discretely now nearly impossible. How did one steal a treasure inside a brightly lit compound surrounded by rifle-toting Marines? The hellish call from the United States President came in a few minutes.

The President opened, "Good evening, Mr. Prime Minister. I assume you are fully aware of events of the past hours?"

"I am, Mr. President."

"I assume the worst is true and the suspect is Becky Fadlallah," said the President.

"The girl is the Senator's daughter, but the Israeli government had nothing to do with her murder. Lower level personnel did take it upon themselves to cover up the evidence out of some misguided sense of patriotism. Charges are currently being filed against them. Israel will cooperate with your country in any way on this sad matter," said the Israeli Prime Minister.

"Undoubtedly. My situation here is tough. American citizens demand action, and Congress is bending over backwards to meet their demands. Congress is reluctant at this point to defend Israel. My influence is at low tide. I have to bring home the Tablets and remaining students. I hope you understand. It's got nothing to do with my confidence in Israel."

"Mr. President, I can't agree. We've done nothing wrong, and my government needs time. To move the Tablets and the students now is to tell the world Israel can't be trusted."

"Prime Minister, I'm nearly alone in defending you. Many are calling for drastic measures against Israel. If a congressional vote were taken today, Israel would not be assured of support. In plain English that would mean your country wouldn't receive a penny. I've already suffered the indignity of being impeached. It's taken time to regain my citizens' trust. If I don't move the Tablets and the students, I'll lose further influence. Right wing speakers are crucifying me on talk shows. If either you or I do anything to slow bringing home these Tablets, the tide of public opinion will sweep us away."

"How can I agree? You're saying my country lacks the right to review these Tablets to judge whether they are a national threat."

"I'm saying nothing of the sort. I've allowed Israel access so the Tablets could be assessed, a concession I didn't need to give. Your scholar had full access. You know more particulars about the Tablets than I do. I don't care what's in them. All I care about is political reality. America won't tolerate more delays. Help me appease America so I can continue to support you."

The Prime Minister paused. "Israel is America's friend and ally. We have always supported United States interests, but my responsibility is to Israel. I must know these Jesus Tablets can cause us no harm."

"Listen, Mr. Prime Minister; neither I nor most Americans care about your country's religion. Religion is personal. However, if Israel resists us on this issue, the United States will abandon you. You have a decision to make. I will address America within the hour to relay it. However, I advise you it will be political suicide to impede the exit of Tablets or students. I need your decision. The American people must have an answer within the hour."

Roth sighed. "Israel will cooperate in moving the students and Tablets. However, we must be part of the planning so we're seen cooperating as part of the transfer team."

"Of course. I'll see to it. You'll be fully abreast of the details. Forgive me, but I must get back to work so I can take pressure off both of us."

Prime Minister Roth hung up and ordered his aide, "Get me Heinz."

***

Within the hour President Straihorn faced the cameras. "My fellow Americans, I promised to keep you informed concerning the Jesus Tablets and recent events in Israel. Most of you are aware there have been shocking developments surrounding this discovery. Two murders of Americans at Sepphoris have been followed by the incredible discovery that their suspected assassin has turned out to be another innocent American. There have been charges of Israeli and Vatican involvement. Senator Fadlallah has made serious charges. That evidence is being examined. As your President, I promised I would be talking to both the Israeli Prime Minister and the Pope himself. The Pope has assured me, and by the use of mass media the world, that neither he nor the Roman

Catholic Church has any involvement with the Jesus Tablets. The Prime Minister of Israel has told me lower level officials covered up the identity of Senator Fadlallah's daughter out of misguided patriotism. These individuals' fate lies with Israeli courts. Prime Minister Roth assures me no one in authority knew of this cover-up.

"We are, of course, conducting our own investigations, results to be made public. The Nation of Israel is our long time friend and ally. Prime Minister Roth has long and close ties not only with the United States Government but with me. Our dealings have been honorable, and I consider him a trustworthy friend. It is our consensus that the American students and the Tablets would be safest in the United States. They will leave Israel within seven days. The United States government will take further measures to protect the students effective immediately and will send in a special team to prepare the Jesus Tablets for transport. Israel has cooperated during every step as a full partner. With continued efforts of both governments, I am confident the truth will be determined. I will keep you fully informed. Thank you and good night. God bless America."

***

If Israel couldn't succeed in destroying the Tablets, the Church had no choice but to use her own plan. The thought of his own culpability made the Pope ill. Father Tobenhien heard the speech while flying to Israel from his mission in Latin America. As always the Church had unique resources, now needed.

Chapter Forty-three

Noon the next day saw an altered Sepphoris. A team of American specialists arrived. Henry and Alice moved to an officially safe location. Building materials for crating the Tablets arrived on trucks bearing American logos. All work halted, students told to pack. No one had permission to enter or leave for any reason. All native workers were paid and escorted to the gate. A backhoe dug ditches in front of the former Cross home to provide defense trenches for the onsite Marines. The removed dirt was utilized to fill sand bags stacked around the Jesus Tablets and former Cross home. Henry and Alice had no part in the packing, the danger too high for civilians.

By sundown of the first day a Patriot antimissile battery was in place, manned by Americans to protect the camp from air attack. Henry Cross would be allowed to look at the packed Jesus Tablets before the specialists firmly nailed on the lid. Except for meals and showers, students and staff were assigned to quarters. Grief stricken, Andre had just received news of the murder of his Bostonian uncle, Father Charles. Michael entertained sinister premonitions.

***

The Sepphoris accelerations complicated Heinz's destroying the Tablets. When alone, he removed his sunglasses and rubbed dents permanently abutting the bridge of his nose. Attacking Sepphoris was out of the question, but the Tablets must be pulverized. Of course, being clay, they were vulnerable to long-term exposure to water. Methodically, Heinz considered his options. The students and Tablets were to fly on an American commercial airliner from Tel Aviv to Paris. From Paris a commercial flight would take them to Washington D.C. Marines would guard the Tablets until they were safely loaded. The Tablets would be most vulnerable between Sepphoris and Tel Aviv or at the airport itself.

The tactical problem was bad, the politics worse. If the Tablets were destroyed in Israel, political fallout would be horrific. Heinz had little time. At their current rate, Americans would be ready to leave before their seven-day deadline. He replaced his glasses and reached in his pocket for antacids.

***

Heinz wasn't alone in weighing tactical options. Pebbles studied maps and timetables, his plans going well. Pebbles wanted to seize the Tablets intact. Pulling the Jews off their moral high ground as God's chosen people would be the great step in regaining Palestine. Pebbles also knew of the plan to use a commercial flight to transport the students and Tablets. His best chance would occur when it was airborne. America and Israel wanted to maintain the appearance of normalcy, implying Israel was a safe place. Such a silly, but convenient effort to show unity.

CIA Director Albright worried. From the first, he felt sharing operational plans with Israel to be wrong, mixing politics with field operations a recipe for disaster.

Garrett Black of the FBI also worried. Elements in the FBI weren't answering to him directly, but to someone else; most likely President Straihorn. The Arab students in Georgia were not the first victims of professional hits whose instigators simply vanished.

As a staunch Catholic and solid family man, Garrett Black had been offended by the President's sexual excesses. The murdered Catholic Priest, scheduled for interviews by the FBI the day before he died, rankled. There'd been reason to hope the unfortunate Father Charles had key information about the Jesus Tablets. An insider leaked this to others who had the good Father killed. No one even heard the shot.

Garrett Black had considered the priesthood, nearly drowning in guilt when he chose marriage instead. Then a priest from Opus Dei convinced him that God would be pleased if he joined as a member of the Pope's army. Grateful, young Garrett stepped into an organization of extreme power and secrecy. Opus Dei guided him through college, law school, and finally in the FBI. He assimilated its tenets. Over the years Opus Dei made few demands on the FBI director, minor favors easy to grant. Gradually, requests such as confidential reports on rising national leaders intensified. To serve Opus Dei was to serve the Church and to serve the Church was to serve God, so he complied. If anything, he furnished more than asked. The former choir boy provided much of what the Church knew of President Straihorn's personal life.

At Opus Dei's prompting, he'd ordered the interview with Father Charles, intrigued by that Priest's visit with the archenemy Secretary General Jesuit Father Tobenhien. Unfortunately everything Father Charles might have known ended with a small round bullet hole in his left temple. Opus Dei's attention shifted to transport of the Tablets.

***

In Brazil, Curt Schneider was last to walk down the ramp of the 747 jetliner. Captain Curtis Schneider, he reminded himself, reaching up to keep his cap from blowing off his blond head. He'd flown passenger jets for Delta for twenty-two years, but his license was due to expire in two months, not to be renewed. He'd faced hard moments before, but none matched this. His blood pressure was too high, and no amount of medication made any difference. "Rules are rules," the fat little doctor said.

Curtis had safely landed four jets that experts swore should have fallen from the sky like rocks. No injuries on his watch. His appeal to the pilot licensing committee included testimony that five hundred people were alive thanks to his skill. It didn't matter. Walking on the hot tarmac toward the main terminal of Rio de Janiero he reflected on how empty life seemed now.

Not that long ago he was a twenty-year- old helicopter pilot in Vietnam, going in under fire to haul out shot-up Marines who should've still been in high school. None of that mattered anymore, the bravery, hardships, and deaths all meaningless today. No one cared and few remembered. His blue eyes dulled. He'd done his best to adapt to civilian life, to hide his recurring depressions and the nagging feeling he should have died. He could hardly endure the blatant materialism of his peers, the immaturity of the generation that followed the Vietnam years, slugs who'd never seen battle- hardened Marines of eighteen with their haunting vacant stares.

Only flying and his Catholic faith kept him alive during the disorienting days of readjustment to civilian life. Only flying brought that sense of freedom. Only in the sky Curtis felt in God's world. He piloted for small private outfits who valued men who would fly barely running planes into hell for the right price. Curtis often flew unscheduled flights out of Latin America to remote landing sites in farmer's fields throughout the Gulf States. Cool under pressure, he credited his war time experience for commonly making landings guided by a single flashlight.

Curtis never sampled his cargo. Fools used drugs. He flew for excitement. Of course, the money was also very good although Curtis never needed much. In three or four years he'd saved plenty. Drug running never posed a problem for his Christian faith. Drugs were ubiquitous, his involvement impersonal. His job was to fly, and he enjoyed this combination of barnstorming and combat. How else could he fly so many miles in so many different planes? These wildcat days taught him how to make those later impossible landings with malfunctioning passenger jets, his best flying on flights never officially charted.

Schneider married because he wanted children. She was a good mother, but understood nothing of postwar trauma, calling his mood swings and depression senseless. Granted custody of their six children, she divorced him. His only involvement with his kids now was canceled checks. He'd tried hard to save the marriage, but no effort could change a scarred man. His wife didn't see marriage as for better or worse until death. Even when he pleaded with her to counsel with their priest, she refused. All talk over, all love lost, she abandoned him to a lonely world.

Then Opus Dei found Curt Schneider and gave him a mission. Opus Dei, expert at handling extremists, explained that sin caused the state of the world. His wife had violated God's laws, causing suffering. What happened allowed him now to serve God alone. Membership in Opus Dei equaled priesthood sans collar.

In a real sense, Opus Dei trained each member as a valuable soldier of God. Curtis Schneider had been a very good U.S. Marine, now a very good Opus Dei Marine. For three years he'd prayed and prepared for the day God would call him to the front. Like many who'd survived too many battles, he sought that elusive peace with honor among those who'd gone so long before. On this last trip, Schneider felt like an old warrior raised from slumber by the call of a distant trumpet. His suffering would soon be over. He'd been chosen by God to save the Roman Catholic Church in her hour of peril. Chosen to destroy the Jesus Tablets.

***

In the Oval Office President Straihorn reviewed his plans, satisfied. He felt no qualms about spending lives, the price to pay for the Jesus Tablets. Of course, the Pope lied, likewise Prime Minister Roth. All this palaver of friendship and loyalty! Nothing in politics had to do with loyalty and friendship. Power alone counted. No one knew that better than the man at the historic desk in the Oval Office, every word, action, and signal calculated to advantage.

There would be surprises, but he'd already anticipated his enemies' logical moves. Like a chess master, Straihorn controlled the board. The end game would start in just days. Confident, he knew how and when his enemies would strike. Like a spider in an intricate web, he waited for activity. Soon the Jesus Tablets would be ensnared.

***

At Sepphoris, trained specialists constructed a solid crate for the Tablets. Measuring and cutting materials outside the former Cross home, they carted finished components into the study for assembling. No one neared the study except the evacuation team. Henry finally spoke to the team leader who made it clear everyone would be out the next day, two days ahead of schedule.

Caught by surprise, Henry sought and gained assurance he could view the Tablets before builders closed the lid.

Henry informed the students that an Israeli convoy of covered trucks would appear at the Sepphoris gate before dawn. American experts would thoroughly inspect them for explosives. The crate with the Tablets would be loaded in an unmarked truck, students in the others, for a hot, but short ride to Tel Aviv. Marines would provide convoy protection while Israeli military forces lent extended flank protection. At the airport the trucks would head onto the runway, and the students would enter the American airliner. An Israeli ground crew would unload the Tablets and load them on the airplane in the Marines' presence. Then, the airplane would take off en route to Paris. Israeli air cover would be joined by American airpower three miles offshore. This airpower comprised part of the American fleet barely in international waters off Israel's coast. The Tablets would be loaded on a scheduled international flight.

Although all students had to vacate Sepphoris, no one had to return to the States who chose not to. Henry and Alice could go home or remain at Sepphoris in a custodial capacity. Nearly all the students wanted to stay with the Tablets; Michael, among a few others, felt accompanying them was closer than they wanted to be.

"Andre," he begged that night as they ate dinner with the others, speaking in low tones. "It's like they're cursed. My father died because of them. I don't want to lose you, too. You're my best friend and," his voice dropped, "the love of my life. Please, take a separate flight."

Andre shrugged. "What danger could there be now? There's Marines all over the place."

"You have to trust me. In my heart, I know the Tablets mean mortal danger. I know it."

***

Henry couldn't decide whether to go or stay. Stein's and the Ambassador's bodies had been flown to the States, their funerals over. Alice argued time alone at Sepphoris would be good for them. Harvard hadn't urged them to return, and without direct instructions their duty was to maintain a presence at the camp. Henry needed to think.

***

"What do you have to show me?" Roth asked when Heinz arrived in a dapper, three piece suit.

"We have one option. There are several ways the Tablets could be destroyed between Sepphoris and Tel Aviv; however, each would mean high losses. The U.S. reaction would be atrocious. The Tablets should be shattered only once off Israeli soil. The jet must destruct over Mediterranean waters, spreading wreckage and debris with no recovering even traces of the Tablets. They'd be reduced to dust with the right explosives. It's the only practical solution."

"How will you place the explosives in the plane?" Roth wondered if Heinz' eyes were shining behind the glasses.

"The operational plan is in this outline." Heinz pushed it toward Roth. "This will save time."

The Prime Minister accepted and studied one sheet of paper. "Under projected casualties, loss of life is total."

"Correct. Explosive experts say a charge heavy enough to pulverize the Tablets will shatter the plane. The force of the primary explosion coupled with that brought on by the secondary one from volatile jet fuel precludes survival."

"Two hundred college kids, normal travelers, and the crew, destroyed," murmured the Prime Minister as he studied his Mossad director.

"Yes."

Roth felt the particular horror of leaders who hold lives in their hands. *So this is what it comes down to. Killing innocents to preserve a history no rational person would believe anyway? Do I have a choice? Do I just count noses, then make a decision for the good of the larger number or is right and wrong greater than simple arithmetic? Can one simply divide the world into 'them and us' and justify any actions against 'them' so long as it benefits 'us?' Did Hitler use that rationale when he lit the world afire? Did Truman use it when he dropped the atomic bomb? When was it right to kill the innocent?*

"Is there no other way?"

"None viable," Heinz answered.

There it was. The beliefs of tribalism versus the dream of a universal ethic of right and wrong. The law of the tribe prevailed. In the nuclear age, political decisions resorted to the rationale of semi-erect cave men, the old pattern not to be denied. The Prime Minister sighed.

"Let it be done."

"It will."

When the door closed after Heinz, the Prime Minister murmured, "And may God have mercy on our souls."

***

The night before departure Sepphoris filled with light-hearted camaraderie and excitement, most of the students more than ready to go home. Fall classes approached. The prospect of a little fame before hitting the books titillated them. They cheerfully imbibed bottles of wine. Henry tried to smile at their youthful excesses as students sang and danced. Why did he feel so uneasy? After all, he was no longer responsible for the kids or the Tablets.

Andre finally agreed to stay in Israel with Michael for a few days before booking a flight to America. Likewise Henry Cross yielded to Alice's arguments, deciding to remain at Sepphoris. The excavation leader told them they wouldn't be allowed back into their former home until the protective trenches had been refilled. The site would be returned to its former state in three days.

Henry viewed the crate holding the Tablets before the construction team secured the lid. No doubt they were perfectly packed and crated, the crate constructed of oak, the packing substantial. Each tablet nestled in its own container row upon row exactly like the egg crates he'd seen as a boy on the farm. As Henry was escorted from the study he heard the sounds of hammering sealing the lid. He should feel at peace, but peace eluded him.

He left the barracks to stroll the site, chilled and grateful for his woolen shirt. Cresting Sepphoris hill, he saw lights of scattered farm houses. Mary must have walked this ridge. He felt connected to that woman who lived so long ago. In his musings, he neared where his team discovered the Tablets. Where Mary had hidden them so long ago... Henry thought, for centuries the Tablets lay buried here. She couldn't have dreamed that someday they would be excavated in a world of space flight and the atomic bomb. Mary hid her Tablets from a world too dangerous to receive them, and we haven't progressed far. Was it ever safe to tell people their religious beliefs rest on myths and psychological need? Would it have been best if the Tablets remained buried for another two thousand years? Henry sat on a boulder gazing at the stars over Palestine. Even now, two thousand years later, the world could not acknowledge religion as hope. All that was certain was the unknown.

Henry shivered, unable to escape his foreboding. The students wanted to go, and America wanted them home. A professor with no evidence wouldn't be a deterrent. Henry rose, trying to shake the chill, so unusually cold this evening. He meandered down, trying to ignore his unease. Finally, by force of will, he stopped and looked back on Sepphoris ridge. The clouds scudding across the half moon made shadows skitter like quick fingers from rock to rock. The breeze quickened. Dust swirled. Something terrible reached from the future, and he could do nothing. At home he lay by Alice but couldn't sleep, holding his sleeping wife close until the alarm clock warned of the coming day.

Their late-night partying left students subdued. Twenty trucks would take them to the airport, all assigned Marine escorts. Henry noticed each Marine carried more ammunition.

Henry watched the trucks load, the last assigned to carry the Jesus Tablets. The crate had been loaded on massive skids. Even outdoors everyone's breath caught when near the Tablets. The crate radiated danger. People lowered their voices. A big forklift hoisted and slid the precious cargo into the back of the truck where muscular men secured the load with binders and retaining blocks. Henry again reminded himself that the Tablets were out of his hands, and whatever their effect, it wasn't his responsibility alone.

Once loaded, trucks wove in and out as if performing a giant mechanical dance. In moments Henry lost track of the exact truck carrying the Tablets like a carnival hustler moving shells to obscure which held a pea. As quickly as the trucks began this maneuver they stopped, forming a queue for departure. Someone had planned superbly. Henry watched the trucks depart the gates. After two silent millennia the Jesus Tablets would speak.

Intrigued, *New York Times'* John Martin, along with the other journalists, hoped to get pictures and story material at Tel Aviv. Martin's plans changed abruptly when he discovered a note under his pillow advising him to stay in Sepphoris near Henry Cross.

Chapter Forty-four

At Ben Gurion Airport, a Lebanese entrepreneur, Abu Abbai, scion of an old, prominent, and secular Beirut family, sat in the waiting area reading the *London Times*. His family, prophets of capitalism, warned their government that war would break out due to religious hatred. In 1975 civil war erupted between religious factions. For fifteen years, Christians murdered Muslims in the name of their Prince of Peace, Jesus, and Muslims murdered the Christians in the name of their benevolent prophet, Mohammed. During lulls Sunni Muslims killed Shiites. Not to be left behind, the Christians splintered, occasionally killing each other.

The young Abu grew up in Beirut watching his family lose millions in infrastructure investment along with relatives. Many fled to safer havens: Paris, London, and New York. However, Abu's father rejected the easy route. Stubborn, he stayed in Beirut trying to hold his family and nation together. All the divided Muslims hated Israel. However, the Abbai family had investments there and tried to remain realists in the quagmire of Mideast politics.

Impatient and independent, Abu differed from his stoic father. A scholar and inherent problem solver, he chose a new direction. To the intellectual Abu, rampant hatred in the Mideast originated in tribalism coupled with religion. Abu saw the endless warfare and generational hatred as simply stupid; those more educated tended toward tolerance. The worst of the less educated became fanatical killers, believing one only had to read the Bible or the Koran.

Abu saw education as primary for Mideast peace, prosperity second. But only prosperity could provide time and money for education. He studied Christian and Muslim literature, both, he concluded, based on a hodgepodge of visions, detached voices, and improbable tales.

The Abbai family maintained varied connections. After all, one had no idea which fringe group today might become the ruling government tomorrow. Abu grew up exposed to radical leaders of every faction. In raw disgust, he watched 'people's parties' come and go. Abu knew all about Hezbollah, the alleged Party of God. He knew all about Hamas, the so-called Islamic Resistance Movement. He was painfully familiar with the Palestine Liberation Front and the Popular Front for the Liberation of Palestine. All reduced their flowery names to acronyms: PLO, PLF, PFLP, SLA, and UNIFIL.

All Abu's thoughts solidified on April 10th, 1996, when Israel conducted a massive air attack on southern Beirut and the ancient city of Tyre. His father lay among the Beirut dead that sunshiny day. According to the old warrior of peace and tolerance's wishes, no clergy officiated at his funeral. Abu said the final words over his father's grave, reminding mourners how hard his father had tried to preserve peace even at the loss of much of his own fortune. His father had taken food to the ailing widow of an employee when he was killed. This man who could afford to be anywhere chose to stay and aid his friends in his beloved Beirut. His son closed with, "This was a peaceful, tolerant man. God, if there is a God, will accept him."

From that day on, Abu, determined to make a difference, searched for means to weaken religion's hold in the war torn Middle East. When news of the Jesus Tablets broke, he considered them his answer. Pouring money into learning about them, he drew Pebbles' notice.

Perhaps with the Tablets Abu could weaken religion in the Mideast. Certainly, the United States couldn't be trusted to reveal their contents. Crippling Judaism and Christianity would discredit two-thirds of the region's religious players. Abu shrewdly concluded that Islam would also have severe doubts thrown against it. After all, if two out of three religions were clearly wrong, might it not follow that the third was also a human creation?

As he eagerly pursued information about the Tablets, eventually another shadowy player showed his hand. Soon, an agent assigned by Pebbles approached Abu proposing he take a major role in Arab possession of the Jesus Tablets. He accepted. However, what the agent said next left him shaken. They wanted him to hijack the plane, diverting it to Tehran. When Abu protested he could have nothing to do with weapons or violence, his contact assured him neither firearms nor violence was necessary. He must only pretend to be armed to divert the flight.

Once the Tablets arrived securely in Tehran, international scholars would be invited to inspect them. The Iranian government would donate copies of the Tablets to all major universities. He would be a hero to the Muslims. America and Israel would confiscate his assets in those countries. However, Europe, the Mideast, and most other parts of the world wouldn't honor such an indictment.

Abu agreed if workable plans were in place and the plane with its passengers allowed to leave Tehran once the Tablets were unloaded. His contact assured Abu it was the Tablets that had value, and the moral thing was to release the plane. Iran would announce that the Tablets' were seized only because of fear of their destruction in the West. By permitting international access, Iran would take the moral high ground. Since the United States had made the same promise, moral outrage would fizzle.

Only governments had networks privy to flight plans and cargo manifests. Iran had enough power to protect and properly display the Tablets. No radical, Abu had to be convinced the plan was sound enough to justify the risk. The agent protested that Allah respected caution, the plan foolproof.

Their conversation took place at an upscale restaurant in Tel Aviv. Abu only had to book his Paris flight. He'd be at Ben Gurion at the scheduled time. Once airborne, a flight attendant would inquire if he'd be flying to Hamburg after changing planes in Paris. In ten minutes she would walk past again. He was to rise and follow her to the cockpit. She would pretend terror because the man behind her, ordering the plane be flown to Tehran, had a gun. The pilot would divert the flight, its passengers ignorant until the final moments.

As Abu waited at Ben Gurion he conceded his handlers' efficiency. A frequent traveler, popular even with lower level airport personnel, Abu tipped heavily. When first-class passengers of flight 217 to Paris were directed to board, Abu embarked. Comfortably seated, he recognized some of the flight attendants. Which was his?

As Abu arranged his carry on, Captain Curt Schneider checked the instrument panel in the cockpit. International intelligence agencies would never forget his name. He prayed silently. For the sake of the Holy Roman Catholic Church and Opus Dei, the forgotten Vietnam warrior prepared to be an instrument of destruction.

The plane rolled to a halt at an out-of-the-way spot near a runway. Military trucks pulled near and Abu watched soldiers surround the plane. Students clambered out of trucks and clustered, visiting, blinking in the sun's glare. Two vehicles approached from the main terminal. A mobile boarding ladder coupled with the jet as the students boarded. They filed through first class toward coach. Abu concluded they came from Sepphoris. The second vehicle, a forklift manned by two Israelis, drove to the back. It must be loading the Jesus Tablets, Abu thought, trying to relax.

***

Father Tobenhien watched from the main terminal, assured by Mossad that everything was on schedule. Tobenhien had lived too long amidst politics. Only actions counted, and the Tablets were still intact. Thank God the Church had its own plan.

At the airplane, the forklift operator gently hoisted the crate carrying the Jesus Tablets from the truck toward the open cargo door. Observed by Marines, it rested on rollers, then electrical winches attached and it was drawn into the cargo hull. In the cargo bay, blocks stabilized it. Israeli personnel covered it with thick blankets and bound the load with web binders, rechecking their work. Marines continued to watch as the cargo bays were closed and sealed.

The airliner fired its engines, taxiing down the runway. Flight 217 lifted off. Father Tobenhien prayed for the Tablets' destruction, as well as the salvation of each soul aboard.

The jet was to climb to cruising altitude, flying north by northwest until close to Cyprus, there to turn west over the

Mediterranean, keeping far from shorelines. To its flanks and directly overhead F-14s from the American task force had picked him up after he left Israeli airspace. Nothing these escorts could do would save the plane with Schneider at the controls. Approximately two hundred miles east of Sicily, in the middle of a broad empty space of the Mediterranean, Schneider would plunge into the sea with impact at over five hundred miles per hour. At such speed the water would be solid as a steel slab, shattering all aboard. The brittle Jesus Tablets would smash into thousands of shards to settle into deep sediment at the Mediterranean floor and dissolve. Recovering bodies would hinder any hunt for the Tablets.

Momentarily, Schneider would tell his copilot to check on some minor matter, then he'd go into a strong barrel roll. Since few passengers would have their seat belts fastened, this would throw everyone into the aisle. Stunned or unconscious, they'd have little awareness of the dive. Schneider would still be accelerating when they hit.

He checked his position. Crete would come up shortly. Schneider felt comfortable, just like his Vietnam days. Once he'd accepted a mission, he didn't worry. He'd always felt safe in God's hands. Today was no different. Why linger on earth when the doors of heaven open so near?

A uniformed Texas blonde paused by Abu. Smiling broadly she said, "Mr. Abbai, good to see you again. Are y'all flying on to Hamburg after Paris?"

He felt a frisson of excitement. "Yes. I have business there."

"I'll bring you a pillow."

Only thirty-three, Bonnie had come a long way from the two dog town of Bencreek, Texas. In Bencreek her big family lived hungry, good looks Bonnie's only asset. Her break came when she went to work for a woman who ran several Texas beauty salons. From this older mentor, the ambitious Bonnie discovered she could be quite happy as a bi-sexual. For high school graduation, her mentor gave her money to move to Dallas and on to stewardess training.

After years of freewheeling fun, Bonnie noticed fine lines on her pale skin. Aging, she couldn't depend on beauty much longer.

She redoubled her search for a route to the good life. Opportunity crooked a finger. On a recent flight to Athens a dapper Arab invited her to dinner. Over roast lamb Mr. Danar asked if Bonnie might be interested in making $250,000.00 with very little risk. Bonnie listened, shaken. Mr. Danar wanted her to take part in a hijacking. He explained she only had to pretend fear. The tough Texan thought it over.

"This doesn't seem like much money for something as all-out-important as the Jesus Tablets," drawled the former country girl. At his flicker of surprise, she knew she'd guessed right.

After some hesitation the Arab said, "We can be reasonable. What in your estimation is a fair return?"

She flashed to an image of the crowded shack of her fly-specked childhood. Did she have the courage? "I'll do it for one and one half million American dollars deposited in a Swiss numbered account of my choosing."

"A great deal of money," said Danar. "Are you sure you won't reconsider?"

This hard scrabble country girl's instinct took over. "Honey, the Tablets are worth a lot more than that. Tell your pals that's my price."

Thus, Bonnie Eakins swayed down the passenger aisle a rich woman. After a reasonable amount of medical care, she planned to sue the airline. The suit would be profitable because the airlines were sensitive to hijackings. Of course she'd quit, claiming fear of flying. In a year or so she would move to Geneva.

***

On Crete, Mickey the Wire squinted through thick glasses at his instrument monitor. Mickey kept his past to himself. Few in Mossad knew he'd been an orphan found abandoned on a refugee ship originating from a Russian port on the cold Black Sea. Passengers claimed to know nothing, and Israel became the baby's de facto parent.

That was in 1974. The disastrous Yom Kippur War had just ended. Israeli intelligence hadn't operated at their usual efficiency so were conducting intense reviews resulting in new thinking. Few leaders were ruthless enough to place agents in hopeless situations. However, postwar analysis showed assets in doomed situations likely to produce information leading to victory. Expendable assets decision makers could view as less than fully human were ideal. This worked best when the agent was an orphan of unknown origin, having always been property of the State. Thus, the Son of Nun experiment.

Israel selected three hundred such orphans, including Mickey. All were four to six-years-old, testing at average or slightly below average intelligence and reared in collectives. State psychologists theorized these children could be indoctrinated to high patriotic intensity. The State assigned them to areas of extreme peril, and they felt privileged. They embraced death for country with the zeal other fanatics sought in martyrdom. Dubbed Section Sixteen resources, they were sixteen when final selections were made. Their value was well proven in 1996 when Israel invaded Lebanon based on intelligence obtained by Section Sixteen personnel.

Mickey had been in position for two days.

According to vital statistics of Flight 217 everything was preceding apace, the aircraft climbing to cruising altitude, its course exactly what Mickey's briefing had projected. He pushed another keyboard button. In eleven minutes thirty-seven seconds the aircraft should be in position to self-destruct. Mickey monitored a two-way radio attached to a simple computer programmed to operate automatically, Mickey was backup. It monitored the aircraft's position by mini-burst transmissions to an on board transmitter connected to electrical detonation devices to fire the main charge of Semtec explosives. The main charge consisted of one hundred twenty-five pounds of explosives constructed into flexible strands woven into sheets covered with duck canvas marked with Star of David insignia. Thick, soft blankets covering the crate were really sheets of spun explosives.

When they detonated by radio command, the Tablets would be vaporized, the aircraft blown to random pieces. Mickey was to visually confirm destruction and manually override the computer if the target displayed any abnormal pattern prior to programmed destruction. The countdown timer now said four minutes, seventeen seconds. He glassed the sky. The target should appear in minutes.

***

Captain Schneider cruised at twenty-one thousand feet above Crete. They would clear the south south-west corner soon. At that moment the blonde stewardess paused next to a jumpy Abu. "Here's your pillow, Mr. Abbai."

This is it! he thought. "Could you help me to the restroom please? I don't feel well."

"Certainly. Steady yourself on my shoulder,"

As they staggered forward Bonnie whispered, "Push me hard when I stop." Abu understood she wanted others to see force before they reached the cockpit. They'd almost left first-class when she stopped and quavered, "Please, don't do this!"

Abu rammed her against the cockpit door. "Shut up, and get moving!"

Bonnie cried hysterically, pounding the door. "He's going to kill me unless we turn the plane east! Please Captain Schneider, he's going to kill us all. I'm afraid to die! Please don't let him kill me!" Bonnie sobbed, scratching pathetically on the door.

Abu shouted, "Turn toward Tehran immediately, or I kill everyone!"

In a millisecond Captain Schneider analyzed. The raghead bastards want to hijack the Jesus Tablets! "Go screw a camel, you idiot! You're on your way to hell!" He threw the jet into a plunging barrel roll. Passengers toppled from seats. The cabin filled with tangled chaos. Luggage and people bounced crazily, no more up or down, everything a spinning madhouse. The copilot's head smashed into the instrument panel, and he slumped. Screams filled the cabin as the jet dove to the Mediterranean. Curtis Schneider began, "Holy Mary mother of God,--." The forgotten veteran never finished his prayer.

Mickey sighted the plane. His computer showed twenty-seven seconds to destruction. Then to his astonishment it rolled and began a vertical corkscrew down. Instantly Mickey pushed the manual detonation button. A flash engulfed the airliner. Witnesses reported the explosion from thirty miles away. None of the accompanying F-14s crashed, although the concussion tumbled them like windborne seeds. Fishermen reported seeing rags tumbling toward the water. Later studies revealed them to be bodies and body parts.

Mickey packed up, checking to be certain he left no trace.

The explosion was heard around the world. Doomed Flight 217 hadn't hit Mediterranean water before voices sent word of the destruction. Seven boat crews witnessed it, mouths agape. Of these all but one had direct communication to shore. Four of the seven crews called for help on radios. The F-14 pilots regained control over their own aircraft, radioing the U.S. task force. Since Flight 217 crashed so soon after departing Tel Aviv, reporters were still at the airport. The fate of Flight 217 reached them in moments. The news hit nation after nation. Years afterward, nearly everyone could remember where they were and what they were doing when word reached them, a sense of the surreal as the news broke. Anchors interrupted scheduled programming with tremulous announcements that the Jesus Tablets and all aboard Flight 217 had been lost.

In the United States, broken-hearted households learned their students had been on the doomed flight. Neighbors and relatives rushed to give support. Weeping groups hunkered around television screens. At first, tantalizing reports of survivors issued, giving hope to families praying for miraculous reprieves. Hope faded as boats raced to the crash site only to witness a watery version of Dante's *Inferno*. Devastation spread over a two mile radius of lightly rolling sea.

Clothes, books, letters, pillows, and any part of the plane that could float drifted meaninglessly. Ample signs of death, bodies and pieces of bodies floated on the ripples. Some seemed uninjured and the coldly objective camera lens suggested life. However, pulled aboard, bodies showed organs shattered on impact. Others were torn to pieces, like floating limbs of broken statuary. Repulsed, reluctant crews lashed bodies together and tied them to the sides of their boats, unable to bring them aboard for fear of swamping. Rafts of floating bodies trailed boats. One crew member spotted a girl on the warm water's surface, auburn hair floating around her face like silk ribbons. When the seaman grasped that hair to draw her to starboard, he saw in horror that the head wasn't attached to a body. As the seaman vomited into the sea an older man quietly tied the head by her beautiful hair alongside the boat. For the rest of the rescue operation she haunted them, a macabre cork bobber.

Hysterical aides rushed into both houses of Congress with the appalling news. Congress recessed. For the first time the President groped for words. The record later showed he asked aides for advice. Finally responding to one suggestion, he ordered all military units placed on red alert status. He agreed with another aide to call an Oval Office emergency session with his highest advisors. Aides scrambled, setting up chairs.

Practical questions arose. The remains had to be gathered, identified, processed, and prepared for burial. Investigation had to be made into the cause of the crash, possibly taking months. Nevertheless, the American people must be assured their government had taken control. President Straihorn appeared shocked, indecisive. The Navy argued for a quick burial at sea. Political advisors' reactions were frantic. There must be a place under American control with facilities for the burial personnel and experts examining the wreckage. Although close, Crete's government had strong Arab sympathies.

A junior Army officer asked what was wrong with Sepphoris. After all, it had facilities for a number of people, and the United States already had military in place. This brought heated debate. Some argued that Israel might be found culpable; others that there was no evidence Israel had anything to do with it. It had been an American plane, crew, and cargo. Political advisors liked Sepphoris which would display Israeli and United States unity at a time of tragedy. During this debate more than one set of eyes glanced at the dazed President.

The Secretary of State took the matter in hand asking him, "Would Sepphoris be an acceptable base of operations for body preparation and the investigation?"

President Straihorn seemed awakened from a dream. "Sepphoris? What do you think, Mr. Secretary?"

"Most of us in think it's workable, Mr. President."

"Call Prime Minister Roth and explain."

"Right away. Would it be proper to recess for two hours to give everyone a chance to collect information and think?"

President Straihorn waved his hand in summary dismissal. "Yes, good idea, very good. I need a little time."

As they left, his advisors noted President Straihorn rubbed his face wearily.

Prime Minister Roth was also alone. Told of the mission's success, he'd not yet read the full report. Apparently there'd been a glitch, but nothing that deterred the operation. The Tablets and the airplane crashed leaving no survivors. Roth felt a dull, sick, emptiness. Guilt would be his companion for life. At that moment his secretary announced the White House calling. Roth dreaded the moment, but had to answer. "Prime Minister Roth speaking."

"Prime Minister, this is Secretary of State Anderson calling on behalf of the President concerning the crash of Flight 217."

Roth leaned forward, surprised. "Mr. Secretary, good to hear from you, but certainly not under these circumstances. I've been expecting President Straihorn's call. Israel will offer any aid during this tragic time. What can we do?"

"The President is absorbing the shock and will communicate with you shortly. The United States and Israel must stand together."

"Of course. How can we assist?"

"We need Sepphoris for holding victims' bodies and housing investigation teams. We'll need refrigeration units and help transporting the remains. Israeli airspace would remain sovereign since only your helicopters would carry our dead to Sepphoris. The United States will supply body preparation personnel, but they'll need temporary visas. We hope to conduct an international memorial service at Sepphoris before flying the bodies here. We want to finish this grim business in a week. Will Israel cooperate?"

"I'll order helicopters into immediate service. Refrigeration trucks and generators will be in place today. Israel stands with America. Please tell President Straihorn I share his distress."

Within the hour arrangements were made with Crete to use a section of shoreline to gather and load the remains. The civilian fishing population threw every asset into the search. Fortunately, the sea was calm and the crash occurred early that morning. Soon, one hundred-fifty torn bodies lined the beach. Many wept as they peered at the youthful faces. Four American helicopters ferried bodies to a remote beach in Israel. In Israel, they were taken to Sepphoris by Israeli helicopters. As the first arrived, refrigeration trucks already waited

Chapter Forty-five

It is a remarkable coincidence that almost everyone has the same religion as their parents and it always just so happens they're the right religion.
Richard Dawkins

A man is his own easiest dupe, for what he wishes to be true he generally believes to be true.
Demosthenes

There is a fundamental difference between religion, which is based on authority, [and] science, which is based on observation and reason. Science will win because it works.
Stephen Hawking

Stunned, Henry and Alice Cross clung to each other. These were the laughing boys and girls who not so many hours ago drank too much wine and played childish jokes. Alice's heart broke. The kids didn't deserve this. Ashen faced, Henry, never before at a loss for words, moved like a sleepwalker. This was all wrong.

But Henry reasoned. Right now, so far as he knew, only three living people had ever read the Jesus Tablets: he, Alice, and Dr. Gold. Whoever killed the others might not rest until they, too, were eliminated. The Tablets were gone, but Henry and Alice still had the translation notes, the knowledge, and possibly one extra hope, none of which would bring back the dead. If men of integrity failed to speak the truth, the murderers won. Henry still had the power of speech, more than those silent bodies in the freezers had.

He spotted John Martin jotting notes near the refrigeration units. Leaving Alice, Henry strode over to him. "Mr. Martin, as you know. I'm site supervisor here. You ought to ask me for an interview."

Martin brightened. That expression always meant someone eager to spill everything.

"Sounds great. Where?"

"We'll have more privacy in our quarters. What I have to say will take time." With that Henry beckoned to a worried Alice. Martin followed, certain of another front page breakthrough.

***

Pebbles perused the reports on his battered desk. The Tablets were gone. Five independent agents' reports matched. The ways of Allah were not the ways of man. Pebbles prayed for patience in the face of the unknowable. In the end nothing would defeat Allah's justice. Perhaps this was an opportunity to strike major targets, now that the spotlight shown on Israel. He turned to his list of possible operations. Targets were everywhere. New York City – that hotbed of commerce. A blow there would be a true blow for Allah.

***

Pope Jerome sat alone in his chambers. When the plane crash was confirmed, he canceled all appointments to meditate and pray. If he'd only spoken, it wouldn't have left the runway. Passengers of Flight 217 would still be alive on this sunny Italian day. However, the Jesus Tablets would have destroyed the Church. Ashamed, he acknowledged relief overshadowing guilt. As before, the Church could shelter those needing spiritual guidance. God could forgive what humanity could not. The Pope clung to this wispy straw as he prayed for himself, the innocent dead, and the rescued Holy Roman Catholic Church.

***

In Jerusalem, the contented Heinz also read reports. Destroying the Tablets had been the most vital task of his career. Israel would survive. Of course, she would have to walk lightly. Allowing the bodies to be processed at Sepphoris was a start.

Second, Israel must counter inevitable conspiracy charges. Lastly, Mossad had to tidy up loose ends. Dr. Gold would have to go. The Cross couple, too, but a little more patience had to be exercised there. It didn't do to give conspiracy theorists ammunition. Of course, the dangerously astute Father Tobenhien must follow Father Charles. He scheduled his list: Tobenhien within two months, Dr. Gold soon, the Cross couple within a year, the students Andre and Michael within two years. He shuffled through his reports again. The Section Sixteen asset had been eliminated along with his handler in Crete. That cutout isolated the rest of Mossad. The agents who killed the cutouts had simply followed orders.

Initial reports from America looked excellent. The President, clearly under stress, would stick with Israel being innocent. The Prime Minister expected his call within three hours.

President Straihorn called the Prime Minister two and three-quarter hours later. Roth spoke first. "Mr. President, how are you? These are such horrific circumstances."

"Frankly, it's taking time to absorb it. My intelligence doesn't have a clue what happened to that plane. Our critics will be after us. Losing the Tablets is one thing, but loss of young lives is tragic. I need your help. Any ideas would be much appreciated."

President Straihorn had certainly turned more tractable. "Mr. President, I assure you our intelligence is turning over every stone. It's not clear whether the jet crashed due to mechanical reasons or sabotage. Do you have any feedback on that?"

"I do not. Witnesses say the plane exploded, but some say it entered a downward spiral before it blew up. We won't know until we recover the black box from the cockpit. It might be two weeks before it's recovered with debris spread so far. Frankly, I'm at a loss as to how to handle Sepphoris. My advisors felt the bodies could be best processed there. What do you suggest now that most have been recovered?"

Prime Minister Roth sighed in relief. Mossad estimates were accurate. He'd never seen Straihorn unsure of himself or so open to suggestion. "Mr. President, the quicker the bodies are processed and returned to the States, the quicker we can put this catastrophe behind us. I suggest American and Israeli intelligence combine to investigate the crash. Then we'll decide how justice will be served. The quicker the bodies are laid to rest, the quicker the media will move on."

"My advisors tell me our body prep team should land in Tel Aviv in three hours. Would your people see they get to Sepphoris ASAP?"

"Mr. President, Israel will do everything possible to help you and the United States."

"I'm exhausted. I'm going to get some rest. I'm not in the Oval Office today. My Vice President is covering essential tasks. If there's nothing more I'll close now."

"By all means, Mr. President, rest. You can depend on Israel's cooperation here and in the United States." Roth could have sworn the President's voice quavered as he hung up. Later study of the recording confirmed the President's voice did, in fact, break with emotion, reconfirming Cliff Straihorn's being in shock.

***

In reality, President Straihorn felt fine, everything following his expectations. He would have the black box in twenty-four hours. He'd know his enemies' names and the exact cause of the destruction of Flight 217. He'd never doubted the plane would be destroyed, had based strategy on it. However, it would be interesting to know who pulled it off. The deaths didn't bother him, necessary lubrication for his plan. What a game this is! the smug President thought.

***

The next hours produced tumultuous news. The Henry Cross story to John Martin exposed the Jesus Tablets' contents to an astounded world. Henry emphasized that all on Flight 217 were murdered by parties unknown to prevent the Tablets' exposure. His conscience wouldn't allow the truth to go unrecorded. Alice, outrage trumping reluctance, corroborated with her account of translating the Tablets.

Many Protestant Churches responded predictably by denouncing the Cross couple as exploitive heretics. To nonbelievers and academia Henry and Alice became overnight heroes. Rank and file believers went from one end of the religious spectrum to the other. The more liberal didn't feel the Jesus story had much to do with their faith, tending to believe in a vague God. More imaginative believers condemned Henry and Alice as satanic manifestations sent to tempt and deceive. Pope Jerome took Father Tobenhien's advice and directed Catholics to pray for them in their mistaken desire to draw fame from tragedy. Other leaders issued secret orders to discredit the story.

In a thousand ways the Catholic Church and Israel reiterated the Cross couple had no real evidence absent the Tablets. Little did the Church realize, but stroke by stroke it painted itself into the tightest of corners. The Arab States promoted the Cross interview as another message from Allah showing the falsehood of Jewish claims to Palestine. Many promised sanctuary for Henry and Alice to write their memoirs and teach in Arab universities, predicting their unnatural deaths if they didn't accept. The couple proved hard to discredit. Past and present colleagues attested to their competence and integrity. Harvard cautioned that Henry's was not necessarily its viewpoint. No statements would be made by the U.S. government or Israel until the Flight 217 investigation concluded. However, "official public sources" were quoted saying the Church was correct. Henry and Alice Cross had no direct evidence.

Identification and body preparation proceeded. Bodies were sorted, arranged, and identified in the study, each checked for all its parts: missing hands, arms, legs, and even heads matched to owners. The flight manifest was used to check off identified bodies with those missing. Faxed dental records confirmed questionable identities. All work had to be performed under controlled temperatures of refrigeration units connected to special trucks and rooms of the Cross home. One by one the identified bodies were taken from the chilled trucks to the study for identification one last time, stripped, washed, embalmed, and clothed. A team of six placed each in its military casket. Finally, the caskets were sealed, numbered, and placed in other refrigerated trucks.

In America the question "why" ballooned. Citizens demanded answers. Airlines and airports scrambled to deflect negligence charges. Congress swung among varied positions. Within forty-eight hours, five votes approved special committees with extraordinary investigative powers. President Straihorn hadn't addressed America. Many saw this as an admission of guilt. Grief-stricken parents filed Federal Tort Claims, believing the Cross interviews.

Senator Fadlallah urged America to let the system take its course, to bury the dead, then seek the murderers. This wisdom helped stabilize the citizenry. Nevertheless, suspicions peaked. For the first time, a majority of Americans blamed Israel for Mideast unrest. Jewish groups pointed out Israel's cooperation and that Flight 217 was an American plane under American control. Prime Minister Roth lay low. Crackdowns on Palestinians paused. Every Israeli newspaper touted the blessings of peace and friendship. Israel hinted at possible concessions to help the peace process. Finally, Roth called President Straihorn, appealing to him to speak to America to publicly reject charges against Israel.

***

A drawn, gray President Straihorn looked into the cameras. After one false start, he spoke. "Good evening, my fellow Americans. Tonight I address you about Sepphoris and the Flight 217 tragedy. Much is yet to be discovered. The exact cause of the crash remains unknown, but experts are on site working round the clock recovering and studying evidence. It is unclear whether the jet crashed for mechanical reasons or due to sabotage. The possibility of a bomb or even a missile cannot be discounted. We will determine the cause of this disaster. If sabotage, we will not rest until we find and bring the guilty to justice. The Jesus Tablets' destruction is a loss, but the Tablets are not preeminent. The tragedy here is the innocent victims. My heart breaks for you who have lost loved ones.

"Emotions are understandably running high. Each of us is outraged. It's natural to want to strike out at any who might be at fault. I urge you to remember that all are presumed innocent until proven guilty. Some have unjustly blamed Israel for this tragedy. Israel has been our ally throughout this disaster. The Jesus Tablets were an American responsibility. Flight 217, the students, and the Tablets have always been under United States control. Israel never interfered; quite the contrary, supported us and is protecting those preparing our dead. Israel has committed millions in equipment and manpower to help, not accepting any payment. At all times, Israel has been our trusted friend. No evidence indicates we have misplaced that trust.

"Our dead leave Sepphoris day after tomorrow after a brief interdenominational service. The United States looks forward to placing these young citizens to rest. We will relentlessly pursue our search for answers. I will keep you informed of our progress. Until then, using the powers vested in me I order all American flags flown at half-mast until our dead are on American soil with their families. Thank you and good-night. God bless America."

Prime Minister Roth felt gratified at Straihorn's strong defense of Israel. Mossad's operation would never be discovered, the chain of knowledge severed.

***

The following day passed quickly at Sepphoris, all but six dead accounted for. Trucks carried coffins to Ben Gurion Airport after the brief service. As before, the Israeli Army provided flanking security while Marines covered the transport trucks. In a country of daily violence, no one broke this peace.

Isaac Gold watched from a roadside boulder a few miles from Sepphoris. There were no laughing students today, no knowing looks between lovers, only the Israeli sun beating on late-summer Galilee. How many forgotten had been lost on this embattled ground? How many mothers wept for children in this land of tears and hatred? How many plots made and destroyed between adversaries reduced to dust? How many men and armies made their last stands on some forgotten hilltop or tiny valley? Many swore they heard battling armies on far hilltops during stormy nights, the screams of dying men on Roman crosses. Even the educated had their doubts when they walked alone at quiet places like Sepphoris.

In a century when science had conquered many diseases and sent astronauts to the moon, truth was still withheld. Perhaps it's hopeless, thought Dr. Gold as he flicked his cigarette away. Apparently they needed their virgin births, improbable miracles, and dead bodies rising along with their glowing angels, demons, and unlikely heavens. Like a nightmare from which we cannot wake, people murder and die to defend improbable tales. He started back, depressed.

Nearing his car he saw the well-dressed young man leaning against it. Smiling, the man pointed a black pistol. Gold, strangely at peace, only nodded when the young man asked if he were Dr. Gold. The silenced bullet struck Gold in the forehead. His assassin still smiled as he holstered his pistol and walked away. All watching the trucks, no one saw the honorable old scholar's red blood clot and blacken the rocky soil. The breeze picked up, sifting dust from Sepphoris gently across Isaac Gold's body.

***

News coverage showed trucks unloading coffins next to the waiting jet liner, armed Marines protecting the dead. Honor guards stood side by side next to the open cargo door, American and Israeli flags dipped in mourning.

Tension eased when the jet, surrounded by heavy security, landed at Charles De Gaulle Airport for refueling, then made the long flight across the cold Atlantic, finally landing at the old, well used Reagan National. When it nosed downward, landed, and finally rolled to a halt, journalists made copy of parents weeping for their lost children. President Straihorn directed the bodies taken to nearby Fort Meade where he would speak during a memorial service. By unanimous vote of Congress, all costs for flying the dead to their homes would be at governmental expense.

The worst was over for Roth. Investigation of the crash would exonerate Israel. Sepphoris would fade into the fog of history. Harvard indicated Sepphoris would be under custodial care indefinitely. With luck it would return to a sleepily silent hill. Mossad would tidy up any loose ends, and the less Roth knew, the better he would sleep at night.

President Cliff Straihorn was happy. The dead rested under guard at Fort Meade, Mossad turning to other matters.

The black box recording the final conversations in the cockpit of Flight 217 had been secretly recovered within three hours of the crash. Straihorn listened to the tape over and over. Arabs had wanted the Tablets badly, and intact. How ironic their move was countered by another fanatic in the person of the pilot. Straihorn had long known of Captain Schneider's affiliation. Opus Dei had bet their cards on a Vietnam vet. In all likelihood Schneider intended to ditch the plane in the Mediterranean. The hijacking just brought it sooner. The actual explosion was done by Israel. Interesting! Old Roth, all love and kisses, had ordered the deaths. After the memorial service tomorrow, Straihorn should know more.

* * *

The next day dawned hot and humid as August days often are on the Potomac. Hundreds attended the nation's farewell to those on the fatal flight. Congressional members appeared with other key politicians and reporters. President Straihorn wore a somber face as each speaker droned on, seemingly certain each student had been on the verge of greatness. Drivel, thought Straihorn. If his plan worked, the deaths were worth the gain. Trading lives for advantage what government was about.

Looking around, Straihorn inhaled the cloying smell of hypocrisy. Although many Senators spoke against senseless death and needless violence, Straihorn could pick out those who lobbied for armament factories in their districts. Americans made deadly weapons designed to kill and maim as many fellow humans as possible. Yearly deaths from landmines were in the thousands. America was the world's largest seller of military weapons. Straihorn almost laughed.

Observers remarked on President Straihorn's conviction and passion. He moved listeners to tears, intoning the loss these students were to their country, stressing again and again the truth would be found out about Flight 217. He consoled grieving loved ones and emphasized how the victims' deaths affected him personally, appealing to Almighty God that humanity might learn the wisdom of peace. With perfect timing, he brushed tears away before leaving the podium.

***

The sergeant in charge of outside security at the Fort Meade mortuary couldn't help but be on edge with the new moon only a hazy suggestion. At 0230 hours, normal base activity seemed far away. He'd been warned security would be tested and better not be found wanting. A high ranking person would seek entrance sometime between 0200 and 0400 hours. Guarding a big dark building containing bodies from the infamous Flight 217, Sergeant Blake remembered how during the day the big shots had been everywhere, the place teeming with mourners. Now it gave him the creeps. Blake had to shake off the weirdness. Semis full of civilian coffins sat in back. Inside, personal inspected each body, transferring them to final coffins. Thank God he didn't draw that duty!

A military-green government sedan, windows tinted, approached. Not the type high ranking civilians used. Sergeant Blake asked the driver for his authorization. It had been signed by General Dobbler, Base Commander. Blake demanded the password. The driver said, "Robin."

Blake waved the car on saying, "Proceed with care." The sole back seat passenger, wearing sunglasses at night, hadn't said a word, probably some spook. Sergeant Blake watched the taillights recede into a drive-in bay of the cavernous mortuary.

The man in sunglasses knew his way and climbed two sets of stairs to a balcony overlooking the work arena. He sat, shrouded in darkness. This mortuary had been a teaching hospital before its conversion during World War II. Down below, workers rolled military coffins into the room, seals broken, lids opened for corpse identification. After that, bodies were transferred to civilian coffins requested by each deceased's family. The onlooker above approved such orderliness. In every case, once a coffin was opened, the body was removed and objects from the coffins placed in a packing container on a dolly. From his elevated position the silent man withdrew binoculars from his suit jacket and glassed the container nearly full of flat rectangular objects. He smiled, withdrawing a Partaga Corona. The lighter's flame illuminated Cliff Straihorn's satisfied face. Savoring the sweet taste of that Cuban, he possessed the prize of his life, the Jesus Tablets, with the next move his.

Chapter Forty-six

Henry and Alice moved back into their former home, its ambiance now foreign. With no ongoing excavation, they had little to do. They spent hours walking over the Sepphoris site, lonely in abandoned silence. Everywhere they looked they expected to see tanned young people sweating in the sun, yet finding time for jokes. There was something so healthy about youth working on a common project. Alice had marveled at their energy. Now there was nothing but ancient dust disturbed by sullen wind.

The government said they were investigating, but no one sought out Henry and Alice who'd cried murder. In the end, they grew fatalistic. Two Marine squads remained as onsite security and Israeli soldiers still guarded the camp's perimeter although fewer in number with nothing left to guard. Only Henry, Alice, and their personal effects remained. The study still housed a good library but neither felt the old drive to study. They craved rest, even their love-making tepid. Their Sepphoris sojourn had drained away joy.

On the fifth day life changed. Both Harvard and the government ordered them back to the United States. Harvard wanted them to take a month's vacation, but also offered Henry chair of the Archaeology Department. The government wanted them in Washington, DC. Alice found herself unexpectedly eager and liberated to be returning. Religion in the States was a part of life, not all-consuming.

D.C.'s traffic and activity disoriented them after Sepphoris' isolation. Housed at the Omni Hotel, they tried to relax before meeting with the FBI. Next morning's debriefing wasn't difficult. Henry and Alice retold polite agents what they'd said to John Martin. They again swore they had no idea how information in the Jesus Tablets had leaked out. The interview ended amicably, Henry and Alice told to remain in DC for further questions.

The FBI interviewed Alice once more by herself, Henry twice more, then encouraged them to take in the sights. For the next few days they visited memorials, the Smithsonian, and the White House. On a Friday evening Henry received a message that he'd been scheduled for a final interview at 10:00 p m., after which they were scheduled to take a next day flight to Boston and Harvard. The story of the Jesus Tablets entered its final chapters.

***

At 10:00 p.m. sharp the government vehicle picked Henry up, its driver quiet, professionally courteous. When Henry asked their destination, the driver said nothing. Henry was escorted into a building painted that flat gray for which the Navy is so famous. An officer escorted him to a helicopter pad. Again Henry felt misgivings, but saw no logical reason to refuse. In thirty minutes the helicopter landed in an illuminated circle ringed by woods. A tall man escorted Henry to a building hulked in the darkness, then to a small auditorium.

Alone, Henry waited for whatever was to happen next, unable to lose the itch of being watched. He stilled himself to conceal his discomfort. After ten minutes, he considered getting up and walking out just as he heard the door behind him being locked. He struggled against the urge to jump up, but wouldn't give his captors the satisfaction of seeing his fear. The lights dimmed. In a matter of seconds, only the square object on the dais remained faintly lit. Henry resolved to endure this battle of nerves. Someone had entered.

"Dr. Cross, good of you to come. Courageous in the face of such surroundings. This won't be another interrogation. We're just here to work out a problem. I know your background and followed your reaction to the Jesus Tablets. In my line of work I've known few with integrity, but honesty is my best course with you." The voice morphed into a bark of laughter. "Honesty is rare being so often useless. Your interview with the *New York Times* intrigued me. You accused unknown parties of murdering the students to destroy the Tablets, perceptive for an academic. In fact, you're right. The kids were murdered. Those blessed Tablets were so damned dangerous. So many, powerful Catholics, Protestants, Jews, even Muslims, wanted them for practical reasons. Reasons that, for some, made even murder practical. The most powerful Christian faction is the Holy Roman Catholic Church. Likewise, Israel was established on the basis of Jews as God's chosen people. All that divine money and heavenly power so threatened. The theological winners might have been the Muslims, at least for a time.

"Islam might have consumed the Middle East, putting an end to Israel. Western nations would lose our only sure military presence there. Arabs would have a stranglehold on oil. Almighty oil means money, the true divinity, what people really worship. Surely you can see that the Jesus Tablets were too dangerous for this world?"

Appalled, Henry remained silent.

"Wise, Dr. Cross. You see I'm in a talkative mood, so you can learn by listening. Understand, the number who died on Flight 217 is a low price. Worth nothing, they couldn't be considered in the equation when dealing with the fate of nations. Six thousand die every day in the United States alone. Innocent thousands die daily and no one of importance cares. Did you know that one hundred fifty thousand die every day worldwide? That comforts we who cause death so handily. How often do you dwell for even one second on the three million murdered in Cambodia just a handful of years ago? You're an educated man, Dr. Cross. You know the average American has never even thought about the tens of thousands who died in one day in the trenches of World War I. Is it really a surprise that leaders seldom worry about the fate of average citizens? We don't have time because such folk have no value to the government. You grasp my point.

"America didn't kill those on Flight 217. Others saw to that. Don't misunderstand. I would have given such orders to gain the Tablets. However, other major players destroyed the carrier. The Catholic Church was one. Israel, too. After all, half earth's Jewish population lives in America, mixing practical acuity with being God's chosen. Influential American Zionists parlay two to four billion annually, desperately needed to float Israel. Since Muslims would have used them to discredit Judaism, Israel couldn't permit the Tablets to survive.

"We were the final player. America needed the Tablets for peace in the Middle East to buy oil. Peace will never be obtained while Palestinians are mistreated. This is tricky. What the United States needs is an Israel that exists, but on our terms. As matters stand we have limited ability to influence Israeli policies. It all comes down to money and power. Concepts of right and wrong bandied around by ordinary mortals really don't apply to world leaders.

"The practical problem was how to get a ton of material out of Israel without one of the other players destroying or stealing it. My first thought was to surround the Tablets with innocent people on the theory that their lives would block the destruction. On reflection such a strategy wasn't sound. No number of innocent lives would prevent it. Flight 217 confirmed that rather dramatically, wouldn't you agree?

"The murderers believe they succeeded. They gave me over two hundred twenty-five handy boxes in the form of coffins. The dead didn't mind sharing their spaces with the Tablets back to America. Want to see them? After all, this operation took extraordinary planning. I'm proud of that. Please, remove the covering."

Henry slowly rose and walked to the platform under the lights. It only took a moment to remove the blanket and there, before his eyes, were hundreds of clay rectangles, The Jesus Tablets.

"Dr. Cross, find your voice. I'm lonesome. Are these the Tablets you and your wife examined?"

Henry ran his fingers over the letters on the Tablets, stunned that they were here and mortified at the lives so casually spent to bring them. Henry turned and said, "These are the Tablets. No doubt."

"Dr. Cross, don't sound so despondent. After all, isn't this what you wanted? The Tablets are intact and in the United States. If you'll return to your seat I'll tell you the rest. It's short, but interesting. As you might imagine, I'm unable to share it with many.

"Dr. Stein and the Ambassador's deaths confused me. Did Israelis kill them in order to storm the camp, or did Arabs do it to force the Tablets' movement? I correctly decided on the latter.

Once Flight 217 was airborne, the Arab faction played their card in an attempted hijacking to Tehran. Two things went haywire with that bold thrust. First, the Tablets weren't actually on board, and second, the fanatic Catholic pilot planned to destroy them by crashing.

"The hijack attempt prompted him to head into a fatal dive. This was the Catholic card, a good one. Nevertheless, the dive never got far because the Jews destroyed the plane and what they thought were the Tablets from a radio signal to a bomb on board. I will spare you names, methods, and histories. It's complex and just comes down to a bunch of nuts.

"Obtaining the Tablets at this point was easy. Hand-picked agents loaded the coffins with bodies and the appropriate number of tablets in each. The Tablets are now in front of you. Try not to mourn for Dr. Stein. He was dead the second he read them. The Israeli Secret Service has permission to tidy up any loose ends, and Dr. Stein was one," the voice stated. There was a sharp laugh. "Not that Mossad needs orders to perform vital actions."

Henry felt cold when he asked, "What about Dr. Gold? What's his fate?"

"Dr. Gold was found dead near Sepphoris. Apparently, Mossad decided to move fast in his case," said the detached voice.

Nausea gripped Henry.

"Don't be so dejected, Dr. Cross. Mossad is efficient, and Dr. Gold didn't suffer. Perhaps you wonder how the secret of the Jesus Tablets escaped Sepphoris. Among your many intelligent students was a young man, Andre, cursed with the ability to detect lies. You lied after the Tablets' discovery. Curious, Andre discovered the secret by breaking into your study. His Catholicism drove him to inform his uncle, a Baltimore priest. From there the secret traveled to the Vatican. Andre, in turn, is the homosexual lover of Michael, son of Robert Steward, the late, renowned Baptist preacher. Michael made the fatal mistake of telling his father about the Jesus Tablets. He appealed to me and thus my quest for the Tablets began. Interesting how the world works, isn't it, Dr. Cross?

"Michael was a sleeper. He sensed the danger of Flight 217 and persuaded his lover, Andre, not to take it. Apparently, your wife Alice is equally astute and persuaded you to remain in Israel. Andre is marked for death by Mossad because he also read the Tablets. Michael is on the thinnest of ice thanks to confused loyalties. He's the CIA agent who passed the message on to John Martin of the *New York Times*. Nevertheless, divided loyalties are dangerous in the intelligence business. By warning his father and Andre, Michael signed his own death warrant. I bought Prime Minister Roth's secretary for a mere two million, adding pressure and confusion to Israel. Her escape to France was vital. Mossad will decide her fate. All of which brings me back to you and Alice.

Silence hung for a long moment. "You must guess that you and the lovely Alice are also marked for death by Mossad. It's unpredictable when they'll strike, but in view of Dr. Gold's sudden demise it's likely to be soon. I considered standing aside, but I need you. After all, you're both qualified not only to provide in depth translations, but are impeccable witnesses to the Tablets' validity. Of course, you have every reason to cooperate. If you don't, you won't survive, and I assure you all deaths are not as quick as Dr. Gold's. You would also be an ever present reminder to Prime Minister Roth and Pope Jerome that their cooperation with the United States is advisable.

"You'll be free to live your lives. I understand Harvard is offering you the position of Chair of the archaeology Department. Our government will be generous. After all, the Jesus Tablet question has convinced many in Congress that archaeology in the Holy Land does serve our national interest. How would you feel about such an arrangement, Dr. Cross?"

"You're a blackmailer, a murderer, and an accessory to murder. The truth of the Jesus Tablets belongs to the world. Nobody has the right to nullify…" Henry's voice shook.

The voice across the room chuckled. "Blunt integrity is refreshing. Let me clarify. If you refuse to cooperate, you won't leave here alive. In a few days your wife will be repeatedly raped and then strangled. Andre will be castrated, then shot. Michael will be sealed alive in a forgotten room to starve. On these points you have my word, and I have the power to make my words reality. Don't disappoint me. You're intelligent and reasonable. I'm powerful with no shred of morality. My past speaks for itself."

Henry paused. "I'll cooperate on certain conditions."

"Your self-possession is impressive. What do you want?"

"Would it be too much to ask what you intend to do with the Tablets now that you have them?" asked Henry.

"Excellent question. Most in your position wouldn't be so practical," answered the voice from the darkness. " I'll thoroughly enjoy seeing the Catholic Church renounce its stranglehold on the masses and make serious changes in dogma. In addition, I'll force the Church to make changes in how it conducts business. The idea of a spiritual dictator in this day and age is ridiculous and dangerous. The Pope will change his Church's power structure. If he doesn't, I'll show what a hypocrite he really is. If the Catholic Church doesn't renounce its right to interfere in secular politics, I'll reveal the Tablets. Pope Jerome will be happy to deal with me just as his predecessors coexisted with the Nazis."

"How can you be sure the Pope doesn't claim ignorance of the Church's involvement in all this? What if he pleads underlings deceived him?" Henry asked.

"Very good, Dr. Cross! You may have missed your calling. You'd have done well in politics. The Pope blundered by joining forces with the Jesuits. My aims for a more rational Church are also held by Jesuit dissenters. Father Tobenhien contacted me early concerning my ultimate intentions. Tobenhien saw that allegiance with me would destroy papal power. His goal and that of his do-gooder Jesuits was to accomplish that yet save the Church. Therefore, he joined forces with me to trick both Pope Jerome and Roth. Tobenhien taped and videoed every conversation he had with Pope Jerome concerning the Tablets and destruction of Flight 217. If necessary, the Pope will be exposed as a knowing party to murder. The Holy Father will be reasonable. Don't you agree?"

Henry couldn't absorb the magnitude. Here was a genius of deception. However, a more rational Catholic Church would go far toward international peace. One major religion relaxing its inflammatory claims would lower tensions. Such a show of tolerance might even strengthen humanity's spirituality. Was it possible that the man speaking from darkness could actually benefit humanity while pursuing his own sinister goals?

Henry pushed a little more, "Smart, but what about Israel?"

"Well spoken! You're not just honest, but brave. Israel is a problem, but I'll approach it the same way. I'll force Prime Minister Roth to declare a schedule for displaced Palestinians to rejoin Israel as equal citizens. Israel will agree in the United Nations to a time frame during which Palestinians will reclaim lands in the same percentage they owned them before the 1967 War. The United States will protect her interests and the terms of the Arab-Israeli agreement by buying barren hill country and deserts, approximately one-fifth of Israel. We'll turn it into our largest overseas military base. Once we purchase it outright, we'll colonize it with Americans, protecting it with our arsenal. This military outpost will go a long way toward stabilizing the region. Jews and Arabs will be forced to cooperate for a working economy. If Israel refuses, I'll use the Jesus Tablets to discredit their religion, economy, and ultimately their country. What do you think of those broad strokes?"

Henry squinted in confusion. The vision's scope impressed him. A United States outpost on its own soil in the Middle East would transform the power equation in that troubled region. "Frankly, I've got to think. Peace in the Middle East would go a long way toward world safety."

"At last you respond like the reasonable man I know you to be. You think me insane. However, what is insanity, Dr. Cross, except a different way of thinking? You might be reassured to know America has a clandestine panel to evaluate the standing President's sanity on a regular basis. My rating among those esteemed shrinks is climbing. Granted my sexual tastes are a little off the well-trodden path, but what genius hasn't sought his own pleasures? Proclivities have varied so much among cultures, times, and individuals, who's to say what's normal? Besides, do normal people seek world leadership or spend a hundred million dollars seeking a position that pays only four hundred thousand?

Those like me want power. To rise to where I am, a person lies, cheats, compromises, and, yes, sometimes, kills. Do you surmise the rich advanced millions to get me elected without expecting a return? Part of the game is that moneyed people think they're buying me when, in reality, I'm using them. I love games. Surely it's good if I prevent humanity from wars that kill in the hundreds of thousands at the cost of a few hundred. I might spare lives of millions. Give me your thoughts, Dr. Cross. We have time."

Henry, reared to think in terms of right and wrong, reeled. The difference is supposedly plain, with most choosing the right. On this gigantic scale, right couldn't be so easily defined. Certainly a more reasonable Catholic Church would be an improvement, any resolution between Jews and Palestinians a great relief. Henry had never considered that evil people can sometimes accomplish good things. It didn't seem right, but was obvious. "How can you guarantee the lives of the people you said Mossad has marked for death? After all, even your power has limits."

"Good point. I'll tell the relevant players if any of you die for any reason, I'll reveal the Tablets. They won't risk calling my bluff. After all, I'm a fruitcake. In any event, the changes I plan to force the Church and Israel into making will be accomplished in under two months and once made, never retracted. Odds are all the potential victims will live out normal lives."

"Is it correct that I'm speaking to my President?" Cross asked softly.

"It's true. For the time being I'm the most powerful person alive."

"Your term is up soon. What happens to the Tablets then?"

"It only appears that presidents change. Inside we're all the same and understand each other. I'll pass the Tablets on to my successor who'll see the same advantages to possessing them. Voters are naïve, fretting and fuming, debating virtues of their candidates. All candidates adhere to the ancient rules of power. In effect, the choice has always been between me and me. I personally will retire to a privileged position in society where I can enjoy my debaucheries knowing that, in fact, I did leave the world a much better place. Isn't that ironic?"

It is indeed, Henry, never political, thought. "What about the Tablets' scholarly value? Will the world ever learn the realities?"

"You won't like this. Unfortunately, the Jesus Tablets are too dangerous. Folks must have their simple answers, and leaders see to it the folks are tranquil. The Tablets will never be generally known. Those in power will never release such an unsettling force. Think about it. We're merciful. The Tablets will exist and exert their force, but in clandestine ways. Don't be upset. Confirming suspicions would serve no constructive purpose. Do we understand each other?"

Henry considered. The hidden President waited. Henry had no choice. He'd no right to condemn the innocent and he, himself, wanted to live. Perhaps the Tablets might be able to do what Jesus never could: bring peace to tortured Palestine. Maybe the truth was too disturbing. After all, the Jesus Tablets had lain silent for two thousand years while the world survived. Henry had time on his side. The Tablets were well protected. Eventually, he might find another way. Henry remembered the biblical phrase "peace beyond all understanding." Perhaps this was God's way to bring peace to a weary world.

"I condemn your methods, Mr. President, but we all need the end result. I agree to your terms." The lights sprang on. Both rose and walked to the dais, meeting on opposite sides of the Jesus Tablets, their differences unbridgeable.

However, this understanding between scholar and madman changed the planet.

Chapter Forty-seven

Henry accepted Harvard's promotion even before he and Alice left on their much-needed vacation. Alice, who'd been through enough, never knew of his agreement with President Straihorn. The investigation of Flight 217 concluded that a bomb placed by parties unknown destroyed the aircraft. President Straihorn addressed Congress, stating his intent to dedicate his remaining term to achieving peace in the Middle East. He joined the grieving father, Senator Fadlallah, to appeal to Israel to come to the United States to discuss options. Offended and concerned about this new twist, Prime Minister Roth and his government could do little. Their delegation arrived in Washington a week later. Zionists flooded the media with statements that the United States President naively underestimated Israel's complex situation.

Political experts intoned the peace effort would be dead on delivery. Initial discussions deadlocked. President Straihorn and Prime Minister Roth flew to Camp David where a miracle occurred. Prime Minister Roth emerged from their private discussions a different man, agreeing to peace being not only desirable, but eminently possible. Stunned insiders acknowledged peace between Arabs and Jews within reach.

It didn't make headlines when Mossad head, Heinz, was found dead in his Jerusalem home of an apparent heart attack, his funeral sparsely attended.

On September 23, 1996, President Straihorn and Prime Minister Roth presented their joint peace plan to the United Nations Assembly. Israel agreed to withdraw to the boundaries prior to the 1967 war. Palestinian refugee camps were to be dismantled and displaced Arabs returned and granted title to former properties or their equivalent if seized prior to 1967. Israel would be a representative government of Arab and Jew, discriminatory laws based on sex, race, and religion abolished.

Every adult would be enfranchised, minorities' rights protected by a constitutional Bill of Guarantees. United States aid would be reduced so every citizen, both Arab and Jew, had reason to unite to make a viable nation. To assure peace and adherence to these agreements, the United Nations would oversee all elections. Israel's survival would be guaranteed by a United States military base on property ceded by Israel. The military outpost would be partially funded by the United Nations to insure stability in this volatile area, allowing the United States greater latitude to deal on an evenhanded basis with all Middle East countries.

Palestinian organizations immediately endorsed the agreement and initiated the treaty. Private Jewish investment in the occupied lands received offsetting tax credits. This allowed the new Israeli nation to discourage displaced Jews from leaving since they wouldn't want to lose gains from years of labor and investment. The Holy Lands had never known a greater miracle.

Within weeks of this historic signing, Pope Jerome called a conclave of cardinals at St. Peter's Basilica to prepare the Church for its role into the twenty-first century. Rumor and speculation abounded, but talks occurred behind closed doors. No one was prepared for the conclave's brevity. The Catholic hierarchy's wheels virtually spun. In twelve days Pope Jerome spoke from a balcony overlooking St. Peter's Square. The Pope and Father Tobenhien had conferred about the speech earlier in the Pope's chambers.

"I have prayed during my every waking hour for the welfare of the Catholic Church and of my own soul," the Pope, visibly aged, said to the invigorated Jesuit. "The peace agreement between Jews and Palestinians was a sign from God to us all."

"The crowd will listen enraptured as Your Holiness explains how misused religion has been the basis of tragic events in the land of Jesus, a sad part of the history of even our Roman Catholic Church."

"I'll say I summoned the conclave to remedy those errors. The Mideast peace treaty was signed because God's strength is greater than we can conceive. The impossible is possible if men and women rise above their own selfish natures."

The Jesuit's eyes twinkled as he lowered them. "Add that all things are possible if we change for the better to singly and collectively admit mistakes. Confession of sin is still the only path to God's approval. Therefore, Your Holiness, tell the faithful how you wish to confess your sins and those of the Roman Catholic Church for a new beginning in the world God created."

"I do wish to confess my pride," the Pope said sharply. "One alone can never know what is best for God's people. That false belief led me in unhelpful directions. God has forgiven me. I hope those listening can also forgive."

Father Tobenhien leaned forward, "Say the Church is not the province of an elite group in Rome. In truth, she belongs to God, and all who seek to live a life worthy of a just Creator."

"I know I must say, too, the world can no longer endure one man rule in any sphere. Forthcoming changes will trouble some, but we should accept them gratefully. From this day, we renounce the belief that the Roman Catholic Church is the only path to God. The claim of papal infallibility was a sinful practice of mortals who wished to replace God and the collective wisdom of believers. From now on, Cardinals will collectively make overall decisions of the Church."

When the Pope spoke from the balcony to listeners who hardly dared breathe, his words continued the rehearsal with Tobenhien. He explained that Papal influence would now be advisory, voting only to break deadlocks. Local matters would be decided locally. The Church renounced interference in secular governmental decisions. As the New Testament stated, man could not serve both God and money. The Church would serve as a moral compass and spiritual advisor. However, following Jesus' example, she would allocate the greater portion of her resources to helping the poor. All earthly governments were to take notice that the Church, using all the nonviolent methods at her disposal, would resist poverty of the many for the benefit of the few. Although the Church would render her collective opinion as to the morality of any policy, she would refrain from interfering with the individual's right to decide. Hence the Church would no longer delve into family planning. She nullified her prohibitions against birth control.

"The Church admits error with regard to who may serve as her priests. God made men and women equal. From this day forth, the Church accepts all who wish to serve at all levels. Marriage is an institution created by God. Priests may both marry and serve their flocks.

"The Roman Catholic Church embraces all who seek God. May other religions respect everyone's right to seek God without coercion. Peoples of the world can no longer tolerate violence in God's name, and God will be pleased if all see the wisdom of tolerance and humility in matters beyond mortal understanding."

Having spoken, the Pope removed his tiara, then his pallium and fanon, and formally set aside his papal scepter. Pope Jerome stood before his gathered thousands in his plain white cassock, head bared. He lifted his hands toward the crowd. Those nearby could see he wept. There was silence. Then cheers rocked the very stones of that holy place. Clouds parted on that gray day and sturdy shafts of sunlight shone on that joyous multitude and radiant face of their leader.

World reaction veered from astonishment to delight, the connection to the peace treaty in Israel apparent. International intelligence agencies knew the Jesus Tablets had exerted force, but lacked details. Neither Israel nor the Catholic Church was talking.

Henry Cross comprehended. Although surprised, Alice agreed to ignore the Jesus Tablets professionally for the foreseeable future. After initial curiosity the subject of the Tablets faded among their colleagues. Daily work of lecturing on archaeology to new students soon pushed the Jesus Tablets deeper into the realm of dead ends. Curiosity moved to new discoveries. The issue slept. Henry occupied Stein's old office, hoping his mentor would have approved.

In the evenings after harried days, Henry would gaze at students lounging about the campus greens, innocently drinking sodas and socializing. Memories seized him. How similar these kids were to the victims of Flight 217. What a price they'd paid for proximity to the Tablets. Henry also lived under the shadow of death, never knowing when his fragile bargain with the mad President might fall through. He didn't want Alice or any others to join the long list of victims. Yet the story of Eli, the escaped slave, and Mary, the tortured mother, harried every dream, stirred the backwaters of every day.

Henry hoped the truth would out someday. Perhaps God used the Tablets to test human willingness to accept truth violating hope. This generation failed. He wondered if someday humanity could accept the difference between hope and certainty. Didn't Ecclesiastes say that there was a time for everything? "A time to search and a time to give up." "A time to keep and a time to throw away." He smiled, remembering from childhood, "A time to be silent and a time to speak." Now was a time for silence. Henry was at peace. The Jesus Tablets could wait until that time for speech. Moses, Eli, Mary, and all the rest would understand. God willing there would come another day.

Chapter Forty-eight

Forty Years Later:

Heat waves distorted the sinewy old man's vision as he gazed across the arid Sinai Mountains, the Red Sea glimmering in the far distance. This forbidding land hadn't changed since the time of Moses. Henry Cross sat on the crag's lip overlooking the desolate land, two porters far below tending to his base camp. Nearly eighty, Henry gave thanks to an active life of teaching and field archaeology for keeping him fit enough to still hike these rugged mountains. White-haired, retired for ten years, he'd concluded an illustrious career.

Blessed, he'd supervised major sites in Palestine, but nothing ever equaled Sepphoris. What a find! After retirement, Henry and Alice moved to Cairo. Henry loved searching for artifacts of raiders who dwelled in the Sinai so many centuries ago. He'd found many ancient campsites; perhaps, even Moses and Eli's main encampment, uncovering military artifacts, fire rings, and ancient implements. An encampment of hundreds. Henry even found Moses' cisterns, but kept that to himself.

How he missed Alice, taken by an aneurysm four years ago. The doctors said she felt no pain. Henry would soon cross that line between the quick and the dead. They'd been lucky. Few so near the Jesus Tablets had died of natural causes.

He was not far from where Eli and Moses killed the scouts on the road to the Egyptian mines. After searching three years, he even found their hidden pool. The time would come to share it, but not yet. President Straihorn allowed Henry and Alice to keep their notes and translations of the Tablets, only reminding Henry to remember the rules. Henry suspected it gave the unbalanced man pleasure to know he didn't dare share the information.

***

Israel had been stable for over forty years now. Arabs and Jews coexisted in the rough and ready arena of commercial competition. Peace granted enjoyment of property, available to any who earned it. Palestinian resistance was a thing of history. Young Arabs and Jews hung out in shopping malls. Peace allowed them carefree days rather than the hell of combat.

Memories turned to mysteries, one of a legendary, even spectral, Palestinian resistance leader known as Pebbles. No one knew what happened to Pebbles or where he was. Rumors spread of sightings in Latin America. Some assumed he returned to America. Others claimed he died of disease in North Africa, or had been captured and held in an unnamed dungeon. Was he still planning world domination for Islam? Rumors came to nothing.

Pebbles had ordered the Fawn to lay down her rifle. Amal married a farmer and reared six lovely children. Her handsome husband never knew that his modest wife had been the most sought-after sniper of the end days of the Arab-Jew conflict.

Nightmares from combat experiences stormed Amal's sleep. She prayed daily for herself and the souls of those she assassinated. She visited General Kessler often in Tira now only to chat of lilies and the blessings of peace, until one warm night he slept away. Amal and her husband prayed to Allah that their children would never know war's horror.

Andre matured into a compassionate priest in his uncle's parish. Catholicism enjoyed tremendous rebirth in America. Strong assets, women now served as priests. The changes of forty years ago increased lay Catholics by thirty per cent in the United States alone. Evangelism was up, the modern Church a monument of reason, a haven from the harried pace of life. Its new emphasis on poverty forced Latin American and Mexican governments into meaningful economic changes. The relaxed position on birth control let families plan their way out of poverty. Workers could demand better wages and working conditions. When one could earn beyond bare subsistence, education was within reach.

Michael quit government service to become director of a system of Peruvian orphanages. He used his substantial inheritance for his work.

Henry never knew of Prime Minister Roth's role in the Jesus Tablets. Roth and President Straihorn shared the Nobel Peace

Prize in 2000 for their efforts to end the Arab-Jewish conflict. Roth never wrote his anticipated memoirs, saying only that he did what any rational person would have. He lived another fifteen years before dying in a one car rollover, his funeral a national day of mourning. He rests in the family plot next to his beloved brother.

Father Tobenhien dedicated his life to helping the poor in Latin America, declining numerous teaching offers in prestigious Jesuit colleges. He passed away in Brazil, beloved servant of the common people.

Pope Jerome lived eight years following his historic reforms. He was the only Pope to be awarded the Nobel Peace Prize, albeit posthumously. Although he had many enemies in the old guard of the Catholic hierarchy, none doubted how the rank and file believers loved him. He left the Catholic Church far stronger than he found it. The Church began the process to have Pope Jerome canonized. Vatican insiders told reporters it was a sure thing.

Dr. Gold's murder was never solved. He was buried in Jerusalem, his contributions to archaeology noted in nearly every textbook. His old friend David Roth visited his grave annually until his own death.

Clifford Straihorn lived on for eighteen years. Few presidents generated as much controversy or displayed such inexplicable behavior, yet benefitted so many while hated, maligned, and vilified. Books appeared charging him with vile sex offenses, misuse of power, and even murder. Nothing came of them. His many defenders noted that he'd brought peace to the Middle East when all others declared it impossible. Many suspected he was behind reforms of the Catholic Church, although nothing was proven. Ironically, he died of AIDS in 2018, rumored to have contracted it from a vengeful cousin he allegedly raped in her youth. Straihorn sought her company after stepping down from office. She failed to tell him she was infected with the virus, dying two years before him. During his final months the President remained cheerful, adamant he'd done more good than harm. Henry Cross was one of his last visitors. A nurse remembered President Straihorn reminding Henry to heed his promises. Henry said he would.

***

Henry did remember those promises as he sat on this lonely ledge in the burning Sinai desert. He also heeded his obligations to truth and to the dead who'd honored it, obligations that began with Eli and ended with Mary, then him. Yet, the world had to be ready. Modern proliferation of knowledge and new ideas defied imagination. It was no longer possible to enclose islands of ignorance. How far could humanity evolve in two more centuries? If people survived the impulse to destroy each other in the nuclear age, the Jesus Tablets should find a favorable reading by then.

The tablet Henry and Alice hid had never even been suspected. On it, Mary described her recurring dream of the family library seized by evil people and withheld. Mary hired two scribes from Egyptian Ashkelon, city of antiquity and scholarship, housing them in her servants' quarters. It took them nearly two years to copy the family library in Sepphoris. They fired the Tablets in a kiln in the family garden. These scribes returned to their city wealthy men who died keeping silence. Mary's old friend Joseph's grandson carried on his family's trading ventures. He accepted Mary's request to take the second set of Tablets deep into the Sinai, hiding them in a man-made cave high on a remote mountain. He hired illiterate porters of no knowledge and less curiosity. The grandson kept silent, the porters dispersed, the journey into the Sinai lost to memory. Mary slept dreamlessly at last. The crude description of the Tablets' location suggested key geographical features. With these, Henry found the Tablets in his seventy-ninth year. Thanks to arid conditions, they were perfect. Only thick layers of dust suggested their antiquity.

Henry wept as he gripped one of the Tablets of Moses, Eli, and Jesus in his ropy-veined hands. Trembling, he replaced it and made his long trek to the base camp.

He'd planned well. If the human race survived it should be ready in two hundred years. For a story begun nearly three thousand years ago, another two hundred didn't seem long on

God's time scale. Henry would soon put the last step in place. He was to return to Harvard to celebrate the opening of the new archaeology building. There he would accomplish his last duty.

***

The sun shone on Boston as dignitaries and students gathered to dedicate the new building, the Stein Center of Scientific archaeology as pronounced in granite lettering. As he walked to the stage, many watched the retired Professor Cross fondly. They knew he'd been exploring the Sinai in his retirement and wondered why he hadn't published any findings.

Old Henry Cross would have the final words, a vintage lecture. His platitudes drawing smiles, Cross reminded every supporter of archaeology that nothing counted more than to tell the Creator's truth. Many no longer believed in a Creator, but listened patiently. Henry had the privilege of sealing a two-foot square time capsule to be raised by crane and bricked into the base of Samuel Stein's statue. He chose several items for the future. Doctors Cross and Stein had been as close as father and son. Henry held each item up before the applauding crowd to view before settling it in the container. First was a copy of Dr. Stein's massive work, *Archaeology and Science*, Dr. Cross's biography of his mentor entitled *Dr. Samuel Stein: Father of Modern Archaeology*. There was a collection of Dr. Stein's original manuscripts. Dr. Cross carefully sealed the lid as the crowd stood. Everyone watched as the capsule was raised seventy-five feet to its final resting place.

Few noted Henry stride away. His work finished, he had no wish to socialize. He'd placed Mary's Tablet disclosing her concerns and the geographical location of the second Jesus Tablets collection within Stein's hollowed out book. Likewise a baked clay tablet showing the exact GPS coordinates of the Tablets he had located in the Sinai Wilderness rested within his hollowed out volume. Last, he placed Alice's original Jesus Tablets translations preserved in archival conditions with Stein's manuscripts. He had no doubt Mary, Stein, and Alice would approve. As he departed, no one there guessed the Jesus Tablets would reenter the world in two hundred years. Perhaps it would accept them then.

Henry Cross died three years later in Cairo, recognized as a giant of archaeology, laid to rest next to Alice near his family's farm in Nebraska. In time, most forgot their names. Students saw them only in footnotes with no way of knowing that in the distant future Henry and Alice Cross and The Jesus Tablets would be remembered as long as truth and history coexist.

Epilogue

The wind rose over the Red Sea's waters. Gaining power and velocity, it moved north under the silvered moon that faintly lit the Sinai Mountains. Fingers of wind swept through tangled canyons and somber mountain wastes unchanged for millennia. So much had happened here, but the wind could not speak. Hot dust swirled and the dry desert scrubs swayed in the grip of this invisible current. There was no sign of those who lived, loved, and died here so many centuries before, sounds of battle and dying men long vanished. There was only the wind, and it spoke a language none understand. Timelessly, the elements of wind, sand, and stone interacted in a transformation unchanged since cosmic dust formed a small planet in the midst of the endless cosmos. Even stars in the clear Sinai sky were silent reminders of countless suns, each burning in splendid isolation. The wind swept around a twisted peak in the depths of this heated wasteland, its fingers entering a shallow cave where they sifted feathers of dust upon a stack of clay tablets arranged by long forgotten hands. Here the Jesus Tablets silently wait for the day when people are ready to face themselves. Perhaps God waits for that day also. Until that time, the silent earth abides.

Acknowledgments

Many good friends supported my writing with their wisdom, perception about good storytelling, and general enthusiasm for literary efforts. My dear husband Jerry had the original plot idea and then turned it over to me as a loving gift. His knowledge of the Middle East and biblical history made the work so much easier. Debbie Burke's editing and enthusiasm were a blessing. Cindy Dyson kept me trying to make it better with her proven sense of what enriches the experience for readers. Karen Feather, who suggested the title, let me know where it needed reworking, as did Tim Ness. Members of Authors of the Flathead, a writing group in Kalispell, Montana, have been a tremendous influence in my bringing the book to publication. I am grateful to all these and the authors of all the books I've devoured since childhood.

Many books provided helpful information in the writing of events of Moses through Jesus, particularly David Noel Freedman's *The Anchor Bible Dictionary* (6 Volume Set), Jun 1, 1992;Richard Elliott Friedman's *Who Wrote the Bible?* HarperOne, 1989; Burton L. Mack's *Who Wrote the New Testament? The Making of the Christian Myth,* 1996; also by Burton L. Mack, *The Lost Gospel: The Book of Q and Christian Origins;* 1994; Dr. David Friedrich Strauss' *The Life of Jesus: Critically Examined* , [Classic Reprint] 2012; James Barr's *Fundamentalism;* Westminster John Knox Press, 1978; Dennis McKinsey's *The Encyclopedia of Biblical Errancy,* Prometheus Books, 1995; John Dominic Crossan's *The Historical Jesus: The Life of a Mediterranean Peasant,* Harper Collins, 1993; Rudolf Bultmann's *The History of the Synoptic Tradition,* Blackwell Publishers, Revised Edition, 1972; Bart D. Ehrman's *Misquoting Jesus: The Story Behind Who Changed the Bible and Why,* HarperOne, 2007; also Bart D. Ehrman's *Forged: Writing in the Name of God: Why the Bible's Authors Are Not Who We Think*

They Are, Harper Collins, 2011; Richard N. Soulen's *Handbook of Biblical Criticism*, Third Edition, Revised and Expanded, Westminster John Knox Press, 1976; and *The New Analytical Bible and Dictionary of the Bible, Authorized king James Version*, revised by the International Council of Religious Education, John A. Dickson Publishing Company, 1950

ABOUT THE AUTHOR

Karen Wills lives with her husband near Glacier National Park in Montana. She will be publishing a children's book, *Tinker's Glory*, in the near future and is currently working on a historical novel set in the area of the North Fork of the Flathead River.